DASHING ALL THE WAY

CELESTE BRADLEY   EVA DEVON   ELIZABETH ESSEX
HEATHER SNOW

DASHING ALL THE WAY

Copyright © 2017 by Celeste Bradley, Eva Devon, Elizabeth Essex and Heather Snow

A RAKE FOR CHRISTMAS

Copyright © 2017 by Maire Creegan

UP ON THE ROOFTOPS

Copyright © 2017 by ERB Publishing

THE VERY DEBONAIR LADY CLAIRE

Copyright © 2017 by Heather Snow

A LIAR UNDER THE MISTLETOE

Copyright © 2017 by Celeste Bradley

Cover Design: The Midnight Muse

All rights reserved.

No part of this book may be reproduced in any form or by any electronic or mechanical means, including information storage and retrieval systems, without written permission from the author, except for the use of brief quotations in a book review.

A RAKE FOR CHRISTMAS

EVA DEVON

Lady Evangeline Pennyworth is done with being a wallflower. Determined to leave the unkindness of her family, she turns to London's most notorious rake, demanding he teach her how to be desirable.

After witnessing the love of his parents devolve into pain and anger, Anthony Basingstoke has vowed never to be swept away by passion. But when Lady Evangeline charges into his world, he finds he is taken by this wallflower in a way he never has been before. Now, he must decide if he will let the past rule his future or if he can choose love.

For Anthony and Evangeline, only a Christmas miracle will make true love a gift that will last forever.

DEDICATION

For Elizabeth Essex
Who is the best of women, dearest of advisors, and loveliest of friends.

CHAPTER 1

Lady Evangeline Pennyworth only had one wish for Christmas and that was, quite simply, not to be the Season's absolutely most awkward and unwanted wallflower. Again. The unique state had been hers for three years now. The unpleasantness of it could not be stated in flowery enough terms. It might have been bearable if society noticed her in any way. But she had fallen into that hideous position of invisibility. She had gone the way of the elaborate furniture of many a *ton* home, there but unremarked upon. It had not been a surprising condition. Her own parents had ignored her for years. Still, she was no longer willing to accept it as her fate.

So, it was with great trepidation and a fortitude passed down from her grandmother, who'd escaped the terrors of the French Revolution, that she stood in the shadows of their library and made the boldest move of her rather short life.

She cleared her throat and stepped forward from the edge of the room.

The shockingly handsome man sipping mulled wine by the fire turned to the noise, without surprise, for it seemed a young lady popping out of the woodwork to seek him out was a normal occurrence in his existence. Then he smiled. An oh so terribly slow and delicious smile. A wolf's smile.

It thrilled her to her slippered toes. But even as that feeling raced through her, reason did not abandon her. Anthony Basingstoke, brother of the Duchess of Hunt, looked that way at everyone.

Which was exactly why she had chosen him.

Even so, now that she'd so boldly headed into the firelight, her tongue twisted and she couldn't speak. Perhaps it was years of believing no one thought she had anything worthwhile to say which was untrue. But now, the words she'd prepared froze in her throat.

His absolutely gorgeous mouth, a mouth which suggested it adored kissing and kissing well, only curved into a broader smile. "Looking for a spot of adventure?" he asked with remarkable kindness. There was nothing sinister or affected in his tone. He meant the very words he said and passed no judgement with them.

She blinked. That voice. Goodness. It rolled over her like heated honey and it was incredibly difficult not to let her brain go wandering. But she'd always been sensible and she wasn't about to start gibbering now.

"Not exactly," she replied, winding her fingers together. It was a terrible habit she'd had since childhood.

He cocked his head to the side, dark locks falling over his brow. "No? Pity."

Pity? Surely, he didn't mean that. She was. . . Well, she was not exactly the sort that men such as he had adventures with.

Here it was. The moment she'd prepared for. She couldn't botch it now. Squaring her shoulders, she declared, "I need your help."

At that, his brow furrowed with surprise. "Mine?"

"Yes," she confirmed and gave a nod as if to add her determination.

His brow furrowed even deeper as he eyed her. He remained languid in his chair, completely at ease in their odd encounter. "Forgive me, are we acquainted?"

Her spirits sank. Indeed, they were. They'd been introduced. But it was the nature of her existence. To be forgotten. Just as she was about to reply, he leaned forward.

Recognition dawned on his strong features. "Lady Evangeline? Do forgive me."

He knew her name. Or at least he'd had the good graces to recall it. Mentally, she battened down her relief, determined not to let such a little thing thrill her. How sad that such a little thing could.

She nodded.

"Come out of the drafts." He lifted his glass then pointed to the wine warming over the fire. "Join me?"

That invitation, so kind and easy, stunned her. "Join you?"

"If you prefer standing over there, in the cold, do. I do not mean to be critical, but your house is rather cold." He gave an exaggerated shiver.

Could he feel that the coldness was not just the lack of abundant fires but of the people inside the stones?

"Why not venture near," he asked. "Especially if you've sought me out, as you've clearly done."

"Right," she said. Then crossed to him and somehow managed to sit in the chair opposite him. It occurred to her how abrupt she was being, how lacking in grace. But there was nothing to be done about it.

The beauty of his face. . . It was difficult to describe. He looked like the devil's son. A man who adored mischief but had never been engaged in the sort of scandal that might cause anyone harm. He looked like the sort of fellow who'd lead a lady down a very windy but exceptionally exciting path.

His shirt was open at the neck, a positively shocking thing, but it was late. Very late. In fact, she'd waited hours and hours, knowing that he'd taken to sitting in the library by the fire long after everyone else had gone to bed.

The fact that he'd chosen this room, her favorite, to hide away in had ultimately convinced her that he was approachable.

He frowned suddenly. "Your mother isn't about to walk through the door, is she? I don't mean to flatter myself. I'm not a remarkable catch but—"

She laughed brittlely. "No, sir. My mother has no idea I am here."

How she longed to counter that he was a far greater catch than she could ever hope for. His lack of title could not challenge his immense wealth or proximity to one of the most powerful men in England, his brother-in-law, the Duke of Hunt.

"I think you'd make a terrible husband," she replied immediately. Though as she said these words, the thought *but what if I am wrong*, blazed through her mind. The shocking thought *what if he would make the perfect husband* hummed through her in a succession of madness.

His eyes flared and then he chortled. "Smart young lady."

Keeping her wayward line of thinking to herself, she replied, "I think so, if I do say so myself."

"I'm glad." He winked. "I can't bear a silly piece."

Goodness, how could he be so easy? It was something she'd never learned though longed for. "Silly, I am not."

His gaze, that wicked gray gaze, traveled the length of her then returned to her face. "No."

It irked only ever so slightly that he so readily agreed. But then again, she was never going to be a frothy miss. She knew. She'd tried. It had been horrifically unpleasant. Her mother still insisted on dressing her as if she were, as if by adorning her in the plumes of a colorful bird, she might somehow become one.

He cocked his head to the side. "You don't strike me as someone able to undertake hours of inanities."

She gaped. "Is it so obvious?"

He waggled his brows. "Yes."

Turning to the fire and lifting the handle of the simmering pot, he poured a steaming glass of spiced wine.

The process and movement of his body, a body that was lithe and strong and hidden only by his linen shirt and a pair of tight breeches, caused her throat to tighten with an unfamiliar feeling.

As he held the glass out to her, he said, "This is incredibly inappropriate, you know."

She nodded, biting on her lower lip as she dared to take the wine.

Their fingertips brushed and a wave of sensation traveled up her arm and took root in the vicinity of her breasts. She glanced to their fingertips, half-expecting to see that strange and scientific phenomenon, electricity.

He seemed completely unmoved as he settled back in the chair, as languid as a satisfied marmalade cat.

"Now, do tell me what has you throwing yourself into such a shocking meeting."

"I need to get married," she blurted.

"You assured me that I wasn't about to be trapped, did you not?" he intoned with mock horror.

She grinned at his teasing and the fact that he had not run from the room. "I did. And it won't be to you."

"Glad to hear it. Go on."

Drawing in a deep breath, she braced herself. "I'm unmarriageable."

"Are you?" he asked, astonished.

"Yes."

He shifted slightly in his chair, his absolute maleness seeming to fill up the space entirely. "I can't see why. You're young, unmarried, from a good family, with no doubt a good portion. You're pleasant to look upon. Wherein lies the difficulty?"

"You find me pleasant to look upon?" she asked, stunned.

"Of course." He took a long drink of wine, the ruby liquid staining his lips for a moment before he licked it away. It was an absolutely, transfixing gesture before he continued, "Don't you?"

No words would come from her mouth, no matter how she tried. To her horror, tears stung her eyes and she gulped a large swallow of wine to hide them.

"Bastards," he hissed.

"I beg your pardon?" she piped up, drinking deeper than she ever had in her life. Instantly, warmth pooled in her belly. She'd not eaten dinner and she suddenly felt delightfully light.

"Bastards," he growled now, his sincerity deepening his voice. "Whoever clearly made you feel unattractive."

"Ugly," she said, her tongue loose. The word had escaped her so quickly, she could barely countenance she'd said it.

"Bastards," he gritted again.

"Be careful," she whispered conspiratorially, peering at him over her wine glass. "You're besmirching an earl and a countess."

He stared blankly then asked, "Your parents?"

She lifted her glass in mock salute. "Yes."

He winced and gazed at the fire. "Some people aren't fit to raise dogs, let alone children."

She choked on a sip of wine.

"You be *careful* now. You don't want to explain a wine stain to your maid. Not having received it at this late hour."

"You are far more familiar with such things than I."

"I won't deny it." He groaned. "Oh, God. That's why you're here."

"It is," she agreed, suddenly feeling buoyant.

"I won't deny my experience," he sighed. "But it's not with young, untouched ladies."

A grin pulled at her lips. When had she last felt so light? Was it simply his presence? "All the better."

"Is it, by God?" he asked, his brows shooting up.

She cleared her throat. "I need to know how to be appealing."

Once again, he stared at her.

She felt the hot blush even though, to her surprise, she did not feel truly embarrassed. "You must think me mad."

Silence stretched between them as he took her in again. "Not mad. Desperate."

Desperate. She closed her eyes. What was she doing? Dear God. That lightness she felt leached out of her in one sudden heave, leaving in its wake an appalling feeling of self-reproach. "Forgive me. I shouldn't be here."

She lurched to her feet, glass in hand and started for the door.

He grabbed her hand and held her still. "It was not an insult. I've been desperate in my life."

"You?" She twisted toward him, taking in his carefree frame. "But you seem so. . . Happy."

"I am." He shrugged. "Now."

"Can you teach me?"

"Happiness?"

The feel of his hand wrapped around hers was. . . Well, it was like being shown heaven but being barred at the gate.

"Tell me what you really wish to learn. It's not happiness," he said softly. "Desirability isn't happiness. I can tell you that now and save you a great deal of trouble."

Slowly, she took her courage in hand. She had to make him understand. "I want to find a husband. A good husband. But I cannot make a man notice me. No matter what I do. I. . . I am entirely forgettable."

"Though I struggle to believe it, I do see how you feel."

"You strike me as the sort of man who knows about desirable women."

"I shan't argue. And you wish me to teach you?"

She nodded.

In slow degrees, he pulled her back to stand before him near the fire.

The hem of her plain gown brushed his boots.

Gazing down at her through half-hooded lids, he said, "I can't teach you to be happy."

She gave a curt nod. "I understand. Very foolish of me."

Starting for the door again, she was stunned to find he had not and would not let go of her hand.

He held it firmly, gently, with purpose.

"I can teach you tricks. I can teach you how to tease. I can teach you how to play a man's emotions. But that won't make you happy."

"At least, I will leave this place," she said softly.

"Ah. So you don't wish to marry. You wish to escape. That is a different thing altogether."

"I beg your pardon?"

"You feel your only option is to marry," he stated.

"Isn't it?"

He sighed. "Quite possibly. It's deuced hard to be a woman."

"I have never heard a man say such a thing."

He scowled. "I don't think you've been mingling with the right men."

"I cannot bear it here," she proclaimed. "Not another Season. Not another year."

The intensity of her words seemed to strike him. "Then, of course, I will help you."

"You will?" The words tumbled out of her. Hope was in her sights now.

"I've been lost. In pain," he admitted. "I'm honored you'd ask."

"When can we begin?" she asked breathlessly, barely daring to hope.

"Now," he said, his voice a subtle purr.

"How?" she asked. "Should I fetch paper? To take notes?"

"You won't need paper." He cocked his head back, his gray eyes piercing. "You must trust me."

"I—"

"I promise not to hurt you," he said, his eyes blazing with purpose.

"I trust you can help me."

Those lips of his. Those devilish lips of his curved wickedly. Slowly, he stood, his hand still wound about hers. "Lesson one then."

"Yes?" she prompted, eager to begin.

"Kiss me."

CHAPTER 2

The look of pure astonishment combined with consideration was worth posing that absolutely wild demand. Anthony gazed down at the pert lady that he found himself admiring more and more with every passing moment. He realized, to his astonishment, that his demand was something he desired.

Such a thing made no sense. Ladies such as this one were not in his domain. At least, not for seduction. His own past had ensured he would never, ever put a young woman at risk of ruin. For he had no desire to wed. Yet, here they were, standing before the fire, drinking mulled wine with Christmas a little more than a week away. The clock had long struck midnight and this was, perhaps, the most inappropriately he'd behaved with an unmarried lady in his entire life.

And it wasn't for the inappropriateness of the conversation. But it was rather because he found her quite the opposite of what she had claimed. She was, indeed, desirable.

Very.

Oh, not in the traditional sense. There was no guile to her. No batting of the lashes or pursing of the lips. She did not bow her head and gaze up at him. Nor did she speak in anything but the frankest tones he'd ever heard from a woman of her years.

No, it was her boldness. By God, it thrilled him. She'd decided she wanted something and she'd seized it.

The world needed more ladies like this one. As he gazed down upon her plain but intelligent face, he hoped beyond all reason that she would comply.

Instead, she arched a golden brow and smirked. "Whatever for?" she asked.

Whatever for? *Whatever for?*

"I have been known to be quite good at the proposed activity," he teased.

She gave him the oddest look then. "I have no doubts. But I cannot see how it will assist me."

He laughed. "Kissing will teach you about desire. And desire often makes a woman desirable herself."

"I already know about desire," she stated.

He blinked. "Indeed?"

"Don't be rude. I'm not inhuman."

He blanched. "I do beg your pardon. That was not my intent. But so many ladies don't seem to take that into account."

She nodded. "Young ladies are meant to be ignorant."

"Alas," he agreed. "May I ask how you have gained such knowledge?"

She tsked. "I read, of course."

"Of course." It was all he could do not to laugh, but he knew if he did so she would be both indignant and hurt. He didn't wish to elicit either emotion. "And when you read, do you merely learn about desire or feel it?"

She frowned. "That is a very strange question."

"You see, I ask because theory and practice are two very different things."

"I suppose," she hedged.

"No supposing," he cut in. "I can understand that desire is pleasant for I have felt its unyielding pull."

Her eyes rounded. "I confess I have never felt compelled by anyone."

"No one?" he asked, stunned. Most young people, at some point, found themselves desiring someone. It was the nature of youth.

She bit her lower lip lightly, not in seduction, but in curiosity as she clearly thought back on her short life. Then she shook her head and shrugged. "No. No one has come that might take my fancy. The men I meet are either intolerably dull or conceited beyond all recovery."

He laughed again. "Which category do I fall in?"

She blushed. "Goodness. Badly done of me. Neither, if you must know."

"I'm relieved to hear it."

"You're odd," she clarified and then her blush deepened.

He laughed. It was all he could do to muffle the sound lest some wandering soul down the corridor hear and grow suspect.

"Oh dear," she whispered, blushing. "You see? I am no good at this conversing with men."

"You excel at it," he countered, quite truthfully.

"You jest, sir."

He shook his head. "If you spoke as you do now to all, men would flock to your side."

She snorted. "They'd shut me up in a madhouse."

That gave him pause. Was she correct? "It would all depend on the men, but I'd like to think most of us are admirers of bold ladies."

Her eyes narrowed. "How many men do you know?"

He bit back a laugh again. "Quite a few, but I do eschew certain company. I find a great many dull, myself."

She grinned. "Do you?"

"Oh yes. There's a reason I spent most of my life abroad and with artifacts."

"You seem like a man at complete ease in company."

"Oh, I am," he agreed. "I know my place in it and it is not to be like so many Englishmen who venture little from hearth and home."

"I can only imagine venturing from it," she said, her voice a soft lamentation. "All my life, I've lived in my parents' house. London is my greatest adventure."

"It is a great city."

"Yes, but. . ."

"But?" he inquired.

At long last, she said passionately, "There must be more."

"Oh, my lady, more than you could ever imagine."

At that, she gave him the funniest smile. "You might be surprised at my capacity for imagination."

"In reflection, I doubt it. What else have you cultivated if you read as you do and have traveled so little?"

Her smile faded, replaced by a sort of awe. "Forgive me, but how do you understand me so well?"

"I. . . I don't know." And he didn't. But when he gazed into her eyes, he felt as if he could see deep, beyond the surface and into her longing soul. It was like staring into a great sea that he might throw himself into.

"It is most disconcerting," she stated.

"Unpleasant?"

Her lips parted. "The opposite."

The silence that fell between them crackled with the same clarity as the logs on the fire. All about them stilled and he looked at her again. Seeing.

Plain, dressed in a frock rife with too many furbelows, she was, at first glance, the sort of lady he would acknowledge but never pursue. What a fool he and all men were. For she? She was the one who had depth. Not the saucy, smiling, fan fluttering fools that pervaded the halls of the *ton*. She was the one who would lead a man in a merry dance through time.

"Come to my sister's for Christmas."

She gaped at him as if he'd grown a second head. "I beg your pardon?"

A soft laugh rumbled past his lips. "Come to the Duke of Hunt's for Christmas."

"I understood who you meant. Your brother-in-law."

"The same."

"I have no invitation," she protested.

"I'm inviting you."

There it was. Excitement lit her eyes. The promise of escape. "How—"

"I shall tell your mother that my sister longs for a new and young companion to add to her flock of important women." He bent down and whispered conspiratorially, "How could she refuse?"

She glanced to the fire. Considering.

The truth was, if he went to her mother, the woman would be a fool to say no. Entree to a duchess' intimate society was elusive. Such an exclusive acquaintance would be the greatest feather in any mother's cap. No doubt, his affinity to the Duke of Hunt was the sole reason for his invitation to this house party. His invitation for the daughter would be a victory for the family.

A duchess would ensure a powerful marriage if the girl came from the right family... Any family, really, if it assured a political alliance.

"Why would you do that?" she asked.

He scowled, thinking of the unfeeling austerity he'd felt during his visit. In truth, he'd been counting the hours until he might leave. Until now. "I can't imagine you spending Christmas here. You are clearly desperate *and* miserable."

"Oh, dear."

"I did not mean to offend."

A great sigh escaped her. "I had no idea it was obvious from my person."

"You're standing in the library with a bachelor after midnight... Asking for help to leave your oppressive situation."

"A valid point."

"It will be a very large party. You might even find a husband amongst the numbers, and I will assist you."

"You will?" she asked eagerly, her face lighting up. "How?"

"My sister will help me choose the most likely fellow, and then I'll help you get him."

As soon as the words left his lips, he felt an odd sort of bitterness at the idea that she might be the possession of another man. That was ludicrous. She was not for him. No virgin was.

She beamed up at him, but there was still a lingering doubt, as if she'd had too many opportunities dangled before her and seized away. "It would be quite a Christmas gift."

"One that would last a lifetime," he quipped.

Her gaze turned back to him, her brow furrowing. "Then let us make an agreement."

He nodded, though he wondered if he'd been swept up by a complete madness. "An agreement, then."

"Do you still wish me to kiss you?" she asked, eyeing him as if he were the door to freedom.

His heart slammed against his ribs at the question. He'd been largely in jest, hoping to shock her. As he studied her intelligent and slightly curious face, he breathed, almost without his own reasonable consent. "Yes."

Then to his utter astonishment, she tentatively placed her hands on his shoulders, raised herself up on tiptoe, tilted her head and oh so gently pressed her lips to his.

The world spun at that light touch and he wondered, even as his mind went dancing away from him, what the hell he had done.

CHAPTER 3

*E*vangeline did not swoon. Swooning was not something she was capable of but just the soft meeting of their mouths did something to her that she could not reckon. It was meant to be but a token. A beginning to their quest. A show of her commitment to her escape from her home.

But as their mouths met, her hands softened on his arms, her eyes fluttered shut and it was like. . . Coming home. Home to a place she'd never even known could exist.

It had been her intention to pull back immediately. She found she could not and his hands slid to her waist, pulling her close, lifting her higher onto her toes, until she felt she barely touched the ground at all.

The kiss deepened, his mouth teasing over hers until, much to her astonishment, her lips opened of their own accord.

Breath for breath and kiss for kiss, he held her until, at last, she felt the touch of his tongue.

She gasped against him and stepped back.

His eyes, his startling dark eyes, studied her as if she were a wild thing come into his chamber. To her shock there was a hint of amazement in his eyes as if he, too, could not fully understand what had just transpired.

Slowly, he lowered his hands to his side. "I think. . . I think it is likely you will be married before the New Year, Lady Evangeline."

Her heart thudded loudly in her breast as it hit her that the only man she wished to wed was the one standing before her. And that, she knew, would never happen. Not for Christmas. Not for New Year. Not for anything. For Anthony Basingstoke was the sort of man who would never marry a miss such as she. No matter how she might suddenly wish for it. Even at Christmastide, such a miracle would never occur.

~

"I KNOW you're not mad, but have you taken leave of your wits?"

Anthony Basingstoke did wonder. However, he wasn't about to admit such a thing. "She's desperate. Surely, you recall that state. You traversed on a continent, alone, because of it."

His beautiful and sharp sister gaped at him. "Anthony, I know it well. As do you. But. . ." She sighed then grinned ruefully. "We do seem to be drawn to odd characters, do we not?"

"Our whole family," he agreed.

"My new family, too."

"That is an understatement of grand proportions," he drawled, his voice traveling down the long salon.

She laughed. Her husband, the Duke of Hunt, and his family could be described as nothing but mad-capped. Notorious was the wrong word to describe them, but their reputation for their outrageousness was known throughout Europe.

"Lady Evangeline is the sweetest creature," she said. "I have seen her from afar, sitting amongst the wallflowers but I have never spoken with her. She seems to eschew company."

He cringed. "Sweet is not the word I'd use."

Surprise softened his sister's face. "No?"

"I believe she is held captive by her frills."

"Ah." Understanding, instant understanding, darkened Cordelia's eyes. She arched a brow, surveying him. "And you hope to free her?"

"Not like that," he boomed.

"Are you certain? You've not always been sweet yourself."

A substantial degree of outrage overtook him. "I do not debauch innocents."

She shook her head and tsked. "Some say there is a first time for everything and you do seem to grow bored of your lot."

He scowled. He was bored. He should have left London some months ago, but he loved his sister and her young children. The siren call of history did beckon, though, as it always did.

Their father had been an adventurer. Their mother, too. While Cordy had longed for stability, he had thrived in chaos. Perhaps not in the witnessing of their parents' turbulent marriage but, at least, in the climes which they had spent their childhood.

"She needs your help," he said softly. "She's miserable. So miserable she sought me out."

Cordelia nodded, taking up the mantle of a new cause. "I can't fault her taste even if I fault her sense."

"I do not think she likes me," he supplied. "Not that way."

She rolled her eyes. "What lady does not?"

"Quite a few."

She grinned again. "She seeks a husband?"

"She does. I. . ." He frowned, really quite amazed at the turn of events. "I agreed to help her."

"As her matchmaker?" Cordelia guffawed.

He winced. "No. That is what you are for."

"I'm glad to know my position in this debacle," she said lightly. "How did you know I would comply with your scheme?"

"Because of your heart." To others it might sound a cliché, but Cordelia was a strong woman drawn to those in need.

She groaned. "Dear brother, this is a right mess."

"It is not," he argued. "I do not make messes. I sort them."

"While I'd agree with that usually, this—"

"If you had seen her," he broke in, needing her to see as he had seen. "If you had felt her clear unhappiness, you, too, would have swooped in to do something, anything to assist her."

"Anything?" she challenged, her arms folding over her elegant day gown.

He held his hands up. "Within the bounds of propriety."

"And all is proper?" she challenged, serious now. "Nothing has occurred between you?"

He hesitated. He wasn't a liar. He never had been.

"Anthony!" she exclaimed, throwing her own hands up.

"It was only a kiss," he protested. "The smallest of kisses."

She narrowed her gaze and pointed at him before she accused, "You liked it."

"How do you know?" he asked, shocked that she could see it.

She pointed her finger into his chest. "I know."

"It matters not," he brushed off, capturing her hand and pulling her into a hug. "She doesn't want me. I don't want her. But I do. . . Like her. She is. . . She is. . ."

Cordelia groaned. "Oh, Anthony, I've never seen you like this."

"There is no *this*," he protested vehemently. "She is a young lady of intelligence who has been shunted to the shadows of her family and she knows so little of men that they will shackle her to the worst sort of boor. The only sort who might take a wallflower of such proportions."

"You truly wish me to find her a husband?" she clarified.

"Yes."

"Good God."

"Surely it won't be difficult," he said, hugging her tightly to affirm his admiration of her abilities. "You know everyone."

She leaned back. "I am not in the habit of arranging marriages."

"This once?"

She stared at him as if he'd lost his last wit. "If it means so much to you, of course, I will help. I loathe the fact that any young lady be in such a position. So many are. But if I can help. . ."

He swept her around, her skirts belling out. "I knew you would."

"Put me down. Put me down."

He did as asked, but teased, "The dignified duchess now, eh?"

"Ha," she retorted. "The Hunts clan is anything but dignified. Grand? Yes. Dignified? No."

"She'll be here this afternoon."

"You invited her to the house party?" Cordelia exclaimed.

He really had blazed away at his determination to assist her. He was quite lucky to know Cordelia and her generosity so well. "I have."

"How?" she demanded, though not angry.

He gave her a guilty smile. "I maneuvered the truth a bit."

"A bit?" she scoffed, her blonde curls bouncing at her neck.

"A great deal," he confessed. "But I couldn't leave her to face that lot this season. You know what a misery Christmas can be in a difficult family."

Instead of answering, she reached up and touched his face.

That soft touch of understanding was almost too much, so he took her hand and squeezed it.

"Well, it's too late to say no," she said at last. "We will welcome her to our merrymaking."

"Thank you."

"No more dark rooms," she warned.

"I had nothing to do with that," he reminded.

Cordelia gave him that stare she possessed that put a fellow right in the place he belonged. "You let her stay."

So he had. Though risky to confess all to his sister, he'd felt it imperative to make plain the circumstances in which Lady Evangeline had sought him out.

"I will do nothing to impede her marriageability," he declared firmly. And he wouldn't. He wanted Evangeline to achieve her wish.

She arched a brow. "That's rather vague but it will do. I think it best you let me take care of this now. You've done enough."

He winked.

"You are a devil, Brother."

"You adore it."

"I do." She gave him a playful hit to the shoulder. "Luckily for you. Come then, let us have a glass of champagne."

"Now?" he asked, looking out to the late winter sunshine spilling through the tall windows.

"As my mother-in-law would say, is there ever a better time?"

He laughed again, something that happened a great deal whenever Cordelia was present. Her mother-in-law was famous throughout England as a woman who loved life. Cordelia had become one, too.

"I could think of nothing better," he replied.

"Wonderful. And then you can go out and do whatever it is gentlemen do before dinner."

"Whatever you command."

"I should say so," she teased before ringing the bell.

THE COACH RACED up the icy drive, rattling along the raked gravel and Evangeline could not help but peer at the massive country home sprawling before her.

Her companion, Miss Treadwell, sat across from her, chattering away.

The two had been friends since childhood, but Miss Treadwell had always been in that dubious position of paid employee. A companion for Evangeline since she had so few. Miss Treadwell had made the long, painful years bearable.

She had barely heard a word of her friend's excitement as they crossed the boundary of the Hunt Dukedom's vast estate. They'd been on the duke's land for the better part of a day and, finally, the house became clear after a long drive through a copse of oak trees.

It was not just the house, grand by even the standards of her father, that had her shaken.

Him. She would be seeing him again. Her kid-gloved fingers curled in anticipation.

As soon as the coach rolled to a stop, she found her heart had leaped into her mouth. Speech barely felt possible. The coach door opened and she took the footman's offered hand.

Charlotte followed her down and they both took a moment to take in the opposing edifice of the house before mounting the steps.

The oppressive weight that had pressed down on her for so long lifted as something deep within her whispered that it was in this house, at this Christmas party, that she was about to find her freedom.

The smile that turned her lips nearly hurt her cheeks.

They hurried into the foyer and it was all she could do to keep from spinning about with glee.

A voice called from an arched door, "Lady Evangeline."

That spinning sensation came to sudden halt. That voice raced over her, calling to her. Calling her home. But that was absurd.

Anthony Basingstoke was not, and never would be, her home.

Still, there he stood, his dark hair disheveled. Today, he was dressed to perfection. His ruby cravat only seemed to exaggerate the devilish look of his strong face. He smiled that slow, wolfish smile.

Once again, she reminded herself it wasn't particular to her. She knew that. It was a smile she'd seen many times over many parties. Yet, she couldn't help but feel exceedingly pleasant to feel its force upon her.

"My sister should like to meet you," he said simply.

She blinked. All of it suddenly came to her that this was truly happening. Just as he had promised. Her absolutely shocking action had actually worked!

She nodded and passed her cloak to the waiting footman. Charlotte stood transfixed by Basingstoke and his proclamation.

"And your companion, of course," he added, his smile turning to the other young woman.

They both hurried forward, aware how rare and wonderful it was to be summoned by a duchess.

As her traveling boots padded over the marble floor, she drew in a slow breath. It struck her that she was traversing into an unknown encounter. What had he said? What did the duchess know?

Once she reached the arched door, she brushed past him and she did not miss the way the folds of her gown brushed his leg. It nearly made her heart stop. Such a simple thing. A thing which, with anyone else, would have given her no pause.

Yet, at that moment, she suddenly felt herself standing alone with him before the fire, his arms wrapped about her waist.

Heat immediately suffused her features and she barely looked at him, lest she lose her composure.

Upon entrance into the long hall decorated in various shades of blue, she couldn't help but feel that this house, which should feel cold what with its enormous proportions. . . Did not.

If anything, it felt entirely the opposite.

Unlike her own residence, this grand house effused warmth and welcome.

Holly and greenery had been decked upon every surface, giving the room the most delicious of aromas. As if one was walking through the forest.

Christmas was in a mere few days, but one would have thought from the festive ribbons and colors that it was here. Her parents did little to decorate. A Yule log and mistletoe on Christmas Eve. Perhaps a little mulled wine. But they did not have merry hearts.

The moment she laid eyes upon the Duchess of Hunt, Cordelia, she knew the woman must have a merry heart, indeed. For she was smiling kindly, a strange twinkle in her eye.

Blonde curls danced playfully about her face. And her gown was a deep red; the bodice accentuated with a gold braid just beneath her breasts.

"So, you are Lady Evangeline," the duchess greeted with unreserved welcome. "My brother is quite taken with you."

A strange note trumpeted from Anthony Basingstoke.

What had been said? Evangeline longed to know.

"Indeed?" she managed as she curtsied.

"Oh yes." The duchess held out her hand, a ruby ring winking. "He said I could not go another day without you for a companion. So, here you are. We are drinking champagne and, now, so shall you."

She gestured to the footman who had quietly followed them in and, before Evangeline could make reply, crystal flutes filled with the bubbling honey-colored wine were passed into her and Charlotte's hands.

Basingstoke reclaimed his glass from the ornate fireplace mantel and they all raised their glasses.

Just as Evangeline took a sip, the duchess declared, "You are in want of a husband."

She sputtered, barely managing not to make a fool of herself. Her eyes burned ever so slightly as she swallowed the delicious wine. "What lady is not?"

The duchess laughed. "I have known a few that had to be veritably hauled to the altar. But you're correct. Most ladies do see it as their lot in life."

Basingstoke gave his sister a playful hug. "Sister, you make marriage sound like a noose."

"And if you disagree, why are you not married?" she sallied.

"Too true," he replied while laughing.

As the two exchanged words and filial affection, Evangeline's heart ached. She had never known such an interchange. It was magnificent to behold, their clear love for each other.

"If you must know," the duchess began, unwitting to the effect her relationship with her brother had, "which you will in any case quite soon, I adore marriage. If everyone could have a marriage such as mine, I should wish everyone to go through this life two by two."

To her astonishment, Evangeline blurted, "And if not?"

"Then if they have the funds, they'd best stay single," the duchess said as if proclaiming from the gospel. "Especially a woman."

Anthony Basingstoke again let out a barely suppressed, strange noise.

"Do you think so?" asked Charlotte.

The duchess smiled. "Forgive me, you are?"

"Miss Charlotte Treadwell. What terrible manners I have," Evangeline exclaimed.

"Not at all," the duchess assured. "These are most unusual circumstances. And yes, Miss Treadwell, I do think so. Now, we shall have no secrets. A secret is well and good when it's a present. But when it comes to the heart, secrets are odious things."

Evangeline's eyes widened, feeling as if she'd fallen into a wild but most exciting storm. "Oh?"

"Yes." The duchess turned to Charlotte. "Is Miss Treadwell your friend or your companion?"

"Both, I hope," piped up Charlotte with surprising force, her red hair glinting in the light.

The duchess nodded. "One always hopes it to be the case, but I do know quite a few young women with spies lurking about them. Are you a spy, Miss Treadwell?"

Charlotte's mouth dropped open. "I do not know if I should be offended or pleased that you think me capable of artistry."

"It is merely the way of things," the duchess said.

"She is my friend," Evangeline defended quickly. "Perhaps, my only friend."

"That is most definitely not the case," the duchess said firmly. "Not now. For I am your friend, as is my brother."

And there, in that one declaration, Evangeline felt her world change. Friends. She now had *friends*.

This time, tears of gratitude stung her eyes and she had to blink quickly lest they be seen.

"Anthony, will you see that Miss Treadwell finds her room? I must have a moment with your young friend."

Wordlessly, he bowed and took Miss Treadwell's hand.

Just as Evangeline was sure he was going to behave as if nothing at all had transpired between them, he gave her a subtle wink.

Inexplicably, she felt a rush of relief. He wasn't done with her. He wasn't merely handing her off to his sister.

They were, indeed, friends.

CHAPTER 4

The champagne laced through her veins, giving Evangeline a brilliant feeling. It was a feeling she couldn't recall experiencing in years as she checked the ruffles of her dinner gown.

She stared at herself in the mirror, eyeing the pink lace and bows. Her mother had picked the design, hoping to make her more feminine. She looked like a cake. A cake decorated by a mad chef pâtissier.

But there was little she could do... Or was there?

Biting her lower lip, she turned to her small box that held her embroidery. Embroidery was well and good, though she was quite terrible at it. Her mother sent it with her everywhere, desperately hoping she'd give up novels. But there was something in there she might use. Did she dare?

A wicked, little smile curved her lips. Indeed, she did!

Perhaps it was the conversation she'd had with Duchess Cordelia wherein the slightly older woman had treated her with kindness and respect and plied her with wine and told her that a bold and intelligent woman was the best thing to be.

Perhaps it was the sudden freedom of being away from her parents. But she strode to the box, flipped the lid and slipped out a small pair of scissors. She stared at them for a long moment then called to Charlotte.

Her friend, who was in the adjoining room with a door opened between them, hurried in. Her own teal green gown was simple yet beautiful. The clean lines gave her red-haired friend the most beautifully sophisticated air, even if she'd made it herself.

"I need your help," Evangeline said, her voice catching, hardly believing what she was about to request.

"Of course. What can I assist you with?"

She extended the scissors. "Cut."

Charlotte's brown eyes bulged. "*Cut?*"

"This frothy monstrosity." She gestured at the gown, her hands fluttering. "I think we can separate the over gown and tie a ribbon about my waist."

Charlotte's eyes widened with horror and intrigue "But— But—"

"If you count yourself my friend, please."

It was the note in her voice that had Charlotte stepping forward.

Carefully, she took the scissors. "You're certain?"

"Certain," Evangeline said, her voice hard with determination. "Free me."

And with a suddenly cheeky grin, Charlotte did just that.

ANTHONY CHATTED with the Duchess of Aston, adoring her Scottish accent and blunt humor. The lady was as good a company as one could hope for. Witty, beautiful, married, and absolutely uninterested in straying from her slightly dangerous and boisterous husband.

They had become friends since her marriage.

To her husband's good credit, he'd encouraged it. Anthony had always disliked men who walled their wives away from the society of other men. Trust, he was certain, was extremely important to a successful marriage.

They stood near the fire, the light dancing over them. The room was bustling with the joyous conversations of well-entertained people.

The Duke of Aston, himself, sat in the corner, quiet for once, playing the pianoforte. Mozart.

As he launched into a sprightly *Voi Che Sapete*, there was a lull in the conversation.

Someone had just entered, garnering attention.

He turned and his jaw slackened.

"Basingstoke, are ye well mon?"

He could not even shake his head. He was transfixed as was every other damned man in the room.

Lady Evangeline stood in the doorway... Veritably naked.

Not naked. But good God... She might as well have been.

The silk of her pink gown clung to her breasts, stomach, and thighs.

The thin silk fabric had mere straps at her shoulders. It dipped, exposing the amount of flesh he expected from the most fashionable debutants. After all, bosom was de rigueur. Unmarried ladies even dampened their skirts to make them cling, but Lady Evangeline had seemed far from such an action as well as the exposure of her breasts.

She'd clearly embraced hers.

But he never would have imagined she'd own such a piece in her wardrobe.

A silver embroidered ribbon shimmered just beneath her breasts only emphasizing the pale swells and hourglass shape of her waist.

Her hair... Her hair had been curled, a wild riot that seemed barely contained by a matching silver ribbon woven through in the Grecian style.

Half the room was gaping at her.

The women were smiling with admiration and approval. It was the sort of gown that could start a fashion. Perfection.

And yet, he had no bloody idea what to think. Except that, somehow, in one short afternoon, Evangeline had turned into a stunner.

Oh, she wasn't pretty. Her face was and always would be unusual.

Her nose too bold, her lips slightly too plump, her eyes too big. But by God, she'd stopped the room.

And as if she had absolutely no idea the effect she'd just had, she entered quickly, Miss Treadwell on her heels.

Lady Evangeline's wickedly intelligent eyes darted over the room, looking for a familiar face.

And then, she spotted him.

Her eyes, those damned blue eyes that had always burned with a hidden fire, blazed at the sight of him. Her lush lips parted in a delighted smile.

He knew he should back away. He should run. In all his life, he'd never felt so completely frozen. Not out of fear, but out of amazement and... Desire.

He'd already admired her. Her spirit. Her fire. But now?

Now, he wanted to haul her to a room somewhere in the house, pull free the fragile scraps of her gown and expose the body she was teasing them all with.

Mine, his mind growled silently and then he blinked, appalled by the thought. What the devil was happening to him? Whatever it was, it was so foreign he had absolutely no tools in which to make sense of it.

Miss Treadwell and Evangeline stopped before them.

"How do you do, Mr. Basingstoke?" Charlotte said brightly.

He did not make an immediate reply. He couldn't. For once in his whole life, he'd been struck dumb.

She gave the slightest curtsy which caused the firelight to play over her face and breasts.

And he could not breathe for the magic of it.

"Sir?" Lady Evangeline said. "I hope you have made merry this evening."

He blinked again.

"Have you gone deaf, Basingstoke?" asked the Duchess of Aston. The redheaded duchess elbowed him slightly then smiled. "Well, since his wits have gone the way of the chimney, I shall introduce myself. Shocking, I know. I am Rosamund, Duchess of Aston."

Both young ladies curtsied again.

And he suddenly realized what a total ponce he was being. "Forgive me, Your Grace. May I introduce Lady Evangeline and Miss Treadwell."

"A pleasure." The Duchess of Aston leaned forward and gestured with her fan. "I quite admire your frock, Lady Evangeline. From Paris?"

"Yes," Lady Evangeline said, smiling. "Though it has had alterations since it arrived."

"Whatever you've done, it's marvelous. And Miss Treadwell, I always feel an affinity to other redheads. People will accuse us of having the worst tempers. But I'm mild as a lamb."

Anthony choked back a laugh.

She tutted and hit him lightly with her fan. "Now, don't you be giving them any ideas, Basingstoke."

"I'd never dream of such a thing," he drawled.

"You dream more wicked things in an hour than most in a lifetime," the duchess quipped.

"No doubt I will suffer for my sins."

"No doubt," she agreed. "But your company is excellent. You know the young ladies well, then?"

"Miss Treadwell I met today," he informed her. "Lady Evangeline and I are friends."

The duchess' brows rose ever so slightly. "Are you, indeed?"

"Yes."

"Well, a lady can always use a rascal as a friend," the duchess said pleasantly before she gave a sly smile to Evangeline. "They always know the fellows to avoid."

"He has promised to point them out to me," Evangeline agreed.

"Has he?" The duchess looked from Evangeline to Anthony. "Most cordial of you."

He cleared his throat. "I am nothing but the height of cordialness," he managed even as he stared agog at Lady Evangeline.

Who was this woman? For Seasons, she'd barely spoken a word. A few hours with his sister and she seemed transformed. No, not transformed, for she'd been quite a lady before. But now? Somehow, she seemed as if she'd shed shackles that had weighed her down like stones in a river. Had simply leaving her family done that?

Such a thing was possible. If it was true, it was a crime what her parents had done to her.

Just at that moment, the butler unfolded the doors leading into dinner and pairs were made.

His sister suddenly swept up beside them. "Dear Lady Evangeline, I will escort you to your dinner companion. Brother dear, I've paired you with Miss Treadwell. You will know how to tell her the dearest gossip about every single one of us."

"You wound me to the quick," he exclaimed, pressing a hand to his chest.

"I do not believe that possible," his sister quipped as she whisked Evangeline away. As she was rushed, she looked once back over her shoulder.

It was beginning, what he'd promised. Once his sister took up a project, nothing stood in her way. He should be feeling joy. He wasn't certain what he was feeling but it bloody well wasn't joy.

"Och. This will be an interesting party," the Duchess of Aston laughed.

Suddenly, her husband's booming voice cut in. "Where's my wife? I can't go in without my wife."

"I thought it wasn't the done thing for husbands to take their wives in," Charlotte said with genuine confusion.

The Duke of Aston, who'd crossed the room in a few quick strides, gave his famous tiger smile. "It isn't. But I can't have her from my side above fifteen minutes. She is that which makes my life worth living."

It would have sounded absolutely nauseating from anyone else. But his words rang true and Basingstoke himself knew the way the two had become not only lovers but the dearest friends. They were one of the only happy couples he knew. Most of which were in this room.

He offered his arm to Miss Treadwell. "Shall we?"

She smiled up at him. "We shall. And this is the most entertainment I've had in the whole year."

"It will only increase," he said, half with dread, half with anticipation at how Lady Evangeline might surprise them all next.

CHAPTER 5

If precedence had reigned at this dinner table, it would have been a most incredible sight. It took Lady Evangeline little time to realize that there were four—four!—dukes at the table with their duchesses.

A smattering of earls, marquesses, and a few of those without title graced the long table.

And much to her shock, she'd realized that the duchess had not seated them by rank. It was. . . Astounding and remarkably egalitarian.

Her father would have been horrified.

So it was that she sat beside the Duke of Aston and the Earl of Ellesmere, who'd led her in.

The glittering table with its cut crystal glasses, gold-rimmed plates, and hundreds of hot house flowers interspersed with holly gave the room the jolliest of airs. In fact, everyone seemed to be full of goodwill.

Perhaps it was the good wine already poured and being drunk with good cheer, or perhaps it was the conversation filled with ideas, not gossip, which did it. Whatever it was, the duchess was an excellent hostess. Evangeline could not recall a better gathering.

Aston laughed loudly and chatted a good deal with his wife across the table, another shocking thing.

Ellesmere, a good deal quieter, had proved most amicable during the first course. He'd regaled her with his fascination with Greece and his man of business' trip there to purchase several antiquities to be shown at a new wing of his ancient abode. The Ellesmeres had survived the War of the Roses, turmoil of Henry VIII, and the Glorious Revolution. Not many families had claimed a title and a seat for so long without interruption. They were clearly exceptional at picking the right side.

Ellesmere himself could not be above five and thirty. His ash hair shone icy in the candlelight and his eyes were a most remarkable shade of green.

In all her years in her Seasons as a wallflower, he'd never once spoken to her. He was a man far from her league, until tonight.

Tonight, the world had opened to her and she'd decided that the only thing to do was embrace it with open arms. It had been no easy thing, eschewing her often quiet attitude. But as she parried ideas with the earl, she'd come to the stunning realization that quietness was not her nature. It had been inflicted on her by being so trodden upon by her family for so very long.

Here? Here she could be anyone she wished.

"You enjoy the hunt?" Ellesmere asked.

"Not particularly, but I do love riding," she said, trying to hide her wariness at this particularly dangerous topic.

"I love riding myself," he replied, "but I'm surprised to hear you say it."

She fought a frown as she felt her first wave of dismay. "Are you?"

"Oh yes," he said, clearly confused. "Isn't your father an avid fox hunter?"

"He is," she admitted, her smile freezing.

He smiled apologetically. "I've always thought it rather odd myself."

Her smile softened. "Have you?"

He nodded his golden mane. "Can't abide the idea, you know. A pack of dogs and men after one small animal. They're vicious, foxes, but I'd not wish that fate on any creature." He hesitated. "I hope this gives you no offense."

"Not at all," she rushed, delighted to find he was of like mind. "Perhaps it is unfilial but I do not approve for the reasons you mention."

"How refreshing."

She fought a frown. Anthony had told her men admired boldness, but she'd not really believed it. "In what way?"

"That you voice an opinion opposing your father's," he declared. "Ladies usually do go in line with the pater familias."

"I suppose they must," she ventured, knowing she'd kept silent for far too long.

"But not you?" he queried, clearly pleased.

"No," she declared, loving the feeling of the word on her tongue.

"Bravo." He inclined his head. "No easy thing though, going the route of rebel."

"I am not quite that far gone," she protested.

Ellesmere laughed.

"Damned shame," the Duke of Aston drawled as the next course was served and it was time for her to turn and speak to him.

It was a nuisance and she'd wondered if this tradition would also be ignored but it appeared not. Ellesmere was a fine conversationalist.

Ellesmere grudgingly turned to the lady to his left.

"What's a shame, Your Grace?" she asked, taking a swallow of the brisk red wine that went with the game fowl laid before her.

"That you're not so far gone as a rebel," he said. "I do like a rebel."

His tone was so teasing but also so grand that she couldn't stop her laugh. Laughter appeared commonplace amidst this company. How had she gone so long without it?

"No laughing matter, Lady Evangeline," he countered with dramatic seriousness. "Not at all."

He grinned then. A wild grin as he dared her to argue.

"You're right, of course."

"Always am."

There was a clear snort from his wife. Her eyes were dancing as she glanced at him across the table.

"Now, my love," Aston tsked. "I'm speaking with Lady Evangeline, urging her to the path of rebellion. It is noble work."

"I'd tell you not to listen to the mon, but he speaks true." With that, the duchess turned back to her own conversation.

"The duchess is a rebel then?" Evangeline asked with genuine surprise.

"She always has been. Couldn't have married her if she wasn't."

She gaped at him but then quickly forced herself to rescind the role of codfish. "Truly?"

Aston gazed at her pointedly. "Only boring fools marry boring women."

The statement caught her so off guard that she held her wine glass aloft.

"Drink, my dear, drink," he urged brightly. "Only thing for my company."

"I doubt that very much, Your Grace."

"Kind of you to say so, but it will make your evening merry. I used to say my life was wine, women, and song."

"And now?" she asked, doing his bidding and tasting the wine.

"I have one woman and she has me." His eyes and gaze filled with so much love it was hardly believable. "So, we delight in wine and song together."

She drank again, suddenly envious, the bold notes floating over her tongue. She could hardly give it credence, the kind of marriage the duke spoke of but given the way he was looking at his wife, her doubts had to be mistaken.

"Don't look so shocked, young lady," he waggled his brows. "We are not all fools."

"I beg your pardon?" she queried, not quite following.

"Men," he clarified.

"Oh."

He grew more serious and said gently, "I've seen you, you know."

She flinched.

"It's what I do," he informed without importance. "I notice things. Can't help myself. I've seen you over the years. And tonight... Tonight you're finally yourself, aren't you?"

Her head reeled. "Do you always say such shocking things?"

"True things," he corrected.

"Still shocking."

He laughed again. A barrel sound. "Oh yes. I can't help myself. It's my nature."

"I've seen you, too, of course. Everyone has."

"It's the curse of being a duke," he said simply with no self-pity. "One's watched like an exhibit."

That was also true, but she had a strong feeling that the Duke of Aston would be watched no matter what rank he held.

"Now, I'm going to be more shocking still," the duke informed, leaning his head slightly toward her.

She sat on the edge of her seat and took another sip of wine, feeling as though she would need it.

"Remember how you feel tonight. Whatever it is that has made you this way. Remember it and don't let it go."

Her gaze slipped first to the Duchess of Hunt and then, without meaning to, she looked to Anthony Basingstoke.

He was engaged in conversation with the lady to his right, a beautiful lady in emerald green, a jade stone resting between her breasts.

"It's not him," Aston whispered amidst the din of the conversation.

"I beg your pardon?" she gasped, horrified to be caught.

"It's never another person that makes you act yourself," he said firmly as if determined that she should truly understand him. "It's something in you."

She blinked back sudden tears and wondered how such a man could believe that she was capable of so much.

He lifted his glass in salute. "To the rebels, Lady Evangeline."

She raised hers again. "To the rebels."

Now if only she had the courage to see it through.

THE BLOODY EARL OF ELLESMERE.

His sister had picked the bloody Earl of Ellesmere. The man was walking perfection.

Well, not perfect. No man was. But he was milk toast. Bland. Completely without an interesting thought in his head. Which wasn't actually true, damn it. The man was intelligent, cultured, and good company.

"You're pouting."

"I do not pout," he replied immediately.

His sister swept around his side. "Your lip is out. That denotes pouting, dear brother. This is what you wanted, is it not? I think she's already made a conquest."

"I'm delighted," he gritted.

She nodded. "Of course. Hence your expression of joy."

"What the devil did you say to her this afternoon?"

Dramatically, she raised a hand to her breast. "I? Nothing of note. Only that at I admired her boldness, her determination, and that if a woman wanted anything in this life, especially happiness, she couldn't sit idly by. She has to take it."

Lady Evangeline had listened well and he wasn't about to be a ponce about it. She wasn't his. She never would be and, well, he was delighted for her. Delighted. Ellesmere was a marvelous catch.

"But he's so boring," he said suddenly.

Her lips twitched with amusement. "Ellesmere?"

He nodded.

"Anthony, not everyone can be born in a tent deep in the Ottoman Empire."

"That is not the point," he bit out, realizing he was in a ridiculous humor.

"Is it not?" she returned. "All our lives, we grew up like wild ones. I've tamed a bit. But you? You still desire the great beyond. Anyone who doesn't is average in your eyes. An impossible standard, don't you think?"

"He'll lecture her for the rest of their life," he informed his sister, seeing it now, the two of them talking about Herodotus as he instructed her on Greek conjugations.

"I've heard he's quite good with his tongue. Very clever."

The words, though meant as a harmless jest, twisted like a knife.

"What the devil do you mean?"

Her eyes flared with amusement. "Only that to the contrary of your reports, I've heard he's quite a good conversationalist. Whatever did you think I meant?"

"Nothing," he sighed. "I think I shall take a bit of air."

"Don't," she warned suddenly.

"I beg your pardon?" Anthony asked, stunned by her directness.

"Don't go off on your own. It's Christmas."

"Not yet," he said softly as he headed away and towards the hall.

∽

THE ENTIRE EVENING had sent Evangeline into such a state of happiness and complete disbelief that she'd felt compelled to find a moment to herself. Stepping out into the hall and hoping to find the library, books being her sanctuary, she failed to notice the man exiting the salon at the same moment.

She charged straight into Anthony Basingstoke.

Stumbling ever so slightly, he caught her in his strong embrace.

The wise man and lady would immediately have stepped apart.

They did not.

The scent of leather, soap, and some unknown spice surrounded her.

The scent of him.

She tilted her head back and he held her. Held her carefully, his strong hands wrapped about her arms.

In that moment, she could have sworn she could count the beats of her heart. As she gazed up into his eyes, the silence between them filled. Filled with unspoken hunger.

Before either of them could speak, he pulled her against him and crushed his mouth over hers.

She tasted red wine and desire.

In all her life, she'd never been so possessed. Their mouths met, danced, gave and took.

The riot of it nearly threatened to undo her but, just as she was tempted to yield to the madness, to pray he'd take her into another room, she forced herself back.

Panting, she whispered, "You must let go, sir."

Out of breath, as if he'd run to London and back, his usually devilish face hardened, not with anger but with pain and he whispered, "Yes, I must."

And then he did exactly what she asked.

He let her go, heading off down the dark corridor, an angel fallen.

It was, she understood, one of the most painful moments of her life. For though she'd known she could not give in, she felt more alive with him than she ever had in her life and that was something she never wanted to let go of. Not ever again.

CHAPTER 6

Anthony grabbed the decanter of brandy, no doubt many years older than himself, and headed out onto the freezing terrace.

What the bloody hell was he doing?

This wasn't what he'd promised her. He'd promised to help her. Kissing her in a dark corridor where they could be discovered at any moment? That was as far from helping a lady as a man could get.

He winced then took a drink.

"Pass the bottle."

He whipped around.

Aston.

"What the devil are you doing out here?" he demanded, his tone far rougher than it should have been.

Aston twirled a hand, gesturing to the falling snow. "I still love the night air."

"It's freezing." As if to confirm it, his breath blew out in a white cloud.

"Only by your standards. Man of the East and all that. I've spent most of my last years on ships, sailing into frigid gales."

They were both adventurers of different kinds. It was one reason he'd always liked the wild duke.

He took a long drink, then passed the crystal decanter to the man perched on the stone balustrade, seemingly oblivious to the wind and weather. A dusting of snow had settled on his evening coat.

Aston took it, then took a smaller drink. He handed it back and said, "You're fighting a losing battle there."

"With the bottle." Anthony swirled. "I promise I shall be the victor."

Aston arched a brow, then said, "I saw."

"Saw?" His chest tightened.

"The way you looked at her."

"I've no idea what you're on about," he said, flooding with relief that Aston had not seen the kiss.

Aston snorted. "Of course you don't. But I'll tell you this, if you let that one go, you're a bigger fool than all those peers you disdain."

"Who?" he asked, even as he knew he was a bloody ponce for obfuscating.

Rolling his eyes, Aston drawled, "The lady of the hour. Lady Evangeline, since you make me be so precise."

His shoulders sank. "It's so obvious?"

"Not to most," Aston said easily. "Probably not to anyone but me... And probably your sister. Wise woman that one."

"I've known Lady Evangeline for a few hours combined."

"Doesn't matter."

"Does it not?"

"Indeed, no." A look of pure, nauseating bliss transformed Aston's rough features. "I knew the moment I saw Rosamund. It terrified me. Oh, I didn't know I'd marry her. But something deep within me knew she was mine and I hers. All it took was a moment."

"You've been at the brandy," Anthony said.

"Brandy and I are good friends, but I am not three sheets to the wind, as you seem determined to be."

He lowered the decanter and stared out into the black night. The clouds parted for a moment and stars danced overhead, pure crystals in a black velvet curtain.

Aston slipped down from his seat and headed back for the door.

Before he slipped inside, he paused. "Give it thought, before you cast that feeling aside. Once it's gone, you will not find it again."

With that, the duke slid inside, always a tiger, always prowling, yet with a grin upon his face.

Was it true? Was he casting aside his chance?

He'd seen love. He'd seen the darkness of it and where such passions could lead.

Surely, to acknowledge the power of what she'd invoked in him would only be the path to ruin. For them both.

∽

The Earl of Ellesmere had danced attendance upon her the last two days. The strangeness of it did not make it unpleasant. But for all that she looked at him and passed the time in friendly banter as they surveyed the many books in the library, she felt no affinity for him. Nothing like the soul-searing passion that Anthony caused within her.

Was that something to take lightly?

Anthony would never marry her. She'd barely seen him since their stolen kiss.

So, she had pushed the thought aside and continued on her perusal of the vast collection of ancient tomes, reveling in the fact that a man was happy to discuss *The Odyssey* with her.

Christmas was on the morrow. It hardly seemed possible.

A whole day had passed. She and Anthony had steadfastly avoided each other. Wisely, they had not continued in his promised education. For she knew as well as he that, alone, they were a dangerous pair. Something she never would have thought possible for herself.

The relentless placidity of her life had seemed impenetrable. How mistaken she had been.

"Do you read Greek?" Ellesmere asked brightly as he turned a page.

She shook her head, not just in answer, but in the hopes of clearing it. "I do not."

"Would you like to learn?"

A laugh rippled past her lips. "Would you teach me?"

"If you'd like."

"Of course," she crowed. "A Greek tutor was for my brother, not me."

Ellesmere's face creased with annoyance. "Too little is made of the intelligence of ladies, in my opinion."

"When you have daughters will you feel the same?" she asked before she could think better of it.

Ellesmere grew serious. "Yes."

The sudden intensity of the moment made it clear that he was seriously considering that she could be the mother of these hypothetical daughters.

The thought should have caused her elation. Why didn't it? Why? It was not fair that the very man she'd sought to help her find someone like Ellesmere had taken up her thoughts like a conqueror.

No, not a conqueror. Anthony was not violent or cruel. He had seduced his way into her mind with his devilish smile and his pure belief in her that she could achieve her desires.

"Do you plan to marry soon?" she blurted.

His eyes flared but then he laughed. "If you must know, yes. I am not an old man, but it is time. I have spent enough time at play and wish now to make a family."

"I see," she breathed.

He studied his book too carefully. "Do you?"

"An earl must marry."

After several moments, he lifted his gaze. "We are to prevaricate?"

"I have known you little, my lord. What would you have me say?"

"Do you think I'd make a welcome husband?" he queried.

"I am certain any lady would be most fortunate to have you."

A smile lifted the seriousness from his brow. "I'm glad to hear you say it."

The entirety of their conversation was so jarring she had no idea how to continue. Even if this is what she had desired, she felt at sea. "Now, I do believe I must meet the duchess for tea."

"Must you?"

"I cannot be an ungrateful guest," she replied. Which was true. "She has been nothing but kind."

"Then go. But I look forward to this evening."

"As do I," she agreed.

Suddenly, he laughed. "I hope you enjoy singing."

"I do. But may I ask why?"

"The duchess is a lover of carols."

"Then we shall be a very merry party."

"I do hope so."

As she hurried away down the hall, she could scarcely think. This was all a dream. An impossible dream. Days ago, she was a wallflower that no one noticed and now the world had noticed. She had no idea what to do. To suddenly and finally have such opportunities was bewildering, but she would not throw this away. Not when going back would be the end of all her happiness.

∼

It wasn't usually common to be on a given name basis with a duke. Anthony was with several. The strange set of dukes who were friends and had descended on the house were all intimate acquaintances by chance circumstances. His sister had been married to a duke in the most curious circumstances and then, well, he'd fallen in with their set.

The rarity of dukes together at Christmas was also strange, but the friends were so close that they often chose to spend such important days together. It had been a revelation to him that there could be such gatherings. Usually, he was delighted to take part.

Today, he was completely at a loss for the events unfolding before him.

What would have been a joy was now a precipitous battlefield. Several gentlemen, including Hunt and Aston, had headed out into the falling snow. Several of them had been giving him knowing looks.

It was damned disconcerting.

Often, a party of servants would be sent to find the Yule log but

Hunt and Aston did not do what was often done. He admired them for it. For years, he'd had a dubious opinion of the English nobility, not truly certain what they were for, beyond ruling the lower orders and keeping them, well, low.

But after his sister had found happiness in her marriage and Anthony had met the group of boisterous men, which included three other dukes not in attendance to this party, his opinion had improved. Over the last two years, he'd learned that his original opinion was still correct regarding most of the ruling class. Still, these dukes were different. Remarkable, really.

The Duke of Hunt fell into step with him. "You've taken quite the young lady under your wing."

"I beg your pardon?" He nearly tripped and did his best to hide his surprise.

"You don't think Cordy and I keep secrets, now do you?" Hunt asked, his lips twitching.

Anthony sighed. "I had hoped."

"Alas."

They marched through the snow, studying fallen trees, looking for the perfect log.

"You're wise," Hunt said.

"Am I?" Anthony sighed. "I don't feel it just now."

"You've avoided her," Hunt said pointedly.

"I have," he confirmed. It had been hell, turning away every time he'd seen her enter a room. Because in all truth, whenever he saw her, he desired to be near her. It was perverse.

Hunt nodded. "Well, that's wise if you do not intend to offer for her."

The statement, though correct, rankled. "I'm aware of my reputation."

"Is she?"

"I do believe so."

Hunt paused. "I won't have any ruinations happening at my house."

Anthony stopped. "Do you think so little of me?"

"Of course not," Hunt rushed. "But I know passion. I know how it can seize a man's wit and unless you're willing to do the right thing. . ."

"Nothing of that kind will occur," he stated flatly. He'd had this discussion with himself several times in the last two days. "I promise you that."

Hunt let out a relieved breath. "Glad to hear it."

"Are you happy?" he asked suddenly.

"What kind of a pox-ridden question is that?"

"It's just. . ." Anthony turned away, staring out into the vast wood. "I struggle to truly believe that married couples remain happy."

"Ah."

How could he say this? "My parents—"

"Your parents were creatures of fire," Hunt cut in. "The both of them. They were bound to burn each other out."

Was that true? My God, as a child, he'd watched their love burn bright to the exclusion of almost everyone around them. Their lives had been as stars blazing for each other but that love had turned to bitterness and cruelty. He, his brothers, and Cordelia had watched it, victims of its wildness.

Suddenly, Jack grabbed his arm. "Do not be afraid to be happy because of your parents. It is a mistake many of us make. I almost made it. My brother almost made it as well. We would both be miserable men without our wives."

As if they had been discussing naught but the weather, Jack suddenly pointed at an enormous fallen tree. "There!"

The men vaulted towards the potential Yule log and after several bouts of discussion of size and girth, and a great deal of laughter, they agreed.

Christmas had truly begun and Anthony felt more shaken than he had since he'd been a child.

CHAPTER 7

Once again, she'd been at the opposite end of the resplendent dinner table to Anthony. It had not stopped her from sneaking quick glances at him.

He did not seem his usual self. In fact, a strange seriousness seemed to have settled over him.

When they all retired, the ladies to the sitting room, the men to port, she wondered what could be troubling him.

Biting her lip, she gazed at the Duchess of Hunt who had stepped away to speak to a footman.

If she was to make her inquiry, now was the time.

Taking courage in hand, she crossed quickly.

The duchess seemed surprised by her sudden presence.

"Is anything amiss, Lady Evangeline?"

"No. I. . ." Now that she stood here, she felt foolish. To hide her embarrassment, she smoothed her hands down the front of her gown. "It is that I worry."

The duchess' face softened.

"Is. . . Has something transpired. . . Your brother seems distressed."

"You are kind to inquire." The duchess hesitated then said carefully, "Anthony is well. Though I think he is off foot just now."

"Off foot?"

The duchess pressed her lips together, clearly weighing whether or not to impart private details. "Since our parents died, he has been a rock. Oh, he gives the best of appearances that he is nothing but a rogue, but deep in his heart he has always been kind and a little sad. But he always hopes for the best."

How did she reply? That she wished things were different? That he wasn't a rogue? The very fact that he was had led to their meeting.

"Do you like Ellesmere?" the duchess suddenly asked.

"I do."

"I'm very glad. I knew you would."

She nodded. Was the duchess very kindly telling her to cease thinking of her brother? Most likely.

Could she? It seemed impossible.

Just at that moment, when she was about to press, the gentlemen strode into the room, making their way through the artfully arranged chairs, settees, and Adams tables.

The duchess gave a wave of her hand and trays of mulled wine appeared as if from nowhere and the footmen began effortlessly offering them to the guests.

The soft notes of a pianoforte filled the room. Evangeline expected to turn and see Aston playing, for he had done it every night.

But when she looked to the instrument, it was Anthony.

The music which poured from his fingers, filling the space, soon had everyone transfixed. The beautiful notes of the carol filled her heart with an intensity of emotion, and before she even knew what she was doing, she was walking towards him.

As if compelled by a force greater than herself, she began to sing about the promised rose which sprung from the ground. The German words had been taught to her as a child and she softened the hard consonants as she walked forward.

Anthony suddenly looked up and their eyes met. Her voice nearly hitched but she allowed the deep love she felt of the song to press her onward. His fingers didn't falter as they continued.

Her voice matched seamlessly with his playing and she stood

beside him. Wishing with all her heart that she could stand beside him forever.

As she sang of the prophecy that would bring about the Prince of Peace, the entire room seemed to fill with awe and kindness.

Tears stung her eyes. In all her life, she'd never known such kindness. Nor such an affinity to another person.

When the last note had left her and the pianoforte hummed to silence, those listening stood in an absolute hush for a long moment, then the applause began.

Anthony immediately began another song, the Latin words filling her mind. Still, she questioned the wisdom of staying there, with him, before so many. When she started to venture away, Anthony whispered, "Stay. Stay here with me."

And she did. Come rack or ruin, she stayed. For she could not give up this moment as the hush of Christmas Eve filled them all with warmth. Not for anything.

∼

THE CRYSTAL PURITY of her voice nearly undid him. Anthony had learned to play in Paris and the pianoforte, wherever one was about, was his refuge. He had eschewed it these last nights, knowing Aston, too, sought it out.

But tonight, the darkness had pressed in. His feelings had been too many. His confusion too deep. And so, he had walked straight to the instrument and sat.

As she sang the words *O Come, O Come Emmanuel*, he felt peace. Perfect peace. As if their talents had always meant to be bound.

Surreptitiously, he glanced at her. Radiant. She was radiant. Why had he never heard her sing? If it had been up to him, every gathering that she attended would only begin with her voice soaring high, blissfully above the difficulties of this world.

After they had performed several pieces for the rapt audience, he stood and led her away.

Ellesmere watched carefully but not obviously, as he spoke with the Duke of Hunt.

"I did not know you sang," he said softly.

"I don't usually," she informed him. "At least not in public."

"Why?" he asked, amazed that her talents had been so hidden.

"No one ever asks."

"Tonight was different?"

She looked away, her breasts rising and falling quickly. "Tonight, I heard your playing and could not stop myself."

"That is a compliment that I doubt I truly deserve credit for."

"It is true, and you shouldn't make light of it." She licked her lips. "When you played... I felt it in my soul. I know you did, too. You play with such emotion."

"It is one of my few solaces," he admitted, wondering how she had found her way into his soul. How she had felt him so deeply.

She took a glass of wine from a passing tray and sipped it. "The world does not always make it easy to reveal our true selves."

"And what do you think of my true self?" he asked, half-afraid of her answer.

"I see pain and sorrow."

He looked away. Did she see so much?

"And joy," she added. "Your love of the music walks hand in hand with your other feelings."

"When you began to sing, I felt joy. That you had been so called." Dear God, he wanted to take her hand. To twine her fingers in his to breach the unwanted gulf between them. "You answered my plea."

She studied her wine. "And that plea was?"

"That someone hear my pain," he admitted. God help him, his voice broke slightly and he took in a shuddering breath. "I've never been able to put it into words. But you heard it."

She gave a single nod.

"You are a marvel, Lady Evangeline," he breathed.

"I feel—I feel as if I know you. And you me. Why is that?"

"You do know me," he whispered. And God, it was true. She looked into him and saw past the rogue to the man beneath.

There was no point in contradicting it. Rather, she gazed up at him and replied softly, "As you do me."

"You two are having the most fascinating of tête-à-têtes," the Duchess of Aston said, her burr soft as she suddenly interjected herself into their conversation with an overly bright air. Then she leaned in and said, "And you are drawing a great deal of notice."

Evangeline winced.

The world had disappeared for them both. It was the only explanation. Just as when they had been playing and singing they had continued in a world of their own. But it had not been a world of their own but one very much on display.

"Laugh now," the duchess said, her eyes flashing with intensity.

Evangeline did but the sound held no mirth. "Excuse me, I need..."

But she did not finish the phrase. Instead, she turned on her heel and, to all appearances, fled.

"Do not follow," the duchess warned, her voice kind but hard.

"But she is distressed," Anthony protested.

The Duchess of Aston's eyes were filled with sadness. "Because she knows."

"Knows, Your Grace?" he queried, though he wished he could disappear.

"That her hopes will be disappointed."

Anthony shook his head, not understanding. "Ellesmere will fail her?"

The duchess narrowed her gaze. "No, you great fool."

And with that, Rosamund whipped away, muttering, "I need a cup of wine."

What the blazes was she speaking of if not Ellesmere? For it was clear that the earl was infatuated and everything that Lady Evangeline had hoped for at this gathering was about to transpire.

His breath caught in his throat. Rosamund had accused him of being a fool. She couldn't possibly mean...

Despite himself, he gazed in the direction that Lady Evangeline had disappeared. She couldn't possibly be hoping that he...

No. She couldn't. And if she was, he had to make her understand that he would not be the man she hoped for. No matter how secretly he had begun to wish it in the deepest part of his soul.

CHAPTER 8

⚜

*E*vangeline attempted to read her book, hoping that the novel written by an anonymous lady would sweep her away from the man who'd stolen her wits. But every time she read of the mysterious, lordly hero on the page, Anthony's face came to mind.

"Blast," she muttered then flung her book down. The pages opened and she felt immediate guilt. Her poor book was not to blame. Just her foolish heart.

Slowly, she bent and picked the tome up from the ornately woven red rug and placed it carefully down on the polished mahogany table. All her life, she'd dreamed simply of escape. But something had happened in recent days. She'd dared to dream of something more.

The soft knock at her door jarred her away from the fire and she stared at the wood panel, certain she'd imagined it.

But then it came again. So soft she'd have missed it if she'd been engrossed in her book. She glanced to the door separating her room from Charlotte's. Her friend had sought sleep hours ago and was, no doubt, deep in Morpheus' arms.

Heart hammering in her chest, Evangeline walked to the door and opened it cautiously.

It was almost as if she had conjured him with her imaginings.

"What on earth are you doing?" she hissed.

"May I come in?" His voice was barely more than a rough breath.

Wisdom bade her to shut the door in his face. Desire made her do something very different. She opened the panel but lifted her fingers to her lips in the acknowledged gesture of quiet. "Miss Treadwell sleeps in the next chamber. I've shut the door but I don't wish her to hear voices."

He nodded as he strode quietly in. He sought out the fire, his gaze fixed on the ruby flames which gave him an otherworldly glow.

She shut the door then slowly crossed to him.

"What has possessed you?" she asked, desperately glad he had come yet terrified by the prospect of the consequences of being found.

"You know," he said softly.

"I don't."

"*You*. You have possessed me."

She gaped at him even as his words stole through her, burning her with their intensity and meaning.

"I don't believe you," she replied even though she did. There was something wild about him just now, his hair ruffled, his gaze dark.

"Don't you?" he asked, hunger roughening his tone.

She bit her lower lip then nodded. "It is hard for me to believe you could want me but I see you do."

Pain tensed his features. "I hate to hear you speak thusly. I saw your worth the moment you came to me alone. I wish the world had seen it sooner."

She smiled then. "So do I."

"Even so." His face hardened. "I've come to tell you nothing can come of this thing between us."

There. There it was. Her dream, the fantasy she had barely acknowledged, dashed.

But then, she lifted her chin. Seizing her newfound boldness, she looked him squarely in the eye and said, "I don't believe you."

"You should."

"*Let me not to the marriage of true minds admit impediments*," she blurted, her voice hushed despite the abruptness of it.

A wry smile twisted his lips. "Shakespeare? I did not realize you were such a romantic."

"Shakespeare isn't romantic," she corrected. "Not really. Beautiful, poignant, true, but romantic? No. He saw people for what they were."

"Oh?" he challenged. "And what was that?"

"Imperfect."

"Ah." He drew in a long breath. "I cannot agree."

"Indeed?" She was surprised. She had not thought him to be a man who'd given it such thought.

"Not to him understanding humanity but his lack of romanticism."

She frowned impatiently. Were they to argue the merits of The Bard at such a moment?

He hesitated then began in the gentlest of tones whilst slipping his fingers around hers. *"What light is light, if Silvia be not seen? What joy is joy, if Silvia be not by? Unless it be to think that she is by, And feed upon the shadow of perfection. Except I be by Silvia in the night, There is no music in the nightingale; Unless I look on Silvia in the day, There is no day for me to look upon; She is my essence. . ."*

She gasped, for it seemed with every "Silvia" he was, in actuality, speaking her name, Evangeline.

"Do you do that with all the women you long to seduce?" she asked, trying to hide her bitter disappointment that he could at once tell her she could not have him then speak so beautifully to her.

"I've never done this with anyone."

"Then kiss me," she urged, madly. For she was afraid that if she did not ask him to do it now, she never would have the chance again.

"I came here to tell you we cannot have any illusions about our friendship."

"Since I cannot have you, as you claim, let me have this. And then you shall go and we shall think no more upon each other."

Had she truly just spoken so boldly? Had she demanded a parting kiss when they had never even had an understanding? But they did. Even he knew it. For there was no other reason than to choose the verse from *Two Gentlemen of Verona*. They were, inexplicably, two halves of the same coin and yet seemingly condemned to be apart.

The unfairness of it galled her, but she would not beg him to see reason. For reason had little to do with the heart.

"Kiss me," she whispered again. "Or go."

This was her last chance to know such passion and record its every detail, and she would not turn it aside.

∼

ANTHONY HATED HIMSELF. Standing before the fire, her fingers entwined with his, he hated himself more than he ever had in his life. He hated himself for telling her they must part, even as he took her hand.

For now that he was here, he found himself wondering if he'd known exactly what would transpire between them.

Despite recent claims, he was no fool.

He wanted her just as she did him.

The ancients had believed in the forces of the stars. He had not. Until this moment, where he felt as if he were on an irreversible course that had always been ordained.

So, despite the doubts, he could not deny her or himself.

When would they have this chance again? Never.

So, he lingered, angling his head, savoring the line of her throat, the curve of her lips, the almond shape of her eyes and the promises therein. He had to remember every nuance of her.

With aching slowness, he lowered his mouth to hers. This had to last. It had to last a lifetime.

Without hesitation, she kissed him in turn. Her free hand slid up his arm. Her fingers wound into the hair at the nape of his neck.

Holding him close, as if he might suddenly disappear, she opened her mouth to him.

Intoxication had always been something created by wine or discovery. But Evangeline was more powerful than any libation, any bit of knowledge, any unknown land.

He tasted the line of her lips then tangled her tongue with his. No passive participant, she gave him kiss for kiss until, once again, what little mind he had with her was scattered.

Nothing else mattered but the feel of her body pressing into his. God, how he wished he could make them one and never let this go.

He lifted her against him, leaving her toes barely brushing the floor.

Her head dropped back, an invitation.

An invitation he could not resist. So, he pressed open-mouthed kisses down the line of her throat, unable to bear the exquisiteness of the hollow of her throat.

Her scent of lavender undid him as he buried his face against her neck, biting the fragile skin ever so lightly.

She gasped and her hands dug into his hair.

The sensation, both pain and pleasure, pushed him further. Kissing lower now, he touched the swells of her breasts.

With her head back, her neck arched, she was the most perfect offering. Except he realized Evangeline was nothing like an offering.

She was partaking.

Her hands slid down his back then paused at his waist. "I have never wanted anything as much as I want you."

The confession, compelling and powerful, jarred him.

The passion that raced through him, like wicked fire, broke his hold of her.

"I beg your forgiveness," he choked.

"Forgiveness?" she echoed.

He backed away, his hands leaving her body as if she'd scalded him. But he knew, it was he who burned. Years ago, this had been done to him. He could not want someone like this. As if he would destroy worlds just to have her.

That was the path to ruin. To cruelty.

"This was not my intent," he bit out. "I cannot. We cannot."

"Oh, Anthony." Her whole body seemed to exude acceptance and sadness. "I am the one who is sorry."

"You're innocent."

"Yes, I am," she agreed. "But you are not. I see the pain in you and I wish you would let someone help you heal it."

"You cannot heal me," he said firmly.

"No," she said bitterly. "No one can. I think only you can free yourself. It is what I have done. But you did help me."

He swallowed. It was there in her last words. Could he not just allow her to help him?

But he had never taken help from anyone. He feared it too much. Needing someone.

Carefully, he backed away. "Accept Ellesmere. You will be happy."

She smiled sadly. "I am not yours to give away, Anthony. Just because you do not want me does not mean I will marry Ellesmere."

"Don't want you?" he breathed. "I want you more than I want to see the sun again this dawn. But I know where that wanting goes."

"Where?" she pled quietly.

"To hate," he spat.

"Oh, Anthony."

"Hate walks hand in hand with love," he rushed quietly, "waiting to destroy its opposite."

"But Anthony," she began. "Hate is not the opposite of love."

"It is," he growled lowly. "I've seen it."

She shook her head. "I know what it is, I have felt it. It is indifference. Hate means you care. The opposite of love is to be banished from all care."

"I cannot do this. Forgive me," he said again and he bolted from her side, less careful now, opening the door and rushing out into the hall. Away from the past. Away from her. Away from hope.

CHAPTER 9

"You lied to me, you bastard."

Anthony came to a halt in the hall. Though desperate to outrun the demons chasing him, he could not go. Not now. Another wave of self-loathing crashed down upon him as he slowly turned to face a man he respected more than most.

Jack Eversleigh, Duke of Hunt, stood at the end of the hall bathed in the light of a single taper, his face a mask of fury and grave acceptance. "You lied," he said again, the words a barely audible crack down the hall.

He had. Not intentionally. He'd promised to stay away from her. He had not.

"My study," the duke instructed. "Now."

They descended quietly, Anthony having no will to argue. He was in the wrong and there was nothing for it. What was to be done? His mind thundered with the possibilities; all grim until one rang clearly.

He would marry her, of course.

That's what a man did when he compromised a woman's virtue.

They entered the large study, its fire crackling. Holly and pine decked the mantel and bookshelves.

Jack placed the taper down on his desk then glared. In fact, he said naught. Worse, he allowed the weight of his disdain to weigh upon him.

It filled the room with its darkness.

Yet, Anthony didn't truly feel it. He was feeling something else. That thing that he had been so certain he'd forsaken. Hope. It was lifting him up.

It hadn't been what he wanted. To marry. But this was his chance, was it not? Now that the choice had been made. All along, that had been there. The distinct possibility that he would be caught.

"I will marry her," he said, giving his thoughts voice.

"Will you, by God?" another voice called from the shadows.

The Duke of Aston popped up from a chair facing the window. "And what debauchery have you done tonight, young Basingstoke?" Aston inquired, though his usual joviality was gone.

"None," he defended before he realized the inanity of it. "Almost none. But I behaved as a cad does."

"You are a cad," Aston pointed out. "A likable cad and a good fellow but—"

"Yes," Anthony cut in, ready to take responsibility. Ready to do what he must and make the very best of it. "I don't deny it. But I've never hurt anyone and I won't start now."

"Then you won't marry her," Jack said tightly.

Anthony whipped to the Duke of Hunt. "I beg your pardon?"

Jack's lip curled. "Is that what you thought when I caught you? That I'd force you to do the honorable thing?"

"That's not what we do, lad," Aston drawled. "Forcing. And if Jack says you're not marrying, then he's likely in the right."

"But—"

"But what?" Hunt demanded, his voice a whip. "Now that you're forced, you'll have her? Good God man, what do you think of her? You wish to shame her? Or do you think she'll leap with joy that now you'll deign to take her?"

His gut clenched. "No. But you saw me leave her room."

"Yes," Jack drawled with a shocking amount of disdain. "*I* saw you. No one else."

"Someone could have seen me enter," Anthony pointed out.

"You wanted to be caught, didn't you, old boy?" Aston said softly. "Take the whole thing out of your hands. Not well done. But I understand it. I've done something similar in my life. But you might find the lady will not cooperate."

"If she were ruined then she'd be trapped with her awful family."

"You should have given that more weight before your clandestine meeting." Jack folded his arms over his broad chest. "I take it she didn't invite you?"

Anthony shook his head. "I went to. . ."

The words stuck in his throat. What an arse he was. He'd gone to push her away. Instead, he'd taken her in his arms. The lies he'd told himself were astounding.

"What do you wish me to do?" he asked. "I cannot abandon her."

"Ellesmere is best for her," Jack said tightly.

"She won't marry him," Aston said with a smirk.

"The devil you say," Jack retorted. "They seem a good match. It's early days."

"No spark," Aston declared with no room for question.

Jack rolled his eyes even as he seemed to retract from his certainty. "Many people marry with no spark."

"Fools," Aston condemned.

Jack pointed to Anthony. "Well, they could start a blaze and that would be a terrible marriage."

"Would it?" Aston challenged softly. "The way he's gone about it, I suppose you're correct."

"I thought you were on my side," Jack replied impatiently.

"I'm on the side of the lady," Aston said. "I always have been. I always will be. The three of us standing about deciding her future makes me long for a drink."

Jack shifted uncomfortably then cursed. "Cordelia will murder me if she hears I've been acting like this."

"Only after she kills me," Anthony said.

"You're deserving," Jack gritted.

"True." He wouldn't argue. He'd behaved abominably.

"This will make for a most interesting Christmas dinner," Aston quipped.

"Sod off," Jack snapped before wiping a tired hand over his face. "What's to be done then?"

"Let her decide."

Aston and Jack swung their gazes to Anthony.

Aston laughed. "*Let* is not a word to use with ladies. You can't *let* them do anything."

"Poor choice of words," Anthony agreed. "But, she can still choose."

"I still say you should cry off," Jack said, "if this is the only way you would have married her."

"I can't explain it," Anthony said, his voice rough. "I want her more than anything and yet I'm—"

"Terrified," Aston supplied.

"Bewildered," Jack added.

"Yes."

"Welcome to love, old boy. Welcome to love," Aston said, but he wasn't grinning now. "But if you can walk through this, then there will be quite a reward on the other side."

Anthony nodded, still struggling to believe in happily ever after.

But somehow, he was going to have to learn, because he did not think he could learn to live with the hell that had opened up before him as soon as he'd strode from her arms.

CHAPTER 10

One would have thought that tears would come after the man of one's dreams had walked away. Instead, Evangeline strode to Charlotte's door, knocked quietly and waited.

It took several moments, but Charlotte opened the panel, blinking sleepily. "Are you unwell?"

"You heard nothing?" Evangeline inquired, astonished but grateful.

"Only the sounds of tonight's carols in my dream," she said, half-smiling but clearly worried. "Shall I come in?"

Evangeline stood back.

Her friend entered, clutching a wool blanket about her shoulders.

Charlotte frowned. "What transpired? You seem distressed but oddly calm. It is a most confusing state."

"If it looks thus it is because I am both."

Charlotte's eyes widened.

She snatched up a shawl from the chair and hauled it over her shoulders as if its warmth could shield her from the pain falling upon her now. "Anthony visited me."

"Here?" Charlotte yelped.

"Yes."

"You let him in?" she gasped.

"Yes."

"My goodness." Charlotte remained silent for several moments then asked in quick succession, "Did he? Did you? What did you two *do*?"

"Mostly we spoke, but we kissed."

Charlotte's eyes grew to the size of saucers. "Well, you've certainly thrown yourself into your new boldness."

Evangeline collapsed into the chair by the fire feeling so very tired. "I must confess that I am now at a loss as to what to do next."

"Do you think anyone saw him?"

"I had not even thought of that," she confessed, horrified.

"Let us hope not. But why did you let him in? He is handsome, I grant you." Charlotte shook her head, her red locks glinting gold in the firelight. "But the risk—"

"I love him." The words were out and true. It felt so good to say them even if they would come to naught.

"But you barely know him!"

"I cannot explain it. I love him." She gazed at the flames leaping in the fire, wishing they would give her answers. "When I am with him, I feel so alive, so true."

"Is that not because he is handsome and exciting?"

"While I agree he is both of those things, that's not it. I swear, he sees me. He saw me first. When everyone else ignored me, somehow, he saw beneath it all and knew I could be more. That I am more."

"Oh, Evangeline." Charlotte crossed to her and knelt down. "Did he ask you to marry him?"

She gave a tight shake of her head. "I don't think he shall. Even the idea of passionate love seems to upset him."

"Are marriage and passionate love synonymous?" Charlotte inquired. "I do not think I've seen such a marriage until this house party. We are surrounded by loving couples. It is most alarming."

Evangeline laughed and then a tear slipped down her cheek. "I want that. I want it so much. To have more than just a passing existence."

Charlotte squeezed her hand. "You could grow to love Ellesmere."

Holding her friend's hand, she tried to see Charlotte's logic. "I should be lucky to have him."

"Evangeline! He would be lucky to have *you*."

"Thank you, dear friend. I would not have agreed until now, I suppose. I always felt deep in my heart that my existence was so small, that there were grander chances for me than my parents thought. But now, seeing it is true? I want more than a marriage of convenience."

Charlotte sighed. "They seem rare."

"That doesn't stop me longing for it."

"Whatever will you do?"

Evangeline swallowed. "I will not push him. He has made himself plain. So, I must accept it. But I do think I shall go home and plan anew. Now that I know I can be myself, that my parents cannot rule my every moment, I think I will wait until. . ."

"Until?"

She lifted a hand to her eyes. "Charlotte, I cannot help but feeling my chance at love has abandoned me."

"I do not believe it," Charlotte decried. "Something will happen. You deserve love."

"We all do. But how shall it occur?"

Charlotte smiled ruefully. "I do not know. It's a mystery."

"Life is."

"Men are a confusion to me," Charlotte said suddenly. "They say women are the emotional sex, but men seem to be every bit as silly as women."

"I couldn't agree more. Logic is a delusion we all cling to." She shook her head. All the logic in the world could not save her now. "Still, I cannot regret any of this. It has given me myself."

"I have always liked you." Charlotte stood and hugged her then. "I like you even more now. You've given me a great gift."

"Have I?"

She nodded. "Now, I see that when a lady is herself and speaks, there are men who will listen and company that will admire her for it. I won't forget."

"We have both been given something priceless then." Evangeline clung to this, desperate to see something good in this terrible mess.

The clock chimed, a soft gentle ding, twelve times.

"Just in time for Christmas."

"Merry Christmas, my dear friend."

Though her heart was heavy, she could not feel sad. Not when she had gained so much. "Merry Christmas, Charlotte."

Now, she only wished it could be merry for all.

∽

UNLIKE HIS PARENTS, Anthony adored children. He always had. They were magnificent beings, always in the present, always laughing, running, feeling their emotions to the fullest. They had not yet learned to hide their hurts, but expressed them. They understood that play was not a pastime but the vital thing of life and every moment was a discovery to them. They did not avoid leaping because they feared the fall... They thought of nothing but the leap.

How he wished he could still be like that, seeing the world for the first time, not mistrusting that it would hurt him.

As he gazed at the children making short work of their Christmas presents, he held a slim volume in his hands. Was he about to commit a grave error?

He'd had this book since he turned fourteen and had fallen in love with The Bard. He'd carried it with him wherever he went. Now, it was time to let it go.

Evangeline stood across the room, speaking with his sister, dangling a silver ball for the baby to play with.

She looked so merry and happy that one would never have the thought that the events of the previous night had occurred at all. Had he imagined the sheer disappointment on her face?

Ellesmere bent down beside her and whispered something.

She smiled, a beautiful, kind smile.

His heart sank. He had told her she could never be his. She had taken him at his word. As an intelligent woman must. And Evangeline was the wisest woman of his acquaintance.

Even so, he found his feet taking him across the room.

Once there, he stood silently. He was uncertain what to say, so he did not try to say what he could not yet. He extended the volume and said with as much joy as he could muster, "Merry Christmas, Lady Evangeline."

With that, before she could reply, he turned away and strode to the huge fire which now hosted the Yule log. There was nothing he could do now. He had acted the fool and now had to pay the price for it. But by God, he would not make the mistake again. No. Now, he would leap and not fear the fall.

∽

THE BOOK FIT perfectly in her palm. She turned it carefully. The leather was worn with years of reading and obvious use in harsh climes. Instinctively, she knew he'd been carrying it for years.

The audible gasp from the Duchess of Hunt confirmed it.

Slowly, she lifted the cover. The pages had been kept perfectly straight except one. She turned the leaves until she came to the dove-eared page.

"My dearest Evangeline, there are no truer words than these,
Let me not to the marriage of true minds
Admit impediments. Love is not love
Which alters when it alteration finds,
Or bends with the remover to remove:
O, no! it is an ever-fixed mark,
That looks on tempests and is never shaken;
It is the star to every wandering bark,
Whose worth's unknown, although his height be taken.
Love's not Time's fool, though rosy lips and cheeks
Within his bending sickle's compass come;
Love alters not with his brief hours and weeks,
But bears it out even to the edge of doom.

If this be error, and upon me proved,
I never writ, nor no man ever loved.

Evangeline's throat tightened. It was the poem she had referenced in one of their conversations. But why would he send her a sonnet which spoke of love unchanging? Was he being cruel?

The Duchess of Hunt leaned forward and placed her hand on Evangeline's. "The moment I saw you, I knew you were the one for him."

"But the Earl of Ellesmere—"

"Is a very fine man," the duchess said truthfully. "But when you two stand next to each other, the stars are in the heaven, and the fish in the sea. It is right."

The duchess' words wrapped her up in a hope for something she knew she could not have and the pain of it was excruciating. "But he—"

"He won't admit it," the duchess supplied brokenly. "If you wish admission of his love, that book is it. He has carried it nigh twenty years. He has never leant it to anyone. It has been his comfort during many a storm. All through the years of pain he weathered when our parents were at the worst. This was the book he'd turn to."

"And he has given it to me?" she marveled.

"And with it, his heart, though he seems not to know how to say it or how to give it."

"What am I to do?" she asked, truly at a loss.

"I cannot tell you, but I can tell you this. He is stubborn. But if anyone is to conquer that, it is you."

"You wish us to be together?" she asked, astounded.

The duchess smiled through the bittersweetness of the moment. "Since the moment you rushed so nervously into my salon, his eyes following you like a man who has seen a raft in a storm, I knew. You are the answer to his heart's call."

She gasped. "And he to mine."

"I know it." She took her hand. "I only hope he can admit it in time. What did Ellesmere whisper to you?"

"He asked me to meet him in the library after we were finished here."

"Ah." The duchess nodded as if to seem content though she clearly was not. "I wish you happy."

The proper reply was to thank her, but the words wouldn't come because the wrong man was waiting for her. A wonderful man. But the wrong man nonetheless.

CHAPTER 11

*E*vangeline entered the library, her head high, even as she desperately wished to twist her hands together. This interview should have been everything she'd hoped for. It was the culmination of her very reason for meeting Anthony alone that night, so many days ago.

It was hard to believe that she had fallen in love and lost that love in such a short space. But there it was.

Ellesmere glanced up from his book.

"Is it interesting?" she asked, thinking of nothing else to say.

Those green eyes studied her carefully. "In truth, I have no idea what it is about. I've been staring at the same page for some time now."

"You are preoccupied?" she queried.

She expected him to smile but he did not.

"Lady Evangeline, I do believe that you and I are to be good friends."

She sighed which should have given her relief. It did not. For she knew what she had to say. But how did she say it? "I am grateful that you think me your friend."

"And I had thought we could be more."

Thought. That gave her pause. For this was not the way a proposal was begun, was it? She had no experience of it.

"But I think it would be a great mistake," he finally said, closing the book as if he were closing the possibility of them shut as well.

"I see." And she did. Ellesmere was a wise man.

"I—" He looked askance. "Your heart is elsewhere."

The words rushed to the tip of her tongue to deny it but, instead, the feeling that overcame her now was, indeed, relief. "Is it so very obvious?"

"Yes," he confirmed without joy at his correct observation. "Last night when the two of you played and sang, I don't think there was a soul in the room who did not know it."

"Except for Anthony Basingstoke."

He frowned. "I beg your pardon."

"It matters not," she hurried. "I am, of course, sorry, because I think we could have been content. But you are right, and I must admit that I am happy you have said so. I think I would have said it, too. Though most would think me mad."

The silence that followed was only broken when he pushed back his chair and crossed to her.

Towering over her, he took her hand in his. "We could be content, I agree. But you and I, we both wish for more than pleasantries, I think. After all, this is the only life we have. Should we waste it on what is only enough?"

"No," she replied softly but with surprising confidence.

He lifted her hand to his lips and kissed her fingers. "If you ever have need of a friend, do not hesitate to call upon me. You are a wondrous young lady. Do not forget it."

Tears stung her eyes as she cursed fate. Cursed her feelings, and fought the urge to curse Anthony, too. "I wish things were different."

"If wishes were horses, beggars would ride, Lady Evangeline. But I am happy for the time we have shared, little as it is."

She nodded.

Ellesmere inclined his golden head then left her alone in a room which usually lifted her spirits.

She took out the book Anthony had given her and opened it at random.

"All alone I beweep my outcast state. . ."

Tears stung her eyes now. How had this happened? How had she found herself alone? Stronger, true. But alone.

"Should I offer my congratulations?"

She whipped around to that voice.

Anger sparked in her then. "What the deuces are you doing here?"

He strode further into the library. "I came—"

"Anthony, you cannot do this," she suddenly proclaimed, unable to take the emotional upheaval. "You cannot reject me at one turn and seek me out in the next moment. I had thought this to be the happiest Christmas I would have known, but for this. For this, I cannot—"

"I haven't rejected you, Evangeline."

She blinked. How could he deny it! "You have. You have pushed—"

"I have rejected myself," he cut in simply.

Her mouth dropped open. "Yourself?"

He nodded. "I have been so afraid of pain. So utterly stupid. Last night, I was discovered leaving your room."

"My God," she gasped. "Am I ruined?"

"No," he assured quickly. "It was the Duke of Hunt. Aston knows. And I was so. . . Well, so happy because I thought that was the end of it all. I would have to marry you."

She flinched. "That sounds absolutely horrid."

He smiled wryly. "That's what they said, too. But, I think I went to your room, desperately hoping to be discovered, no matter what I told myself. For, if I could have you without myself giving in, then at least it wouldn't have been I who inflicted pain on myself."

Sadness filled her then. But she had to hear him out. "Is that what our union would be? Pain?"

"My parents loved each other," he began, his eyes shining. "Deeply. But by the end, watching their fighting, it undid us children. They insulted each other. Used us against each other. Our lives were a storm."

The raft. The Duchess of Hunt had said he looked upon her as though she was his raft in a storm.

"Every time I pushed you away, it was myself I was punishing," he gritted, his eyes alight with agony and something else, too. "Unfortunately, I punished you, too."

A tear slipped down her cheek. "Yes."

"But I cannot live afraid," he continued, his voice gaining strength as he stepped forward again. "Because I am already in pain. In pain at losing you and what we could have. Can I throw that away? The chance? What a mad thing to do. Because I believe that you and I, we are two halves and when together. . ."

"We are whole," she breathed. "I never knew anyone could feel like that," she said gently. "I never knew I could feel so intensely for a person in such a short time."

"What will I do without my other half?" he asked, his voice honest, plaintive. "Suffer. That's what I will do. What you will do. So, I can either suffer now, or be brave and choose to love you every day. And choose to never let the darkness take over our love."

"Anthony, we do not ever have to let that darkness in," she said. The sadness that had taken her was now ebbing away as she realized that he was choosing hope. "We are both strong. And you are too kind to ever be cruel as your parents were. Look how you showed me myself. You showed me what I could be. You knew when I stood before you alone that night that I was more than just a desperate wallflower. And somehow, your knowing allowed me to make it so."

"And you knew that I was more than a rake," he added. His gaze lost its agony and filled with something else entirely. "More than a man who lived his life drinking and making merry."

"We shall still make merry but together, our whole life long. . . That is. . . That is if that is what you are saying."

Smiling, he knelt before her. "Marry me? Give me a gift this Christmas that we will share forever."

His words, upon their meeting in another library, many nights ago, echoed through her mind. She had hoped then it would be him.

"Why did you let me meet with Ellesmere?" she asked suddenly.

His brows shot up. "I could not take your choice from you. It's why no one knows I came from your room last night. I wanted you to have the freedom to choose what you wanted. At first, I longed to allow the circumstances to force our hands. But nothing will be forced between us. Ever."

"Then yes, I will marry you. Today. Forever."

He stood and folded her into his arms.

"Say it," she declared against his chest.

Without instruction, he answered, "I love you, Lady Evangeline Pennyworth. I love you from your sharp mind, to your witty, wicked eyes. I love the way you gave yourself without fear whilst I hovered in the shadows. I love you for giving me all the light I ever needed."

Resting her head against his chest, she closed her eyes, a wave of perfect peace falling over her. "I love you, too. I love your teasing, your strength, your devilish grin, and I love that, despite all the hurt, you never allowed yourself to grow bitter. That you were willing to help me despite the risk."

"You will always be worth the risk, Evangeline. Always."

Down the hall, the piano rang out a sprightly carol, and the house was full of children's voices singing.

She tilted her head back. "Merry Christmas, Anthony."

"Merry Christmas, Evangeline. Now, let's go find the bishop."

EPILOGUE

The Duke of Hunt had written to inform her parents that Evangeline was to be married. Though she had reached her majority the year before, it had been agreed that such news from a duke would be inarguable.

And given that the wedding had taken place the day after Christmas in the duke's own chapel, they had not been able to attend, ensuring the happiness of the affair.

They had received a brief note of felicitations. She could only imagine how stunned they were that *she* had made such a match.

But none of that mattered now.

The quiet days after Christmas had been spent almost entirely in the small house near the forest of the duke's estate. A house he kept for his favorite guests needing time alone.

They had gone up for several dinners, whereupon they had been teased mercilessly about the joys of married life. They had enjoyed every moment of it, for they truly had discovered joy in each other. And then they would return to the place where they could be alone, together, and in awe of what they had found.

To call the love nest a house was almost laughable for it was equipped with every luxury and necessity including a pianoforte near the fire.

When not in the bedroom, she and Anthony had spent a great deal of time at the instrument, making music at it. And making more music together before the fire; their bodies melding into one as did their hearts.

Love with Anthony was a revelation. Every waking moment was a new discovery. Yet, it was also like she was coming back to something that had always been hers.

Now, Anthony held her on his lap, sitting before the pianoforte, playing easily. His fingers touched the ivory keys as reverently as they had caressed her.

She let her head rest upon his broad shoulder as she hummed. The soft fall and rise of his chest, the warmth of his body, the feel of his arms about her. How could she describe it except that she knew after years of feeling as if she had no place, that she was well and truly home.

With Anthony, she knew they would not stay on England's shores. It was something she anticipated with great happiness for not only was their love an adventure, so would their lives be. And wherever they went, they would make it their refuge.

As the notes changed to a more poignant tone, she began to sing.

"Should auld acquaintance be forgot
And never brought to mind
Should auld acquaintance be forgot
And days of Auld Lang Syne
And here's a hand, my trusty friend
And give's a hand o' thine
We'll take a cup of kindness yet
For Auld Lang Syne"

And as the words rang out, she knew that she and Anthony would go hand in hand through life, their hearts full, always risking, always chancing, and never turning away from love.

The End

ABOUT EVA DEVON

USA TODAY BESTSELLING AUTHOR, Eva Devon, was raised on literary fiction, but quite accidentally and thankfully, she was introduced to romance one Christmas by Johanna Lindsey's Mallory novella, The Present. A romance addict was born. She devoured every single Lindsey novel within a few months and moved on to contemporary and paranormal with gusto. Now, she loves to write her own roguish dukes, alpha males and the heroines who tame them. She loves to hear from her readers. So please pen her a note!

For more information about Eva's books, visit:
evadevonromance.com/books/

UP ON THE ROOFTOPS

ELIZABETH ESSEX

Caledonia Bowmont longs for London's Christmas cheer, but a string of jewel thefts has brought the festive season to a standstill. Society accuses the Scottish Wraith, Tobias McTavish, yet Cally knows he has given up his thieving ways and paid his debt to society.

Toby is determined to clear his name and reclaim the life he's built, so with Cally's help, he heads up on the rooftops to trap the thief.

Will they stop the high-carat crime, or find the hidden gem of lasting love instead?

CHAPTER 1

DECEMBER, 1813 — LONDON

*O*ld Christmas came but once a year, the country carolers sang. Caledonia McAlden Bowmont was sorry the holiday did not come much more often than that. Because the festive season filled London with the most delicious sort of excitement—parties, musicales and balls that made the world merry and bright.

But come Christmas Eve, those amusements would come to an abrupt end, and like the princess in the French fairy tales, Caledonia would turn back into a country pumpkin. Or perhaps a Scottish turnip—rather more bland and entirely unexciting on the palate.

Such was the life of a widow. People—even well-meaning people like her own family—expected her to retire to the quiet gloom of her late husband's house at the foot of the Cheviot Hills, where nothing ever happened—nothing was *allowed* to happen.

Nothing was *supposed* to happen to a widow.

Other people lived exciting lives—her brother Hugh, a Senior Post Captain in the Royal Navy, and his wife Meggs wrote Cally the most exciting letters from all over the world. Cally's older sister Catriona accompanied her diplomat husband to exotic and interesting foreign lands. And even Cally's widowed mother had somehow managed to fall in love—in her fiftieth year, no less—and re-marry a viscount.

But at four and twenty, nothing so exciting ever happened to Caledonia. Her widowhood stretched the calendar round with little respite. For nine and forty weeks a year she was a dutiful, competent daughter-in-law, managing her late husband's farming estate to her mama-in-law's exacting satisfaction. But without her much-loved—and much-missed—late husband, who had loved to tease and make merry, there was neither comfort nor joy to lighten the relentless load.

Which was why, when Cally's own mother invited her to London for a little Christmas cheer, she spent those three weeks ever on the lookout for amusement, or some small adventure. She longed for some unplanned excitement—she pined for a diverting mis-chance. As a girl she was never so happy as when she was neck deep in some ridiculous scheme—like the time she sneaked into the New Club in Edinburgh disguised as a gentleman, complete with fake whiskers, or when she had impersonated Princess Charlotte of Wales at a garden party at Holyrood Palace.

"Punching over her weight class," her father had chuckled.

Her mother had been aghast, and taken on a stricter governess.

Caledonia had of course grown up since those days. She had married and been widowed—which was, she reckoned, singularly aging—but she still had a soft spot for the excitement of the hurly-burly, and took pleasure in the topsy-turvy.

And so she would enjoy all that London had on offer whilst she could—she would dance and laugh and enjoy every last bit of excitement until she was packed back off to Scotland. She would marvel at each new sight, relish each new experience, and listen to each tidbit of juicy gossip—like the lurid tale of thievery one of her acquaintances was telling now.

"Did you hear, Cally?" Claire Jellicoe asked. "They took everything—very last pin and pearl."

"I had not heard." Caledonia had not yet caught up on all the London newspapers—in Scotland, her mama-in-law depreciated the newspapers as being fast and loose with the truth, and un-fit for a lady's eyes. "Tell me all."

"All the Peverston diamonds," her young friend related with relish. "At least two full parures."

"They?" Caledonia tried to moderate her unladylike curiosity at such larcenous daring. "Who are they?"

"I've heard it's a criminal ring—a gang of Romany," another young lady whispered in scandalized tones.

"Who break in at night," Claire went on, "while the victims sleep soundly in their beds. Imagine that—sleeping while thieves prowled your home. My papa would sack all our servants if a sneak thief got by even one of the footmen."

"Surely not," Cally demurred. But she felt an intoxicating rush of excitement—as if she'd bolted a glass of sherry on the sly.

It all sounded so wonderfully daring and intrepid. And decidedly familiar. "There was something very similar—a string of dazzling jewel thefts—some years ago. Do you not remember?"

But it seemed the young ladies were all too young to remember a scandal that had waxed and waned before they were entirely conversant with the world. Caledonia herself had been a young girl when the so-called Scottish Wraith had ghosted his way through the Beau Monde's baubles, but she had a long memory. "It was all London, and even Edinburgh, could talk about!"

"Well, my father thinks it's the Society thief the broadsheets call the Vauxhall Vixen." Claire's whispered tone was full of respect for father, the Earl Sanderson's, information.

"Oh, no!" Caledonia couldn't keep her disappointment from her voice, but the fact was, she didn't want the thief to be this Vixen. She wanted the thief to be a different person altogether—for no other reason than it was too quiet in the Cheviot Hills. Too bloody quiet by half. "I rather think it smacks of the McTavish touch."

"The what?" The young people stared at her, mouths agape.

Caledonia warmed to her subject—she hadn't thought about McTavish in years, but those girlish fantasies had etched themselves indelibly in her imagination. "It has all the hallmarks of the Scottish Wraith—the Cutty Purse—don't you think?"

At their blank looks, she continued. "I suppose it was years ago, but the broadsheets and newspapers called him the Scottish Wraith—gone like a wraith at midnight, into the Prince Street Gardens, or down the Whitehall Stairs, or over the Mayfair rooftops, the papers used to report. But his real name was proved to be Tobias McTavish, a Scotsman of some great skill in the gentry lay—that is, stealing from well-to-do houses."

"*Gentry lay*! Was he ever caught?" Claire Jellicoe asked.

"Indeed. The case was infamous—the popular support for his derring-do was so enormous, the beak at the Old Bailey feared the mob would rise up if McTavish were sentenced to be hanged. The broadsheets made him into a folk hero, the same as they are doing to the Vixen now. So the judge gave McTavish the choice of transportation or the navy, instead of being hanged. And of course McTavish chose the navy—but be-damned if he didn't go on to become a great naval hero in his own right."

Caledonia was so caught up in her tale, she only just realized she had cursed in a ballroom. But she was weary of censuring her true self—she was the product of a large, rambunctious and linguistically colorful family, and not even three years under the rule of her censorious, straight-laced mama-in-law had entirely rid Cally of her colorfully-spoken ways. She couldn't always be watching every word like a hen harrier, never letting herself have any real fun.

So now was her chance. "He served at Trafalgar, where he was mentioned in dispatches—singled out for praise. I know because my brother, Captain Sir Hugh McAlden, was his commanding officer at one point. McTavish became even more famous as a hero after the navy than he had ever been before."

"Now I remember." Claire clapped her hands. "He redeemed himself with his bravery. But was he not killed whilst in the navy, in one battle or another, and buried as a proper hero?"

"Oh, no!" Caledonia could not let such disinformation pass. "Not killed—invalided out, as they say. He lived to retire from his rating—for he had risen to the rank of warrant officer, which was quite a feat—after he was wounded during the bombardment of Copenhagen. He came home with his reputation reformed, if not entirely redeemed, and settled to farm a tract of land up river, swearing to never thieve again."

"Until now?" asked Claire.

"It could be." Caledonia forced herself to hedge, because she really didn't want the Scottish Wraith to be behind such thefts. She wanted him to remain the gritty, reformed hero of her imaginative memories. But she had to admit, the jewels that had been stolen sounded exactly to his taste.

Yet the tricky question was, why? Why would he come back now? McTavish was said to have been out of the game for years. And, to be fair, no one mentioned that any of these sensational burglaries involved his particular signature. "The Scottish Wraith used to leave a sprig of white heather in the empty jewel boxes. The unsuspecting victims would unlock their cases in the morning, and there would be nothing inside but a sprig of sweet and innocent white heather proclaiming they'd been cleaned out."

"Oh, yes," Claire breathed. "That's exactly what the broadsheets say is happening now!"

The rush of emotion through Caledonia's veins was a dizzying combination of vindication and disappointment—to leave a sprig of heather now was nothing short of grossly inept. The McTavish she had admired had been far cannier than to proclaim himself in such a fashion.

"If you suspect him, surely the Bow Street Magistrates will have done," Claire sagely opined. "They'll have Runners after him now."

Caledonia let out a ridiculously wistful sigh. "They'd be fools if they don't."

CHAPTER 2

Tobias McTavish could hear them coming—the Bow Street Runners. They announced themselves in a clatter of carriages drawn by steaming, tossing horses, heading at speed for the gate of his farming estate in Isleworth, an old Anglo-Saxon village upriver, to the west of London.

He been expecting them, of course—he read the broadsheets, same as anyone in London. He had seen his name connected to a string of Mayfair robberies, and he had reckoned that it was only a matter of time before the Runners would come to roust him out, even as he hoped that perhaps, just perhaps, this time they wouldn't jump to unfounded conclusions.

But hope was a spurious thing for a man in his position. And protesting his innocence would do him no good. Once a man had a certain reputation, nothing in the world—not heroism, nor duty, nor honor—could wipe the slate clean. Devil knew he had almost died trying.

"Show the gentlemen of Bow Street in when they arrive, Ella," he instructed his housekeeper. "You know what to do."

The stout-hearted woman—the widow of a former shipmate—tipped him the wink. "I'll see to 'em right 'enuff, sar." They had long ago made contingency plans against such a day—when the law would come barging its way through his gates.

Toby left his loyal ally to her work, and quickly retreated to his personal chambers, where he primed the pistol he habitually kept loaded in his clothes press—a man never knew when the past was going to try to creep up on him. Except, of course, when the past was loudly hammering its mittened fists upon his front door.

Toby set the stage as best he could before Ella's knock sounded upon the chamber door. "If ye please, sar, they's fellas as want to see ye. From the Bow Street Magistrates office, they say."

"Thank you, Ella." Toby dismissed his housekeeper with a nod, and took his time descending the stair. "Gentlemen," he addressed the three men ranged to stand between him and the doors. "I've been expecting you. Would you care for some refreshment after your mad dash out from the city? I hope the roads were not too filthy or rutted this unseasonable time of year?"

The Runners looked nonplussed to be so greeted.

"No?" Toby took a comfortable seat in the drawing room. "Then let us get to the business at hand."

The chief amongst the men puffed himself up to stand before Toby, as gruff as a bulldog before a bear. "Someone has laid an information against ye, Tobias McTavish."

"How devilishly irresponsible of them." Toby continued to smile as if he was as innocent and blameless as all the angels and saints—some of those saints had led similarly colorful careers before their apotheosis. "May I know what crime is alleged against me?"

"As if ye didn't know," the Bulldog scoffed. "Robbery, wouldn't it be—thievery of jewels! Ye're to be taken to Bow Street, to answer the magistrate's questions, whilst we search this house for the valuables what's been stolen."

Toby spread his hands wide in invitation—there wasn't much he could do to stop them—and since he had hidden no such gems, they could search all they liked.

Still, he couldn't let them have their way entirely. "How do I know you won't steal something of mine, whilst you're wandering about my house?"

"By jove!" The Bulldog's face turned a meaty shade of red. "That's enough of that palaver. Ye're to come with us."

"Of course," Toby demurred with all politesse. "I won't but be a moment to finish dressing." He gestured to his shirtsleeves. "I'll just get my coat and hat." He took his time ascending the staircase, as if he had nothing better to do than while away his afternoon getting dressed and going to gaol, though he was very conscious of the lead Runner crowding closer to the foot of the stair so he might keep his eye on Toby.

As well he might. Toby slipped into his room, letting the door lock fall with an audible snap—immediately, he could hear the Runners start to creep up the creaking stair.

Perfect—they were so easily led.

When he judged they had crept about halfway up the long flight, Toby opened his window and fired off his gun.

A cry instantly went up from below, "Jeesus God! He's kilt hisself!"

Immediately, their feet began to pound up to the top of the staircase.

Toby propped the smoking gun on the open window sill, and whisked himself up the hidden staircase cleverly concealed behind wood panels, heading for the roof, from whence he could see that the Runners who had been stationed outside guarding the drive had abandoned their positions, and were running into the house toward the source of the sound.

They really were so easily led.

Within the house, the sounds of the fellows throwing themselves at the bedchamber door grew until the wood surrounding the locked bolt gave way with an audible crack, and the Runners crashed through the door in a din of flailing limbs and scraping boots.

"Where is 'ee?" one of them howled.

"Gone, dammit—out the winder."

"But I thought he'd a-shot hisself? There be the gun."

And while they were doing their utmost to parse together the disparate clues, Toby signaled down to his housekeeper, who waited in the stable block, and who immediately set off down the now-abandoned drive in a covered carriage.

The Runners heard the clatter of hooves upon the gravel, and ran to the window. "By jove! He's scarperin'!"

"After 'im, lads."

And away they all went, thumping back down the staircase and out of the house in full cry. "Get after that carriage!"

Which gave Toby all the time in the word to do exactly as he had said he would, and change into appropriate clothes—appropriate for a nice long row downriver to London.

To get some bloody better answers.

CHAPTER 3

Toby rowed easily, riding the tide running downstream as if he were an idle undergraduate up from Oxford out for an afternoon's chilly but invigorating exercise. Within the hour, he had fetched up handily at the Adelphi Wharves below the Strand, where the warehouse of Grindle Brothers Wine & Coffee Merchants perched on the quay like a fat cat next to a goldfish bowl.

It had been almost a year since Toby had visited the place. The dim confines looked just as prosperous and seedy as ever. And populated with the same seedily prosperous fellows—a number of his former shipmates in the Millbank Prison as well as on His Majesty's Royal Navy frigate *Vanguard*.

All of whom eyed him with something rather stronger than disfavor.

"Well now, would ye look what the cat drug in?" Bolter—a former landsmen, or unskilled sailor, aboard the *Vanguard*, whose injuries had been even more severe than Toby's, costing him his leg—hitched up his woolen pants, and spat into the sawdust at Toby's feet. "Come down in the world enough to visit uz, have ye?"

"I haven't come down yet, Bolter. And I won't, if I have anything to say about it."

"Runners chase ye outta yer plushed-up riverside pad, now did they? Been nosin' round 'ere, they 'ave, making life a misery for uz that still has to work fer a livin'. All cuzza ye."

"I have done nothing to invite or warrant such nosing around, Bolter. You can tell the rest of our mates that it isn't me robbing these Mayfair kens. Got out of the business and stayed out of the business just like I promised I would. Just like we *all* promised."

"A likely story, McTavish." It was Grindle himself, former assistant purser aboard *Vanguard*—hence his knowledge of both cargoes and wine—moored up against the doorframe in his scarves and mittens.

His open disdain for Toby seemed to embolden the hostility of others—Mott, another thick-armed landsman from their ship, stepped forward and drew out a rather wicked looking blade from his heavy boot. "I'll 'ave a go at 'im," he muttered. "I'll carve 'im up handsome like."

"Easy, Mott." Toby immediately backed away, holding his hand out as a caution. He had come here looking for help, not a knife in his back. "Handsomely with that sticker—someone's liable to get hurt, and I don't want any trouble." But Toby slid his own knife down his cuff and into his hand as sweet and silent as a snake—if Mott wanted trouble, Toby was prepared to help him find it. He might look like a toff, but under his gentry togs, he was still a hard man.

"Mott." Grindle growled. "Enough."

"Not e'nuf, if'n he gets uz all stretched."

"We'd all have to be *doing* something to get ourselves stretched," Toby reasoned. "And I, for one, am not."

"My eye," the big fellow swore, and advanced.

"Enough, I said," Grindle barked. "Come in here." He motioned Toby into the window-lined office overlooking the warehouse floor. "Back to work, the rest of you." Grindle regarded Toby with a sour, dissatisfied look upon his beaked face. "Why've you come?"

"You know why I'm here—everyone in the city, including the Runners, thinks that I'm the one behind these Mayfair jewel thefts."

Grindle shrugged as if such a conclusion were entirely forgone. "Are you not?"

"No." This was one of the drawbacks in being a former thief—no one believed *former*, not even his friends. "The last time I stole anything was for the benefit of His Majesty's Navy, and we all benefited then." The prize monies Toby had helped to earn for *Vanguard*'s crew had allowed them all to buy shares to start the business under Grindle's direction.

"And we all benefit now, if we hew to the straight and narrow," Grindle observed, gesturing to the stevedores working below. "I have beat it into their thick sculls like a bosun. But it will all be for naught if you don't keep your nose clean, as well—we'll all be tarred with your brush of pitch."

The thick skull that had saved Toby on more than one occasion was still fully functioning—no one in Grindle's warehouse did anything without profit, including accusing a former shipmate of theft. The suspicions that had buzzed at the back of his mind flew to the fore. "I tell you," he swore, "it isn't me."

"Then who could it be?" Grindle threw up his hands. "We all read the broadsheets—these thefts bear your mark, the sprig of heather."

The damn sprig of heather—it had been a stupid bit of pride, that long-ago impulse to make the white heather his calling card, so the rich Englishmen he robbed would know they had been bested by a Scotsman. "That is what they say, isn't it?"

But what the broadsheets were reporting now was that the current thefts were marked by a bloom 'as purple as the Scottish hillsides from whence McTavish hailed.' So whoever was behind the new thefts knew a great deal about him, but they did not know all.

It wasn't much to go on, but it was the only sliver of advantage he had at the moment.

The other advantage was that he distrusted Grindle implicitly—Toby had learned the hard way that no one could betray a man like his friends. "But clearly you believe the broadsheets, Grindle, and have said as much to the men. No wonder Mott and Bolter want to carve me up."

Grindle turned aside the question of his flexible scruples with a shrug. "They think *you* have broken your word, your bond."

It wasn't the thievery that counted against Toby with these men—they couldn't care less if some rich toff were robbed—it was the breaking of his word, his very honor. But if he could not convince his friends, what chance had he with the magistrates, who would see the few years he had spent as a prolific thief as evidence of his guilt, no matter the many more years he had spent expiating his sins in the Royal Navy? His heroism would be forgotten in the rush to judgment.

And whoever was robbing Mayfair of its best baubles certainly knew that. "What I can't understand is how this thief could imitate me so perfectly," he mused. "How they know my technique so well as to duplicate my methods."

"Perhaps it is a former Runner," Grindle offered with a shrug. "Bow Street made a study of you before, to capture you. And now perhaps they use this knowledge."

It was likely enough for Toby to consider the possibility—and reject it. "The Runners who laid information against me in the old days were old men even then—and thievery of this variety is a young man's game. People our age fall and die coming down from ladders, not going up drainpipes."

Grindle laughed. "You're only nine and twenty."

"It's not the age, but the sea miles, Grindle." They all had fathoms of aging experience under their belts. "And I shall use that experience to catch this thief—the devil knows the Runners won't."

"You?" Grindle's mouth gaped open in shock before he gave way to laughter. "How will you do that? Especially if, as you said, you've been out of the game?"

"I have been out of the game," Toby admitted. "But I may have a way or two to get back on terms."

But he wouldn't get any help doing so at Grindle's. Toby saw now that there was always going to be an unbridgeable chasm between him and his shipmates after he had risen out of their ranks to become an officer—even a high-ranking warrant—though he had paid for the privilege in lead.

Yet, he had recovered from his wounds, unlike others—Bolter's uneven gait on his peg was pronounced. They had all kept their distance from one another for their own reasons.

Toby's reasons had him speaking to Grindle with every appearance of candor. "The old ways haven't left me entirely." Toby had kept his hand in, practicing his skills in the comfort of his own home, picking locks and breaking into strong boxes for his own amusement —a gentleman ought to have a hobby.

Which was now catching the thief. All he had to do was reckon where the crafty fellow was going to strike next, before the man himself had even thought of it.

But the problem was that Toby no longer had the information he needed about society—about just who had jewels worth stealing. He needed to know where they lived, in which rooms they kept their jewels, and what time they went to sleep. He needed to know if they had dogs, or guns, or vigilant servants, or took extraordinary precautions against theft.

And he wasn't going to find that information at Grindle Brothers.

"I'll see myself out, Grindle. Thank the lads for not carving me up, will you?"

"You'll stay away?" the merchant asked. "So there won't be Runners sniffing around here daily, putting people off? Makes my men nervous, puts them on edge. Makes customers think I'm not running an honest establishment."

Toby felt a wry smile carve up his lip. "And we certainly wouldn't want that, would we?"

CHAPTER 4

Cally all but stuck her head out the window of the Balfour town coach as it maneuvered its elegant way through the carriages, carts and drays coming and going, jostling for position in the yard of Grindle Brothers Wine & Coffee Merchants like bees busy at the entrance to a hive.

She was more thankful than ever that her kind mama understood her need to be up and about and doing—being useful while also exploring all of London, not just the hundred acres of Mayfair frequented by the *Ton*.

But being frequented by the *Ton* was also what had led her to Grindle Brothers—the wine merchant was fast becoming the purveyor of choice to the Beau Monde. Grindle's would not only supply and deliver the vast quantities of wine and spirits needed for her mama's Christmas masquerade, they would also provide the raft of trained extra footmen that such an evening required. The strain on the Balfour House staff would therefore be minimal.

Cally alit from the coach with the assured assistance of Balfour House's most imposing footman, Tom Dancy, who attempted to shield her from the fray. "If you'll come this way, ma'am."

But Cally delighted in the fray. She loved the hurly-burly atmosphere

—especially when the cacophony of sights and sounds was made more dramatic by the arrival of a coach of foaming, tossing horses that disgorged a bevy of rough looking fellows all attired in red waistcoats.

Bow Street Runners!

"You'll want to steer clear of those Robin Red Breasts, ma'am," the poor footman advised, trying in vain to herd her back toward the coach.

"Nothing of the kind," Cally insisted as she deftly sidestepped him to plunge after the Runners, who had spilled into the open building like rats seeking grain, and were greeted and treated as such by the even rougher-looking denizens of the warehouse, if the shouts and curses assaulting her ears were any indication—she was surprised to see no one swinging a shovel.

Cally made for a nearby stair in hopes of gaining a vantage point from which to view the warehouse floor, when a peg-legged fellow clambered hastily past, gripping the wooden railings hard enough to make them shake as he hoisted himself upward, toward a glass-fronted office that overlooked the floor.

"Mr. Grindle!" The man called out while he was only half-way through the office door. "They's Runners 'ere now." He shot a vicious glare at a dashing-looking bearded gentleman seated at his leisure in a chair before the desk. "Poking around, lookin' fer 'im"—a thick finger jabbed at the gentleman, who eased to his feet, unperturbed by such bristling hostility—"an' no doubt. Makin' trouble for uz, he is."

The greasy, nip-cheese looking fellow who must be Grindle was up and out of his chair, and at the window in a shot. "Where are they?"

Cally pressed herself into the wall at her back to make herself as invisible as possible as a lady could while eavesdropping in a fur-trimmed pelisse and a feather-capped hat.

"Swank carriage out the front." The peg-legged fellow hooked a thumb over his shoulder.

Grindle was all efficient alarm. "Best leave by water." He turned and pointed the still self-possessed gentleman the way down a back stair. "Bolter will ensure you aren't seen."

They were gone from Cally's view within moments, but so determined was she not to miss a moment of the drama playing itself out across Grindle's warehouse that she snatched up her skirts and ran around the outside of the building, past the astonished footman —"Come on, Tom!"—and through the maze of stacked sacks of aromatic coffee beans, to reach the quayside at the river.

She was just in time to see the intriguing gentleman—such a look of keenness in his bright blue eyes—descend into a serviceable wherry minded by a cherub-faced imp of indeterminate age.

"Take 'im up river, quick-like, Betty," the man Bolter ordered her.

"Wot? All the way to Islewerf?" the girl protested. "Tide's turning, and besides, I'm meant to take Grindle's scribbles downriver, to Vinner's Hall."

"No, not to Isleworth." The rather dashing bearded gentleman took command as he jumped nimbly into the boat. "Three Crane Stairs will do nicely. Just give Grindle's orders to me." He held out his hand. "I'll take them and save you the trip, Betty. Smartly now."

But the contrary child scampered to the oars. "Ain't givin' you nofink. And whatchu want 'ere? And why should we help ye, when yer giving everyone such trouble with yer thievery?"

The keen-eyed gentleman looked none too pleased with that declaration. "I'm not about to argue with a gamin barely out of pigtails." He took his place at the front set of oars. "If you're coming, just put your back into it without any lip."

The girl Betty did so with a flurry of batted lashes. "Ye outta like my lip—I like yers. Yer 'andsome enough. For a toff. And a thief and a rogue."

And so he was handsome enough, with his bright, mischievous eyes, and well-formed lips nearly hidden by a rough beard. Especially if he were a thief and a rogue.

Most especially if he were the thief and rogue she sought. Along with all of London, it seemed.

"Tom?" Cally asked without ever taking her eyes from the departed wherry. "Where is Three Crane Stairs?"

"The City, ma'am." He pointed eastward. "The stairs give out to the gates of Vintner's Hall."

"Excellent. Fetch me a wherry, if you please."

"But what about the wine, ma'am?"

"Bolter!" she called to the astonished giant who nonetheless turned obediently to her service. "Here is my order for the Viscountess Balfour." She thrust the folded foolscap with the listing she had made of bottles of claret and Madeira to be purchased. "Pray give it to Grindle and have him wait upon Mr. Withers, the butler at Balfour House, tomorrow morning."

"Very good, madame," the giant stammered.

"Thank you." She turned back to the footman, poor lad, who gaped at her like a dumbfounded Cheviot sheep. "Well then, Tom, let us get off to Three Crane Stairs with all due speed."

He handed her into the wherry even as he muttered. "Sure to cost me my job, this is."

"Don't be silly or lily-livered, Tom," Cally assured him. "I take full responsibility."

She always took all responsibility for her adventures. Because if there was one thing she had learned in the long, lonely course of her widowhood, it was always easier to ask for forgiveness than it was for permission.

CHAPTER 5

Toby kept his eye on the warehouse as he rowed away, diverting his mind from his imminent peril with the sight of the beautiful young woman who had appeared out of nowhere on Grindle's quay. There was something about her, besides her beauty. Something strangely familiar.

Behind him, in the forward seat, Betty seemed determined to turn his attention with chatter. "So, are ye gonna flee off to the continent to escape the beak of Bow Street, for 'e'll surely give ye the noose?"

"No." Of this Toby was certain—he would not abscond like the biblical thief in the night. He had worked too hard to earn his good name, his parole, and his comfortable, calm life to give them all up now.

The girl sighed with the melodramatic fervor of young women who want to appear older than they are. "Always wanted to go to the continent meself. Ye should take me with ye. I can keep house right good, and I know how to keep my gob shut good and tight." She smiled at him. "And I can fence yer stolen bits and baubles with no one any little bit the wiser."

Toby faltered at the oars—why on earth would a girl of no more than five and ten know how to peddle jewels to a fence? Unless

Grindle, or the men at the warehouse, like her father, were doing something other than supplying the taverns, inns and coffee houses of London with drink at market rates?

It was something to think about. But so too, was the more pressing problem of his current situation. "I have nothing to fence—because it isn't me."

She scoffed. "O' course it is. 'Oo else could it be?"

"Is that really what you and the rest of them think? That I would betray you all for a few bob?" It offended his scruples to find that with friends like the Bolters, he had a ready-made set of enemies.

"O' course." Young Betty cared nothing for his scruples. "But I'm not angry at ye like them, even if ye live out there in the country in the lap o' luxury while we all work like navvys for our crust of bread."

"Your father should talk to Grindle if he works him too hard, not to me." But Toby also felt compelled to make another point. "And I do not live in the lap of luxury—I work, too. I farm."

"Sell me another one, darlin,'" she drawled. "Yer never a farmer— yer a gentleman wot owns a farm, is wot you are, living out there in Islewerff with all the baronesses and earls."

"There are no baronesses and earls at my farm," he assured her. "And I've earned my peace honestly—I paid my debt to society."

"Yeah, big hero in all the broadsheets. Must be nice."

It had been nice. It had been lovely and peaceful and rewarding. Until someone started imitating his former technique, and leaving him to take the blame.

He had no scruple in abandoning Betty at Three Cranes wharf, where Vintner's Hall was located. Toby used this wharf fairly often, as it gave him close access to the financial heart of the City, where he hoped to find that which he yet lacked—information.

He slipped through the Vintner's elaborately wrought iron gates, and headed north up College Hill toward Cheapside, and the Royal Exchange.

Toby liked the narrow hodgepodge of honest streets of the old city, with their names that meant exactly what they did—Poultry Lane, Cloak Lane, Cowgate Hill. No grand pretension here, though hidden behind the modest brick walls might be an ancient abode just as replete with porcelain, plate and gemstones as any Mayfair mansion-come-lately, but without the crass desire to show off that characterized the newer West End. Which was why he had never, even at the height of his powers, stolen from the richer denizens of the ancient City—he had too much respect for the honest labor that had gone into building the businesses and enterprises that dwelt there.

Toby walked purposefully into the chilly shaded courtyard of the Royal Exchange where syndicates of investors gathered to insure such different commercial enterprises as maritime trade and personal property. And where the Honorable Arthur Balfour, third and final son of Viscount Balfour, kept offices in the Society of Lloyds.

Like all the best things in Toby's life, the navy was responsible for this acquaintance—his superior officer and eventual commander, Captain Sir Hugh McAlden, had seen Toby working relentlessly to better himself, and had done all he could to assist Toby's rise. Even after he had been invalided out of the navy, it had been the captain who had introduced Toby to his step-brother, Arthur Balfour, who was now Toby's man of business, and the reason he could afford a farming estate in bucolic Isleworth instead of toting casks in Grindle's warehouse.

Toby applied to the porter to have a note sent up—and just in case the law was about, his note asked the young gentleman to meet him at a discreet coffee house near Exchange Alley where he knew the lay of the land—a good thief always knew three ways in and five ways out of any room.

In a very few minutes, the young gentleman appeared in the coffee house. "Mr. McT—"

"If you please." Toby held up his hands to keep Balfour from publicly divulging his identity. "I won't waste your time, Mr. Balfour —I am in a pickle not of my own brining, and I require assistance to see my way out of the barrel."

"The press—"

"Yes, the press. The broadsheets are in the business of selling stories, not in making sure such stories are necessarily reflective of the truth."

"But the magistrates—"

"The magistrates find me the most expedient answer to a vexing question—the fact that I am not the correct answer is both inconvenient and immaterial to them."

"I must say, I am relieved to hear it. Not that I believed the stories," Balfour hastened to add. "But my opinion is not the one that matters."

"To me it does." It was a balm to Toby's battered and abused scruples to know at least one person didn't think the worst of him.

"Thank you. Now how can I be of any assistance?"

"By helping me to stop this thief who is impersonating me—therefore helping the Society of Lloyd's by preventing any further loss of property of the gemstone and jewel variety."

"How can *I* help you do that?"

"As I am no longer in the business of knowing who has jewels worth stealing, I require two things—the first is information."

Balfour visibly paled. "You want me to entrust to you the names of our clients—"

"Not their names—just their addresses, and their basic worth, and the general description of their jewels, so I can judge for myself." Toby smiled to mitigate his gall. "If you don't mind."

"Good Lord."

Toby didn't know if it was the baldness of his request, or his brass in asking for it in the first place that struck young Balfour so. But he didn't have time to flatter or massage the information out of the man —his cravat felt enough like a noose as it was.

"We have a common interest, Mr. Balfour—you and I both want to see these robberies ended. We need to work together or we will both surely lose—you will lose business and money. But I, Mr. Balfour, will lose my life."

"When you put it that way…" the young man hedged. "But you are, if you don't mind my saying so, what we would call a bad risk."

"So I am." Toby accepted the fact calmly. "But I'm a safer risk that doing nothing."

"Perhaps," Balfour hedged.

"And if I am able to find the real thief sooner, rather than later, there is a greater chance that I can recover some of the stolen jewels." It was, in actuality, a rather slim chance—a good professional thief would have, to use young Betty's words, 'fenced them with no one the wiser.' But Toby would use every last bit of leverage he could pry into the Honorable Mr. Balfour. "And you'll get the all credit."

"Well yes, I suppose that would be nice—rather a boon to one's prospects."

"Indeed. So think about putting your hands on that information I need." Because Toby already had other things to think about—a constable was peering through the window at the front of the coffee house. And behind him, damn her sneaky eyes, was the very young woman with whom he had rowed downriver. Betty had peached.

Who said there was honor amongst thieves?

Toby immediately stood to take his leave. "Good afternoon, Mr. Balfour. My second requirement will have to wait, as I'll be making a timely exit through the back."

"I wouldn't, if I were you." The cool voice belonged to an astonishingly beautiful young woman who stepped between their table and the window, blocking the constable's line of sight.

"Hello, Arthur." She smiled at Toby even as she greeted Balfour. "What interesting friends you have. But as I was saying, you'd best find another means of escape unless you mean to meet the Runner lurking in the shadows of the alleyway. And I can't imagine that should end well."

It was the strangely familiar woman he had glimpsed on the quay as he had escaped Grindle's. But what she might have to do with either Grindle, Betty—who was clearly everything petty and thorough, exactly like her father—or Balfour, Toby could not fathom.

He only knew good advice when he heard it. "Thank you kindly. I believe I'll head for the roof. And hope to hell the drainpipes aren't frozen over."

CHAPTER 6

Toby took a small set of rooms at the Inn of the Three Kings off Davies Street, right in the heart of merry, Christmasing Mayfair. The cheerful, bustling inn was large enough to make him no more than another well-heeled traveler in the seasonal crowd, and provided him a comfortable, warm place to rest his head while the Runners stalked his cold farmstead.

He immediately wrote a note directing his housekeeper to close up his house, take down the knocker and take herself off on an extended Christmas visit to her sister's in Norwich, which was sufficiently far away to seriously inconvenience the Runner who would most assuredly be assigned to follow her.

It was the little things that gave him pleasure.

Like his beautifully made skiff—Toby sent another note round to Grindle, asking him to store the boat until further notice. And then, he took himself off to a barber, followed by his tailor in Saville Street, so that the following day, Toby might join the well-dressed crowds in the galleries of Somerset House, where he parked himself in front of a gorgeous bronze by Verrochio, and waited until the Honorable Mr. Arthur Balfour made his nervous way across the parquet floor.

"I almost didn't recognize you after the other day," Balfour said by way of greeting, as he admired Toby's beautifully cut bath superfine. "You have exquisite taste."

Toby tried to school his expression into a smile. "Thank you."

Balfour had the grace to color. "Not that I'm surprised."

"And yet you are," Toby concluded in the same wry tone.

"I am," Balfour admitted. "I've never met someone of the criminal class with…" He let the thought lie unspoken.

"Such good taste?" It wasn't the first time Toby had heard such a charge. "And you're wondering how a man like myself—low born, and Scots to boot, would acquire such good taste, but you're too well-bred to ask. Go ahead—ask."

"Well, why did you take it up in the first place?"

"Farming? A man has to have a profession."

"I meant"—Balfour lowered his voice—"jewel theft. You're a man of obvious sense as well as taste—you must know that in the end, crime doesn't pay."

"Ah, but it does, my dear boy—ask any banker. But to answer your question, I took up theft to acquire this good taste that you are so obviously admiring—and which I admire as well—to afford the things that a crofter's son could never dream of if he didn't take shortest route off the moor."

"And how *did* you get off the moor?"

"Strong legs and natural agility—I walked. And then by virtue of those same endowments, I joined a traveling circus to make my fortune. Unfortunately, the circus folded just before we reached London. I was destitute and hungry, and although such a state was hardly new to me, I decided to put my agility to a more commercially rewarding use."

"So you stole."

"I did indeed." He would not deny that which had long ago been lawfully proved. "Very successfully."

Arthur Balfour shook his head. "You claim your lack of scruples honestly."

"If it helps your judgement of my scruples, I only stole from those whom I judged would never go hungry."

"Ah, so you're something of a present-day Robin Hood, are you, stealing from the rich?"

"But not giving to the poor," Toby corrected him. "No. I kept every single thing I stole for myself—or at least kept the money from the sale. I admit I was a thief—just like you."

"I am nothing of the kind, sir." Balfour was all sudden effrontery. "My profession is to assesses risk and—"

"You make wagers on other people's money—and sometimes *with* other people's money. When you make a mistake, do you give the money back?"

"I work within the bounds of the law."

"At the moment, I don't have that luxury, because the law will condemn me no matter that I have not actually stolen anything in years. I paid my debt to society with my own blood—and the blood of other honest, true men—and I still have to prove my innocence every day of my life." Toby took to his feet to exercise his feelings. "But it is a far harder thing to prove that you haven't done something than to prove that you have."

"But this is England, and the rule of law is fair."

"Only if you can afford to make the rule of law work for you. The law shan't be fair to me—the magistrate will condemn me by reputation alone, without any shred of actual evidence."

"Yes. I suppose he will…" Balfour's voice trailed off in a way that prompted Toby to take a closer look at him—the poor fellow looked a little too green around the gills.

"What is it? What is it you aren't telling me."

"I'm afraid I told the magistrate what you are planning to do."

Toby would have sworn a blue oath had he not been standing in the middle of a public gallery. "Well, that is at least refreshingly honest. I suppose I ought to have expected it." He really *had* been out of the game for far too long—he had gone soft. "They swore against me, I suppose?"

"No, actually, they thought it was a wonderful idea for me to set you up. They think you're going to hand them the evidence they seek —they think they'll catch you red-handed, as it were."

Toby took that news with a dose of navy fatalism—there was no avoiding the coming battle, so a man had best make peace with the cannonballs. "They think it's me anyway—though I thank you for the warning. And it may even prove a boon to have two sets of eyes watching the right places—mine and theirs. Perhaps their zealousness will be useful, after all. And speaking of useful—I'm being useful to you in trying to put a stop to these thefts, and therefore your losses. But you have yet to be useful to me—especially after you've 'peached on me,' as we of the criminal class would say."

Balfour colored again. "I needed some assurance that you wouldn't play me for a fool. So if the Runners do catch you stealing from these people I'm about to give you—"

So Balfour did plan on assisting him—the realization mitigated some of Toby's annoyance. "My loyalty to your brother was your assurance. But I had hoped my word alone might have been."

Balfour was apologetic. "I'm sorry, but I didn't think I knew you well enough to take you solely at your word. As I said, you're a rather bad risk."

That was also refreshingly honest. "Enough weighing out of scruples. Give me your list or don't, but decide now."

Reluctantly, young Mr. Balfour reached into the breast pocket of his coat and withdrew a folded and sealed paper.

Toby felt the strange sort of anticipatory tingle he used to get before handling precious jewels as he broke the seal. "Very nice," he said as he scanned the document. "Very thorough. Excellent." He folded the paper away into his own well-concealed pockets. "Now, the second thing I require from you is an entrée into Society."

"Me?" Balfour was all astonishment. "You mean you want to appear in public with *me*?"

"I am a former officer and friend of your step-brother you chanced to meet at Somerset House galleries. We struck up a friendship. Don't worry—I shan't embarrass you. I do know how to behave in polite society. Though I was only a warrant officer in His Majesty's Royal Navy, your Captain McAlden saw that my training included the fine art of being a gentleman."

"I see." If Balfour objected to equating a warrant officer with a gentleman he kept it to himself. "Well, I do have family connections who aren't too high in the instep, and who have not yet left for the country. I might be able to include you in one of their evening parties. But after that, receipt of any invitations will be entirely up to you."

"Say no more." Toby touched his hat in politesse. But young Balfour wasn't going to be let off so easily—where would be the fun in that? "Thank you for such valuable information, though I must trouble you for one more thing—an introduction to that intriguing sloe-eyed blonde from the other morning."

"Cally?" The poor fellow choked on his own breath. "I—"

Toby patted him solicitously on the back. "My dear fellow, take a good long breath—you look like you could use it before you accompany me to meet this Cally this evening."

CHAPTER 7

Caledonia recognized him the moment he entered the room by her step-brother's side—the dashing, then-bearded man who had rushed out of the wine merchant's on Adelphi Wharf. The same man that gamine girl had taken away downriver in a boat before the Bow Street Runners had scurried and nosed all the way through the wine merchant's warehouse.

The man she was sure was Mr. Tobias McTavish.

Caledonia would bet her fastest mare—the one she rode to escape her mama-in-law's lamentations—on it. He was exactly as she had always pictured him—minus the rough beard, which was now gone, revealing a smooth, freshly-shaven jawline—from her brother's descriptions. A man of "fine mettle and loyal heart," with those marvelously keen eyes. And that tall whip-cord form. And a lean, tensile strength that emanated from him like steam from a boiling kettle.

And why else would Runners have been pursuing him if he were not McTavish? Why else would young Betty have brazenly called him a thief as well as a rogue?

He had to be Tobias McTavish.

Mostly especially because she wanted him to be.

Even more so when poor Arthur turned as red as a winter radish when Caledonia separated herself from her mother, and went straight to him. "Arthur. So nice to see you." She kissed her step-brother on the cheek without waiting for a reply. "Do introduce me to your friend—you know how much I like making new acquaintances."

Arthur's mouth opened to protest, but Cally was already reaching out to shake hands with the handsome stranger, so her step-brother reluctantly complied. "Caledonia, may I present Mr. Ansel Smith of America, a man of business from that country, whom you chanced to find me with the other day." Arthur gestured to her. "Mr. Smith, my step-sister, Mrs. Caledonia *McAlden* Bowmont."

"Ah." The gentleman—for that was his appearance in a beautifully tailored, if somewhat austere suit of midnight dark evening clothes—invested a world of understanding in that simple syllable. "Mrs. Bowmont." He bowed deeply even as he smiled up at her through his blunt lashes. "I am honored."

"Gracious, what an introduction, Arthur. How do you do. Mr. Smith, was it? And all the way from America?" Oh, this was already such fun. "We're honored. Though I thought your accent was rather more distinctly Scots."

The gentleman's eyebrows rose infinitesimally before he schooled his expression back to blandly social. "How clever of you to notice. I was originally from Scotland, ma'am, but emigrated as a child."

"How very interesting. But let me introduce you to my mother, for I am sure you'll want to know her." Especially as Mama was wearing her Balfour diamonds.

Wasn't this the most delightfully rum to-do!

Cally quickly closed the distance to her mother's small circle. "Mama, I should like to introduce you to a new friend of Arthur's. Mr. Ansel Smith is from America, Mama—quite the exotic."

Her mother responded to Caledonia's cheek with a raised eyebrow of delicate warming—which Cally ignored. "My mother, Mr. Smith, the Viscountess Balfour."

If Mr. Smith found it hard to bow over her mother's hand without ogling the exquisite confection of pearl and diamond stones that made up her necklace, it didn't show—he didn't hesitate in the least or flicker so much as an eyelash. Which were rather more thick and dark than ought to be allowed on what was otherwise so masculine a face.

But nature was cruel and capricious in that fashion—Caledonia's own hair was as fair as all the McAldens', yet her brows and lashes were distinctly darker. It was a look quite out of fashion and therefore entirely vexing.

As was the intriguing Mr. Smith, who rather vexingly gave Cally entirely too little regard.

"An honor to make your acquaintance, my lady," he was saying to Mama.

"I do hope you've come prepared to dance, Mr. Smith." Caledonia inserted herself back into his notice. "The young ladies shall all want an introduction to someone of such intriguing foreignness."

"Alas, I do not dance, though I thank you for the invitation. I am a man of business, as Mr. Balfour so kindly said, and I rather prefer the card room, where more business might be done."

"Excellent." Caledonia refused to be thwarted. "I do like a game of chance myself."

She set off for the card room without looking to see if he followed, and went to a table with only one chair available for *vingt-et-un*, the advantage of which was her clear view of the rest of the card room, whereby she could watch the so-called Smith do his best to play the less-than-polished colonial.

He did do his best, bless him—hovering at the hazard table as if he had never played the game before, looming over the Dowager Marchioness of Queensbury rather gauchely to place his bets upon the table. He appeared entirely oblivious to the affronted looks and pointed huffs that lady sent in his direction, but after about four plays of the table the most interesting thing happened.

Mr. Smith drew attention to his bluff colonial self by rather adroitly—or clumsily, depending upon one's vantage point—dropping a gold coin directly down the dowager's rather considerable décolletée.

The Dowager Marchioness promptly let out the kind of shriek one might assume she would loose upon seeing a mouse in the marquessorial residence, and clasped her hand across that copious bosom.

And then, in the best aristocratic tradition, she carried on playing as if nothing had happened.

Which caught Mr. Smith out flat-footed. "But my dear lady," the erstwhile rube protested while he actually peered down the dowager's gown for the missing coin. "That was a gold guinea piece."

Caledonia didn't even try to stifle her laugh—it rang out across the room.

Which had the desired effect—Mr. Smith's gaze found hers, as did his frown.

The dowager was so outraged and flustered all at the same time, that she shoved several guineas in his direction without even looking. "Just go away, you odious man."

And he did exactly that.

Cally naturally followed him. "Well, sir, that was educational."

He did not look best pleased to find her on his heels, but he did his best to keep his civil veneer in place. "That was rather badly done of me, I fear."

Cally was having none of it. "On the contrary, I think it was rather cleverly done. I am quite in awe of your sleight of hand—the control—that enabled you to position the coin just so it would slide without obstruction down the deep vee of the dowager's bosom." She gifted him with a smile of congratulations. "No one would suspect your actions were rehearsed—you've established yourself as the dreaded but tolerable colonial. Well played."

His eye brow gave the tiniest quiver—as if he had to physically exert control over it—but he maintained his smile. "I detect, Mrs. Bowmont, that you are a cynic."

"Oh, not at all." It was no trouble to give him back her widest smile—she was so enjoying herself. "Rather more of an *enthusiast*—that is to say I have an enthusiasm for the diverting and the ridiculous."

"And you find me ridiculous?"

"I find you ridiculously intriguing, and the others, ridiculously gullible."

He played his part to perfection, allowing his forehead to crease into the barest of quizzical frowns. "I can't think what you mean."

"Can't you? Well, you had better dance with me so I can explain it." She held out her hand so that the poor man had really no other choice than to accept it.

"Had you not rather dance with Mr. Bowmont?" he asked with an off-putting frown.

"I had, but as dear Mr. Bowmont is unfortunately deceased, you'll have to do. So fear not, Mr. Smith—you're quite safe with a widow."

"How reassuring." But he smiled, and he said no more as he led her out to the dance floor for the entire couple of dances.

To be fair, they were lively dances that both kept them in close proximity to others and required such attention to the figures that she had no chance to talk to him either. But she got the measure of him in other ways—of his hands, which were beautifully articulated, with long, fingers that displayed a fascinating strength when they took hers. Of his eyes, which were a divine glittering green, and which never stopped roving about the room, taking in all sorts of other details, but never once strayed to *her* bosom and the rather expensive Tudor-era pearl cross hanging there. And of his bearing, which was graceful and elegant without sacrificing an ounce of honed masculinity.

In short, Mr. Smith was a handsome man. Remarkably handsome. A man to admire.

And admire him she did—he fascinated her, just as he had done since the first time her older brother Hugh had mentioned his name in a letter all those years ago. She had rather made a hero of McTavish in her mind, buffing him up to a glossy shine without the benefit of actually knowing anything about him beyond his "fine mettle and loyal heart."

But after all those years, she was delighted to find the reality was very near as good as the adolescent fantasy.

So Cally made sure to keep him near to her side by a number of different subterfuges—introducing him to her friends, encouraging him to dance with them so there was no way for him to politely refuse, and being at the precise point to meet him when he came off the dance floor. "Dear Mr. Smith, do be a lamb and escort me back to my mother, would you? And she's talking to Lady Godolphin—who is, you'll note, wearing the famous Godolphin emeralds. They'll match your eyes."

He turned to her with those remarkable green eyes narrowed. "Mrs. Bowmont, is this some sort of ham-handed attempt to flirt with me?"

"Indeed it is, Mr. Smith." Cally nodded encouragingly. "How kind of you to notice."

He appeared both genuinely shocked—his entire face cleared—and genuinely pleased—his eyes crinkled beautifully at the corners. "I'd have to be blind not to notice."

"And you're not blind, are you? Not with that exquisitely timed shot down the dowager's décolletée. I'll also wager you've weighed out the value of my mother's necklace right down to the last stone, though no one would suspect you of doing so, clever man. And here she is." Caledonia kissed her mama on the cheek. "Mr. Smith was kind enough to offer to escort us out to our carriage with Arthur, Mama, now that the evening is through."

So much easier to take what one wanted instead of asking for it like a good girl.

"And of course, we must offer them the use of our carriage, as Arthur's bachelor quarters are so close to Balfour house."

"Indeed," was all her smiling mother said publicly. But while they were fetching their heavy evening cloaks, she took the moment to whisper directly into her daughter's ear. "Whatever game you're playing here, Cally, mind your fingers—you're playing with fire, and I shouldn't like to see you get burned."

As Cally didn't particularly want to catch fire, she minded herself for the time being, staying carefully mum all the way out the door and through the colonnade where the carriage awaited them.

"Thank you for your offer, my lady," Mr. Smith demurred as he handed her mother into the carriage. "But I am going entirely the other way. Mr. Balfour will no doubt see you home. I bid you good evening."

"Thank you, Mr. Smith, and good evening. Thank you, Arthur." Mama let her step-son see her within.

Caledonia refused to be daunted or out-maneuvered—she used the moment her mother's back was turned to edge into the deep shadow of a column, and grasp Mr. Smith by the cravat. "Come riding with me tomorrow. The park. Ten o'clock sharp." She didn't wait for him to agree, but then, to induce his confidence and compliance, she kissed him.

And while she guessed it wasn't the most experienced kiss Mr. Smith had ever received, it was all she had. And she gave it to him.

The moment his hands came up to clasp her arms, she pulled away —discretion *was* the better part of valor. "Thank you, Mr. *Smith*. You've been a delight."

At which point she smiled and turned away, and left him staring after her in the dark.

CHAPTER 8

~~~~

Toby's first thought, as the Balfour carriage trundled out of sight, was that he had never met a more provoking woman. Or one who intrigued him more.

If he weren't so bloody busy trying to keep his head out of a noose, he might be having fun. And it seemed such a devilish long time since he had had any real fun. Perhaps he ought to frequent aristocratic circles more often.

His second thought, was that Mrs. Bowmont had been right about one thing—her mother's jewels were a tempting lure for the damned impostor thief. Between the two of them, the Balfour mother and daughter had been wearing something of a fortune in very old, very valuable jewels. Perhaps not as valuable as the Godolphin emeralds, but Lady Godolphin was rumored to wear her jewels all the way round the clock, never taking them off—a problem for even the most accomplished of jewel thieves.

It were best if he kept his eye upon the Balfour family—he owed it to his friend Captain Sir Hugh McAlden to stay one step ahead of the thief who might target his sister. It had nothing to do with the fact that the provoking woman had kissed like an angel.

An over-exuberant, bossy angel, but an angel nonetheless—he could still feel the soft press of her lips against his.

She was also quite extraordinarily beautiful, in an unconventional way—her coloring was full of contrast, dark and light. And her eyes, such a clear, crystalline blue he could fall into like the sea. Exactly like her brother, Captain McAlden's. But they weren't calm and restful, Caledonia McAlden Bowmont's eyes—they were likely to be turbulent those seas, an uncomfortable passage for a man who wanted nothing more of drama or excitement in his life.

Caledonia Bowmont was the sort of lass who could lead a man far, far astray. And make him enjoy the journey. But it was not a journey Toby could afford to take at present.

He turned away from the colonnade, and walked way into the night.

In the morning he wished he had walked even further than the Inn of the Three Kings, because he awoke with Caledonia Bowmont on his mind—and upon his body, if the rude state of his arousal was any indication. But there was no denying either his attraction to her, or her intrigue for him.

And so he listened to his well-honed instincts, and then ignored them as he went to meet the stunningly attractive Mrs. Bowmont, who, equally stunningly, appeared to be attracted to him.

She began talking the moment he was within earshot of where she sat, dressed in a superbly fitted habit of lush purple velvet, atop her mare at Hyde Park Corner. "Have you heard," Mrs. Bowmont—he would not allow himself the pleasure of even *thinking* about her as Caledonia—asked as soon as he reached her. "But of course you know —you picked her out especially."

"I beg your pardon?" His mind was rather taken up by calculating the proportions revealed by the close-fitted riding habit—all long, lovely curves and uplifting—

"The Dowager Marchioness of Queensbury. Whose bosom—"

Toby's mind was now entirely taken up with thoughts of another bosom—smaller, and perfectly proportioned to fit in a man's hand.

"—you so artfully intruded upon."

Toby shook his head to clear it, and recalled himself to his persona. "I did apologize to her. It was an honest, if gauche, mistake."

"Dropping a guinea straight down her bosom last night, or relieving her of all her jewels this morning?"

"What?" He couldn't keep the near bark of astonishment from flying out of his mouth, while his gut fisted up tighter than a turk's head knot.

So much for his crass, colonial persona.

"Relieving her of all her jewels this morning," Mrs. Bowmont repeated patiently, as if he were a particularly dim child. "They—meaning the broadsheets, whom one assumes have been informed by the magistrates or the Runners, or possibly both—cannot decide who might have done it, the one they call the Vauxhall Vixen, or the old Scottish Wraith. I suppose you are to be congratulated, though I must say I am astonished. I was only teasing you last night, since I was sure you were reformed."

There were many things that Toby was supposing at that moment, with uneasiness crawling up his neck like a spider, but none of them were congratulatory. Several were blasphemous. All were alarming.

He had been outwitted—but so had they all.

"Mama will be next, I assume, though I must wish she wasn't." She was all blithe openness, as if she didn't have an unexpressed thought in her head.

Provoking, dangerous woman.

And damn his eyes, but this thief seemed to have it in for him particularly—almost as if they were setting him up to take the eight-foot fall on purpose. "You should warn her to safeguard her jewels—have her husband take them to a vault."

"I'll tell her you said so."

"It is no more than I should tell anyone who had a fortune in jewels to lose."

"Yes, they do say this thief is particularly ambitious. And avaricious—no one in Mayfair is safe."

Toby couldn't decide if Mrs. Bowmont was teasing again, or if she was simply giving him gum. And as much as he would normally have liked to trade clever witticisms with a beautiful woman, they were in a public park, where anyone might hear her chatter and make unfounded assumptions.

Anyone, including the particular urchin who was approaching them in the guise of selling flowers—Bolter's daughter, Betty. "Violets for the lady, sar? Posey for ha'penny."

"No, thank you," he said automatically, not wanting to have anything to do with the troublesome girl. But then he immediately thought better of it—had Bolter, or more likely Grindle, sent her with a message? "On second thought, violets would suit you and that particular shade of royal purple you're wearing this morning," he told Mrs. Bowmont.

"How kind you are," she said. But her sharp gaze was shifting cutty-eyed between him and Betty in a way that made him uneasy.

"If you'll but give me a moment?" He did not wait for a reply, but dismounted, and turned his horse to stand between the girl and Mrs. Bowmont. "What is the message?"

"Message?" the gamine replied. "Here's a message for ye—Ain't ye the swell, lording it about the Hyde Park while we sweat and toil with Runners breathin' down our necks."

They had sent her to tax him. "You may tell them I'm not the one who set the Runners there."

"Certainly y'are—everyone is talkin' 'bout the robbery from last night—the Marchioness of Queensbury's jewels snatched right outta her house on Green Park. An' ye, hanging about the Three Kings yard, so close by."

"News travels fast." As did Grindle's spies—the man had eyes and ears everywhere, it seemed. And why was that?

"Almost as fast as yer gonna have to travel to the continent. But I'm all packed and ready to go wit ye. Ye just say tha' word."

"I am not going to the continent."

"No? Ye gonna waste yer last moments o' freedom to go ridin' with that upper crust tart?"

Mrs. Bowmont was not, technically speaking, upper crust—she was not a titled noblewoman—though she certainly looked the part seated so magnificently upon her tall black mare. But the distinction would undoubtedly be lost upon a creature like Betty who appeared bundled in rags to ward off the cold. And he didn't have to justify himself either to Betty, her father, or Grindle. "I am."

"What's she got—besides enough jewels to choke a milk cow?"

He was in no mood to give consequence to meddling brats. "She's a lady."

"Why do ye want to buy an expensive cow when all the milk flows as sweet?"

And in even less of a mood, now. "I'm not going to dignify that with an answer."

"Drat. I was hoping to catch a glimpse of your dignity hoofing it about the park."

It was Caledonia Bowmont, who had slipped up behind him as quiet as the sneak thief he was pretending not to be—another young woman who bore careful watching, for a myriad of reasons. "Mrs. Bowmont." He tipped his hat. "I didn't see you dismount."

"I didn't want to interrupt your chat with your little friend. But do introduce me—I so love making new acquaintance." It was the same request, made in the same sunny tone, that she had made to Arthur Balfour to introduce him.

He was even more wary than young Balfour had been. "She's not an acquaintance—she's merely a flower seller." Toby fished a ha'penny from his pocket, made a sharp toss of his head to send the blighty girl off, and passed the posey to Mrs. Bowmont. "Let me help you mount."

"If you say so," Mrs. Bowmont answered his first statement. But her eyes were all for young Betty, who stubbornly hadn't removed herself. "Such an intriguing and memorable face you have, my dear," Mrs. Bowmont said to the girl. "You're quite beautiful—I hope you know that."

"I knows my worth," the little wretch answered.

"I'm glad." Mrs. Bowmont smiled at her. "But you should have put the squeeze on him for at least a full penny, since you know he's got to pay the price. And can afford it."

That was enough of that. "Come, Mrs. Bowmont. The morning grows late. We'd best get you mounted if we're to have our ride."

"Oh, we'll have a ride," Cally assured him as she swung smoothly up into her saddle without waiting for any assistance. "Shall we try to lose them now?"

"Who?"

"Them—those two fellows in the red waistcoats—the Bow Street Runners trying to follow you." She laughed as she threw a meaningful glance over her shoulder. "Shall we give them a run for their money, Tobias McTavish? Or should I call you the Cutty Purse—the Scottish Wraith?"

CHAPTER 9

Caledonia gave vent to her excitement, and gave her mare her head. Off they went down Rotten Row at a pace designed to shred decorum as well as miles. And why not make it miles? Why not get Tobias McTavish all to herself so she could get to the heart of the matter—and have an adventure saving her mother's jewels in the meantime.

So she turned her mare off the well-beaten, hard-packed bridle path, and angled their course northward along the ice-bound line of the Serpentine River. Cally checked surreptitiously once or twice to make sure McTavish followed, before she put him to a real test by jumping the low railing out of the park and across the Oxbridge Toll Road into the fallow frozen fields of Craven Hill.

And gracious if McTavish didn't clamp his hat upon his head and follow, making an effort to draw even with her by the time they reached the outskirts of the small village of Paddington.

"I had no idea you were a jockey masquerading as a young lady," he observed as coolly as if she had not just called him by his real name. "You ought to be working the circuit at Newmarket."

"Wouldn't that be fun." Cally laughed and gave him her sunniest smile as she patted her steaming mare. "One does one's best."

But her companion declined to flirt, and drew rein before turning his mount southward. "We've gone far enough—it's time to turn back. Your people will be wondering where you are."

"I'm a widow of four and twenty, Mr. *Smith*." She used the name he obviously preferred as she turned her mount abreast of him, lest he think she was the sort of girl who could be led. "I'm hardly a green girl who needs to be minded."

He tried to be quelling—favoring her with a ferocious frown. "That is a matter of opinion."

But she could see the twitch of a smile at the corner of his mouth, as if he were working manfully to deny them both the pleasure.

"Have it your way." They rode on in silence until she felt obliged to pick up the conversational reins. "Come now, Mr. *Smith*. I've been waiting all morning for you to ask me about—or even mention—that kiss I gave you last night."

And there was the discernible curve to his gloriously full lips. "A gentleman doesn't like to introduce such a topic."

Cally laughed again, her breath curling in delighted arabesques over her head. "But we both know you're no gentleman. Especially if you really were a Mr. Smith—they've done away with such distinctions in America."

Her blithe response seemed to make him even more quelling—his frown grew into a narrow scowl. "In America—and in Scotland as well—" he added, "you're what we'd have called a headstrong lass."

"Thank you." She touched her riding crop to her hat in acknowledgment. "I know men always mean the opposite when they say that—as if they judge my head not strong in the least—but as I'm from Scotland, I'll take that as a compliment."

He looked at her askance. "It wasn't meant as one."

Cally laughed at his discomfort—she'd teach him to flirt yet. "Nonsense. You're Scots," she pointed out. "And you like me. You'd never have consented to come riding with me otherwise. Unless...you're like the rest of the men, and only after my money. And jewels."

He reacted not at all to the last. "And have you any money, Mrs. Bowmont?"

Now they were getting somewhere.

Cally minded herself enough to safely cross the traffic at the Oxford Road near St. George's Row into the rather more tame confines of the park. "Not enough to make me an object of unscrupulous fortune hunters."

"But you think I'm one of them?"

"I'm not sure just what you are, Mr. *Smith*. But I know you're not American."

"As I said, I was born in Scotland."

"Where?"

"Fife."

"Which is a rather large place—although it does make us neighbors of a sort, as I'm originally from Perthshire—so where specifically in Fife, Mr. *Smith*?"

"And why do you want to know, Mrs. Bowmont?"

"Why, to see if we have any acquaintance in common."

"We do not." His tone was firm. "I come from humble—frankly poor—stock. Not at all the type of people who have acquaintances."

"Nonsense." Cally pulled up, so she might face him. And so he might actually look at her, and *see* that she was sincere. "I come from good solid farming stock myself—my father was a gentleman farmer, not a nobleman like my mother's husband. Viscount Balfour is my step-father only, and as generous and kind as he is, he shares with my siblings and me some of his money, but none of his bloodline."

"All of the benefits, and none of the responsibility."

He was trying to be off-putting again, so Cally switched tacks to agree with him. "I suppose so, when you put it like that. I do know I've been very lucky and very fortunate in my circumstances—though I have known the abject loss of widowhood, I've never known want, nor ever lacked all comfort. In fact, the loss has made me see what matters more clearly—and that knowledge has made me stronger."

"So I see. As I said—headstrong girl."

"Yes, headstrong. And heartstrong as well. I decide what I like and what I want, and I pursue it."

"And do you usually get it?"

She gifted him with a smile. "Usually."

"A singular girl, as well. I hate to be the first to disappoint you—"

"Oh, you're not the first. And I was already disappointed in you—consorting with such a young girl back in the park. Shame on you."

He was honest enough to immediately take her meaning. "There is nothing I can do about the age of a flower seller."

"My dear man, I may be headstrong, but I am not stupid. You were quite clearly more than acquainted with that gawp-mouthed girl—I saw you go out the water stairs from the Thames at the Grindle & Company warehouse with her when I went there to arrange for wine to be supplied for my lady mother's Christmas masquerade. You nearly knocked me down in your haste to escape the Runners. I'll warrant you really didn't see me, but I saw you."

Now she had his attention—he leaned over the pommel of his saddle to openly stare at her. "I beg your pardon. I seem to have greatly underestimated you."

As that was as good as an apology as she was like to get from him, she accepted it with an airy wave. "Men always do—they underestimate all women, I fear. But we do seem to have lost them, the Runners."

He didn't even bother to look around to confirm the truth of her assertion—he still just looked at her. "Very neatly done. You do seem to have your uses after all, Mrs. Bowmont."

He was looking at her with open admiration—his eyes were shining with it.

He was going to kiss her now—she could tell by the way his gaze sharpened and dropped to her lips.

Cally's heart squeezed in her chest, making it a pleasurable discomfort to breathe. It was everything she could do to sit still, and wait for him. To not moisten her suddenly dry lips, or lean toward him in encouragement.

Or maybe she was leaning toward him. Maybe...

"Let's head back." He turned his mount away, quashing her hope. "We've been gone far too long. And the horses will grow cold. Someone will miss me, even if they can't possibly miss you."

CHAPTER 10

Cally followed him docilely enough along the shaded path adjacent to Park Lane until two rather hot-faced men ran into the avenue ahead of them.

McTavish instantly turned his mount. "Let's head this way to Berkley Square."

Cally set her mare to follow. "They are nothing if not persistent, aren't they?"

McTavish muttered something under his breath, and changed his path again, turning down Stanhope Street toward Chesterfield House.

A glance over her shoulder told Cally that the new set of Runners were still determined to follow—darting across the traffic on Park Lane. But wait—these fellows didn't have the red waistcoats of the Robin Red Breasts. So who were they?

McTavish gave her no time to pose her question—he abruptly dismounted and turned sharply into Derby Street and the crowded warren of narrow lanes surrounding the Shepherd's Market. Cally did the same, immediately sliding to the ground and leading her mare directly in his wake as he threaded his way through the throng, cleverly steering toward larger obstacles like drays with teams of steaming, jangling horses, so they might blend into their surroundings.

In no time at all he had whisked them straight through the market, across Curzon Street and into the maze of Clarges Mews, where they were effectively concealed from their pursuers.

"Well done, McTavish." Cally was all admiration at his skill. "You've lost them for good this time."

He looked annoyed at being congratulated. "Did it never occur to you that it might be *you* I was trying to lose? You and your bloody royal purple riding habit, which is undoubtedly recognizable a cable's length away. And stop calling me that—my name is Smith."

"It won't fadge"—Cally enjoyed her use of the vulgar street cant—"this pretension to being mere Mr. Smith when I know full well you're Tobias McTavish, the famous thief."

"Devil take you, woman. If you don't stop saying that name out bloody loud, you're going to put my head in a noose." He glanced around them for anyone who might be listening to their conversation.

Cally belatedly checked their surroundings—thankfully, the alleyway leading out toward Charles Street was empty. "We're entirely alone—alone enough for you to admit who you really are."

"I'm Ansel Smith, from Boston, Massachusetts—"

"Hardly," she scoffed. "I've read all about you in the broadsheets—"

"The broadsheets are full of lies made up to look like news in order to sell copies and make money, not to tell the truth."

While that was undoubtedly true, it wasn't the whole of the truth. "But I also have another source of information. My brother—your shipmate and friend, Hugh McAlden. I thought for sure you would have made the family connection before now."

"I made the connection," he protested, though he looked far too conscious to do it convincingly. "But I thought better of Captain Sir Hugh McAlden than to feed his impressionable baby sister Banbury tales."

"There! You do know Hugh. You are Mr. Tobias McTavish, the hero from Fife. And the Scottish Wraith."

He muttered an oath so blue, Cally was surprised his lips didn't turn color. "Former wraith."

"I knew it." Her triumph was a physical thrill that echoed through her body like a shout across a glen.

"Don't sound so smug," he chided. "It's unbecoming."

She wouldn't let him dim her sense of accomplishment. "I've never caught a jewel thief before—it's exciting. I feel positively clever. I first noticed you as I said, at the wine merchant's warehouse. You got into a boat rowed by that girl you were chatting with today. And then, of course, I followed you to Exchange Alley. That was two days before you showed up at the Marchioness of Queensbury's ball." She gave way to the irresistible urge to gloat. "Mr. Ansel Smith just fresh from America—I wanted to ask if you'd come all that way via row boat?"

"Naturally."

"But more than all that, I thought I recognized you from an old broadsheet I remembered, so I went right out from the warehouse to find a fresh one. And it was full of the news of the Peverston diamonds. But something about it seemed too pat, too easy. And Hugh never mistakes a man. Never. But if you've really come to steal my mother's jewels, because they've been written up in the tattle sheets, you'd best tell me now."

His eyebrows lofted for a moment—as if he were surprised that she had made that connection.

"You see, you're not the only clever one. Perhaps the Runners haven't noticed that particular fact, as they might not read the tattle sheets, but I did."

"You are remarkably observant for such a rattle."

Cally felt her face bloom pink—she didn't know when she'd felt more complimented. "But I knew you couldn't let these accusations against you stand unanswered. And so I waited. Not very long, as it turns out—you came only two nights later, with Arthur in tow. Very clever of you. And of me. As the barristers would say, Q.E.D., *quod erat demonstrandem*—thus it is demonstrated."

"I must assume your own ambitions to take the bar have been frustrated by your sex, else you'd be King's Bench by now."

"Nothing about my sex frustrates me, Mr. McTavish. As a matter of fact, the next thing I noticed about you was remarkable—you only looked at my mother, who is a very attractive woman, I'll grant you, but she is married, quite happily so. She is also a woman of mature age who did not flirt with you in the least, like I did. But you didn't look at me until I made you. And you did not look at my jewels, as any real self-respecting thief ought."

"What do you know about what self-respecting thieves ought? And perhaps I was only trying to be a gentleman. I kissed *you*."

"*I* kissed *you*," she countered.

"So you did," he admitted with a hint of a begrudging smile. "Expertly and efficiently."

"Thank you. But your mind was elsewhere, else you'd never have let me go so easily."

He stopped and looked at her—really looked, just like he had the first time, in the fields. "And do you often kiss men with the expectation that they won't let you go?"

"No," she admitted. "You were the first. Not to kiss me, of course—I'm four and twenty and a widow. But you were the first man I've ever kissed first—the first, besides my sweet husband, that I've ever *wanted* to kiss."

"I'm flattered."

"You should be. If there's anything all those other kisses have taught me, it's to be selective."

"All those other kisses?"

She would have none of his attempt at shaming her—she had earned her right to kiss as she wanted through the grief and loneliness of widowhood. "Don't try to get me off the real topic at hand here, and that's my cleverness—which doesn't get the least bit of exercise at home." But that was a topic for another day. "You're simply not convincing as this rough colonial character you're supposed to be playing—I'm from Scotland and I know a true country man when I see him. You're far too dashing. No man who moves in society with such sophistication could be this rube you're trying to play."

"I'm not a character, Mrs. Bowmont. I assure you, I'm a real person—a real man with real wants and real desires."

She wasn't about to let him be off-putting—she gifted him with another encouraging smile. "Which is exactly what I'd hoped."

"No." He shook his head, warding her off—refusing to be charmed. "I'm sure you're a very nice woman, despite this propensity to let men kiss you, but you've got too great an imagination, and—" He gave up whatever he had been about to say and crossed Charles Street into the mews behind Berkeley Square instead.

She quickened her pace to fall in beside him. "Do you think my mama might be robbed next?"

That knocked McTavish back a peg—he took off his hat and ran his fingers through his hair. "Are you asking if I plan to rob her? Of course I am not going to rob your mother. I should like to live long enough to regret this conversation."

"That's nice—Mama likes you." Relief made Cally optimistic. "She loves a rogue."

"And so, I can only assume, do you."

"I suppose I do—I know I *like* you. Very much." She had for years, ever since Hugh had shared his admiration for his shipmate, Toby.

"You like the idea of me," he countered. "The idea of excitement. But let me tell you there's no excitement—only cold, hard fear and intense preparation."

"That sounds even better—I like a man who is prepared. So how are we going to stop this thief from using your name? I think Lady Meecham will be next—she was just written up last night—"

"Now, stop this." He held up his hands again, as if he might physically try to stop her.

Which was impossible—she was having an adventure and she meant to stick to it as long as possible. "Don't you think she's the one? Why the Meecham diamond and pearl parure alone—"

He kissed her—he looped his arm around the small of her back, pulled her close and covered her mouth with his.

Every bit of the winter cold melted away—oh, now that was more like it.

His lips were firm and smooth all at the same time, and she was nearly overwhelmed by the him-ness of him—the smell of the starch on his collar, the barely-rough texture of the beard beneath his smooth-shaven skin, and the heat of his chest pressed tight against the layers of velvet and wool cloth between them.

Nearly overwhelmed—he was deliciously frightening and absolutely heavenly all at the same time. Because she was normally everything sane and logical and knew that kissing a rogue in an alley was not the done thing. But for the first time in her dull, deadly boring widowhood, she wanted a man—she wanted him, Tobias McTavish.

And he, rogue that he was, could tell—he eased back from the kiss. "Is that what you came here today to get, Caledonia?"

His voice was low and quiet—intimate, even—insinuating itself into her bones. Melting the few inhibitions she had left. "Perhaps." Much as she might want to, she couldn't throw herself into his arms in an alleyway. Or could she?

She gave into the reckless rush of blood in her veins and did exactly that—threw herself at him, relishing the way he caught her as his back slammed into the mews wall. She wrapped her arms tight about his neck and kissed him with all the frustration and desire and thwarted ambition careering around inside her. She kissed him with heat and hunger. With years of longing, and years of wanting and waiting for the second best man.

Because second best was better than none. And because he kissed her back.

His lips and tongue met and tangled with hers, meeting her need with strength and finesse. His hand was at the back of her neck, cradling her head, holding her close and closer still. Teaching her of tongue and taste, danger and desire.

And then it was over—he pushed her away.

She was disoriented and dismayed at so sudden a loss of him, until a jangle of harness and the clop of hooves penetrated her brain. She stepped aside and took up her abandoned reins to draw her mare out of the way, but she was not yet done with him. "Meet me at the Meecham's ball later tonight. I'll be looking for you."

He shook his head as if to clear it—as if he felt as disoriented as she. "I don't have an invitation."

She gave him her best, most conspiratorial smile. "Steal one."

CHAPTER 11

Toby immediately forced himself to shake all thoughts of the devious and frankly delicious Mrs. Bowmont from his head, because who should come out of the service entrance to the Balfour mansion and into the mews but Grindle, looking as fat and happy as an alley cat with stolen cream.

But more interestingly, when Grindle headed out of the mews toward St. James's the two young fellows who had been following Toby and Caledonia Bowmont fell into step with him. So Toby mounted and took himself off through Green Park, getting ahead of the fellow so he was already there when the merchant returned to the warehouse on the Strand.

"You seem to have had a busy morning, Grindle." Toby had made himself at home in Grindle's chair. "Didn't know you were so comfortable in the rarefied air of Mayfair."

"Oh? Ah, yes. What a busy man you are, McTavish. I thought I saw you near Berkley Street but I didn't know your…friend." Grindle gave the word a suggestive intonation. "Or what game you were playing—I did not want to give you away."

"How thoughtful." Toby filed away the information that Grindle had seen him before he had seen Grindle—and ignored the man's question to ask one of his own. "What were you doing there?"

"I—we, the company—have been engaged to supply the wine and spirits for the grand masquerade ball they plan in two nights. I was just below stairs with the butler, bringing him some samples, making sure the wine was satisfactory, and more importantly, arranging to be paid."

"Very good. And the two lads whom you set to keep an eye on me —what was their purpose?"

Grindle was as canny as a shyster, and answered Toby's query with another question. "To what purpose? It'd be a waste of good money to try and follow you."

"I haven't forgotten that your boys have threatened to kill me if the Runners don't get off their backs."

"That's just talk." Grindle waved the threat off. "You know how they are—all hotheaded bluster."

"Then let's keep it all bluster and no blunderbuss." Toby's tone was mild, but his intent was deadly serious. "Keep them away from me, Grindle."

Grindle was not so easily intimidated or influenced. "But what were you doing in Berkley Square so close to the Balfour mansion, McTavish? Were you casing the ken for your next job? Or trying to flatter the viscountess's daughter into giving you a key? The Balfour diamonds are famous, to be sure, but if you try something that night, we'll all be taken up and no doubt about it."

Toby smiled as blandly and menacingly as possible—he would not let Grindle under his skin. Nor would he mention the fascinating Mrs. Bowmont. "You worry about your men, Grindle, and not about me. I know what I'm doing."

"And what were you doing with that society girl?"

"What I was doing was being taken for a ride." Damn his eyes—the gleam in Grindle's eye made Toby acutely uncomfortable. Not only because he wasn't quite sure what he was doing. But because he didn't want Caledonia Bowmont involved in this business in any way.

Because the ride was only going to get bumpier—Toby knew it the minute he saw her later that evening at the Meecham ball.

It was nearly ten o'clock by the time she appeared in the doorway, a vision in supple, flowing lavender silk. And wearing a fortune in baroque pearls. Almost as if she were baiting the thief. Damn her pretty eyes, because in doing so, she was making it damn hard for Toby to stop whomever the hell it was.

Once again he was at Arthur Balfour's side, acting the rough colonial, as if he didn't know a seed pearl from a seed purse. He bowed low over the gloved hand she offered him.

"Mr. *Smith*." She pronounced his name with relish. "How pleasant to see you again, so soon."

"Soon?" Arthur looked from his step-sister to Toby and back. "What do you mean, soon?"

"Mrs. Bowmont means I met her out riding today—a very pleasant morning ride in the park."

"I enjoyed our ride as well, Mr. Smith." Caledonia tossed off a smile like a smoldering firecracker. "I was impressed by your seat." She breezed on, patting Arthur consolingly on the back while he choked on his champagne. "He was very nearly able to keep up with me over the toll road walls. But I've always heard that Americans are good riders."

Toby decided not to let her have all the fun. "We're also good rides, Mrs. Bowmont."

Her eyes lit with pleasure at their banter. "Marvelous, Mr. Smith, marvelous. So are our bets in on who is going to be the Scottish Wraith's next victim? You'll remember I put in a strong vote for Lady Meecham—she's even got the tiara out of the vault tonight. I doubt the Cutty Purse will be able to resist the full Meecham parure."

Arthur visibly paled. "Caledonia!"

Toby took pity on him. "Come, Mrs. Bowmont, we'd better have you dance before you frighten poor Arthur to death."

She rewarded him with one of her dazzling smiles. "I thought you'd never ask."

"I didn't, but this will work well enough," he answered as he swung her into place in the set. "I must tell you that you look conspicuously divine this evening, Mrs. Bowmont. The sweet lavender of the gown and white purity of the pearls contrast so strongly with the reckless black of your heart."

She tipped her head back and laughed up to the high ceiling, and he could feel the strong defensive walls around his heart start to crumble just a little bit, as if the mortar had been surreptitiously weakened, and was suddenly beginning to give way.

"My heart is not in the least bit black—perhaps just a lovely deep, dark purple, like the sunset over the heather-covered Scottish moors."

"Aye, not quite black as night, but drawing well on toward evening."

"Just so," she agreed. "And speaking of night drawing nigh—"

"Which we were not."

"Which I am—can you tell me how you're planning to do it? The broadsheets say you go up the drainpipes and down through the attics, but they haven't said how this impostor does it. I think they would be better off pretending to be drunk and toddling off up the stairs as if they're in search of the necessary."

He had to admire her imagination—it was blessedly fruitful. Perhaps this thief was not of the criminal class—as the magistrates liked to call anyone who wasn't wealthy—but one of the *Ton's* own. That would certainly explain the invisibility of the thief. "Is that what you'd do?"

"Certainly." She nodded, sure of herself. "I should slip away and take whatever jewels the marchionesses and Lady Meecham, and the other matrons had decided they wouldn't wear. I know my mother wouldn't insist that her unworn pieces be put back into the safe until the end of the night, when she was taking the jewels she had worn off."

It was a devastatingly clear assessment, delivered with frank insight into her world. Or was it her world—what had she said about only being a visitor to it? "Careful, Caledonia, you sound almost eager to steal something yourself."

"Do I? I suppose I might be—in theory. And if I were a proper widowed lady I would want nothing to do with any of this." She waved her hand to indicate the world and thievery in general, he supposed. "But I'm not a proper lady. I never have been. And I think this is the most exciting thing I've ever been a part of—I get a little vicarious thrill thinking about it all, and I like the feeling too much to regret any part of this."

There was a wealth of interesting information about the equally interesting Mrs. Bowmont in that statement. "You do seem a trifle over-eager to witness a robbery."

Her eyes brightened. "May I?"

"No. Because I'm not going up any stairs—or drainpipes—and neither are you. I'm going to get a drink. A stiff drink." Stiff enough to keep him from doing what he had really come to the Meecham mansion to do—kiss Caledonia Bowmont silly.

On second thought—

"Come along, Mrs. Bowmont." He tucked her arm in his,

"Do I get a drink, too? That would be wonderfully novel—no one ever offers me anything stronger than watered sherry. So many new experiences. Where are we going?" she asked, though she had already fallen in with him.

"Someplace private, where you can get what you came here in search of."

There was that absolutely delighted smile spreading across her lips like fresh jam. "You?"

He shouldn't be so flattered. "No—a thrill." He backed her into a conveniently empty alcove and lowered his lips to hers.

There was nothing coy or unknowing about her response—she wrapped her arms about his neck and drew him closer still. Her pearls pressed hard into his chest, the baroque baubles coming between them more effectively than a sentry. His hand slid to her nape, unclasping the necklace.

He could almost hear her smile. "You can't resist them, can you?"

"On the contrary." He snaked the odd-shaped beads right down the front of her exceptionally well-fitted, exceptionally uplifting stays. "You know as well as I do that those pearls are fake."

Caledonia McAlden didn't even blush—if anything she smiled more widely. "Oh, bravo, Tobias." She nuzzled along the line of his chin. "They are indeed fakes—but I'm not."

"You are, too," he growled into her ear. "You're pretending to be far more worldly that you could possibly be."

"Why don't you try me, and find out?"

CHAPTER 12

He did. God help him, Toby wanted nothing more than to try all of her—every sinuous curve and delightfully wicked twist. But he would settle for the wicked twist of her lips that put that devious dimple in the middle of her cheek.

He kissed her the way a man kisses a woman he wants beyond distraction—with heat and perhaps a little anger. But he was angry—angry that she tempted him so. Angry that he couldn't stop himself from wanting her just the same. Angry that she kissed him like he'd never been kissed before—as if she knew *she* was the most precious jewel he would ever hold in his hands.

But they were in too public a place. Anyone might come by—her mother, her step-brother Arthur, her step-father the viscount. "Come," he whispered against her lips, and she came willingly, grasping the hand her offered her to lead her down a corridor to the first door that gave out into the courtyard, where the winter wind lashed against her bare arms.

Toby immediately turned back, determined to find someplace indoors.

"No." Despite the cold, she was just as determined. "I think I know a spot."

She led him at a run to the carriage house, which was well-lit on the alley side, with braziers put out to warm the gathered coachmen as they waited for their charges within the house.

But Caledonia Bowmont was as clever as she was beautiful, steering them toward the back of the carriage house, where the Meecham town coach was put up tight and snug. And best of all, dark and inviting.

She clambered in and immediately pulled out a thick, fur-lined rug. "This will keep us warm."

"No," he contradicted even as he wrapped the dark sable around her shoulders. "I'll keep you warm."

He drew her close to kiss her, so close she was almost in his lap. And then she was in his lap, with her arms wrapped tight around his shoulders, kissing him as if it were the rightest and best thing in the world. As if they had always meant to meet in a dark, velvet-lined carriage. As if he had always dreamed of kissing her wrapped in fur and delight.

She smelled of sweet orange blossom—sunshine in the dark of winter—and she tasted of wicked desire and sparkling champagne. Of brightness and light. Of happiness. Of possibility.

That was her allure—that was her danger.

Because she made him think of impossible things.

She made him hope.

She pressed herself to him, all heat and happy ardor. Everything within him, every nerve, every fiber of his being was attuned to her enthusiasm. And her urgency—she slid her hands along the line of his jaw to tip his head more to her liking.

No docile, sighing miss, she. She was all direct appreciation, murmuring approvingly as she took his lips delicately between her teeth, and bit down just firmly enough that she could be in no doubt of his state of arousal.

She was not in any doubt. "I'm flattered," she whispered into his ear, before her hand found him, hard and wanting, while she kissed her way down his neck, leaving a scorched wake.

He wanted to say something arch and suggestive. He wanted to give her as good as he got, but already he was having trouble thinking enough to speak.

So he abandoned all pretense of thought and reason and gave in to the decadent hedonism sliding under his skin like quickfire—he set his hands to her bodice, reaching around to find her buttons before he pushed the gauzy sleeves off her shoulders to bare the top of her stays. His mouth was on her skin above the line of her shift, and she was arching her head back to grant him access, murmuring her approval.

Toby was happy to oblige—kissing and pushing away fabric, layer by layer, working her sleeves down far enough that he could assay the laces on her stays, and free her breasts to tease the honeyed tips with his tongue.

And set her pearls loose to fall into his hands.

But he was interested in pearls of a different type—he placed the necklace in her cupped hand, saying only, "Keep track of these," before he returned to his leisurely perusal of her beautiful breasts.

Devil help him, but she was exquisite—her skin painted golden by the spill of warm lamplight cutting through the chill.

Her breath came in exuberant, visible gasps and appreciative pants. Within the confines of the carriage, the temperature was warming apace—enough for him to shuck the tight restriction of his evening coat and wrap it around her back. She took the moment to tangle her hands through his hair, urging him to her breasts to suck and tongue her over and over, moving from one tightly furled peak to the other, lavishing his attention upon her in the most intimate way.

"And you," she said, and immediately went at the buttons of his waistcoat before she made short work of his cravat.

For the moment he couldn't kiss, so he spoke. "We're going to need a maid and valet to make us even reasonably presentable enough to return—"

"I don't care." She stripped the cravat from his neck and flung it away. "I have no intention of going back."

That she meant every word of her declaration was evident in her haste to bare him as he had bared her, pushing his waistcoat off his shoulders, and opening the neck of his shirt. Tasting him as he had tasted her, setting her lips skimming across his chest, nipping and kissing from the hollow of his throat down. Setting his blood roaring in his veins.

"Your husband was a lucky man," he said before he thought better of it.

She stilled for only the smallest fraction of a moment. "He was. And I was a lucky woman. But he's not here anymore. And you are. So do shut up and kiss me."

He did so, and then he let her go, picking her up and pressing her into the seat opposite. "I'll do you better than merely kiss."

He left her there, leaning back against the upholstery, bared to the waist and watching impatiently while he began to divest himself of unneeded clothing.

Toby stripped his shirt over his head and tossed it into her lap. "Hold on to that for me, will you," he whispered as he reached down and raised her legs to either side of him, resting on the opposite seat. "Because you're going to want to hold on to something."

CHAPTER 13

Cally's heart was already beating a dancing *allegro* within her chest. "McTavish?"

"I mean to impress you, lass. So hold fast. We're in for a bit of a storm." And to prove it, he flipped up her skirts, and ran his hands up and down her legs, over her stockings to the edge of her garters.

Her dancing heart stopped. "Do you promise?"

His smile was all in his eyes. "Aye. The better to impress you with." He let the brogue he had been carefully covering light the edges of his words.

"Oh, Lord help me, I do like a rogue. And I like a Scots rogue best of all."

McTavish slid to his knees in front of her. "Then you're in for a treat, lass."

Caledonia felt heat flash under her skin, and her head felt light, faint with anticipation and need. "Pray God, you don't disappoint me."

"Have I yet, lass?" His grin was sly and confident all at the same time.

"No." And he wasn't disappointing her now. Not in the least.

It had been so, so long since she had felt this kind of focused, physical attention. It had been so long since she could give herself over to the sensations sliding across her skin without needing the memories that went with it. It had been so, so, so long since she had let herself feel this kind of unbridled, unapologetic bliss.

McTavish put his hands upon her knees and pushed them gently wider. He lowered his head to feather kisses on the insides of her thighs, and she felt herself coming undone, inch by tantalizing inch.

Oh, God, yes, he could—Cally nearly shrieked with relief and gratitude at the first warm, wet lick of his tongue across her. But the sound that came out of her mouth was all animal pleasure.

"Yes," he agreed, and she could feel his voice vibrate through her as he tongued and probed her. She was carried away, floating along on a current of soft, infinitely pleasant sensation.

And then with a precise touch she hadn't prepared herself for—and never could quite manage on her own—he kissed her *there*, in exactly the right spot to make all the quiet desperation of her lonely nights in the Cheviot Hills dissipate into warmth and want. Into delicious desire.

A craving, a hungry yearning rose within her, and her hands tangled in his hair, pulling him to her, pressing his lips—his marvelously clever lips—against that most sensitive place. She felt intoxicated with the relentlessly gentle onslaught of his tongue against the center of her very being.

Her fingers curled and dug into the fabric of his shirt, as if they could bind her to this man, but she was untethered, carried off on a journey of passion by his strength and his gentleness. And, heaven help her, his clever, clever hands. Because, with one sweet touch she flew away, blinded by the explosion of light and heat behind her eyelids.

Cally had no time to rest in the afterglow—while she was still wet and all but shaking from the outrageous force of her release, McTavish unbuttoned the flap on his breeches, lifted her up like a rag doll, and just as easily lowered and impaled her upon his ready member.

And they burst into flame.

"McTavish." She didn't know what else to call him. Good Lord, she had never even used the man's Christian name, and here she was, making acrobatic love to him in an empty town coach at the back of a carriage house at a party she could not now return to.

The only sensible thing seemed to be to wrap her arms around his neck and weather the marvelously pleasurable storm.

She did so with a whisper at his ear. "Make it a slow ride, if you please, McTavish. Let it last a good long while." Long enough to see her through the bleak, lonely days that were sure to come.

With her hands about his neck, her skirts pooled down about her waist, covering his lap.

"No, lass," he urged against her lips. "Pull your dress back up so I can touch you."

Cally felt a tremor of something reckless and intoxicating shiver its way deep into her belly as she complied, hugging the folds of supple silk fabric to herself as she pulled them up.

McTavish kept still except for his hands firmly caressing her hips as she adjusted to having him so deeply inside her, letting her find her own desire.

"Well done, lass," he whispered with that marvelously appreciative, and decidedly wicked grin. "You're a beautiful sight for damn sore eyes. Devil take me if you're not."

Cally made a sound that was very near to a groan as he reached around to her bottom, pulling her even more tightly against him, before he let his hands stray upwards. As his palms swept across the bunched silk of her dress she began to arch her back slightly, knowingly thrusting her aching breasts forward for his touch.

He did not disappoint her, stroking the sensitive undersides with his fingers before moving on to draw the backs of his knuckles across her rosy pink nipples, running his fingers back and forth, grazing against the sensitive peaks until they pebbled, and she gasped with the exquisite pleasure.

"Beautiful," he whispered again.

She was drenched in thankful pleasure that poured through her until she had to move, had to chase the bliss that she knew was just out of reach.

"That's right, lass." He kissed her neck, and then her ear, and then kissed her deeply on the mouth.

Cally responded instantly, channeling all her need to touch him into her mouth, into the play of her tongue with his. McTavish moved his nimble, articulate hands to the apex of her thighs, and let his fingers play against the sensitive nub at the center of her being.

She rocked her hips into him, creating the sweet, unbearable friction between their bodies, and clever man that he was, he let her set the pace, let her find the rhythm she needed, until need and knowledge made her move more urgently.

McTavish matched her motion, rocking his hips in rhythm to meet hers, driving upwards into her with his own increased need as she spiraled higher.

Cally could feel her legs start to clamp together, could feel the glorious slippery tension that signaled her need for release. "Please."

He heard her and understood her inchoate plea. He kept one hand on her, urging her towards her fulfillment, while he wrapped the other around her waist and began to urge her up and down, sliding deeper into her slick heat.

She couldn't stop herself, couldn't think, couldn't do anything but try to bring the bliss nearer and nearer, faster and faster toward the rush of oblivion.

The one thought she could form, as her climax blossomed through her body, was to kiss him on the mouth to mute her unbridled scream.

CHAPTER 14

Their parting was swift and nearly silent. Caledonia Bowmont returned to the bench opposite to let her breathing slowly return to normal, and quietly put her clothes to rights, though nothing much could be done for the tousled mess of her hair—she retrieved a pin or two from the carriage floor and pinned it up in a quick twist.

Toby had all he could do not to stop her from tucking the long golden strands away with the rest of her inhibitions.

But they had both best return to their respective places in the world before the collision of their planetary houses was discovered. He picked up the pearl necklace that had fallen to the floor, and returned it to her hand. "Perhaps you had best return first?"

"No." Her denial was quiet but firm. "I don't intend to go back—I'm no card player, and anyone who knows me will suspect instantly that I've been up to no good."

"No good?" He couldn't manage to keep the prick of pride from his voice.

"The best sort of no good," she said as she touched his cheek in reassurance. "But I have an evening cloak I'll need, if you would but retrieve it for me." She sat back, out of his reach and quickly fastened on the pearls. "You can just leave it over the door."

"Just leave it? No speaking? No kiss goodbye?" Was he to be dismissed like a *cicisbeo,* no longer needed, now that he had performed to her satisfaction? His pride was like to burn a hole in his tongue.

"Yes, goodbye, dear McTavish." She leaned forward to kiss him sweetly on the cheek. "And thank you, so very much. Now if you'd retrieve my coat so I might have some privacy to recover myself, I would appreciate it."

"Recover yourself?" Was she ill or upset?

But she was smiling. "Yes, you sweet man. It has been a very long time since I've had the pleasure of such sexual satisfaction, and I have the silliest urge to laugh and cry and dance about all at the same time, but I have grave suspicions about my legs' ability to support me at this time. Thus, I should prefer to simply sit here and smile stupidly into space until I have to force myself to go home."

And now his smile had grown under the influence of hers. There was nothing he could say to such a sweet, silly speech but, "I will leave you to recover whilst I fetch your cloak, but then I will see you home, so I can satisfy myself that your legs do, in fact, still work. You have approximately three minutes." This time it was he who touched her cheek, and he who planted a leisurely kiss on her mouth. "I'll be back."

He did exactly as he promised, taking a moment to check his appearance in a pier glass in the front corridor and wipe the faint smear of her rouge from his lips, before he retrieved her cloak and bundled her quietly out via the mews. "Where to?"

"My mother's house is only a street away. Really there is no need—"

"There is every need." His own gentlemanly satisfaction among them.

Toby steered them out of Grosvenor Square, around the corner and down Davies Street without incident, but as soon as they reached the edge of Berkley Square, Caledonia Bowmont put a hand to his arm to stay him.

"I'll go on from here. It's too cold for you to stay out." She pressed a quick kiss to his cheek and was off, dissolving out of his hands, though he meant to make her stay. At least long enough for a proper kiss.

But it was cold, and he couldn't waste time standing about the pavement when he had better, though less rewarding, things to do than kiss Caledonia Bowmont.

He had a thief to catch.

Toby spent the rest of the uncomfortable night watching the Meecham place from the relative comfort of the frozen rooftop of his inn. From his vantage point with his back to a chimney for warmth and shelter from the cold east wind that drove the freezing fog up the river, he had an ample view of the Meecham Mansion that fronted on Grosvenor Square, but whose garden backed up to the inn walls.

But there was nothing of note to see. Not a flicker of movement, nor a shadow in the night. All was for naught. When dawn finally broke, red and raw in the east, he gave up his fruitless vigil, and made his quiet way down the back stairs to his room. He had just reached the bottom of the outer porch stairs below his room when she came at him.

"Give them back, you horrible, foul man."

He was too happy to see her to understand what she was talking about. He drew Caledonia to him, both for the lovely comfortable feel of her in his arms, and to shield her from the innyard's view—she was dressed informally, or rather intimately, in only a beautiful teal wool redingote over what appeared to be a white cotton flannel night dress, as if she hadn't taken the time to do more than throw the coat on over her night clothes before she left her house. All it would take was someone spreading gossip that Viscount Balfour's step-daughter was seen at dawn in the yard of an inn for Toby to be snared in something even tighter than a noose—the parson's mousetrap.

But still he was amused and impressed—how had she tracked him down?—by her presence. "If you'll recall, lass, I didn't steal anything you weren't freely offering."

She slapped him—a hard, vicious right that sent flaming heat searing across his cheek.

"Mother's jewels," she hissed. "What have you done with them?" She started to pull at his clothes, turning his pockets out. "Where have you hidden them?"

Toby wasn't sure what hurt more—the slap to his cheek or the blow to his pride that she would so quickly distrust him.

He grabbed her by the wrists, and though she put up quite a struggle—she was a strong Scots lass, after all—he managed to half-pull, half-wrestle her into a quiet corner of the stable where the only one awake was a mare who stared at him balefully over the door of the box stall.

"Keep your voice down," he instructed in a low growl as he damned himself for a fool—a diverted, un-thinking fool. This was the second time the bloody, too-clever thief had gotten the best of him. "Now tell me exactly what has happened."

"You know what has happened—you betrayed my trust, cozening me up with kisses, and then stole my mother's jewels." Her low accusation lost nothing of its furiousness. "This is no longer a lark, McTavish—now give them back."

"This never was a lark, Caledonia." He made free with her name—it seemed somehow disrespectful not to acknowledge that they were intimates. "Someone is trying to get me hanged, and they are doing a damn fine job of it. I don't have your mother's jewels—I didn't steal them, damn my unseeing eyes." He deflected a kick aimed at his shin. "Not that you're prepared to believe me."

But perhaps she was, at least a little. She crossed her arms over her chest. "Then who did?"

"That is exactly what I have been endeavoring to find out, but like you, I thought the Meechams were the most likely target—I spent the entirety of last night on the bloody rooftop hoping to catch the thief."

She was not convinced. "The whole of the night? It's near freezing out."

"Below freezing—the river will be icing up around the banks." He offered her his hands in proof. "Look at what I am wearing. Feel how cold my hands are. I've been out all night. And I am tired. So, please." He ameliorated his tone. "Please take me to your mother now."

"I don't think—"

"Fine. I'll go alone. You can stay here and help the inn's maids with the laundry."

She followed of course, practically running down the pavement in an effort to keep up. He took her hand for reasons that were obscure to both of them. There was no time for gentlemanly niceties—with this robbery someone had practically measured him for a coffin and was tying the noose around his neck as they spoke. Toby could all but feel their malevolence drawing tight over his windpipe.

And their jealousy.

CHAPTER 15

The front door to No. 45 was magically opened from the inside just as Caledonia ran up the front step. "Are the constables already here, Withers?"

Toby didn't wait for either Caledonia or the butler, but started for the stair. "Where is her room—where did your mother keep her jewels?"

"In here." Lady Balfour answered his question from the top of the stair. "Thank you for coming so soon."

"Show me." Toby didn't waste time on preliminaries—he reckoned he had less than ten minutes before the constabulary arrived.

"On the dressing table, there." Lady Balfour pointed to a small table topped with a folding mirror. "I usually have my dresser lock them away in the strong box, but last night I thought it was enough to wrap the jewels I'd worn in their small cases and bags, and put them away in the drawers."

"Was anything else stolen? Did they take only your jewels, or were any of Caledonia's stolen as well?"

"Just mine, I think."

"Be careful what you tell him, Mama!" Caledonia appeared at the door still in her coat and night dress. "I'm not quite sure if he isn't playing us all for fools."

"Is he?" The viscountess was remarkably composed for a woman who had lost her finest jewels. "If he is, what is he doing here now?"

"I don't know. Angling for more information, certainly. Perhaps even returning to the scene of the crime in triumph," her daughter answered while throwing looks like daggers his way.

"He doesn't look triumphant to me," the viscountess remarked. "He looks as if he's seen a ghost."

"Indeed." Toby could only agree with her. "The ghost of my somehow not-forgotten past. Where does this door lead—"

He answered his own question by opening the curtained door onto a small balcony that faced the back garden—the dark side of the house, where they wouldn't be seen. "They came over the roof and down onto this balcony. I take it the door wasn't locked?"

"It's some forty feet above the ground." The viscountess's tone told him she'd never considered the possibility that anyone could enter the house from such a height.

"At least," he agreed. "It was neatly done, I'll give him that."

"Just as neatly done as you'll be the moment the constable arrives," Caledonia insisted. "I told Withers to send for them before I went to the inn. So you'd better make a run for it."

"My dear Caledonia, I never 'run for it.' Or more correctly, I never, while I was a professional, ever ran for it. I *was* a professional—I simply disappeared."

"Well, I shan't prevent you from doing so now." She snatched up the fireplace poker and waved it in his direction before she was forced to retreat to the bedchamber door in response to the sound of heavy tramping feet below. "Go on! If they find you, they'll say they've got you red-handed."

"My dear Caledonia. I am not red-handed because I haven't got— Oh, bloody never mind." And because Toby was still a professional, he disappeared himself out onto the balcony and up the iron railing and onto the roof before the constabulary had even gained the top of the stairs.

He lay flat, invisible against the gray slate of the roof tiles and the soot-covered chimney piece, and listened as a breathless male voice asked, "Where is he?"

"The thief? Gone before I woke," the viscountess asserted. "Be a lamb, Cally, and fetch my dresser, and my smelling salts. And take those men out of here so I might make myself presentable enough to deal with them."

Below, a door swiftly closed. And a soft female voice swore, "Bloody hell. Mama, you'll never make a convincing liar—the book you're pretending to read is upside down."

~

Toby laid low for the next few days—with the constabulary and the Runners searching everywhere from Mayfair to Scotland for him, and Mrs. Caledonia Bowmont no longer quite so acutely fascinated by him, he kept quietly to himself, returning to Isleworth to live invisibly out of his own boathouse on the river, hiding in plain sight by fishing every day.

But his nights were taken by constant vigilance—during which he discovered several things. And several enemies.

One of whom was not Arthur Balfour, who came quietly to Isleworth to confirm a few things Toby was pleased to know. "The viscountess has been steadfast that it wasn't you. Swore out a formal complaint in which she most particularly insisted that the thief was not Tobias McTavish."

"How kind." Arthur did not offer what the viscountess's daughter's formal complaint might have been, nor did Toby ask. "You can tell your lovely step-mama privately that she is quite right. And I'm going to prove it."

"How?"

"I've been watching the Meecham mansion—and so has someone else. I've felt their presence in the night—heard them moving on the adjacent rooftops, trying to get closer, but not coming any closer because they know that I'm there."

"So what's going to happen?"

"They are going to rob it anyway—preferably over my dead body."

"What?"

"They know I'm there, so are going to have to go through me to do so—the easiest way is to try to kill me."

"How are you going to stop them? You *are* going to stop them, aren't you?"

"Oh, I'll try—I've gone to too much trouble to stay alive to roll over like a good dog now. But I need help—I need you to inform both the Runners and the constabulary to be on watch at the Meechams' town house tonight. The thief"—although he had a growing theory that this wasn't simply a lone thief—"is angry. So he is going to make a mistake. But he is definitely going to make his move. I can feel it in my bones."

CHAPTER 16

The Meecham mansion was one of London's older, grander houses, and one of the few that still sat apart from the street, surrounded by its own paling and small parkland. It was a grand 17th century beauty, filled with beautiful paintings and portraiture that Toby would have loved to see, but he no longer allowed himself the dark pleasure of sliding unseen along people's galleries on his way to and from their boudoirs.

This evening he stayed off the roof, preferring to find a good vantage point in the shrubbery, where he made himself only a little conspicuous—conspicuous enough for the thief to know where he was, but not so conspicuous that the authorities might find him before he could find the thief.

It was a delicate balance he attempted while trying to keep his neck out of a noose.

He sat quietly, resting comfortably against the wall of the house with his back in the crook of the chimney, and closed his eyes to better sort out the sounds of the night. Sounds of harness brass jangling in the street beyond the high stone wall. The clap of closing doors and footsteps on stairs within the house. The low moan of the wind across the chimney tops. The quiet, shuffling movement of the animals stabled in the nearby mews.

He opened his eyes, now adjusted to the biting dark of the cold, moonless night, and mentally went through his plan, sorting out where he would have entered the grounds, where he would have chosen to make his ascent of the drainpipes, or balconies, or whatever means the house presented.

He heard them before he saw them—muted crunches as they came across the gravel drive. Too many footfalls to be only one person.

And there they were—two large hulking shapes making low toward him. Two men too large to be successful rooftop thieves. Two men with knives already drawn.

It was going to be a brutal business.

Toby drew his own knife in readiness.

They came at him fast, with purpose—no hesitation, no shifting preliminaries. Their faces were blackened with burnt cork, but he could tell they knew him just as well as he knew them—his old shipmates, Bolter and Mott, come to give vent to their jealousies.

The more agile one—Mott—struck first, going for Toby's hair, fisting it up to stretch his neck back—the better to silently slice his throat open.

Toby slashed upward with his own blade, slicing into the soft underside of the fellow's arm—the hand in his hair immediately gave up the grip. He then used the only other weapon he had—his skull—smashing it hard into the bastard's forehead, momentarily stunning him.

Bolter was the bigger, heavier one. But he was also slower, though he had strong, strangling hands that felt as if they could choke a bullock, let alone a man. Hands that wrapped hard around Toby's neck.

Toby had to drop his knife to try to pry Bolter's fingers off, to pull some air down his throat and into his lungs, but the fellow was relentless, holding on with the strength of a butcher, steadily throttling the life from him.

Out of the corner of his eye Toby saw Mott stagger to his feet and raise up his cosh or pipe, or whatever the persistent bastard had armed himself with.

Toby did the only thing he could—he pushed himself into the hands around his neck with just enough force that Bolter reversed his effort to hold Toby at bay, and pulled him closer. Just in time for Mott's strike to land with deadly force.

Toby heard the sick crack of bone, but miraculously it wasn't his bone—the pain he expected never came. Instead, the beefy hands around his neck went slack. Bolter sagged down on top of Toby with dead, crushing weight.

Toby managed to slide out from under him, letting the body down in a scattering of gravel, and turned to meet the stunned Mott still holding the pipe.

In his horror, Mott turned and fled at the first shrill screech of a constable's whistle. A barrage of footfalls sounded on the gravel from every direction, while lights flared from the house, as if they had been in waiting to spill out into the yard, cutting off potential paths, blocking Toby from following his would-be attacker.

But he knew a better escape. Always three ways in and five ways out.

Toby retreated into the dark of the shrubbery at the base of the chimney, and immediately made use of the irregular stonework as footholds. He was up and flattened into the crook of the chimney top in a trice, well out of sight of the constabulary below who clustered like flies around the body of the dead man. As if that poor fellow were the answer to their search.

As if there weren't another still loose in the night.

∼

CALLY DID NOT MISS him in the least. She had not spent most of her waking hours thinking about him, worrying about him, heartsick over her mistake.

And what a dreadful mistake it was.

Because the headline blaring across the frontispiece of the *Tattler* being hawked by a lad on the street corner proclaimed that the Mayfair jewel thief was dead.

Cally felt an awful moment of stunned numbness before the pain set in, as if something within her chest had torn in two, and was spreading hot poison inside her.

She had to grasp her mama's arm to steady herself.

"Cally?"

It could not be. She wouldn't allow it.

"Cally? Where are you going?"

She forced herself to walk the three paces to the corner and dig the necessary coins out of her purse to buy the broadsheet, but she could barely steady her hands enough to read the lines that proclaimed the plague of jewelry thefts that had beset society was not the work of the renowned Scottish thief, but another, who had met his just end, his skull crushed after falling from a Mayfair rooftop.

Now it was mama who clutched Cally's arm. "Who is it? Is he dead?"

No need to ask who 'he' was.

"No." Cally was too sick with relief to say more for a long moment. She could feel the awful emotion wash out of her, as if someone had pulled the plug on all her fears. She had to take a deep, fortifying breath before she could continue. "It says his name was Bolter, and that he worked at the wine merchant's warehouse on the Strand. It says that he was a career criminal of long repute."

Mama clasped a hand to her chest. "Thank goodness."

Yes, Cally agreed. She would thank goodness, or badness, or wrongness—however it was that Tobias McTavish had not been involved, she was glad of it.

Glad she had been wrong about him.

"You're going to have to apologize to him."

"I know." Although knowing it only made Cally dread it more. She was particularly bad at apologies—she had too much experience of being right.

"You were wrong about him."

"I know," Cally repeated with a little more heat. She was also very bad at taking criticism—especially of the I-told-you-so variety.

"Hugh had the measure of him—he said McTavish was an honest man."

"I know," Cally repeated for what she hoped was the last time. "He was right, and I was wrong, and I will make my apology, just as I ought. You needn't tease any further. I'll make it the handsomest apology ever."

"You do that, lamb. And while you're at it—do figure out how you managed to fall in love with such an inappropriate man."

CHAPTER 17

After the debacle of the previous night—a debacle that had left a man dead—Toby decided it was past time for him to beard the lion in his den, and speak to the resident magistrate of the Bow Street Court.

"What a comfortably cozy group." Toby said amiably as he let himself into the office where Arthur Balfour, two Runners, the editor of the *Tattler*, and the magistrate himself sat in conference.

"McTavish." Arthur Balfour rose in some confusion. "I didn't expect to see you here."

"So I surmise—you're far too easy to follow, young Arthur. You'll need to work on that. But I came to congratulate the magistrate's office on their triumph—they have caught their thief. And to ask, now that my name has been cleared, if I may return unmolested to Isleworth and my farm? My profession—my land and my crops—have suffered in my absence. I wish to know if I may at last go back to making an honest living?"

There was pronounced quiet in the room that told him no answer was yet forthcoming.

Instead, poor young Arthur Balfour stepped into the breach. "I told them that you were the one to tip me off, McTavish—that it was you who helped to capture this Bolter fellow in the act."

"Yes, I thank you. Quite surprised me, that—Bolter being the thief. I didn't think he had it in him, what with his injuries."

"Injuries?" the heavy-set magistrate bestirred himself to ask.

"Yes, quite cut up in the war, poor bastard. Lost his leg at Trafalgar. Never quite as nimble on his peg after that." He enjoyed their astonished looks. "Oh, didn't you know that? He had a wooden leg. But I imagine that fact was carefully kept out of the newspaper accounts. But it's hard to imagine him silently crossing London's rooftops when he couldn't even cross the floor at Grindle & Company without making a racket."

"Good Lord," Arthur Balfour was aghast. "Do you mean—"

"Of course I do. This headline is only a sop to Bow Street's pride—a convenient lie to sell both newspapers and their services to a wary public." Toby looked askance at the newspaper man. "And they know it."

"We also know we shall be keeping a wary eye on you, McTavish—don't think we won't." The magistrate's sour tone matched his prune-faced look.

"Thank you." Toby bowed in their direction. "That is what I came here to find out." He replaced his hat atop his head and stood to take his leave. "I'll make it easier for you. You know where to find me—in Isleworth, where you can keep an eye on me. But first, I have a funeral to attend, where I'm going to get a good look at the real thief."

~

THE SERVICE WAS HELD NEARBY, in the sober, newly-restored St. Paul's in Covent Garden. Only a few years ago, the barn-like church had been nothing but a roofless burned-out hulk, raising the empty arms of its walls heavenward in entreaty. The churchyard was still blanketed with the fall of ash—a fitting enough metaphor for the devastation this particular crime spree was taking on people's lives.

Toby knew most of the assembly—men from the warehouse who had all been former shipmates when they had risked life and limb together as Jack Tars for His Majesty, George the Third's behalf. But the brotherhood of shipboard life had given way to jealousy and suspicion in the current circumstance. His friends might have laughed and joked about his prowess as a renowned burglar back then, but they weren't laughing now.

No, they were staring him down, or avoiding his gaze altogether with narrow, downcast eyes. But Toby wasn't about to look down. No, he was going to search each and every face for evidence. These were hard men, accustomed to hurt and deprivation. Many of them had actually preferred the hardships of the navy—at least they had been clothed and fed regularly—before they had banded together to pool their monies and form their company. Toby had given the lion's share of that prize money—for he had been elevated to an officer, and had a greater share—but had accepted only a working share of the company in deference to the others' wishes.

Perhaps it was the memory of that deference that brought Grindle to his side. "It is good that you've come to pay your respects," he said with a low sigh. "A sad end for a brave man."

"Indeed," was all Toby allowed, while he noted that Mott was conspicuously absent. "What will become of his daughter?"

"We will take care of her, of course—her father's share has gone to her."

"Good." Toby kept his voice low and even. "It will be of some comfort to know she will not starve."

"No, indeed." Grindle was all whispered paternal sympathy. "We look after our own."

Toby wasn't sure if that sounded like a promise or a threat—in the present circumstance, he reckoned it was wise to take it as both.

"But the lads owe you their thanks—you risked the gaol to help capture the real thief."

If Grindle believed that, Toby had some swampy acreage upriver to sell him.

"But you've your compensation for the risk," Grindle offered with a faint twist of a smile.

"Do I?"

"Your estate up the river where you live in quiet and comfort. And perhaps the girl from the other morning—I'm told she's quite beautiful."

Grindle was fishing—as if Betty, or the boys he had set to follow Toby, hadn't made Grindle a full and colorful report.

Toby decided to help Grindle along—what better way to play out this particular chess game than to offer up a pawn. "Ah, yes," he murmured appreciatively. "Mrs. Bowmont. Caledonia McAlden Bowmont. You'll recognize the name and remember her older brother, Lieutenant—now Captain Sir Hugh—McAlden, from our days aboard the *Vanguard*."

Grindle's face showed his surprise—his spies were perhaps not *everywhere*. "I see."

"Do you? Her family are old friends to me—steadfast and loyal. Of course you know her mother is Viscountess Balfour, for whom you will be providing wine for her masquerade ball."

"Yes, of course."

"Yes." It was almost like watching a waterwheel turn—Grindle's thoughts were so transparent, Toby was learning valuable information of his own. "Perhaps I'll see you there?"

"Are you such great friends that they have invited you?" Grindle was genuinely surprised, but quickly masked his expression in bland interest. "What costume will you wear?"

Toby allowed himself the pleasure of a very small smile. "I'll surprise you."

"What are ye saying?" The shrill question burst from the lips of Betty Bolter, interrupting the vicar's solemn service. "What must ye talk of like idlers while me father's not yet cold in his grave?"

Hands came to console her but she shrugged them off, spitting fire and ire. "It's on account'a ye 'e's dead," she accused Toby, venting her grief at him. "We all know that," she sobbed. "Get out of here. Get out, ye damn thief. Ye bloody murderer!"

There was nothing for Toby to do but to honor at least this small request, even though she was only partially right—it had not been his hand that had crushed her father's skull, but he was the reason Bolter had been at the mansion that night.

But his former shipmates had begun to close in, crowding round, their thick arms and broad working-men's chests barring his way. If they wanted to beat him to death on the spot as simple-minded revenge for one of their own killing Bolter instead of Toby, there was nothing he could do to prevent it.

Before he could even register the cold heat of fear in his gut, the vicar spoke. "There will be no further blood shed on this hallowed ground, do you hear me? This is not the time."

The wall of men fell back, leaving a gap he was still obliged to push through. But they let him go. This time.

Toby was not such a fool as to think the cold hand of retribution wasn't still coming his way.

CHAPTER 18

Cally was waiting for him outside the churchyard in her mother's sleek unmarked carriage. The newspaper had a notice of the funeral, and it had taken no great deduction to surmise that McTavish would be there. "McTavish!" she called, leaning out the open window of the carriage. "Toby."

He came toward the coach reluctantly, but he came—though he did not come out of the wind into the warm carriage. "What are you doing here?"

She did not try to evade his scorn, but met it straight on. "I came to apologize."

"Have you?" His brows rose in wary surprise. "How novel."

She had the grace to feel abashed—her cheeks must be the color of cherries in the biting chill. "Yes, well. I read about the burglaries being solved, and I— Well, I am so very sorry I wrongly accused you. I'm sorry for all the things I said in my mother's house that morning."

He tipped his head to the side in consideration. "You were upset."

"I thank you, I was, but that is no excuse for such a gross misjudgment of your character. That was very wrong of me to leap to such an unfounded conclusion."

"All the best headstrong girls do it."

There was almost enough warmth in his tone to make her feel he was teasing her. Almost. "I don't think you mean that as a compliment."

"I mean that I accept your apology. I am sorry, too—sorry I'm not the dashing, exciting, faultless person you thought I was."

She would have none of it. "You're exactly who I thought you were." When he looked skeptical at her assertion, she tried another tack. "What are you going to do now?"

"The same as I was doing yesterday—find the real thief."

"But...the broadsheets said it was this Bolter fellow. That they caught him red-handed, as it were, at the Meecham townhouse."

"They did nothing of the kind." His growl was laced with impatience. "They found Bolter's body and jumped to convenient conclusions."

"Such as?"

"That the crime had been thwarted. But the fact of the matter is that Bolter and Mott were there to stop me, not to rob Lady Meecham's jewels. Neither of the two men who attacked me were thieves."

"How can you be so sure?"

"Because I know them just as they know me. And I heard them coming a mile away—they made no bones of it, coming straight to slit my throat with their knives and bash my brains in with their cudgels."

"They came to murder you!" The realization sent a chill sinking deep into Cally's bones like a killing frost. She shivered in her fur-lined cloak. "Why?" she asked, even though she understood him perfectly. "To keep you from finding the real thief?"

"Aye." His voice was nothing but grim resignation.

"Then the broadsheets lied."

"*Lied*," he scoffed. "Surely you're not that naive—they printed a convenient truth." Toby shrugged away the injustice of it all. "Bolter was indeed there, and he was indeed tied to the thefts—as, I reckon, are several others. But the broadsheets left off several other important truths, like the fact that Bolter had a wooden leg, and could never have climbed across any roof to emulate the Wraith—he was definitely *not* the one leaving sprigs of heather in people's jewel boxes."

Cally was indignant on his behalf. "Well, that's not right."

He turned her concern aside. "My dear Mrs. Bowmont, pray don't let my unfair treatment keep you up at night."

"Of course I shall let such injustice to you keep me up at night," she exclaimed before she could think better of it. "I have for years!"

He stilled. "Years?" He narrowed his eyes at her, but the beginning of a smile lit the corners.

"Yes." There was no sense in trying to evade his regard now—things had gone too far, people were being murdered. "Ever since I've known of you—years. Years spent wondering what you were like, how you were faring in your hard naval career, what you were doing once you'd left the navy. I've followed your career with interest."

"It's no longer my career."

"Thievery? I know that—I was only teasing before, so you would admit who you were. I meant farming."

His smile was kind but skeptical. "What do you know of farming?"

"I know that you're very good at it. That your Limousin cattle have taken champion ribbons for beef breeds at the Middlesex Fair, and your blackface sheep have taken Best Wooled Breed three years running. And that your spaniel dogs are prized for their keen noses and merry temperaments. And that you're probably the nicest, most attractive farmer I've ever met. And I rather think I'm falling in love with you."

He stared at her, shocked into momentary silence. "It is very nearly frightening that you know all that."

She felt her skin flame all the way down her chest. "It is ridiculous, is what it is, not frightening."

"The prizes, or that you know about them?"

Cally began to feel some of her normal good humor start to return at his quizzical, almost droll tone. "I had assumed you won the prizes fairly, without any bribery of beef breed judges or paying off of blackfaced sheep men."

"The blackfaced sheep men are notoriously expensive—too rich for my blood."

She feared she heard a warning in his voice, but she forced herself to have the courage to ask, "And me? Am I too rich for your blood, too?"

He took a deep breath before he answered. "I fear you're just lonely and bored with nothing better to do than imagine yourself in love—"

"Is that really what you think of me? Is that why you kissed me? And made love with me—because you think I'm lonely? And bored? Have you no idea of what I'm truly like? That I manage my husband's farm on my own, thank you very much, so my mama-in-law will have peace and comfort and good health all her days, though she wishes with every breath of her body, every single day of her life—and mine—that her son was the one providing those things for her, and not I. That these few weeks of harmless frivolity in London visiting with my mother are the only bloody frivolity I'm like to get until next bloody year. And that I love spaniel dogs even though they are notoriously hard to train properly. And I don't see why I shouldn't be able to love you if I want to."

Tobias McTavish was silent again for a long moment before the corners of his eyes began to soften into a smile. "Well, I suppose there is no gainsaying that."

Hope was like a sunrise in her chest, warming the bleak chill of the morning. "There isn't. And I don't care who knows it."

He rewarded her bravery by reaching for her hand. "In that case, my dear Mrs. Bowmont, I'd be very much obliged of your help."

Caledonia's heart did a little cartwheel of joy within her chest. She felt all topsy-turvy with relief and excitement and just a little bit of fear. Because this really was his very *life* they were playing with—she couldn't let herself forget that. "What do you need me to do?"

He smiled, that knowing, this-is-going-to-be-trouble smile that warmed the improper cockles of her heart. "Get me an invitation to your mother's masquerade ball."

"Done. But you'll have to have a costume," she warned.

"Indeed." He nodded. "What are you wearing?"

"Columbina—she's a sort of Italianate motley—a harlequin." Her mother had arranged it all months ago—the bright colored costume a gift in understanding of the bland sameness of Cally's days in the Cheviot Hills. "Mama will be a Dama Blanca, and Balfour an elegant Clown. The masquerade is really more of a Twelfth Night revel than a sedate Advent Ball, but Mama knows how much I love a revel."

"You would." There was no censure in his smile. "I should like to try and fit into your group if I may."

"Of course. I should like that. Do you want a full mask, so you're not recognized? Or do you want people to be able to tell who you are?" It was so complicated, this trap they needed to set.

He kissed her hand. "And that is why I may, in fact, be falling in love with you, dear Mrs. Bowmont—your delightfully agile mind. You understand things. And as to the recognition and disguise—I think I want both."

"Both," she repeated, beginning to understand. "You want people to *think* they can recognize you?"

He leaned across the sill of the carriage window and kissed her in confirmation.

Cally's lips all but tingled—she didn't know when she had felt more relieved, or more alive. "I think I've got an absolutely brilliant idea."

CHAPTER 19

Cally had never, ever in all of her life, felt nerves like she did the moment she took her place in the receiving line on the night of the masquerade ball—she felt picked apart, as if the pins and needles holding her costume together were falling out and she was unraveling at her seams, when in fact her patch-color Columbina costume fit her to perfection.

But still, she was as anxious as a tethered racehorse—there were so many details, so many particular things they had had to arrange, so many possibilities for things to go wrong—she could barely stand still.

"Ready?" Tobias McTavish appeared by her side attired in his own form-fitting costume.

Cally took a deep breath in admiration of the magnificently honed body the motley revealed. "Gracious, McTavish. I am as ready as I'll ever be, though I think I should check to make sure there are adequate chaises in the withdrawing rooms, so the ladies can recover after ogling you."

He laughed just as she had hoped, dispelling some of her tension. They had spent the previous day in close consultation, working out the details of the roles they were about to play, but the worry—the constant imagining and reimagining all the possibilities—had been exhausting. Cally had hardly slept a wink.

But she forced herself to smile, and be her normal self. "You do look exceptionally fetching in your costume, sir."

"Let us hope I do—and can *fetch* both the jewels and my reputation back this evening." Then he took her hands and spread them out before him, to inspect her costume. "You on the other hand, look stunning. If you were to take up thievery you'd be able to rob men blind just by smiling at them in that costume."

"Thank you, Toby. I'll take that as a compliment."

He leaned in to whisper. "I mean it as such."

Before he could kiss her, Mama was in the corridor. "Come along, children." Her mother waved her mask upon a stick to magic them into place before the ballroom doors.

Together they looked magnificent—all hot patches of bright harlequin color that presented a united theme. Toby was all but unrecognizable as their equally masked and turbaned servant in harlequin, bearing an enormous feathered fan to shade and cool them, despite the fact that it was ten o'clock at night. And inside. And winter.

But masquerade balls were not at all about reality. Cally could only hope the fantasy they had spun would do its work.

"Assume that nearly every man without a partner will be a Runner," Toby whispered at her back. "It will be your job to keep their attention."

They had worked through her step-father, Viscount Balfour, and his son Arthur to give the constabulary what purported to be a tip-off about the ball. The viscount had hired the Runners himself, saying that he wanted the extra protection of Bow Street's men to ensure his guests felt safe—Bolter's death notwithstanding, society as a whole was still nervous of theft.

And even if Toby had no confidence in the Runners' ability to catch the thief, he needed them to witness it when he did.

The viscount followed his wife, nodding to each of them in turn. "Are we all ready, then?"

Cally smoothed her skirts over her nervous tummy. "I think I know now how they must feel on the stage at Drury Lane, just before the curtain goes up."

"Break a leg, they say to one another," Toby laughed.

"Oh, lord, no." Cally wouldn't hear of it. "Please don't break a thing."

"I pray you will take great care not to break *anything*," breathed Mama before she clasped Toby's hand. "But let us hope the best man indeed wins."

And so it began, with costumed guests making their way into the house as if it were all choreographed by an unseen hand pulling their puppet strings.

And with those guests, a number of unaccompanied, costumed men made their way into the ballroom without the benefit of being announced, while Cally and her mother greeted and exclaimed over the cleverness and imagination of their invited guests.

"Aren't you all quite the pretty family group," more than one wag offered. "And so convivial, your beautiful daughter and your handsome step-son."

"Oh, that's not Arthur," Mama began disingenuously. "Poor boy, always called away on some important business. This is—"

And then Cally would interrupt and whisper, or stop Mama with a quick jab of her fan, or speak over her. "How lovely to see you this evening, Your Grace. That plume in your turban— simply the limit! You must tell me how you contrived it. So original and fetching!"

And on and on they went, greeting after greeting, until at last all the guests were assembled, and the family themselves were about to be announced.

"Oh, gracious!" said Mama in a voice that carried well into the ballroom. "I forgot my fan. Cally, do be a lamb—"

McTavish stepped conspicuously forward. "Let me play my part and fetch it for you, Viscountess."

"Oh, Toby. Thank you, you're most kind."

"Mama! You shouldn't have said his—" Cally cast what she hoped was a horrified glance toward the ballroom, where the guests suddenly found they had much to talk about behind their own fans.

And several of the hired footmen in their dark livery from the wine merchant moved from their positions along the walls to speak to one of the lone gentlemen in consultation. After a moment of conference and gesticulation two unaccompanied fellows followed Toby out.

Perfect.

Cally whisked a glass of champagne from the nearest tray. "Here's to success in bold ventures."

Mama took her own glass, and returned, "Here's to you getting your heart's desire, and not getting your heart broken," as she entered the ballroom as if nothing were at stake.

Cally gulped down the wine. She didn't want to think about what might happen if it all went wrong—if even *one* thing went wrong and their plan began to collapse like a flan in a cupboard.

But in another minute her harlequin was back, handing Mama her fan with a courtly bow, and it was time for Cally to act—she went on tiptoe to whisper into his ear as if she were telling him about her mama's slip-up.

He shrugged, as if the mistake was of no account, and then offered his hand in silent compensation.

"Oh, yes." Cally gave him a smile as if she might make up for the error by lavishing him with all her attention. "I'd love to dance."

And so they did. The moment Mama signaled for the players to start, Cally led her harlequin out onto the dance floor where they remained, dance after country dance—with the exception of one short break for the supper at midnight—for the entirety of the ball.

On and on they danced as the others came and went, until at last they were the only pair on the floor, and the musicians finally stopped playing.

Mama had somehow already retired for the evening—it was only the servants from the wine merchant and those loose, unattached men still propping up the walls.

But Cally pretended she had eyes for no one but her partner.

"Come," she whispered just loud enough for every last Runner in the house to hear. "Everyone is gone. Come with me."

She led her harlequin slowly by the hand out of the ballroom, up the grand staircase, and to the door of her room, where she gave her darling swain her best smile for the benefit of the Runners who had not-so-surreptitiously followed them, and quietly took him into her room, and locked the door with an audible click.

Whereupon poor Arthur Balfour pulled the masque and turban from his head and collapsed into the nearest chair. "My God. I've never danced so much in all my life."

"Nor I," Cally agreed. "And let's hope we never have to again."

They had done their part.

The rest was up to Toby.

CHAPTER 20

The grand townhouse was quiet except for the muffled sounds of the servants clearing up—sweeping the floors, packing away the bottles of wine, counting out the silver cutlery.

The Balfour servants were behaving perfectly—snoring in wine-induced slumber from the continuous tipples the hired footmen from Grindle's had urged upon them. It was a nice touch. The rich were normally easier to rob—they stayed up half the night drinking like lords, and then slept their way through the morning, staying abed until noon. But their servants were usually another thing—they worked into the wee small hours, and were still astir and working well before the crack of dawn.

But not tonight. Tonight Toby was the only one in the Balfour household who was astir through the long hours of the night—he and one other. But Toby was warm and relaxed where he waited in the dark of an alcove at the turn of the bedroom wing. Provisioned against the night by the comforts Caledonia Bowmont had insisted upon providing as chill of night reached its cold fingers on wind that rose up from the river and cut like broken glass under the windowpanes.

The thief would be cold with nerves, anxious to get the job timed exactly right.

Even though it was already too late.

Because Toby heard the thief before he saw the dark silhouette sneak down the servant's corridor toward Cally's room—a low creak of the floorboards had Toby crouched and ready when the shadow flitted by, skimming in and out of the pools of light streaming through the windows.

He called to the black-clothed wraith before the small crouching figure could make the door. "It's locked." Toby stepped into the middle of the corridor, blocking it. "I locked the door. That's why I used to prefer the rooftops—can't lock the outside air."

The little thief whirled to face him. "Damn ye, McTavish."

"Yes, damn me. But know that your days—or more accurately, your nights—impersonating the Scottish Wraith are at an end."

"Not yet."

The little wretch was quicker than Toby had reckoned, and more violently determined, too—Toby only just managed to gird his loins before the imp's head rammed into his gut, knocking him back onto his arse, and leaving him grappling for purchase as the nimble shadow fought its way out of Toby's grip, and went pelting down the hall for the grand staircase.

Toby followed in a flash, thundering down the unlit gallery without care for the racket he made—the more witnesses he roused, the better.

He caught up just as the little sneak was about to jump over the baluster to the platform half-way down the stairs below.

Toby caught a wrist in mid-air and hung on tight as the two of them slammed into the baluster—Toby above and the thief dangling below.

There was no hiding or sneaking now.

Betty Botler's shriek of rage and terror cut the night and echoed off the high ceiling and stone-faced walls of the grand staircase, rousing the entire house.

Toby tightened his grip, levering his body against the railing for balance, catching the second hand the young girl swung up at his face in a steely grip.

"Careful there, Betty," he counseled as she hung helplessly over the side. "I'm out of practice, lass. My grip is not near as strong as it used to be. I'd hate for you to die so young and beautiful. But let you die I will."

Toby made good on his advantage by dragging her farther along the baluster, to where the drop to the marble floor below was good and lethal.

For another second the urchin looked as if she would spit fire, or spit in his eye, until she scrabbled for purchase with her legs and feet and came up with only the empty clutch of air.

"Yes, I've got you, Betty. For now." He flexed his grip around her thin wrist, so she would feel the true tentative nature of their connection, so she would understand that she was saved from certain messy, bone-breaking death on the glossy stone below only by the strength of his grip and the grace of his mercy.

Her shriek had roused the house—Arthur Balfour and his father, the viscount, rushed out to the foot of the stair below, followed by men Toby could only hope were magistrates.

"Get a light there," the viscount ordered. "Set the lamps!"

Runners and servants—some from Balfour House and others in livery from Grindle's—spilled up from the bowels of the house, filling the space with their gasps and shouts.

"Help me," Betty choked, rasping and hollow-eyed with fear.

"Stay back, all." Toby made his face ruthlessly blank, though he shifted his feet to gain some leverage. "I don't like being made a fool of, Betty. And you tried to make a fool of me. You tried to get me hanged."

"No," she pled from the end of this arm. "I swear."

"Then swear who taught you to imitate me, Betty," he commanded in his best captain of the watch voice. "Who put you up to this? And don't bother telling me it was your father," he gritted before she could lie. "I knew him—and I know better that to believe that sort of Banbury tale."

"I— I did it alone. I—"

He shook her, dangling her below him like a rag doll to the screams of the women below.

"Don't lie to me, Betty—I'm like to let you go if you lie."

"It was Grindle," she cried. "Grindle put us up to it. Grindle who taught me, and arranged it all."

"How did you do it?"

"Ye know how!" She was crying now, fat tears welling up and stinging her eyes. "Just let me up."

"Not yet—not until you tell them." He nodded his chin toward the watchers below. "Tell *them* how, Betty."

"He made me work at the parties—said I was a handsome girl and should serve with the footmen."

"Then what did you do after?" He shook her again. "Tell them."

"I'd to change out of maid's togs and put on the black, and go up into the house and get the jewels Grindle wanted while the people was asleep at rug."

"And then?"

"Then I give 'em to Grindle, and I go home."

That was more than enough for Toby, and below he saw the Runners move swiftly off in pursuit of Grindle. But whether or not they caught the bastard was not his concern—Betty was. He hauled her up over the railing, whereupon she collapsed into the arms of Cally, who had, somehow unbeknownst to him, been behind him.

And had a front row view of just what a bastard he really was under his civilized veneer.

"There, dear," Cally comforted the girl. "You're safe."

"But what's Grindle goin' to do to me for peachin'?" Betty sobbed.

"Grindle is going to hang, you wretch," Toby answered. He wasn't about to be taken in by this sniveling—Betty had been giving lip and likely stealing baubles since she was a babe at Bolter's wooden knee. And if she and Bolter and Grindle had had their way, he'd have been the one hanged, or had his throat slit.

He would not feel any sympathy for her. He would not. "And you're going to feel the cold hand of the law as well."

"Toby," Caledonia admonished, looking at him as if she didn't quite like what she was seeing. "She's frightened enough."

"She's a wretch," he repeated though he could not shake the cold sickness that coiled in his gut at the thought of her likely fate. But not everything in this life was fair. Not everything was sweet or kind or could be done up in a pretty bow.

He was not. He was, beneath his manners and suits and well-manicured farm, just as feral and vicious as any of them—he had just proved it by his behavior.

Cally would want nothing to do with him now that she had seen who he really was.

"There's your wraith," he said when Viscount Balfour and the Runners came forward to take Betty. "Happy bloody Christmas."

"Toby." Cally's soft tone admonished him. "What's to be done with her?"

"What the law requires." He heard the cold condemnation in his voice, and suddenly he felt old and weary and jaded. "I don't know. I'm tired and I want to sleep and I'm going home." If he could just get back home, to his comfortable, orderly house, and comfortable orderly life, he would be fine. He would have a dram or two or twenty of good highland whisky and sort out how to make his life return to normal then. But not now.

"And what about me?" Cally's voice sounded small, and for the first time in their acquaintance—although she was clearly far more than a mere acquaintance—tentative.

But he couldn't think—the raw rush of hate and rage and fear and vindication left him drained—as frayed and tattered as an old rag. "Maybe you should go home, too."

"Oh. Yes." Her tone was so quiet, he almost couldn't hear her. "I suppose I shall."

And at that, Toby left her, and walked down the length of the grand staircase, and across the wide foyer, and through the door and out into the dark wee small hours of the night without another word, and without looking back.

CHAPTER 21

Toby awoke to the strong smell of coffee. Which was strange, because his housekeeper, Ella, was still in Norwich, and he himself had had nothing but strong whisky to drink since he had arrived home in the dawn, cold and exhausted and entirely spent from the long row upriver in his skiff.

He sat up for a moment and listened, letting his carefully honed instincts and experience sort out the sounds—the steady lap of the river, the murmur of the winter wind through the brittle trees, the industrious bustle of someone below in the kitchens.

He threw on a banyan to cover his nakedness, and to keep out the chill of the cold house, and made his way coffee-ward.

Only to find Caledonia McAlden Bowmont alone in his warm, aroma-filled kitchen, setting a table for breakfast.

"Good morning." She worked away industriously, as if it were the most natural thing in the world that a viscountess's daughter should be wearing an apron over her embroidered woolen frock in his kitchen in Isleworth.

"Good morning yourself," he managed, though his voice was foggy with the clouds of last night's whisky. "Your pardon, but what are you doing in my kitchen?"

"Making you breakfast. And myself as well," She explained, still not meeting his eye. "Making myself at home."

"For how long?"

She looked at him fully then, standing tall even as she swallowed her nervousness. "I suppose that depends upon you. But as for me, I should like to stay forever."

He stood stock still with his bare feet against the floor. "Are you, per chance"—he spoke slowly, feeling his way along this particularly steep path—"proposing to me, Mrs. Bowmont?"

He wanted to be very sure.

She blushed, her cheeks warming a becoming shade of rosy pink. "I am, as you didn't seem likely to get around to it in all the fuss. And frankly, I'll do anything to avoid returning to Scotland."

It was so like her, to use humor to deflect from her unease. But he was not yet in the mood to reassure her—he rather liked keeping such a magnificent woman on her metaphorical toes. So he said nothing.

The silence stretched just as long as it could before she snapped. "Well, if you're not going to say anything, then at least close your robe—it's fallen open, and you are displaying yourself like a Covent Garden petticoat pensioner displaying his wares."

Toby did feel a cooling draft on his nethers, but made no move to cover himself. On the contrary—he pulled the robe back over his hip. "Well, I suppose that is what a husband should look like in the morning when he comes down to find his wife all flushed with the heat of baking."

Her face pinkened with an absolutely gorgeous flush of pleasure. "Know a great deal about husbands, do you, McTavish?"

He rewarded her cheek with a smile. "Not enough. Not yet."

She returned his smile. "You'll do. But since I do have some greater experience in these matters, let me tell you that *that* is not how a husband should look when he comes down to make his wife all flushed with heat."

She advanced toward him slowly, and just as slowly ran her hands up the length of his arms and around across the breadth of his back and down around the globes of his arse. "Now *that*"—she smiled into his ear and she pressed herself flush against him, and felt the exceedingly attentive appreciative reaction of his body—"is much more the thing."

He backed her up to the table, and pushed the steaming porridge aside. Cutlery fell to the floor with a clatter. But he never took his eyes from hers. "And I should very much like to put this *thing* to better use. Inside you. Right now. For I don't think I can wait another minute to have you, Caledonia McAlden Bowmont. So you'd better marry me right now."

She kissed him with an enthusiasm that heated his blood hotter before she leaned back against the table in happy invitation. "My darling man, I thought you'd never ask."

The End

ABOUT ELIZABETH ESSEX

Elizabeth Essex is the award-winning author of lush, lyrical historical romance full of passion, daring and adventure. When not rereading Jane Austen, mucking about in her garden or simply messing about with boats, Elizabeth can be always be found with her laptop, making up stories about heroes and heroines who live far more exciting lives than she. Her books have been nominated for numerous awards, including the Gayle Wilson Award of Excellence, the Romantic Times Reviewers' Choice Award, and RWA's prestigious RITA Award, and have made Top-Ten lists from Romantic Times, The Romance Reviews and Affaire de Coeur Magazine. Elizabeth lives in Texas with her husband, the indispensable Mr. Essex, and her active and exuberant family in an old house filled to the brim with books.

For more information about Elizabeth's books, visit:
elizabethessex.com/category/books/

THE VERY DEBONAIR LADY CLAIRE

~

HEATHER SNOW

When Claire Barton's twin is murdered, she takes his place as a code breaker for the War Department to flush out his killer. Her ruse works perfectly—until the man who once broke her heart becomes her new spymaster. He sees right through her disguise but if he thinks he can stop her from doing what she must, he's in for a bigger surprise than when he'd realized just who wore the trousers now.

The last thing Lord Andrew Sedgewick expects to find when he's asked to root out a traitor is the one woman he's never been able to forget. The worst mistake of his life was walking away from Claire that Christmas six years ago. Now that he's found her again, he doesn't intend to let her go—if they both survive **this** holiday season.

CHAPTER 1

DECEMBER, 1813 ~ THE BLACK CHAMBERS, ABCHURCH LANE, LONDON

Sweat snaked down Claire's face and neck, a slow trickle that did its best to annoy and distract her until, finally, it met the starched linen of her cravat and was absorbed.

While outside this room London was experiencing one of the coldest winters in recent memory, here at Abchurch boiling kettles spouted steam into the air and fires burned to heat wax and wire.

It didn't help that she kept her jacket on when most in the room had stripped down to their waistcoats. But the extra layer covering her chest helped maintain her disguise.

She wished she could spare a hand to swipe the perspiration from her brow, but she needed both for this most delicate part of her task. Should she break the seal while opening the missive meant for the Russian ambassador, the man would know that the War Department was pilfering his post...rather than just suspecting it.

Another droplet started its trek down her cheek, but Claire did her best to ignore it. Pulling her lower lip between her teeth, she slid the heated wire beneath the seal—a precarious operation that required her to move the hot metal slowly enough to melt the wax without breaking it, yet quickly enough not to scorch the vellum beneath.

The seal pulled free of the parchment, and Claire examined the wax rendering of a double-headed eagle closely. Not bad. She saw no cracks or marring of any kind. She should be able to reseal the missive after copying its contents, and send it on to the Foreign Ministry with the ambassador and his aides none the wiser.

Leaning back in her chair, Claire scanned the Cyrillic script, so very different from English writing. She'd need to transcribe it word for word in Russian, of course—any hidden messages would be in the mother tongue, not in a translation. But that was a laborious undertaking, and she was anxious to know what the letter said *now*.

She was running out of time to figure out who had killed her brother...and why.

"Who do you reckon they've tapped to replace Marston?" a voice boomed from behind her.

Claire started, only just stopping herself from crumpling the letter in her surprise. She'd been so focused on interpreting it that she hadn't heard Pike's approach. She blew out a harsh breath, smoothing the vellum flat on the table. All that work preserving the seal would have been for naught if she'd crushed the blasted letter in reflex.

She threw a disgruntled glare over her shoulder at Pike, who only grinned at her as if he'd pulled some great jest. He lifted the cup of tea he'd brought over for her like a salute and then set it on the corner of her table.

Men. She'd never understand them, even after spending the past several weeks living *as* one of them.

A sharp ache pierced her chest as his words registered, followed quickly by a twinge of dread. Who *did* she think would replace Marston?

"I've no idea," she mumbled, turning back to the work at hand, her throat tight.

She still couldn't believe the man was gone.

Lord Marston—Uncle Jarvis to her and her brother, though they'd not been related by blood—had been a great friend to her late parents and a constant in Claire's life since before she could remember.

He'd *also* been the head of the Abchurch offices, where England's brightest minds secretly spent their hours deciphering codes and messages discovered in diplomatic posts, uncovered through espionage efforts on the continent, or relayed from battlefields and naval ships via shutter telegraphs.

More important, Uncle Jarvis had been her co-conspirator these many weeks. Without his help, she'd never have been able to infiltrate Abchurch by pretending to be her twin, nor would she have the chance to uncover the truth behind Clarence's death.

"I suppose there's no point in speculating," Pike mused. "Whoever the man is, he should be here any moment to assess the operation. Take our measure, as it were."

The unease that had started in her chest flared as it settled low in her stomach, jostling for position with the grief from Uncle Jarvis's sudden death. How could she possibly continue this ruse without his protection and aid?

When she'd arrived at Abchurch last month, no one had questioned that she was Sir Clarence Barton. Not when she resembled her brother so closely. Not when she could mimic his mannerisms so perfectly. Not when she was so impeccably tailored, any hints of her femininity ruthless strapped down under her fine gentleman's togs.

Not when Lord Marston, respected spymaster, had declared her to be so.

But Uncle Jarvis was gone, felled by a heart ailment in his sleep two nights past.

And she was all alone.

"I hope they don't send some high-in-the-instep dandiprat," Pike went on, oblivious to Claire's distress. "Some earl's spare who wants to do his part in the war effort, but who's never been outside Mayfair, you know?"

Claire nodded, wishing Pike would be quiet. Or at least go bother someone else. She picked up a quill and pointedly went back to her transcription—and her worries that the new head of Abchurch would find her out and make her leave before she could learn what had happened to Clarence.

"A man of action is what we need. Someone who's seen battle." Pike slammed his fist into his palm with a thwack, clearly just warming to his topic. "Someone who knows first-hand how important the work we do here is to the—"

The click of a lock and the creaking of the heavy oak door at the far end of the room stilled Pike's lips. Indeed, a hush fell over all of the men in the chamber as they waited to meet their new minister.

"Let's introduce you to the men who will be under your charge, my lord," echoed the voice of Greeves, Uncle Jarvis's aide-de-camp, as he stepped into the room, followed by a tall figure.

Claire's stomach rolled, and her heart kicked in her chest. She peered down the long expanse, trying to glimpse the man who would turn her out on her ear if he even suspected she wasn't who she claimed to be.

But it was no use.

The black chambers of Abchurch were, by necessity, clandestine. No windows opened onto the street to allow curious eyes to see in, much less to let in any natural light. Instead, this room resembled a darkened laboratory. The only pockets of light were oil lamps, the fires in the grates, and smaller flames for steam kettles and such, which burned at the tables where the men went about their secret business.

Claire cursed the room's air of obscurity. While it undoubtedly helped her maintain her disguise, it also kept her from seeing the man who held her future in his hands.

She squinted her eyes and saw that the two men had stopped to speak with Peter Finch. Finchy, brilliant at maths, could decipher complicated French codes that used over 1,200 numerals with the seeming ease of a schoolboy doing sums—once said code had been broken. He was also notoriously cantankerous. Yet whatever the new minister said to the man brought a series of nods and, rarer still, an actual laugh.

A moment later, Greeves ushered the stranger to the next table. Claire's station was at the very back of the room, making her the last "man" to be introduced. But they'd get to her soon enough. The knot in her stomach tightened and she turned away, back to the Russian missive and back to her work—for as long as it would remain hers.

So lost was she in the syntax of the language, the foreign ebb and flow of letters and words, that the men were upon her before she realized.

"And lastly," Greeves was saying from behind her, "is our most keen linguist. Aside from English and French, of course, he's fluent in Greek, Latin, Spanish, Italian, and a variety of Balto-Slavic languages. Invaluable, he is, at finding hidden codes within foreign missives for the others to decipher. Couldn't have won the battle of Vitoria without him."

Claire closed her eyes briefly, willing her heart to cease its rapid tattoo. Then she took a breath, pasted on her brother's ne'er-do-well smile, and turned to face whatever came.

And her racing heart stopped dead.

Greeves gestured towards her. "May I introduce you to Sir Clar—"

But the new head of Abchurch interrupted the aide, his voice sounding as shocked as she felt.

"Claire?"

~

AFTER SERVING five years in a brutal war—part of it as a prisoner in France—very little had the power to shake Lord Andrew Sedgewick.

But he must say, finding Miss Claire Barton, dressed as a *man*, in the War Department's hidden enclave of code breakers shook him straight to his polished Hessians.

He blinked once…twice… Perhaps the flickering shadows in this damnably dark chamber played tricks upon his eyes.

But no. Claire definitely stood before him. In trousers. And a cravat. A badly tied one at that.

Her cerulean-blue eyes widened in the awkward silence before she recovered herself.

"Sedgewick," she chided, in a voice so like her brother's that Andrew took another hard look at her.

His gaze touched on her hair, red-golden locks trimmed short in a fashionable men's cut that curled slightly around her face. He took in her wide shoulders and thick waist. Padding could accomplish both, he knew, as well as fill out the boots upon her feet. His eyes drifted to her bosom, or lack thereof. If there were feminine curves hidden under the burgundy jacket and cream-colored waistcoat, they were bound flat.

Yet her breath caught, just slightly, at his frank perusal. And if he wasn't mistaken, pink tinged her cheeks. Definitely Claire.

"You're lucky we're old friends," she went on gamely. "The last person to call me 'Clare' got planted a facer, you know. I detest that blasted nickname." Then she laughed and clapped him on the shoulder. "When did you get back from the continent, my friend?"

Greeves, apparently his new aide-de-camp, looked between the two of them, brow scrunching. "You know Sir Clarence already, my lord?"

Claire's eyes flashed a warning, even as her smile widened.

Andrew still reeled. He couldn't fathom how she'd come to be here. Couldn't imagine a scenario where her brother would allow it. And if she was here, where was Clarence? Myriad questions burned his tongue, but in front of an audience of curious onlookers was neither the time nor the place.

He found his voice. "I do." Turning his gaze back to Greeves, he said, "Barton and I attended Harrow together, which was why I was so taken aback when you presented *him* as your best linguist." He hoped that was enough explanation to cover his blunder. Humor should take care of the rest. He chuckled and tossed Claire a cocky grin. "If I remember correctly, pup, you copied your Latin *and* your Greek off of *me*."

She snorted. "True, but Cambridge cured me of *that*," she said, not missing a step. He had to admit, she played her part well. "Since you had to go and desert me for the Royal Military College, I was forced to learn the stuff myself. Found I actually had an affinity for it, and here we are."

She raised her chin, just slightly, but he recognized the subtle challenge.

"Here we are, indeed," he murmured. *She* shouldn't be here. This place was dangerous enough for grown men, given the secrets that passed through Abchurch every day. Secrets someone was willing to kill for.

A young woman shouldn't even know such a place existed.

But he'd have to be patient. He couldn't reveal her for who she was. Her reputation would be left in tatters, at the very least. But beyond that, if Claire had gone to this kind of trouble, she had a reason. A reason he wanted very much to know.

Still, he couldn't spend time lingering in conversation when he was supposed to be discovering who'd murdered his predecessor. It would draw attention, and that was the last thing either of them needed.

Andrew tipped his head in a quick nod. "Good to see you, Barton," he said. "I'm sure we'll speak again...soon."

Claire held his gaze for a moment, then dropped her chin and turned back to her work.

As Andrew turned on his heel to continue his tour with Greeves, he knew one thing for certain: He wouldn't allow Claire to escape Abchurch Lane tonight until she told him exactly what she was doing here.

CHAPTER 2

Claire hugged her greatcoat to her and pulled the beaver hat lower over her brow as she slipped out into the night. A bitterly cold wind whipped round the corner of the nondescript brick building and stole her breath.

Thank goodness for trousers. Were she wearing a gown, that gust would have blown straight beneath it and frozen her nethers!

There were many things to hate about her current situation, but trousers weren't one of them. And no matter how tightly she had to bind her breasts beneath her lawn shirt and waistcoat, she was infinitely more comfortable than she'd been in boned stays. Yes, aside from the confounded cravats, her new attire was about the only bright spot in the endless darkness she'd found herself in since the loss of her twin.

And Andrew Sedgewick had seen straight through it.

Her chest squeezed with a chilly tingling that had nothing to do with the crisp air she breathed.

What was he doing here? She hadn't even known he was back in England. And why, of all people, had the War Department chosen *him* to replace Uncle Jarvis?

Claire rubbed her gloved hands together, partly against the frigid night, partly to alleviate the anxious energy that had rushed through her at seeing Andrew again. How had he known she was herself and not her brother? What had she done to give herself away?

But none of those questions mattered as much this one: Just what did he intend to do about it?

She reached the hackney and mumbled her address to the jarvey. At his nod, Claire jerked the door open and pulled herself up into the conveyance. A feeble flame flickered from the battered carriage lamp, casting just enough light about to see that no blanket or foot warmer awaited her. With a sigh that sent a puff of white from her lips, Claire settled onto the hard seat, wrapped her arms around herself, and tucked her chin into her chest for warmth.

The carriage rocked, but rather than jerking forward into a roll, it dipped to the side. Claire snapped her head up just as the door whipped open and a massive figure filled the space.

Her heart leapt into her throat. Dear God. She'd known that in taking Clarence's place, she'd become a target herself. It had been worth it to her to flush out her brother's killer. But tonight she'd been so distracted by thoughts of Andrew that she hadn't kept a careful eye on her surroundings.

Would she now pay for that lapse with her life?

She scooted into the corner with an unmanly squeak, pressing herself against the back of the squab as her hackney was invaded, first by a dark head, then wide shoulders that narrowed to a trim waist, and finally by the long legs of a man.

A man who smelled of bergamot and bay…and of memories.

Andrew Sedgewick rapped on the roof of the hackney to signal for the driver to depart, then settled himself beside her as if he had every right to be there.

And before she had the chance to recover from her shock, he cupped her cheeks in his warm palms and kissed her.

∽

CHRIST, Claire tasted exactly as he remembered. A bit like peaches, a bit like honey...sweet, yet not without bite.

He'd dreamt of their last kiss so many times over the last few years that the memory perched on its own pedestal, one that reached all the way to heaven.

And yet this...this surpassed even his most fevered remembrance. Because it was real. *She* was real. He finally had Claire in his arms again and this time, he would not let her go. No matter what Clarence had to say about the matter.

She'd tensed when his lips first met hers, but now she relaxed into him with a soft sigh, opening to his caress with a fervor that was all Claire. He groaned and clutched her to him, fighting to leash years of longing.

Her tongue brushed against his once, twice—and then the minx suckled his into her mouth and he nearly came undone.

"Claire," he gasped, fire rushing through him and obliterating all else. He sent one hand to her nape to hold her to him, another to her waist to keep her from getting too close. He remembered how quickly things could burn between them. He didn't exactly trust himself—or Claire—in this moment, yet he couldn't stop his lips from returning to hers.

He spread his fingers into her hair, knocking something from her head. But instead of the heavy silken locks he remembered, short curls entwined his digits. His other hand, too, encountered strange differences—rough fabric, an unnatural firmness to her side. The oddness of these sensations pulled at his mind, towing him through the lust-filled fog back to the present. Yes, this was Claire. But Claire disguised as a man, for some purpose.

One he needed to know.

He dragged his lips from hers, not without effort. She mewled a protest and tried to pull him back to her, but he resisted and pressed his lips to her forehead instead as he tried to slow his breathing.

"Damn," he murmured against her skin as he came to his senses. What had he been thinking? The last time he'd kissed Claire, it had cost him his best friend. "Your brother is going to kill me."

Claire went very still against him, as if she too were considering the ramifications of these past blissful moments. Then her breath hitched and she slowly pushed away from him.

"Clarence won't do anything of the kind," she said, her voice so thick with emotion that the hair rose on the back of his neck.

He sharpened his gaze on her, peering at her face through the dim flicker of the carriage lamp. Even in the low light, her eyes shown with moisture and he *knew*. Yet he couldn't believe it, even when she confirmed his fear.

"Because he's dead."

Andrew's stomach clenched, as though he'd absorbed a gut punch. The ache spread through him and the air around him went very cold. Clarence dead? "How?" he croaked. "When?" And why had he heard nothing of it?

Claire's eyes went stormy, her eyebrows crashing together as a fierce frown gathered on her face. "What do you care, after all this time?"

He closed his eyes as fresh pain stabbed him. Of course Claire would be angry. He doubted her brother would have told her the truth about why Andrew had walked out of their lives. What she must think of him...

"Of course I care," he rasped, pinning her with his gaze, willing her to believe him. "I've always cared. Things just got...complicated."

That was as close as he'd come to telling her of the horrific fight he and Clarence had had that last night. Over her.

"Please, Claire. What happened?"

She shook her head, but then her shoulders slumped and the fight seemed to go out of her. She scooted back into the corner of the carriage, pulling her knees up and wrapping her arms around them. The gesture made her look so young, so vulnerable, that his heart ached.

Yet her eyes still flashed. "I suppose you need to know," she said, "since you are taking over Abchurch." Her tone clearly said that if it weren't for that, she'd not tell him. That hurt. "Clarence was murdered. Just after All Hallows' Eve."

Andrew flinched, though he'd prepared himself for her answer. He'd gone beyond the place where he could be shocked any more, beyond the place where he allowed himself to feel. During his months of captivity in Paris, he'd learned how to separate his mind from the rest of himself, and it was from that place that he acted now.

"Tell me everything."

∽

Tell him everything?

Blast it all, that was the problem, wasn't it? She *did* want to tell him everything. She *wanted* to pour out her fear, her grief. She *wanted* to rely on him, as she once would have.

But she was no longer that trusting young girl, and she'd learned the hard way that he had never been the man she'd thought him to be.

Shame burned through her at how easily she'd succumbed to his kisses. Reveled in them, even. One touch of his lips upon hers and she'd been swept back to that autumn six years past, when her sun had risen and set in Andrew Sedgewick's moss-green eyes. When merely a glimpse of his tousled brown hair and arrogant grin made her burn in places she didn't yet understand. When she'd lived for the moments they were able to steal away together, as he'd introduced her to pleasure upon pleasure that was certain to culminate in a glorious union of hearts and bodies and souls.

Until she'd found herself alone, waiting beneath the mistletoe at the Danburys' Christmas Eve ball for a man who never came.

The sharp ache of betrayal burst beneath her breastbone, as brilliant and painful as it had been that night and the days, weeks, and even months that followed with no word from him. Damn, she'd thought she'd buried those hurts long ago.

Luckily, fury came to her rescue. How dare he, after six years of *nothing*, come back into her life and, without a word of explanation, kiss her senseless? The bounder!

And now he demanded that she tell him everything?

Claire straightened in her seat, her fists clenching by her sides. She needed to stop acting like some love-struck ingénue and put everything that Andrew had once meant to her out of her mind for good.

She lowered her boots to the floor of the hackney, then bent to retrieve her hat—a convenient diversion as she regained control of her emotions. By the time she sat back up with the beaver smashed upon her head, she'd managed an expression of cool disdain.

"What, *precisely*, do you wish to know?"

Andrew might be the only person she could turn to in this, now that Uncle Jarvis was gone. He *was* the new head of Abchurch. But she'd be damned if she gave him any more of herself than he needed to help her solve Clarence's murder.

He blinked, seemingly taken aback by her response. She'd heard via the marriage-minded-mama grapevine—who kept tabs on *any* eligible bachelor, whether he currently resided on English soil or not—that Andrew had quickly risen in the ranks of Wellington's army, recently being promoted to Lieutenant Colonel. Perhaps he was unused to someone answering his questions with a question.

Well, he'd best get used to it. She'd never toady to him.

He cleared his throat, the sound reverberating in the close confines of the hackney. A deep V formed between his brows as he regarded her for a moment. Then he crossed his arms and threw his right ankle negligently onto his left knee in a pose that said he had all night to discover what he wanted to know. It also left him sprawled into her half of the small bench seat.

Her breath hitched involuntarily, and she scowled at him.

He gave her the lazy half smile she remembered so well, which only made her scowl deepen.

His smile widened.

But then his face turned serious and his gaze sharpened on her, his voice brooking no dissemblance.

"Let's start with how I came to find *you* in one of the most well-kept secret rooms within all of the War Department, shall we?"

CHAPTER 3

*J*udging by the mutinous look on Claire's face, he shouldn't have been surprised when she yet again answered him with a question of her own.

"Oh, let's do," she said. "Tell me…just how *did* you end up in charge of England's crack group of code breakers?" Syrup practically dripped from her voice.

Hell, he didn't intimidate her at all. Not that he ever had, but damn it, his scowl could cow an entire regiment of men.

She raised her eyebrows in sarcastic anticipation.

He sighed. Apparently Claire was made of sterner stuff than even Britain's finest.

Irritated as he was, he did have to admire how deftly she'd turned his words back on him.

"That's not something you need to know," he said. In truth, he wasn't entirely certain himself. Having recently escaped captivity in Paris, he'd expected to rejoin Wellington, who last month had marched over the Pyrenean passes into southern France after his victories on the Peninsula. But Andrew's years gathering intelligence had made a name for him in the War Department, it seemed. When Marston was killed, someone deemed that he was the right man, in the right place, at the right time, and he was sent to Abchurch instead.

Claire, however, was not to be put off. "Lord Marston never once mentioned you in connection with his department," she prodded, "much less as a possible replacement."

Andrew shifted in his seat. He wasn't accustomed to playing from behind and the feeling didn't suit him. He also didn't care for the superior look on Claire's face.

"Privy to *all* of the thoughts of one of England's great spymasters, were you?" he snapped.

Claire's eyes widened, then narrowed into a sly gaze. "More than *you* were, since you didn't know Clarence was dead. Or that Uncle Jarvis had insinuated me into his place."

He winced inwardly. Her jab struck true.

Wait. *Uncle* Jarvis? That's right. Clarence had once mentioned that Lord Marston and his father were friends. That explained some of how Claire came to be here. Still, she knew more of what was truly going on here than he did, and perhaps more than his own superiors, who surely would have mentioned her presence had they known of it.

Fighting with Claire would get him nowhere.

Andrew tunneled his fingers through his hair, steepling them behind his neck as he took a deep breath. "Pax, Claire. Pax."

A dull throbbing beat a tattoo behind his eyes. This damned day had taken a beastly turn. First, he'd been conscripted to go undercover with very little to go on. *That* hadn't bothered him. He'd been in such situations before, and he'd had little doubt he could make short work of it.

But then he'd had a year of his life shocked out of him by finding *Claire* there. He'd experienced the exquisite joy of holding her in his arms once more, only to learn that his childhood friend was dead. And Claire, rather than feeling the same pleasure at their reunion as he, instead seemed to hate his guts...or at the very least, resent his presence.

Oh, and his dead friend had apparently been murdered, which complicated things all the more.

Not one of his best days, indeed.

After another calming breath, Andrew removed his hands to his knees and his feet to the floor. Then he shifted on the bench so that he faced Claire, laying his right arm along the back of the squab. He tried to make his voice soothing, persuasive.

"Let's not fight. If I'm going to have any chance of discovering who murdered Marston and your brother, I need to know everything you do."

Claire's tiny gasp echoed through the cramped carriage. Andrew frowned as her normally robust complexion went ashen in the candlelight, the color leaching from her face in slow degrees.

"Uncle Jarvis was *murdered?*"

Andrew felt the blood drain from his face, too. She hadn't known. He nearly kicked himself. Of course not. How would she? The official story had been a heart ailment.

"I wondered, of course, given our subterfuge, but…" Claire swallowed audibly, and her eyes turned glassy. She wasn't looking at him, but off into the darkness over his shoulder. "But I went to Uncle's house myself, and had it straight from his valet that his death had been natural. Not like Clarence." Her eyes found his, and the sorrow he saw swimming in their cerulean depths stole his breath. She firmed her lips. "You're certain?"

Andrew nodded, once. "Poison."

Claire blew out a breath, then straightened her shoulders. She returned a clipped nod of her own. "Right, then. What are we going to do about it?"

∽

"W̲e̲ a̲r̲e̲n̲'̲t̲ g̲o̲i̲n̲g̲ to do anything," Andrew said, his lips pulling down into the affronted-male frown Claire recognized all too well.

She'd seen it on the faces of men her entire life, right before she was told to stay out of *male business.* She'd seen it on Uncle Jarvis's face, too, when she'd first presented her plan to assume Clarence's identity.

"*You* are going to tell me everything," Andrew went on, "from the beginning, and then *I* am going to handle it from there."

And there it was.

"So we're back to that, are we?" Claire could give an affronted frown right along with the best of them. "Tell you everything, and then what? You'll pat me on the head and send me on my merry way? I think not."

"*Claire...*" he warned, but she didn't let him finish.

"No. Uncle Jarvis tried to tell me he would take care of things, too, but he finally saw reason—"

"Good God!" Andrew snapped ramrod straight in his seat and Claire thought he looked a bit green.

"Are you all right?"

He narrowed his eyes on her. "It has just dawned upon me that if Clarence has been dead since November, and no one has noticed, then *you* have been masquerading as him all that time." His voice had gone from startled to deadly calm.

"Well, yes—"

"What the hell was Marston *thinking?*" Andrew nearly shouted. His body seemed to vibrate with leashed tension. Claire bet that if they weren't cooped up in this hackney, he'd have exploded out of his seat.

Not so calm after all.

"Somewhere out there is a killer who thinks—" Andrew stopped abruptly, his expression sliding from outrage into one of puzzlement. "Who thinks *what?* That Clarence has come back from the dead?" He tilted his head slightly as he looked to her for an answer.

Claire wilted a bit inside, the ever-present ache of losing her twin shriveling her heart another painful degree. "Not exactly. Clarence was knifed, you see. He...he was able to make it home alive. Barely." She took a shuddering breath. "He died in my arms. But for all the killer knows, he could have pulled through."

Flashes of that night invaded her mind. All that blood. The ghostly pallor of Clarence's skin. The horrid rattle of his breathing.

The death grip he'd kept on her hand as she begged him not to die.

Not to go where she couldn't follow. Not to leave her alone when they had always been together—even in the very womb.

But Clarence had been unable to keep his grasp on life, and she'd lost a part of herself irrevocably.

"Don't cry, dearling," Andrew murmured, a scant moment before his arms closed around her and he pulled her to his chest.

Was she crying? Blast it all.

Hot tears spilled down her cheeks as his comforting presence enveloped her. The fresh warm citrus-y scent of him, the familiar strength in his embrace, the connection that came from knowing that once upon a time, she and her brother had both loved this man, albeit in different ways.

So she let herself be consoled by him, just for a little while. She welcomed the pain, rather than shutting it out—let it flow through her into poignant relief as she sobbed, something she hadn't allowed herself to do since that awful night.

And all the while, Andrew held her close.

After she'd cried herself out, Claire found herself loath to leave the protective warmth of Andrew's arms. How easy it would be to stay here. To forgive past betrayals. To forget her fears for the future. To not have to go back to that lifeless townhouse alone.

Wait a minute...

She lifted her head from Andrew's chest, looking up at the underside of his strong jaw, now lightly dusted with evening stubble.

"We've been in this hackney quite some time," she murmured. "We should have reached my residence long ago."

Andrew's head bobbed and his chest rumbled beneath hers as he answered. "Actually, I instructed the jarvey to drive us around the park until I gave him leave to continue on to your destination."

"Why would you do that?"

"Because I had no intention of letting you escape this carriage until we'd hashed things out."

Claire huffed and pulled away from him. He tightened his grip for a fraction of a moment, but released her. Part of her regretted the loss.

As she scooted away from him, she used the backs of her hands to dash away the remnants of her tears, and sniffed. "There's nothing to hash out, Andrew. Uncle Jarvis and Clarence have both been killed, and it has to be because of something they were involved with for the War Department. They were the only people I had in this world, and they were taken from me. I will do anything and everything within my power to find justice for them, with or without you."

His lips pressed together hard and he shook his head. "It's too dangerous for you, Claire." Andrew's voice was raw, gravelly, as if he were holding back a torrent of words that burned to get out. "If the killer thinks Clarence survived, he'll want to finish the job. Only he won't get Clarence this time. He'll murder *you*."

"I've been counting on it," she said, turning her lips up in a grim smile at the look of appalled horror that crossed his face. "How else did you think we were going to catch the man? I'm the perfect bait."

CHAPTER 4

*B*ait.
Bloody bait?

He must have said that last aloud, because Claire clucked her tongue.

"There's no call for swearing," she chided.

Andrew clenched his jaw, clenched his fists—hell, even clenched his toes. Anything he could do to get control of his...

Christ, what *was* he feeling? An awful muddle of lust, sorrow, anger, regret, and a bone-deep fear for Claire's safety, that's what.

Control. That's what he needed. Of this situation. Of Claire. There was no way her charade could continue.

When he trusted his voice not to betray him, he said, "*That* was Marston's plan? To use you as bait?"

"Of course not," she said.

He started to exhale in relief.

"It was mine."

He pinched the bridge of his nose. "And Marston went along with this?" If the man weren't already dead...

Claire, for once, didn't answer his question with a question. In fact she didn't answer him at all. Her eyes shifted to the side and her lips pressed together. The relief he'd almost felt a moment ago finally came. Marston hadn't dangled her in front of the killer after all, apparently much to Claire's frustration.

She took a breath and then her eyes met his again. "I sent for Uncle Jarvis immediately after Clarence died. He was one of Uncle Jarvis's operatives, you see. Not secreted away at Abchurch, but in plain sight in the ballrooms and clubs." A ghost of a smile haunted her lips. "His code name was The Prancer. No one suspected him of being more than a dandified prattler, but they didn't know the real Clarence."

Andrew nodded. He'd known Clarence since they were boys and knew very well he was far from a thoughtless dandy. But he never would have taken the man for a spy. Much must have changed in the past six years.

How strange that their paths would diverge as they had, and yet lead them to the same place. Andrew, too, had been an operative in plain sight, though he'd considered himself more of a reconnaissance officer. Much of his intelligence was gathered while in full military uniform as he carried out his regular duties, even when behind enemy lines. People often believed you were just what you portrayed yourself to be.

Which made Claire, in her disguise, the perfect operative in plain sight, too. Hell.

"When the shock wore off, it occurred to me that whoever killed my brother couldn't know for certain he'd succeeded," she went on. "The more days that passed without an announcement of Clarence's passing, the killer would have to wonder how he'd survived—and what he knew about who'd stabbed him. It only made sense for me to pretend to be my brother because—"

"Because if Clarence was alive, it might force the killer's hand. Push him into making a mistake," he finished, though it cost him to admit that her logic had merit.

"Precisely." Claire's lips spread into a smile of satisfaction. "If it makes you feel better, it took me some time to convince Uncle Jarvis, too."

Andrew nearly growled at her assumption that she'd convinced *him.* No, he was so far from convinced he may as well be across the ocean, fighting the damned Americans instead of the French.

"Eventually we decided to slip Clarence's body into an old family crypt and put out that he was ill. After a few days, I emerged as my brother, and Uncle Jarvis installed me at Abchurch so that I could be useful while I 'recovered.'"

Andrew shook his head reflexively, even as he asked, "Useful, how?"

Claire's eyes flashed, in anticipation of victory he was certain, and she edged closer. "Apart from discomfiting the killer, I *am* fluent in several languages—much better than Clarence ever was."

"Oh, I don't doubt that." He should know. He'd been the one to teach her Latin, Greek, and Italian, after all. The only foreign language that was part of a typical English lady's education was French, but Claire had a keen mind and she'd been desperate to learn anything anyone would teach her.

At first, it had amused him to indulge his friend's sister when he'd accompanied Clarence home from Harrow during school holidays, but Claire had taken to it with an ease that left him both amazed and envious. Soon, she'd quite outstripped him in those languages and had moved on to teaching herself others.

"I'd translated things for Abchurch before," Claire said. "Things Clarence uncovered or that Uncle Jarvis asked me to look at when their language experts came up empty. Turns out I have a gift for noticing odd nuances of phrasing, and plucking code from it."

Her chin lifted when she said that. Just slightly. He didn't think she was even aware of the gesture, but Claire was proud of her ability. And perhaps daring him to doubt or disparage her for it.

He never would. He may not believe women should be involved in such matters, but not because he didn't think them capable. Claire was bloody brilliant, he well knew. But war was the business of men.

He reminded himself of his resolve not to argue with her—not, at least, until he knew everything she did. "That *is* a useful skill."

She quirked a brow at his diplomacy, but let it pass. "Yes, but precious time was lost by the time they realized they needed my help, and then more in having to smuggle things out of Abchurch and across town to me in Bloomsbury and back.

"More than once, Uncle Jarvis's operatives were unable to act on information I discovered because when they finally got it, they'd missed their opportunity. Now, with me *at* Abchurch, I am able to get to things and get them out again much more quickly."

"Wait," he said, remembering something his new aide-de-camp had said when he'd introduced Andrew to "Sir Clarence" earlier. "Greeves mentioned that we wouldn't have won at Vitoria without Clarence's help. But that battle was in June. You've only been at Abchurch since early November?"

Claire nodded. "Yes. But early this summer, Abchurch received several interceptions from the battlefields, missives between France and Madrid that the code breakers struggled with."

The hairs on Andrew's arms tingled. He knew precisely which missives she meant, as *he'd* been the one to intercept them.

"So Uncle Jarvis brought them to me. It took some doing, but I was able to pull out planned troop movements and tactics, which were then relayed back to Wellington." Her voice rang with quiet pride.

It should. Hell, *he* was proud of her. He knew exactly how much that intel had meant.

"I was with Wellington when that information reached us," he said. Vitoria had been the decisive battle in the Peninsular War, where the allies finally broke the French army under Bonaparte's brother and which eventually led to France's retreat from Spain.

But it had been a very close thing. And without the advanced knowledge they'd received from Abchurch…?

"Greeves was right," Andrew said solemnly, seeing Claire as he'd never seen her before. "We couldn't have won the battle without you."

Claire's eyes darted away, even as the tops of her cheeks pinked at his praise. Then she cleared her throat and looked back at him. "Well, as far as anyone was concerned, it was Clarence's work that saved the day. Uncle Jarvis couldn't very well tell people a woman was his secret weapon, could he?"

Hell.

Hell, hell, and hell again.

He was going to have to let Claire continue on as Clarence.

She *was* a secret weapon, not just in his current responsibility of discovering who killed Marston—and Clarence—but in the whole of the war effort.

He might not even be alive if it weren't for her.

And what's more, Claire was the *only* person at Abchurch he knew for certain didn't kill Marston and her brother. Everyone else was suspect. He could use someone there he could trust.

But not as bait. Never as bait.

Andrew let out a gruff sigh and banged on the roof of the hackney, signaling the jarvey to take them on to Claire's home.

"All right, Claire. We'll continue your ruse. For now."

A relieved smile broke across her face and her shoulders dropped as she seemed to relax. "Thank you, Andrew. You won't regret this."

He snorted. "I doubt that."

They rode in silence the few minutes to Bloomsbury, both lost in their own thoughts. When the hackney rolled to a stop, Andrew let himself out, then turned to hold a hand out to Claire.

She glanced pointedly at it and pursed her lips.

"Oh, right!" He snatched his hand back and cleared his throat. "Sorry. I'll have to get used to treating you as I would another man in public." He stepped back and Claire hopped down.

Andrew paid the jarvey, and then followed Claire up the steps of the small-but-tidy brick townhouse.

"You needn't have escorted me in," she said as they reached the stoop. "This may not be Mayfair, but it's safe enough."

Andrew just nodded, taking a protective position behind and to the left of her. His eyes scanned the street, the bushes, and all the very dark corners.

The door opened.

"A bit late this evening, mi—" The butler's eyes widened as he noticed Andrew in the shadows behind Claire. "—m-m-master," the man corrected himself.

Well, that answered his question as to whether Claire's staff knew what she'd been up to.

"It's all right, Wallace," Claire assured the man as they passed into a marbled foyer. "Lord Sedgewick is privy to my ruse," she said, allowing the servant to remove her greatcoat.

Andrew just stood there for a moment, taking in the sight of her for the first time in a well-lit room. If he didn't know better, he'd be damned to think she was anything but a young gentleman about town, albeit a fine-boned one.

It was eerie, how much she looked like Clarence. Her brother had been on the short side, and Claire was quite tall for a woman. He remembered joking once when he'd seen their childhood portraits hanging side by side at Barton Hall that if he just covered Claire's braids with his thumbs, she'd be Clarence. No wonder she'd been able to pull off this ruse. Still, he might never get used to the vision of Claire in trousers.

He shook himself. "Indeed," he said, turning to Wallace. "I need you to send a man to the Clarendon and fetch my things here."

The older man's eyes scrunched in question, but he nodded. "Yes, my lord."

"What are you doing?" Claire asked, her voice rising a notch in surprise.

"I'm sending your man to my hotel—"

"I gathered that," she snapped. "But why?"

He said nothing.

Her eyes rounded. "You can't be thinking of staying *here*?"

"Oh, but I am."

Claire sputtered, color flushing her cheeks. "But I'm an unmarried young lady!"

"Yes, you are," he murmured. Christ, she was beautiful with her color high and her eyes flashing. Even with her hair practically shorn and her feminine curves well hidden, Claire took his breath away.

How had she not married? He hadn't been the only man sniffing around her skirts during her first Season. If he'd have known she'd not be some peer's wife by now... But none of that mattered anymore. Only keeping Claire safe did.

"However, your *brother* lives here as well, as far as anyone knows," he pointed out, "and will serve as chaperone."

Claire snapped her mouth shut. Her eyes narrowed on him as she opened it again, but he cut her off with a wave of his hand that ended with his finger pointed in her direction.

"*You* may not be concerned that there's a killer after you," he said, turning his finger around and jabbing it into his own chest with each successive word, "but *I bloody well am.*"

Ouch. That bloody well hurt. Andrew rubbed at the stinging spot before crossing his arms over his chest.

"I may have agreed to help you continue your charade, Claire, but I have no intention of leaving your side until this entire affair is over."

They stared each other down for a moment, two allied generals on the same side of the war but with opposing battle plans—and an aging butler glancing between them. Andrew wasn't certain, but he thought he spied a look of relieved approval flash over the old man's face.

Then, with a rather feminine huff of disgust that was quite at odds with her attire, Claire turned on her booted heel and marched through the foyer and up the marble staircase.

Andrew relaxed his stance, bringing his arms around and clasping them behind his back as he watched her go. Even dressed in trousers and a man's jacket, there was no mistaking the feminine sway of her hips as she ascended.

He closed his eyes, but depriving himself of the sight of her did little to lessen the tension thrumming through him that had been simmering from the moment he'd seen her again.

He never should have kissed her. He'd had the best of intentions, hoping to put the past behind them and renew their romance. But now that he knew her brother was gone? He couldn't pursue Claire knowing that he would be going back to war and leaving her with no one to protect her while he was abroad.

Yet he *had* kissed her, and his body was not going to let him forget it. Staying under the same roof with Claire was a terrible idea, but he could think of no other way to keep her safe.

Question was, who was going to keep her safe from him?

CHAPTER 5

Claire patted the large pocket of her greatcoat as she descended the stairs, the heaviness of the muff pistol concealed within its depths reassuring against her gloved hand. She moved quietly toward the front door, so as not to alert anyone of her intentions.

In the weeks since Clarence's death, she'd spent many a night walking the streets of London—never without her firearm, of course. She wasn't a fool. She took great care to always be cognizant of her surroundings. Yes, she put herself in danger. But she couldn't just sit around doing nothing while Clarence's killer was out there, alive and free.

But she also walked because facing the endless hours of the night alone in this house without Clarence was often more than she could bear.

Of course, she wasn't alone tonight, was she?

Andrew was upstairs. In her house once more, as he'd so often been when he and Clarence had been friends. Back when she'd thought she'd meant something to him. But she'd been nothing but a plaything to him. Her heart remembered that pain and wanted him out, now. But her traitorous body…

Not only had the overbearing man taken up residence despite her protests, but he'd insisted on staying in the chamber closest to hers. Right across the hall.

Which meant barely eight steps and a panel of hardened oak were all that separated the two of them.

A warm heat flushed through her. Irritation, she insisted, but she knew she was lying to herself.

For hours, she'd tossed and turned in her bed, lost in the memories of past kisses, heated touches, and long-ago desires.

She'd finally forced the memories away and tried to sleep, but when she'd closed her eyes again all she could see was Andrew, asleep in his own bed, mussed hair dark against his pillow, his impossibly long lashes sooty against his golden skin. When she'd started wondering whether he slept in a night shirt or in nothing at all, she'd known she couldn't stay in this house a moment longer.

That, more than anything, was what drove her out into the cold tonight. Not the need to escape from her grief or the desire to lure Clarence's killer, but the urge to run away from her confused feelings for Andrew.

A blast of wintry air hit her face as she opened the entryway door.

"Where do you think you're going?"

Claire yelped, her heart slamming into her throat and then fluttering there like a trapped canary.

She whirled around to see Andrew standing in the shadows at the foot of the stairs.

"What—what are you doing up?" she squeaked, placing her hand on her chest to soothe the flapping bird within.

"That's not an answer." He stepped towards her, passing into the light of a wall sconce. He was wrapped in a calf-length banyan of deepest red silk, with warm black velvet adorning the collar and cuffs. No hint of a ruffled night shirt showed at his neckline. No customary trousers peeked from beneath the hem. And his feet were bare.

He must have heard her leave her room and hurriedly thrown on his robe, buttoning it over…nothing.

She swallowed, her mouth having gone suddenly dry.

THE VERY DEBONAIR LADY CLAIRE

Well, she supposed that answered her earlier musings, didn't it?

He reached her in two long strides, coming so near she caught the scent of peppermint and lemon oil from his tooth powder. Which drew her gaze to his lips, of course. Suggestive, alluring lips—full but not the least bit feminine, the top just slightly more so than the bottom, suggesting long-ago Gallic ancestry. Lips perfect for kissing.

Which was all she could now think about.

Andrew's arm came around her.

A quiver began in her tummy and she let her eyes drift closed in anticipation.

He pushed the door shut behind her and turned the lock.

The slam and click shook Claire from her stupor.

She nearly growled with self-disgust. Stupid, foolish girl. What was she thinking?

She stepped back from him, her back now touching the carved wood of the door. "Out," she snapped, irritated with the both of them. "I'm going out."

His lips pressed together into a line. "Where, Claire?"

She wanted to inform him it was none of his business—which it wasn't—but she didn't wish to sound like a petulant child. So she answered with a sigh. "Just for a walk, to clear my head." No way was she going to tell him what sinful thoughts needed clearing.

His mouth relaxed, but his tone was still quite firm—if one could sound firm and incredulous at the same time, which he seemed able to do. "Need I remind you that someone may be trying to kill you?"

"No," she gritted out. "Nor do I remember asking you to be my keeper." Claire slipped her hand reflexively into her pocket and grasped the handle of the muff pistol. "Besides, I hope the blackguard does come after me."

She pulled the small flintlock pistol from her pocket, twisting her wrist so that the light from the candle sconces glinted off the metal.

Andrew danced back a step in surprise. "Christ, Claire! Is that thing loaded?"

"Of course," she huffed. "All three barrels. That way, if I miss with my first shot, I'll have two more to drop any villain foolish enough to try me."

"Good God," he muttered.

She scowled at his less-than-confident-in-her-abilities-and-possibly-her-sanity expression.

"Don't look so alarmed," she said as she slipped the weapon back into her pocket. "It has a latch that ensures it won't discharge unless I choose to fire it."

Andrew had fallen into a tight, agitated pace. Every so often, he shook his head and mumbled something she couldn't quite hear. Claire barely resisted the urge to mutter some things of her own as she watched him. But all too soon, her frustration turned to a different kind altogether.

The man was rather dashing, prowling around her foyer in nothing but that silk banyan. The cut was more tailored than the robes Clarence had favored, tapering in at the waist in a double-breasted fit more like a waistcoat, and Andrew filled it out nicely. Given that she'd already ascertained he wore nothing beneath it, there could be no pads filling out the wide shoulders, as some men were wont to do. Claire longed to slip her fingers beneath the buttons and feel for herself the changes that years and war had made to the only man's chest she'd ever explored.

The bottom half of the banyan flowed as he stalked about the room, flashing tantalizing glimpses of muscled calf, dusted with dark hair, and the occasional peek of a well-formed knee.

She tugged at her cravat. Was it getting warm in here?

"Claire!" Her eyes snapped up to Andrew's face. He'd stopped pacing and was eyeing her with a narrowed gaze. She flushed. Did he know what she'd been thinking?

"I asked," he repeated, and her flush deepened as she realized he'd been talking to her and she hadn't heard him, so lost was she in thoughts of seeing his naked chest again, "have you gone out alone like this often?"

She nodded, cheeks burning. "Almost every night."

He swore. "And you've noticed no one following you? Never felt like someone was watching?"

She shook her head. "Never." She sighed. She'd hoped the killer would come after her by now, close to her home where she felt secure in her surroundings, but he hadn't. "I don't think I've been trolling the right part of town."

"What makes you think that?"

"Because our coachman told me that Clarence had instructed him to wait a few blocks from the Devil's Den on the night he was killed."

Andrew's brows rose. "The gaming hell?"

"The same." The infamous bastion of iniquity, frequented by all walks of male London society, and the kinds of females who amused them. Unease flickered low in her stomach, the same as it did whenever she'd thought about going there—as Clarence, of course—to see what she could discover. But she'd not been able to bring herself to brave it alone.

"I know Clarence had an informant there," she explained. "He never gave me a name, but he must have gone to see the man that night, and been attacked either at the den or just outside, as he was mortally wounded when he stumbled back to the carriage. John Coachman rushed him straight here, but…"

Some days, it still felt unreal. As though it had all happened in a dream and Clarence would come strolling by at any minute and tug at her curls, which he'd done since they were children and which he knew annoyed her to no end. But Lord, she'd give anything to feel that aggravating yank once more. She'd let him pull until her naturally stubborn curls went straight as a board if he wanted. But the killer had made certain that Clarence would never tease her again.

And she wanted to make the wretch pay for that.

"Did Marston know of your suspicions?"

"Yes. He even went to investigate himself, but turned up nothing."

Andrew nodded, but his eyes wandered somewhere over her shoulder, as if he were lost in his own thoughts. She wondered if he was planning his own visit to the Devil's Den, to see if he could dig up something Uncle Jarvis had missed.

But only Clarence had known who his contact was. Andrew likely didn't stand a much better chance than Uncle Jarvis had. "Clarence" needed to be the one to go.

She dare not go by herself, but...Andrew could escort her there.

Even as the idea formed, her stomach started to flutter. Pretending to be Clarence under Uncle Jarvis's watch at Abchurch was one thing. Even walking the streets as Clarence, armed with her weapon, had felt relatively safe. But the very idea of stepping into the Devil's Den, a world completely unlike anything she'd ever known or probably even imagined, intimidated her.

And intrigued her.

She *hated* that Clarence was gone. She wished she'd never had to play this role. But she was honest enough with herself to admit that she liked the taste of freedom that living as a man had given her.

She wanted to see the Devil's Den for herself, and not just for what she might uncover.

"We should visit the place," she said before she lost her nerve. She tried to sound nonchalant, but ruined the effect by having to lick her dry lips. "Tomorrow night."

Andrew's eyes snapped to her. "We?"

"*Yes*, we." Now that she thought about it, this plan made perfect sense. "Uncle Jarvis discreetly inquired after anyone who'd seen or talked to Clarence that night, but got nowhere. I think that's because Clarence's contact will only talk to him. *I'm* the one who has to seek him out."

"Absolutely not."

"Why not? It's not like I'd be in any danger. You'd be with me." Claire realized the trepidation that usually accompanied her thoughts of stepping foot inside the Devil's Den was absent, leaving only the curiosity behind. Andrew had always encouraged curiosity in her, whether intellectual or physical. She trusted him. To keep her safe, anyway. And not to judge her. The only thing she'd never trust him with again was her heart.

"No, Claire. Even if I was certain I could keep your person from harm—" He pressed his lips together, as if struggling to say or not say something. Then he shook his head. "It's no place for a decent young woman."

She nearly howled in vexation. Had she just thought he wouldn't judge her? And how dare he thwart her best chance for learning something more about what had befallen Clarence because he thought he knew best regarding her moral well-being?

Had he forgotten that she *wasn't* a decent young woman? No decent young woman would have welcomed his kisses and his roaming caresses all those years ago—not without a betrothal. And, good Lord, hadn't she just been clutching him to her in the hackney earlier this evening?

She felt her cheeks flush hot.

No. *Decent* she was not. Not when she itched to pull Andrew to her again, right here in the vestibule. Not when she wished to explore the Devil's Den for herself. Not when she burned to see exactly what was forbidden to her just by virtue of her sex and station.

Claire jutted her chin out in defiance. "Fine. Then I'll go on my own."

Andrew's expression softened, even as his tone hardened. "No, you won't."

She glared at him, but his moss-green gaze returned only an intense tenderness. Andrew stepped close then, and raised his right hand to cup her cheek, his strong fingers caressing the underside of her jaw.

"I understand why you risk it, Claire," he said. "All of it. Impersonating Clarence, going out night after night... If it had been one of my brothers, I'd dare the bastard to come after me, too."

His eyes searched hers as his thumb began to caress her cheek slowly. Seductively.

His voice dipped low. "I even understand why..."

Claire felt as if her cravat had suddenly tightened on her throat, and her breath quickened. Could he see through her? Did he know the curiosity that burned within her? That had since the moment he'd awakened it all those years ago?

"Well," he murmured, his eyes dropping to her mouth. "I understand."

Claire swallowed.

"But it all stops tonight," he said, releasing her.

Her cheek chilled quickly at the loss of his warmth.

"No more late night rambles. No more making yourself a target. And there's no way in hell I'm taking you to the Devil's Den, tomorrow night or *any* night."

CHAPTER 6

Rarely in his life did Andrew have cause to eat his words.

But a mere sennight later, as their carriage joined the blocks-long queue to deposit them at the most scandalous gaming hell in all of London, he decided that words one had to take back actually left a taste in one's mouth.

Something like brackish wine.

"Remember," he said, drawing Claire's attention from the window. She'd been peeking through the curtain for the past five minutes, trying to catch sight of the storied establishment. If she was hoping to see some gaudy exterior, she would be disappointed. The Devil's Den, just off King Street, St. James, catered to wealthy society and looked more like an aristocrat's home than a club.

Claire practically bounced on the edge of the velvet seat, her nervous anticipation palpable in the carriage. Christ, if she acted like a green lad inside the hell, they were sunk.

She turned to him, and in the wash of light from the carriage lamp, he could see the excitement she worked hard to mask behind a ne'er-do-well facade. She rolled her eyes at him and affected a bored look that did her brother proud. That was better.

"Yes, yes," she droned. "Stick to games of chance over games of skill. Hazard, roulette, and *rouge et noir*."

"Precisely. And if you must get drawn into a hand of cards, go for—"

"Faro." She parroted back the words he'd drilled into her for the past twenty-four hours. "Because it moves fast, the rules are easy to grasp, and the chances are better that I won't get fleeced or look a fool."

He nodded, and Claire returned to her window.

He was the fool here tonight, taking Claire to the gaming hell after swearing he wouldn't. It was wrong, on so many levels. If Clarence were alive, he'd certainly shoot Andrew on the spot for exposing his sister to the debauchery and vice she was certain to see tonight.

But he'd been left with little choice. After a week of trying, he'd gotten nothing through his military channels, and several trips to the Devil's Den on his own had likewise turned up empty. He was no closer to finding out who had killed Clarence and Marston or why.

It had been unnaturally quiet at Abchurch, as well. All of the code breakers were on edge. It reminded him of the stillness on the battlefield just before a bloody fight. His gut told him something significant was soon to happen, but they were at a loss as to what.

Clarence's possible contact at the gaming hell was the only viable lead they had left, and it seemed Claire had been right. She had to be the one to follow it.

So he'd relented.

But that didn't mean that the myriad things that could go wrong tonight weren't churning through his mind and turning his stomach sour.

How was a gently bred lady going to be able to brazen through as a man in the Devil's Den and come out unscathed? Much less with the information they needed?

He looked Claire over with a critical eye. Given that most men frequented the gaming hell in the wee hours after circulating through the ballrooms of London, "Clarence" was attired in full evening dress, as if "he'd" been out all night.

Beneath her greatcoat, Claire wore a coat of blue superfine with covered buttons, a single-breasted off-white marcella waistcoat, and cream-colored kerseymere breeches over white stockings. A pair of simple black dress slippers adorned her feet, as was the fashion. She seemed to be padded in all the right places, with no hint of her femininity on display.

To the casual observer, she'd do.

Except...

"Who in the world tied your cravat?"

She turned back to him, her brow furrowing into a slightly offended expression as she glanced at his neck. "Who tied yours?"

It was his turn to roll his eyes. "Can't you ever just answer a straightforward question?"

She shrugged, but her lips turned up just slightly.

He shook his head with mock exasperation, then crooked one finger at her, indicating for her to lean toward him. She raised her brows, but the smile still played about her lips and she obeyed. When she was close enough, he started unraveling the lopsided knot around her neck. "Seriously, Claire. Who massacred this poor scrap of linen?"

She huffed. "Is it truly fair to say 'massacred'?"

He winged an eyebrow at her question-rather-than-answer. "I'd say 'massacre' was a nice way of putting it." He continued to loosen the folds of fabric.

She sighed. "I did, of course. Bothersome things. I'm all thumbs with them. I can't have a man help me dress, and my maid knows less about tying cravats than I do."

He'd love to help her dress. *And undress.*

That unbidden thought stilled his hands mid-tug.

Being in such close proximity to Claire this past week had been a most exquisite torture. They broke their fast together each morning, shared a hackney to and from Abchurch each day, dined together in the evenings, and worked side by side in the library sifting through foreign correspondence and secret codes at night. Apart from her unconventional attire, their time together had such an air of domesticity that Andrew's heart ached for what might have been.

Sure, the first three or so days she hadn't really spoken to him, still furious at his curtailment of her nightly walks and for refusing her excursion to the gaming hell. But she'd thawed, and they'd fallen into an easy—if shallow—camaraderie.

They didn't speak of the past, as too many painful memories were buried there. They didn't speak of the future, as if they both knew that there could never be one between them. But they found things to discuss and eventually to laugh over and tease each other about, as they once had.

And at night, as she prowled through the house unable to sleep—probably in some flimsy night rail that would drive him wild—it took everything in Andrew to stay in his own room and leave her be.

Taking a steadying breath, he resumed working on the cravat. "Hold still," he murmured as he slipped the wide strip of fabric from her neck, careful not to pull the starched material too quickly. He had no wish to chafe her soft skin.

As the cravat peeled away, so too did Claire's disguise. No man could possess such a graceful long neck or such a delicate collarbone, nor flush such a lovely pink beneath his gaze. He swallowed against the overwhelming urge to put his lips to her neck, to trace the faint ridges of her throat with his mouth and press his tongue against the pulse beating in the hollow there.

And just like that, he was hard as stone. Just a glimpse of her hidden femininity and Andrew wanted to remove all of her trappings and rediscover the woman within.

His fingers shook as he stretched the cravat between his arms, and then brought the midline to Claire's throat and centered it on her neck.

"This is a simple Waterfall knot you should be able to learn easily," he said, willing his voice to normalcy. "Take the right side and wrap it around your neck, like so."

As he demonstrated, his knuckles barely grazed the warm skin of her nape, yet she shivered. Her involuntary reaction to his touch shot a thrill through him and stole his breath.

Andrew cleared his throat. Christ, who knew tying a cravat could be so damned erotic? He'd never be able to look his valet in the eye again.

"Now, do the same with the other side." He pulled the cloth around her neck, draping it over her collarbone but being careful not to touch her, much as he longed to. "Cross the fabric over itself and wrap it again and again in layers until it covers your whole neck."

He did this for Claire, his arms going around her, then coming back to the front, again and again. His movements brought their faces close with every revolution, their cheeks almost touching with each pass.

Every time he leaned close he could feel the heat from her skin and smell the hint of ginger, mint, and lemon that made up the cologne water she used. By the time there was only enough of the cravat left to tie, Andrew's breathing was ragged.

Claire's was, too. Her chest rose and fell rapidly and her blue, blue eyes were slightly glazed as she watched him.

Damn, but he wanted to kiss her. He leaned in, just slightly, before he caught himself and pulled back. Claire wasn't meant for the likes of him. He couldn't forget that.

Claire was all alone in the world now. She needed a husband who would take care of her, not one who was off to war again once this mission was done.

"Next," he said, his voice rough as he took up the loose ends of the fabric, "cross the ends into an X, pull the end of the top layer through here," which he did, "and tighten it into a knot."

He tried to sound matter-of-fact about it all, but truth was, he was unbearably close to ripping apart his handiwork and fastening his mouth to her neck, her chin, her lips—anywhere he could reach.

"Th-then what?" Claire asked. Oh, hell...her voice had gone all breathy.

"All that's left," he said, and damned if it didn't feel like he'd run up a hill before uttering each of those little words, "is to spread the top layer over the bottom to hide your knot." His eyes dropped to her breasts—which, though they were currently pressed flat, he could remember were both tender and firm and had once fit his hands perfectly—and he swallowed again, hard. "And tuck it into your waistcoat," he finished in a whisper.

That part he shouldn't do for her. Wouldn't. Because if he touched her again, he couldn't be responsible for what would happen next.

Claire seemed to understand his hesitation. She brought her hands to the neckcloth—were her fingers trembling, too?—and did as he bid. He couldn't tear his eyes away as her deft fingers flattened the linen over her chest, dipping beneath the waistcoat and tucking the folds of the cravat into where he knew her breasts to be. When she'd finished, she smoothed her palms slowly over her chest to her abdomen, and his eyes followed.

He imagined what it would be like to watch her touch herself in pleasure, and nearly groaned aloud.

That was it. A man could only take so much. He reached for her—

"Thank you, Andrew," she said, pulling back from him and settling back against the squabs. Her hands moved back up and she straightened the newly tied cravat. "You'll make someone a good valet someday," she said quite cheerfully.

Valet? Andrew blinked, struggling out of his lustful fog.

Claire flashed him a cheeky grin as the carriage rolled to a stop. "Oh good. We're here."

The door was opened by one of the club's liveried footmen, and Claire hopped out without a backward glance.

Andrew sat there for a second, gathering his wits. And adjusting his falls. It wouldn't do for him to step out of the carriage behind his "male" friend, sporting a half-masted pego.

When he emerged, Claire had almost reached the entrance with eager strides.

Damn it. She was already going against what they'd agreed to. She was to stay by his side the entire time they were here.

Andrew hurried to catch up to Claire, who had just slipped into the Devil's Den alone.

He went in after her, hoping to hell he didn't end up regretting this.

CHAPTER 7

"Ah, Sir Clarence."

Before Claire even had a chance to get her bearings, she was met by a man of middling years, garbed in the evening black of a servant. A man Clarence would know and likely greet by name. Indeed, the man looked at her expectantly.

Her heart pounded in her throat, a rapid tattoo against her newly tied cravat—almost as hard as it had when Andrew had nearly kissed her moments ago.

Any excitement she'd had about getting a glimpse inside this forbidden male realm died. Who was she kidding, thinking to pass herself off as her brother in a place where he was known? What if she made a mistake and gave the whole game away?

Claire's chest tightened and breath became difficult to take in. She should leave, just walk out before—

And then Andrew was there beside her. He didn't say a word, and certainly didn't touch her, but she felt him just the same. Immediately, the knot inside her loosened and she was able to breathe again.

The servant before her was not liveried like the footman who'd escorted her to the door. He was older and more polished. This must be the majordomo of the club, she decided. Andrew had given her his name when they'd discussed the battle plan for the evening.

She nodded to the man. "Good to see you again, Paulson."

"And you, sir," the majordomo replied, and Claire nearly went weak with relief. Pleasantries were exchanged, hers and Andrew's coats taken, and snifters of a sharp amber liquid placed in their hands before they were left to meander toward the large set of double doors at the end of the long chamber.

"You handled that well," Andrew murmured as they made their way into the room.

"Thank you."

She could do this. She could. Still, she felt a little wobbly. And Lord, her throat was dry. Perhaps a little liquid courage was in order. She eyed the snifter. Clarence had always seemed to like the stuff. She brought the cut glass to her lips and took a healthy swallow.

Dear God, the burn!

Claire's eyes immediately started watering as she did her best not to cough up the fiery liquid now scorching its way down her gullet.

Andrew, damn his hide, had the temerity to chuckle at her distress.

She was going to give him what-for...when she could properly breathe again, that is.

But then the burn softened into a glowing warmth in her middle that seemed to be spreading through her limbs, and that warmth felt... nice. Calming. Precisely what she needed. She brought the crystal to her lips once again for another, more cautious, sip.

"Go easy, Claire," Andrew said, no longer laughing. "You need your wits about you."

"Mmm-hmm," she said, the word vibrating against the rim of the glass.

Now that she'd cleared the first hurdle of gaining entrance into the club—and bolstered by her newfound beverage of choice—Claire took a moment to assess her surroundings.

"You know, for a place named the Devil's Den, it certainly seems rather heavenly, don't you think?"

Far from the dim and dubious decor she'd expected, walls of silk damask in the palest cream rose to meet intricate plaster moulding. Claire lifted her gaze to the arched ceiling, painted to depict fluffy clouds in a blue summer sky and—

She blinked. "There are even bloody *cherubs* frolicking up there. Golden harps and all."

If Andrew was taken aback by her swearing, he didn't show it. The word felt a bit foreign coming out of her mouth, but it was expected from a man in a place like this, wasn't it? And if she wanted to pass as a man, she'd need to act like one.

"I suppose they find the juxtaposition amusing," he commented.

"Hmph." Claire took another sip as she eyed the row of intricate crystal chandeliers lining the center of the room. "If I didn't know better," she said, a bit disappointed that the infamous gaming hell was not living up to her expectations of a den of iniquity at all, "I'd think I was walking into any number of Mayfair mansions."

"Indeed," Andrew agreed, nodding to the two footmen who stood poised at the closed doors before them.

The servants turned in unison and pulled on the handles.

A blast of raucous male laughter burst through the opening.

Claire started, but she thought she hid it well.

Another quiet chuckle from Andrew told her differently.

She frowned at him, then walked through the doors.

And entered a world unlike any she'd ever been in before…and yet somehow strangely familiar.

Juxtaposition. That's how Andrew had described the decor in the entryway, and that theme certainly continued into the main part of the hell. The rooms themselves were still rather elegant, though there was a bit more gilt and flourish.

It resembled an aristocratic ballroom more than anything, she realized.

The place was a crush, much like a good ball. Refreshment tables lined the walls on one side of the room but from the delectable smells wafting their way, Claire figured she'd find more than dry cakes and tepid lemonade there. The din of the crowd was as loud as any rout, but more masculine in flavor. And certainly more jolly. Shouts, guffaws, and ribald repartee flew freely around the room and Claire caught more than a few words that made the tips of her ears burn.

It was shocking, thrilling, and bewildering all at once.

"Don't stand there gawping," Andrew whispered in her ear.

Claire coughed to cover her blunder, and got moving.

As they'd discussed before coming tonight, she and Andrew casually skirted the room, giving Claire a chance to orient herself without having to directly engage with anyone who'd known Clarence. While she got the lay of the land, Andrew's job was to quietly observe whether or not *she* was being observed.

There were groups of men gathered around long green tables, hollering and whooping as one or the other of them tossed dice. Hazard, then.

Another table held a spinning wheel which men and their companions crowded around, their eyes fixed on the rotation as if their very fortunes hung on the whim of one tiny bouncing sphere.

There were smaller tables where Claire saw men at faro, *vingt-et-un*, *rouge-et-noir* and even common ballroom fare such as loo, whist, and piquet.

And there were several doors leading to private rooms in which Claire could only imagine what went on.

"I see several of Clarence's friends," she commented, her voice pitched low so only Andrew could hear.

She also saw the women hanging on to many of said friends' arms. Clinging, more like, in a fashion she'd never seen the like of. Laughing with an exuberance no debutante would dare. Touching, and being touched, in ways that would scandalize innocents and fussy matrons alike.

Claire averted her eyes before her cheeks pinked. But she couldn't stop her imagination from wondering what it would be like to be that free with herself.

"As do I," Andrew replied, his lips close as he bent his head toward her to keep their conversation private.

Her chest stilled. Had she uttered that scandalous thought aloud? She couldn't have. Andrew seemed to be able to read her mind of late.

She dared a glance at him, but he was still just watching the room. She let out the air that had been caught in her lungs, and huffed at herself. Ninny. He just meant that he saw people Clarence had known, as well.

Though now that she was looking at him, she couldn't drag her eyes away. She'd not seen Andrew in full evening dress since that night he'd abandoned her at the Danburys' Christmas ball, nearly six years ago to the day. He'd been a beautiful man even then, but now… She had to admit that his tailor had done him justice tonight in his dark-blue jacket, burgundy waistcoat, and close-fitted buff trousers.

But it wasn't the fine figure he cut that kept Claire enthralled. The years and war had changed Andrew, had given him a lean, hard edge he'd not had before.

And she liked it.

The warmth already in her tummy from the brandy flared. If she were at the Devil's Den as herself, rather than as her brother, would she be as bold as the other women here tonight? Would she turn her face and give in to the impulse to kiss Andrew before God and everyone?

And would he return that kiss, while sliding his hand down her back and placing it possessively on her derrière, as other men in this room were doing to their lady loves?

"What I haven't seen," he went on, oblivious to her risqué wonderings, "is any undue interest in you—from any quarter. Or either sex."

His words brought Claire out of her reverie. Her eyes returned to the boisterous assemblage.

She hadn't given much thought to Clarence's contact being a woman, but it was certainly possible. The person they were looking for could just as easily be one of the beautifully dressed Cyprians as it could be one of the patrons or a game operator or a servant or—

Claire took another gulp from her snifter, which she was surprised to find nearly empty.

"It could be anyone," she murmured. The enormity of her task threatened to overwhelm her, but Claire beat the doubt back. She had to find something or someone here that would help her discover her brother's killer. She had to.

She handed off her empty glass to a passing servant and made for the hazard table. "So let's find him. Or her."

For the next two hours, Claire and Andrew haunted the tables. And all the while, full snifters of that delightful liquor kept finding their way into her hands by servants no doubt instructed to keep the players plied with enough alcohol to lubricate the play.

She won at hazard, lost at roulette, and made a killing at faro—which, she discovered, was not really a card game after all, but instead a game of chance that happened to use cards.

Through it all, Claire looked everyone in the eye—friend or stranger, lord or servant, doxy or dealer—searching for recognition or some hint of deeper alliance. But all she'd managed to do was send one aging viscount off in an angry huff, dragging his giggling mistress behind him so that "Clarence" could no longer tempt her with his *soulful gaze*.

"This is hopeless," she groaned. Her eyes burned and itched from all the cheroot smoke and staring. And they were heavier than they should be—from the brandy, she suspected.

Andrew agreed. "Perhaps we should call it a night."

Claire nodded, ready to follow Andrew's lead back through the gaming rooms towards the double doors that led to the entryway. "We'll try again tomorr—"

A manicured hand slid along the inside of Claire's jacket sleeve and clasped her arm with possessive familiarity.

"Clarence, darling," came a husky female purr, as a woman sidled up to Claire and pressed the side of her body full against her—breasts against her arm, hips and thighs touching her own.

For the briefest of moments, Claire froze. That was the best way she could describe it. Her breathing stopped, her heartbeat paused, her mind completely blanked. Then it all slammed back with a jolt that made her suck in air as her heart rabbited and her thoughts flew.

She dared not look at Andrew. She had to play her part.

Claire turned in to the woman with as close to a lazy smile as she could manage and raised her arm to place a kiss upon the back of the lady's hand. She was only stalling, she knew. She had no idea who this woman was, but it seemed Clarence had. How would she possibly bluff her way through this type of encounter?

The beauty—and she was a beauty, with black hair and delicate features and who smelled of rosewater—laughed at Claire's gesture.

"Oh, *mon cher*... *Quel gallant*! But you must know by now," she said, her English heavily accented, "a mere peck upon my hand is not *nearly* enough to satisfy me."

And she tugged Claire's face toward hers.

Oh, God. Oh, Lord! What was she to do?

The woman's lips brushed past Claire's own, bussing her cheek instead. Her hand came around Claire's nape and pulled, bringing the two women cheek to cheek in an intimate embrace.

Then a harsh whisper met Claire's ear.

"Who the *hell* are you?"

CHAPTER 8

Shock rooted Andrew to the spot.

In his life, musket balls had whizzed past his head, cannons had exploded all around him, and once a bayonet had nearly skewered him through. But through all that, he had never once frozen on a battlefield.

And yet he could not seem to move.

He couldn't tear his gaze from the sight of Claire being…what? Fondled? Molested? Nuzzled? And in the middle of the gaming room floor.

But neither could he tear the other woman off of her without opening them all up to dangerous gossip and scrutiny.

Christ, he was supposed to be protecting Claire. But what was he supposed to do in this situation? She must be in a panic right now.

"Ah, darling," Claire said, her voice low and seductive as hell. Andrew's whole body reacted to it, even as his mind wondered what the devil she thought she was doing. "*You* must know by now that *that* was only the beginning."

And then Claire's hands slid down the woman's silk-clad back and grabbed the stranger's arse like it belonged to her!

Holy hell.

The black-haired woman threw back her head with a throaty chuckle and Claire flashed her a rakish—*yes, rakish*—grin.

Andrew could only gape at the pair of them.

"Then we must hurry," the woman said, taking Claire's hand, "as I should hope to find satisfaction at least twice before dawn."

And with that, she pulled Claire towards the wall of private rooms, and away from him.

That finally got him moving.

Andrew pushed through the crowd, staying just steps behind Claire. He had no intention of calling out or making a scene, but neither would he let Claire disappear behind one of those closed doors without him.

He couldn't even imagine what might happen there. Well, he *could*, but—

Claire and the mystery woman stopped at the third door from the back, and had just opened it when Andrew strode up behind them.

"Barton," he said, still at a loss at how to extricate Claire from this folly without giving away her identity.

Both women turned to look at him, cerulean-blue eyes and vibrant green ones pinning him in place.

Now what? He cleared his throat. "A word, if you please."

Claire laughed good-naturedly, as any one of his companions would if his annoying mate was interfering with his wenching. "Shove off, Sedgewick," she said. "I'm busy."

Andrew nearly choked. Had Claire just told him to shove off so she could dally with a strumpet to protect her identity as Clarence?

That was taking the ruse a bit far.

What's more, he had no intention of shoving anywhere.

"Clarence," he warned.

The green-eyed beauty stepped to him then, and put a hand upon his cheek. "Listen, lamb," she purred. "I know I said it took much to satisfy me, but even I can only handle one gentleman at a time." She gave him a pat and a wink. "Perhaps tomorrow night."

Then she and Claire slipped into the private room and slammed the door in his face.

In. His. Face.

Bollocks.

Andrew tried the handle, but it wouldn't give.

He jerked on it again, anyway. Damn it. Now what? Did he break the bloody door down? Did he stand here and wait for the inevitable shriek of surprise and then whisk Claire out of the Devil's Den the moment the door opened?

A few sniggers came from behind him. Andrew let out a growl. That's all he and Claire needed—a group of drunken revelers hoping they would come to blows over a light-skirt for their entertainment. He smoothed his expression and turned his back to the door, sending enough glares that most returned to their own business.

But he couldn't mind his. What was going on in there? He strained to hear, but the doors must have been thick, because no sound escaped.

He raked a hand through his hair as he fell into an agitated pace. He'd known this was a bad idea. He never should have brought Claire here. He should have locked her in her townhouse, hired guards to man the doors, and left her there until this whole thing was over.

Instead, he'd allowed her to continue to dress as a man, work with men day after day, come to a gaming hell, drink spirits, gamble, be a witness to hedonism, and even grab another woman's arse.

He didn't think he'd ever get that image out of his mind. Claire's hands sliding possessively over pink silk... He blinked to clear his head. Who would have ever thought *Claire* would do such a thing? Certainly she'd had more brandy than was wise tonight, but to do *that*?

He stopped pacing, shock wearing off as his brain kicked back in.

Why *would* Claire do something so outrageous?

And then it hit him, and he felt like the slowest arse in five counties.

Claire must think the black-haired beauty was Clarence's contact.

A cold fist knotted in his chest. If that were true, the woman could be dangerous. No one knew for certain where Clarence was knifed, only that the last place he'd been seen for certain was here…and Claire was alone in a locked room with her.

That cold fist turned to fire inside him. Everything in Andrew urged him to knock the door down and get Claire out of there, investigation be damned.

No. No, a more reasoned part of him said. If this woman was their last lead, he didn't want to spook her into running. They needed to know what she knew.

But he couldn't stand out here and do nothing.

Think, you arse.

And then he remembered. When the Devil's Den first opened, all the talk amongst the young bucks had been about the peepholes hidden in the private rooms. If your own carnal amusements weren't exciting enough, you could watch those of the couples next to you. It had been quite a discovery for a bunch of lads who often claimed more experience than they actually had—and rather educational.

Andrew strode to the door of the room directly to the right of the one Claire was in and tried the handle. It gave way and he pushed into the room.

The sound registered first, the rhythmic slapping of flesh on flesh punctuated by the high-pitched moans and deep grunts of pleasure.

Then the rutting man inside the room noticed him.

"What the devil?" the gentleman roared, though he didn't stop his thrusting. His paramour was bent over the arm of a chaise before him, her skirts thrown up over her back.

Hell. It was the viscount who'd threatened to horsewhip Claire earlier for trying to "seduce" his mistress. The silly chit had been flirting shamelessly with both Claire and Andrew at the hazard table. Indeed, the woman now looked over her shoulder and winked at him, even as another man rode her.

"My apologies," Andrew muttered, backing out as quickly as he could. Just before he got the door closed, he stated more loudly, "These doors lock, you know."

He blew out a breath as he hurried to the room on the left of

Claire's. This time when the handle gave, he opened the door cautiously.

The chamber was empty, thank God.

He slipped in and threw the lock behind him. He didn't wish to be caught playing peeping Tom by another amorous couple looking for a swiving spot.

He hoped the gaming hell hadn't plugged the holes in the intervening years. After surveying the wall that separated his room from the one Claire was in, he removed the center painting. Andrew breathed a sigh of relief. The peephole was still there.

He bent, put his eye to it, and waited for his sight to adjust to the light of the neighboring room.

He immediately sought out Claire... There. His chest lightened when he saw her. She was fine, it seemed, standing next to an identical chaise to the one he'd just witnessed being used so lasciviously. He was glad to see Claire was not touching the piece of furniture. No telling what had happened on *it* recently.

Again, he berated himself for ever bringing her here. Claire was too innocent and fine for a place such as this. But he'd live with that regret later.

Now, he tried to hear what was being said.

Because that was what the two women were doing. Talking. Though he'd swear it looked as if both of them had been crying.

"...never..."

"...then..."

"...by..."

"...over..."

Damn. He could only catch the occasional word, no matter how hard he listened.

It was enough, for now, to know that Claire was safe. He'd continue to watch so that if he saw anything untoward, he could break down the door and get to her in moments.

As he watched the women speak to each other, most of the tension that had been building throughout the night began to flow out of him. He'd been on edge since the minute they'd stepped into the carriage at the townhouse and it had only gotten worse as he'd followed Claire into the Devil's Den.

She, on the other hand, had been magnificent tonight.

After that initial wide-eyed hesitation, Claire had navigated the place as if she'd been born to it...and had impressed the hell out of him.

However, the more she'd relaxed into her role, the more agitated he'd grown. He'd thrown himself into watching the crowd with ruthless focus. Yes, because he needed to see if Claire was garnering any undue notice. But in truth, he found he couldn't look at her without fearing that everything he felt for her would be written on his face like an awful gambler's tell.

He'd never felt more protective of—nor aroused by—any woman in his life.

And it clearly wasn't because of her appearance. Her resemblance to her brother when dressed as a gentleman was uncanny and rather disconcerting.

But it hadn't made him want Claire less.

If anything, he wanted her more. Her bravery, her determination, and her fierceness drew him like the lure of a croupier's last call to lay his bets.

And oh, how he wanted to. Claire was worth risking everything on.

If only he were fit to play at her table.

Andrew tensed as the black-haired woman moved toward Claire and reached for her neck. Adrenaline shot through him, and he nearly bolted for the door, but Claire's calm acceptance stilled him. The woman only tugged at Claire's cravat, mussing it thoroughly before reaching into her hair and giving it a tousle. Then she pulled some long black strands from her own coiffure to give them both a just-having-trysted look.

Andrew released a breath.

As a final touch, the woman leaned in to kiss Claire's cheek, leaving a tell-tale imprint of dark rose lip salve on her skin.

And to Andrew's surprise, the two women embraced before

turning toward the door.

He straightened, dropping the portrait frame back over the peephole, and made for his own door. He made it out before Claire and her companion, and had just enough time to lean casually against the wall as they exited arm in arm.

But when he saw Claire, his indifferent demeanor fled. Oh, there was a smile on her face, and damn him if it didn't even look like a sated one, but her complexion had gone pale and her eyes were glassy and red-rimmed. He frowned. What had happened inside that room to upset her so?

He pushed off the wall and went to her. The women halted as he reached them.

"Until we meet again, *mon cher*," the green-eyed lovely said, taking her hand from "Clarence's" arm. She turned to Andrew and tipped her head to the side, giving him a speculative stare. Then she smiled, her lips curling seductively. "Perhaps, dear lamb, we shall let you join us next time after all."

Then with a saucy wink, the woman glided away and disappeared into the crowd.

Andrew didn't watch her go. His one priority was Claire. He dropped his head so only she could hear him. "Are you all right? What happened in there?"

Claire just gave a small shake of her head, all pretense of her rakish smiles gone. Alarm clanged in his gut, and he noticed how tired Claire looked all of a sudden. Indeed, exhaustion and something he couldn't quite put his finger on weakened her voice to a mere whisper when she finally spoke.

"Just take me home."

CHAPTER 9

Claire poured herself another brandy from the crystal decanter in the library. Candlelight winked off the cut glass as she tilted the bottle, giving the impression of tiny flames in the amber liquid. Good. She *wanted* it to burn away this pain in her heart.

She took a swallow.

"Wouldn't you rather have tea?" Andrew suggested quietly from behind her. "Or perhaps even coffee?"

She heard the cautious concern in his voice. He was probably worrying that she was drunk as a broken wheelbarrow by now. And given that this had been her first night drinking hard spirits, perhaps she should be.

But she wasn't. She'd never been more sober. Or more heartbroken.

Or as coldly furious.

Given her moody silence on the carriage ride home, Andrew must surely think her mercurial. But she hadn't been quite ready to talk to him then. She'd learned too much tonight, and she just didn't know how she felt…about any of it.

Still, he'd respected her wishes in the carriage, and now he deserved to hear everything that she had.

"I don't like tea," she said. It seemed like a safe enough place to begin, even if she was admitting to something no good Englishwoman ever should. "Never have."

Andrew feigned shock, then smiled as he realized, "You actually answered my question."

She took another sip of her brandy, relishing the burning bite on her tongue, and said nothing.

His grin faded, the look of concern reclaiming its place.

"Clarence, you may remember," she went on, "loved the stuff."

"I do remember," he answered, the careful tone creeping back into his voice. "Loaded it with more sugar and milk than tea and called it the nectar of the gods. Drank it night and day. The gents ribbed him mercilessly for it."

She huffed. "Yes, apparently his penchant was well-known. I swear, I had to pretend to drink more cups of tea at Abchurch than I could count, whilst finding a discrete place to dump the swill," she complained, pursing her lips in distaste.

Then she took a third swig from her snifter and set it down on the table with a decided clink of glass on wood.

"Did you know Clarence had given up brandy?" she asked.

Andrew's brows shot up in surprise. "What?"

"I didn't know, either."

His eyebrows settled into a V above his nose. "But he enjoyed a nip nearly as much as he did his tea. We drank *barrels* of it in our day."

"Yes, well, apparently he came to…struggle with his need for it." She'd never noticed. Never had an idea that her brother suffered so. Her heart squeezed. She wished he would have told her.

But then, he hadn't told her many things, it seemed.

Andrew's eyes turned down with sadness, or possibly regret. "I had no idea."

A bit of the fury she'd sealed inside her heart slipped out. Just what exactly did he regret? That he'd been gone from Clarence's life these past six years? Or that—

Claire tamped down her anger. She wasn't ready to talk about that part of what she'd learned tonight yet. Nor was she even certain who she was more angry with. Clarence? Andrew? Herself? Until she could figure that out, she had to stick to what pertained to Abchurch business.

"Well, that's one way Rosalie—"

Andrew's eyes narrowed at the unfamiliar name.

"Clarence's contact at the Devil's Den," Claire explained. "That's one of the ways she knew I wasn't Clarence. Clarence, she said, would have nursed that initial brandy most of the night and then set it down nearly full and gone after a cuppa."

"Wait. Are you saying she knew you weren't Clarence *before* you accompanied her to the private room?"

Claire nodded. "When she pulled me to her, she demanded right then to know who I was." She remembered the bolt of fear that had pierced her in that moment. "I nearly shoved her away and ran. But then I decided that if I was already caught, I had nothing to lose.

"So I whispered that I was Clarence's sister and that I needed to speak with her privately. She agreed, and I steered her to the private rooms the only way I could think of with so many people around watching and listening."

Her cheeks burned as she recalled her risqué words, and flamed higher as she thought of what else she'd done.

Dear Lord, what must Andrew have thought of her?

What was he thinking of her now? She peeked over at him.

His lips were pressed together, and he looked to be struggling to contain...laughter?

"Christ, Claire. When you reached down and—" He lost the battle, and a rich chuckle rumbled out of his chest.

Her face was afire now. She must be as pink as the lip salve that likely still graced her cheek. She swiped at it, and indeed, her thumb came away rosy.

Lovely.

Andrew's face, however, glowed with mirth. It made him look younger, somehow, and the sight took her back to when she'd lived to make him happy. "And then," he chortled, "when you told me to shove off?"

Despite the fact that her feelings were gnarled and muddled and terribly conflicted at the moment, she couldn't help a reluctant laugh of her own.

"You should have seen your face," she said, recalling his widened eyes and the look of shock that had nearly made her break character and dissolve into fits.

Despite everything, it felt good to laugh with Andrew again. Impossibly, it made her feel as though all was right with the world once more. Which made everything she'd learned tonight a bit sadder, really.

"You said 'one of the ways' she knew you weren't Clarence…" Andrew prompted when she didn't speak.

"Ah, yes. She also said Clarence would never wear so pedestrian a knot as a Waterfall."

Another sharp laugh burst from his lips. "She's probably right," Andrew said. "He always had a bit of a dandy in him."

"That he did," she agreed.

After a moment, Andrew ventured, "It seems this Rosalie knew Clarence well, then?"

His voice was tenuous and tactful—for her benefit, she suspected. Tiptoeing around the indelicate to spare Claire. Deciding what was best for Claire. Trying to protect Claire, no matter what she wanted for herself.

She was tired of being *protected* by the males in her life.

"They were lovers," she answered bluntly. "That's the true reason she knew I wasn't Clarence. She insisted he would never have gone so long without coming to her unless something terrible had befallen him."

Unlike some men, who could walk away without a word.

And with that thought, all of the emotions she'd been holding back since her tête-à-tête with her brother's lover threatened to burst through the dam she'd built around her heart and drown her.

"Apparently, they were quite close," Claire said, hearing her voice rise with the tide of her feelings, but unable to care. "She claims he even asked her to marry him. Several times."

"Marriage?" Andrew exclaimed. "To his mistress?" Incredulity rang in his voice. Then he shook his head. "Do you believe her?"

"I do," she replied softly. Rosalie had known too much about her brother, things Claire had never fathomed. That was one of the many hurts afflicted tonight. She'd thought she understood Clarence better than anyone, being his twin, but how wrong she'd been. "She says she turned him down each time, but he persisted."

She watched Andrew closely to see how he took the next statement.

"He told her that life was too precarious to live it without the person you loved by your side, everything and everyone else be damned."

Andrew's face went unnaturally still, as if he were suppressing something he didn't wish her to see. But he couldn't hide the flash of anger that darkened the green of his eyes.

"That…doesn't sound like Clarence," he said carefully.

Too carefully.

God. It was true, wasn't it?

She should just come out and ask him.

But now that the opportunity was upon her, she found herself afraid of the answer. No matter what he said, it would taint forever the way she saw him, or her brother…or herself.

Claire strode back over to the sideboard and swiped her brandy glass, finishing off the last bit with one large gulp. Then she turned back to him before she lost her nerve.

"Why did you desert me at the Danburys' Christmas Eve ball?" She swallowed the lump that was threatening in her throat.

Rather than answer her, Andrew closed his eyes.

Oh, no. She wasn't going to let him dodge her question. She walked the few steps to him and grasped both of his hands—and by God, she meant to hold him there until he answered her.

His lids flew open and his eyes locked with hers.

"Why did you never come back into my life?" she demanded with a squeeze. "As if I'd meant nothing to you, when you *knew* how much you meant to me?" Her voice broke on that.

The flat expression he'd been trying to maintain melted, every feature drooping into one of pain. "Claire…" he said, his voice raw.

She waited, but he said no more.

She licked her lips, which had gone dry.

"It was because of Clarence, wasn't it?"

CHAPTER 10

"*W*asn't it?" Claire repeated, unwilling to let this night pass without knowing the truth.

Andrew flinched and tried to pull away from her. "Why would you think that?"

"Oh, no," she said. "You will *not* answer *my* questions with a question."

And still, Andrew remained mute. Who was he protecting? Himself? Clarence? Her feelings? She *had* to know which it was. All of these years, she'd thought he hadn't wanted her. If that weren't the case…

She thrust his hands away. "Fine. If you won't tell me, *I'll* tell *you*. Clarence saw us together earlier that night, in the garden."

It had been uncommonly foggy that Christmas in London. Wet, but not overly cold. It had seemed so wonderfully exciting to slip out into the night, knowing the walks around the Danburys' London mansion offered many cozy niches amidst the shrubbery and trees, made even more secluded by the blankets of fog. She'd felt so deliciously wicked.

Of course, being in the heart of London, the gardens weren't overly large, so they couldn't go far. Or be *too* wicked.

"After we slipped back into the ballroom" —separately, of course— "Clarence found you. As I was dancing my obligatory sets to make certain I was seen behaving as an innocent young miss should, he confronted you in Lord Danbury's study about what lay between us. He knocked you flat with a punch, and when you refused to fight him, he challenged you to a duel."

"How do you *know* this?" he rasped, and a flush of triumph washed over her. Finally, she'd know *why* she'd lost Andrew. "Surely Clarence didn't—"

"Rosalie told me," she interjected, and the momentary rush she'd felt deserted her at the reminder that her brother had trusted a stranger with the truth of what he'd done, but had never seen fit to tell *her*.

Tears pricked the backs of her eyes—tears of betrayal, yes, and of loss. But also from the fear of learning what she didn't yet know. She straightened her back and looked him directly in the eye.

"Did you truly ask him for my hand?"

Andrew's entire body seemed to relax into resignation. He tilted his head, his eyes closing briefly. When he opened them, there was relief and a tenderness in their depths that squeezed her heart.

"Yes."

Her heartbeat trilled in her chest, then settled into a quickened rhythm as she asked the question she really wanted to know. Had he *wanted* to marry her? Or...

"Because you felt honor-bound to?"

"Yes."

She winced. Who knew one tiny word could sting so?

Andrew blew out a breath and raked a hand through his hair. "And no. Of course I felt honor-bound, Claire, but..."

He shook his head, then stalked over to the sideboard, picked up the decanter of brandy and a fresh glass, and poured himself a healthy portion. He held the bottle out in question, and she nodded. After he refilled her snifter, he brought both glasses back to where she stood before the fire and handed her one.

"Let us sit." He nodded to the brocade settee nearest the hearth.

Feeling as though another Claire moved the few feet to the settee, she nonetheless found herself perched upon it, Andrew sitting tantalizingly close. His heat warmed her right side, and in addition to the sharpness of the brandy, she smelled his all-too-familiar-after-all-this-time scent. Bergamot and bay rum. She'd never forgotten.

"What you were told is true," Andrew began, his voice rough and quiet in the flickering firelight. "Clarence did strike me, and I would not fight back. Nor would I accept his challenge. He was fiercely angry, but I knew he didn't truly wish for us to take up arms against one another. Luckily for us both, no one bore witness to his words, so it cost him little to back down from them."

Claire tried to imagine the scene in that long-ago study. Clarence had loved Andrew like a brother, and vice versa. That *she* had come between them...

"My eye was swelling badly from one of the punches he landed, however. I couldn't return to the ball, not without starting the gossip mill churning. Nor could we expect privacy to hash it out in Danbury's study that night. So we agreed to meet at our club the next morning, where we could discuss the matter civilly in one of the private rooms there."

The morning she'd spent fretting over why he hadn't met her beneath the mistletoe as planned, Claire realized. Her mother had still been alive then, and had insisted she help with the many Christmas preparations, so she hadn't had time to dwell. But even now, she remembered the sick foreboding she'd felt all day.

"I wasn't certain how Clarence would be when I arrived. Still angry, I imagined. Or perhaps, I'd hoped, he'd had time to get over the shock of knowing his best friend was in love with his sister."

Claire's heart jolted, and she nearly sloshed her drink over the rim of the snifter in her surprise. Had Andrew just said he'd loved her?

"But I never expected the absolute coldness he showed that day." Andrew paused for a swallow of his brandy, his chest rising with a deep breath.

She held her own breath as he collected himself, only letting it out when he started speaking again.

"He scoffed at my request for your hand. Told me that a fourth son who was destined to be nothing but a bloody spot on a battlefield had nothing to offer you."

Clair gasped at her brother's cruelty.

The corner of Andrew's mouth turned up in a wry smile. "Don't think too harshly of him," he said. "I can see now that he was more than just angry. I'd betrayed his trust by sullying you."

"You never sullied me," she protested, then added with a bit of a grumble, "no matter how much I begged."

He smiled at that, a welcome sight amidst all the tension. "Oh, I sullied you plenty," he said, and the look he gave her nearly scorched the breath out of her. Flashes of memory of his hands and mouth upon her heated her skin.

"But I assured your brother that I had not ruined you," he went on, snapping her attention back to their conversation.

Claire's cheeks pinked that her virginity, or possible lack thereof, had been spoken about between her brother and Andrew, even though the conversation had taken place years ago.

"He was relieved, of course, but still furious. In his mind, I was the worst sort of bastard. He'd not thought he had to protect you from *me*, you see, and blamed himself for letting a fox into the henhouse."

Claire scoffed. As if she'd had no part in the matter. "Men," she muttered.

Andrew winged a brow, but continued. "I won't go into everything that was said between us, but suffice it to say that I left that interview certain of two things: that I would never be allowed to see you again, and that my friendship with Clarence was over."

Pain etched Andrew's voice, and Claire swallowed against the answering ache scratching at her throat. All three of them had suffered such terrible loss, of friendship and of love. Over what?

She barely noticed as Andrew slipped her glass from her limp grasp and took her hands in his.

"Of the two, Claire," he said, his gaze intense upon her, "no longer being with you was what gutted me the most."

Tears sprang to her eyes at the realization of what her brother had taken from her.

Andrew had wanted to *marry* her.

And she...

She understood better now what happened that night, but he had still left her with no explanation.

"If you'd already lost Clarence's friendship regardless, why did you not come for *me*?" A tear slipped down her cheek. "I'd have gone with you."

Andrew dropped his head, but after a deep breath, he looked her in the eyes again.

"Because your brother was right. You had other suitors, better prospects who could give you much more than I ever could."

"I didn't care about that!"

"I know," he said quietly. "But it wasn't just about what I couldn't give you if we'd eloped...it's what I would have taken *from* you."

A sharp ache pierced her heart as true understanding came. "Clarence."

"Yes. I never could have come between you. Your home," Andrew continued, "was like an oasis of love and laughter for me—so much different from the cold halls of Sedgewick House."

Claire nodded. She'd asked Andrew once why he came down with Clarence every single school holiday, rather than going to his own home. After all, his father was a wealthy marquess. Her family lived modestly by comparison. Andrew had made some jest about Sedgewick House having a horrid cook, but she'd seen how he'd watched her family's interactions with longing.

"I couldn't be responsible for ruining that for you," he said. "Or for turning you against your brother, whom I loved also."

Andrew brought one of her hands up and pressed her knuckles against his lips for a long moment in a chaste kiss that nonetheless sent heat straight down to her toes.

"So, as I *hadn't* yet ruined you, I just...I thought it best to let you forget about me and move on to another. Someone your brother approved of. That way you could be happy not only in your marriage, but in your *life*."

Claire blew out a tight breath.

A noble sentiment, she supposed. And in the end, could she truly have been happy with a man who *would* have been willing to destroy her family, even for love?

She didn't know.

But Andrew was wrong. He *had* ruined her. Oh, not in the literal sense, but after loving him, no one else had compared. Not a single suitor who came after him had been able to make her laugh as he had, or encouraged her intelligence and wit, or inspired her to dream of a future together.

She'd not been able to bring herself to accept any offers those first two seasons. Then her mother had died, and after she'd sat out her third season in mourning, Claire had refused to run through the marriage-mart gauntlet again.

Because no one else was *him*.

"What a bloody Greek tragedy," Claire muttered. She'd been miserable for years, thinking she loved a man who didn't want her. Andrew had apparently been miserable as well, having lost both her and his best friend. And if Rosalie were to be believed, even Clarence had suffered terribly over those long-ago choices.

"Not that it changes anything, but Rosalie told me that Clarence's greatest regret in life was how he'd separated us," she said softly.

Andrew's moss-green eyes darkened with emotion.

"And...he missed you, terribly. He was sorry for what he'd done. He just didn't know how to fix it after all these years."

Andrew swallowed, his eyes blinking as he looked away from her.

She'd been right earlier tonight when she'd feared that knowing the truth would change everything—what she thought of Clarence, and of Andrew, and even of herself. She had much to consider in the days and weeks to come, but she knew that she could never look at her life, or her memories, the same way she had just hours before.

"We can't undo our past," she said, laying a palm against his stubble-roughened cheek and turning his face back toward her. "And as much as we both wish that Clarence was with us, he is no longer part of our present. Only *we* can decide our future."

And she brought her other hand up to cradle his face and pulled his mouth to hers.

CHAPTER 11

*S*he tasted of brandy. Slightly sweet yet incredibly rich—like the darkest red plums steeped in caramel.

Intoxicating, heady, and altogether irresistible to a man who'd been dying of his thirst for her for six long years.

"Claire," he groaned against her lips, even as he tried to hold himself back from her kisses.

"Andrew," she whispered. Then her tongue delved into his mouth once more, and he knew in his soul that this thirst for Claire would never be quenched.

Ah, Christ, he was lost. Lost to the intimate caresses of lips and tongues and hands. Lost to the sharing exchange of their very breath.

Lost...

"We shouldn't," he murmured, even as he pressed tiny kisses to the corners of her mouth.

He had to keep his head about him. Claire was his to protect, now.

"Too—" *kiss* "—much—" *kiss* "—has happened—" *kiss, kiss* "—tonight."

He dragged his lips away with the last bit of self-control he possessed, and pressed his cheek against hers so that his lips were close to her ear.

"Too much has been said," he whispered. "Too much brandy has been drunk. And the future is too uncertain. My duty is to the war, and when this mission is over, I'm going back there. *You* need time to—"

Claire pulled back from him and her eyes shone fierce and clear.

"I've wasted too much time already," she said, and kissed him once more.

He groaned again, then gave in to the need that had been building for years.

Andrew pulled Claire to his chest, turning and lifting her as he did, so that she sat atop him on the settee. Without long skirts to tangle around her legs, her knees spread naturally around him, leaving her trouser-clad bottom pressed against the tops of his thighs.

Claire gasped into their kiss. With only her layer of kerseymere and his of buckskin between them, there was no way that she did not feel his hardness. Then she moved experimentally against him, and his own gasp echoed in the room.

She pulled away from him then, which only served to settle her more tightly against his groin. A seductive smile spread over her face as she looked down at him, and in that moment he thought he'd never seen anything so beautiful. The fire crackled behind her, its light wreathing Claire's short red-blonde curls like a corona of flame on a goddess queen.

If a goddess queen wore a cravat and a waistcoat.

Andrew burned to see Claire in all her feminine glory.

He reached up and tugged at the half-tied strip of cloth that hid her neck from him, growling as his trembling hands fumbled at the task. "Damned knot."

Claire chuckled, pushing his hands away and taking over herself. "Apparently, you tied it too well."

He watched her deft fingers at work, and couldn't help imagining those fingers on him, caressing, tugging...

At last the knot came free, and Claire started unwinding the cravat from around her neck. Her eyes never left his as she dragged the cloth slowly, slowly around her, revealing her skin bit by tiny bit.

The minx was teasing him, completely in control while he shivered with lust beneath her.

Well, that wouldn't do.

His hands slid up her thighs and he gripped Claire's hips, hooking his thumbs in her falls and sliding her over him as he pressed upwards.

A low moan tore from Claire's throat and her head tipped back.

That was more like it.

Andrew's whole body screamed for him to take her, to flip their positions and put her beneath him. To drive between her thighs and finally know what it was like to be inside her.

His arms shook with the effort to hold back. No. He wanted to savor Claire. When he'd left six years ago, he'd thought never to see her again, much less have her in his arms once more. And now that he had a second chance?

He clenched his eyes shut, willing himself to take things slow.

Claire was pulling at *his* cravat now. He joined her, yanking at the linen, not caring that it scraped his skin raw when he whipped it off of his neck too quickly.

"Tsk," Claire murmured, her thumb brushing tenderly over the angry mark. Then she bent over him and touched her lips to it and he nearly came undone.

He cupped her face and brought her mouth back to his for a voracious kiss. Once their tongues had caught a rhythm of thrusts and caresses, Andrew let his hands drift down Claire's chest and undid the fabric-covered buttons of her waistcoat. He slid it off of her shoulders, helping her slip her arms free, and then groaned as he slid his hands back up her still-too-covered chest.

He pulled back from their kiss, breathing hard as he glared at her remaining clothing. "What I wouldn't give to have a bodice to yank down, or a skirt to ruck up."

He needed her skin bared to him.

Claire gave a seductive laugh, her eyes heavy-lidded as she squirmed against him.

She needed it, too.

He gently lifted her from his lap, setting her on her feet between his spread knees. He reached for her falls, undoing the buttons before slipping the trousers over her hips and letting them drop to the floor.

The lawn shirt she still wore settled mid-thigh, and it was seductive as hell. Who would have thought a man's shirt on a woman would be so arousing? But damn it all—it was.

Still, he couldn't wait to get her out of it.

He grabbed the hem and pulled it upwards, almost laughing as he remembered her words earlier in the carriage. Perhaps he *would* make someone a good valet someday.

As long as that someone was her.

He peeled the shirt off with ease, anticipating the sight of a naked Claire before his eyes, *finally*.

And discovered all the padding that helped disguise her curves.

"Christ," he muttered, then attacked her bindings with a vengeance. He turned her between his legs, unwrapping, untying, undoing, until at last...*at last*, Claire was revealed to him.

She was utter perfection. Longer and leaner than was typical of her sex, but uncompromisingly feminine still. Her hips flared prettily below her nipped waist, and above that—

"Andrew?" she whispered, and he lifted his eyes up to hers. Her bottom lip, pink and swollen from his kisses, was caught between her pearl-white teeth, and she ran a hand nervously through her shorn locks.

Did she worry he did not find her pretty?

"If I died tonight, Claire," he murmured, encircling her waist and pulling her to him so that he could lay his cheek just below her breasts, "I'd consider myself lucky for having lived to see such beauty."

Then he turned his lips to taste her skin.

For a long time after that, nothing was said between them. Not with words, leastways. Her sighs guided his mouth, telling him where she most enjoyed his kisses. His moans of pleasure encouraged her to explore his body fearlessly.

And when at last he bore her back down onto the settee, this time spread beneath him, her whimpers of need let him know she was ready for him to come to her.

Andrew held himself poised at the brink of making them one, and slid his hands up to entwine with both of Claire's where they lay above her head.

She opened her eyes then, the cerulean-blue now cloudy with passion.

He joined them, then, his gaze locked with hers as he entered her, possessed her. She gasped, gripping him tightly at the invasion, then relaxing as they moved together.

Then they were kissing as they drove one another higher, their tongues mimicking the thrust and acceptance, the push and the pull, between them.

When he knew he couldn't last much longer, Andrew released one of Claire's hands and slid his between their bodies. He found her tight nub with his fingers and rubbed in rough circles, thrilling as she gasped and stuttered.

"Come for me, Claire," he whispered harshly, his breaths coming hard and fast as he started losing his rhythm. His thrusts felt frenzied now, as did Claire's cries. So close. So close…

And then she keened her pleasure and he knew he'd never heard such an incredible sound. Claire shook and quivered beneath him, and as she gripped him tightly in her release, Andrew let go, driving himself one last time into blinding release of his own.

~

CLAIRE NESTLED BACK against Andrew's chest as they sat on the floor before the fire some hours later. She'd donned her lawn shirt again for modesty's sake. It barely came mid-thigh, but it was loose and comfortable without all the padding beneath, and she felt more at ease being at least somewhat covered after all she'd just done.

Which was silly, really. Andrew had seen, touched, and kissed every part of her in the three times they'd made love. Heat touched her cheeks as she imagined how she must have looked—and, dear God, *sounded*—as he'd driven her to completion. Liquid warmth spread through her at the very memory.

Andrew, for his part, remained gloriously nude. He wrapped his arms around her from behind and hugged her to his chest, while the soft hair of his legs tickled her skin where she sat cradled between them.

They'd been thus for some time, both keeping their thoughts to themselves in sated, if not completely easy, silence.

Perhaps he, like she, wasn't certain what to say after all that had happened tonight.

"Was Rosalie able to tell you anything that might help us find Clarence's killer?" Andrew's breath brushed by her ear, causing a warm shiver.

"Perhaps," Claire replied, grateful to have something to discuss other than whatever now lay between the two of them. "While she was Clarence's lover, she was also his contact. She received tidbits of intelligence from France and passed them along to him. She said the night Clarence was killed, he'd only been at the Devil's Den to be with her, however."

Claire had been terribly disappointed by that revelation, until Rosalie had continued her tale. "*But*, a fortnight *before* that, she'd told Clarence that someone named San Carlos had been seen in Paris."

She felt Andrew straighten at this news. "The Duke de San Carlos?"

"I believe so. I'd not heard of the man myself," she went on. "Rosalie said he'd been the Spanish ambassador to Lisbon, London, and Paris, but that he'd—"

"—been imprisoned by Napoleon five years ago, along with King Ferdinand of Spain," Andrew finished.

She half-turned in his arms to look at him. "Yes. She said rumor was that Napoleon had set San Carlos free."

Andrew had released her, and now planted his hands behind him, scooted back and rose to his feet in a fluid movement that flexed long, lean muscles all over his body. Claire's breath caught at the sight, quite unused to having a large, nude male in her library. One who was now pacing before her fireplace.

"Napoleon is up to something, then," Andrew said. "He doesn't set anyone free, not without a reason." He stopped and turned to face her.

Claire did her best to keep her eyes above his waist—though, oh, it was tempting to let her gaze dip down in curiosity to the part of him that had brought her such pleasure. What did it look like when they were not—

"My sources have mentioned nothing about this," he said, and Claire snapped her eyes up to his face guiltily. "Nor did I hear anything of the sort while I was in Paris. Which means whatever Napoleon is about, it's being kept very, very quiet."

Claire rose to her feet, Andrew's heightened interest sparking through her as well. "If the French are going to such lengths, then they must be hiding something considerable," she concluded.

Something worth silencing Clarence over?

"Have you decoded any messages that mention San Carlos? Or Ferdinand?" he asked. "Because I have to wonder…if Napoleon has freed San Carlos, he may be working some arrangement to release King Ferdinand as well."

As he'd been speaking, Claire had moved to the settee and rustled through the pile of men's garments to find his trousers. She tossed them to him now. They caught him off-guard, hitting him in the face before sliding to drape over his shoulder.

He blinked at her.

She blushed. "Sorry. It's just…I can't talk dastardly plots when you're standing there—" She couldn't bring herself to actually say the word *naked*. "—like that."

A slow grin spread across Andrew's face and she felt the pull of it all the way down to her toes. He slid the trousers off of his shoulder without breaking eye contact, shook them out, and slowly stepped into them—one leg, then the other—before sliding them up over his hips and fastening his falls.

Good Lord, he might be even more distractingly sensual in just the trousers. There was something incredibly arousing about knowing what those six little buttons on the front barely contained. And his chest was still on full display.

She shook her head. "You were saying?"

His grin spread a bit wider. "I said, if Napoleon has freed San Carlos, he may be using him to broker an arrangement to release King Ferdinand as well."

"But why would he do that?" she asked. Admittedly, she knew little of military tactics, but… "Didn't he conquer Spain and put his own brother on the throne?"

"Indeed. However, Spain allied themselves with Britain and Portugal, and together we recently broke Napoleon's hold on the Iberian Peninsula—thanks in no small part to you," he said, nodding at her.

She knew he meant her decoding of the troop movements that helped win the decisive battle of Vitoria.

"Napoleon can't stand weakness. It's rumored he blames Joseph for deciding to engage Wellington against his field marshal's advice, and for fleeing back to France when defeat was imminent. I would not put it past Napoleon to betray his own brother if it served his ends."

"How awful of him," Claire murmured, hating that she could empathize with Joseph Bonaparte, even a little bit. Though Clarence's betrayal was much, much different, she now understood what it felt like to be hurt by one's brother.

"Particularly since Napoleon himself was also recently defeated in battle at Leipzig," Andrew said. "Now that British and Spanish troops have invaded France for the first time since he started this bloody conflict, he has to be feeling cornered."

Claire's eyes went wide. "If Napoleon brokers some sort of treaty with Spain to put their own king back on the throne, he would want something in return. And I'd bet every shilling I won at Faro tonight that it would be for Spain to break her alliance with Britain and pledge it to France."

Andrew's eyes had darkened, any semblance of his suggestive smile given way beneath a clenched jaw. "It's an idea."

Claire stepped to him, raising a hand to his cheek and using her thumb to soothe the tense muscle there.

"It's more than we had before," she said. "Tomorrow, we start combing the coded intelligence for anything regarding Spain, San Carlos, or Ferdinand."

She felt him relax beneath her touch, and then that half smile of his lifted her thumb as he brought his arms around her. "And tonight?" he asked, winging one brow in suggestion.

Claire swallowed. She knew what he was asking, and her body, at least, wanted to fall in line. Her mind, however, was still riddled with doubts. After all she'd learned tonight, she understood Andrew's reasons for walking away from her six years ago.

But, her heart whispered, *wasn't I worth staying and fighting for?*

An ache twinged in her chest, but she shoved the pain away. She'd think about that tomorrow.

"Tonight?" she repeated with a sensual smile of her own, and Andrew shook his head at her question-rather-than-answer.

Then she gave him her true answer by pulling his lips to hers.

CHAPTER 12

Three nights later, Andrew nodded to the plain-clothes soldier who now guarded the interior entrance to the Black Chamber. Two new men he'd personally chosen were also posted at the exterior of the building, front and back, though very discretely. He'd wanted to increase security at Abchurch, not draw undue attention to it.

He lifted his arms when asked, shaking snow from his greatcoat onto the tile floor and trying not to show his impatience as the soldier patted his pockets and such. Since he'd become head of Abchurch, anyone with access to the secret rooms was searched coming or going —himself included.

The code breakers had grumbled and fussed for a few days, but Andrew had held his ground. He'd wanted no weapons going into the place—for Claire's protection—and, nearly as important, no documents being smuggled out.

He hoped that diligence would bear fruit and that Claire would be able to find something relating to San Carlos or Spain in the stored copies of correspondence.

"Thank you, my lord," the guard said.

Andrew nodded and pushed through the door, anxious to be inside.

While he and Claire had a plausible theory for *what* may have gotten Clarence and Marston killed, they had no clues yet as to *who* had done it. The culprit might very well be within Abchurch itself. Every time he had to leave Claire here without him set his nerves on a knife's edge, even with the additional security measures. He wouldn't be able to breathe fully until he saw for himself that she was safe and sound.

He scanned the room…

…and there she was, hunched over her table in the back, her eyes squinted as she analyzed the missive before her. She was one of only a couple of "men" still in the Black Chamber this late in the evening.

Andrew's chest lightened at the sight of her, and he took a deep breath, bringing his chilled hands to his mouth and blowing out his relief to warm them. Then, he quickly looked away from her.

They'd been very careful that "Clarence" got no undue notice from Andrew. Not only could it be disastrous for the killer to discover they were working together, but Andrew also doubted he could hide his feelings for Claire if he watched her overlong.

And that could get awkward.

He went about his routine of checking in with the other remaining code breakers in turn, leaving Claire for last.

"Did you learn anything new today?" she whispered when he reached her.

"Perhaps," Andrew murmured beneath his breath. He'd been out in the frigid cold most of the day and into the evening, hunting down a rumor that San Carlos might have crossed into England last week. He relayed that to Claire.

She glanced up at him. "So he's here, then?"

"Quite possibly," Andrew said. A shiver caught him by surprise. Even in the unnatural warmth of Abchurch, he'd yet to recover from the bone-cold of his hours in the out of doors. He spied "Clarence's" customary cup of tea, untouched on the table beside her. Perhaps a hot cuppa was in order. He nodded to it. "May I?"

Her eyes flicked to the tea. "I wouldn't," she said. "It's been sitting there for hours. I imagine it's cold as ice by now."

Andrew pressed his lips together and picked it up, walked over to the tea tray and deposited it with the other used china, and got himself a fresh hot cup of tea. What he wouldn't give for a warming shot of brandy right now—not here, but in the library of Claire's townhouse. Sharing it with her.

It had been their routine the past couple of days. He stayed out tracking leads and setting men to follow key Spanish diplomats and influential French nationals known to the War Department, while Claire remained here looking for anything that had been missed.

Then they'd return home together each night and debrief over brandy.

And yet…since the night following their visit to the Devil's Den, their conversation rarely veered into the personal. Oh, their relationship did. *Quite* personal. But while Claire seemed to revel in being in his arms, she dismissed his every attempt to bring up their future.

He knew what he feared. Chances were he was still destined to end up a bloody spot on a battlefield. With her brother gone, he'd be leaving her with *no* protection other than that of his name if he died. And even if he survived, he'd take up no telling how many *more* years of her life as she waited for him to return from this seemingly unending war. Was that fair to ask of her?

As he crossed back with his tea, he wondered if she felt as conflicted as he. Was that why she distracted him with kisses whenever he so much as mentioned tomorrow?

What was Claire afraid of?

"I may have found something," she said when he reached her table again. She held out a scrap of vellum that was covered in coded scrawl. He could make neither heads nor tails of it.

"A little over six weeks ago, there's a brief mention of a secret meeting being held in Paris between a 'Ducos et Dubois'." She pointed to a bit of translation. "I asked Finchy what he knew about it, as he's the one who handles most of the preliminary French correspondence. I usually only see the very difficult."

Yes. Andrew had learned from Greeves that Claire's expertise was often a point of contention for Finch, who resented the idea that he ever needed help. "And?"

"He told me to leave it, that it was nothing of importance. I pressed him for more, asking whether he'd written a report on the matter." She winced. "I fear he thought I was second-guessing him…which I suppose I was. He got quite surly with me."

A surge of anger warmed Andrew better than any cup of tea ever could at the idea of Finch being rude to Claire. He glared over at the man, but Finch wasn't at his table. A quick glance around the room didn't locate him either. He must have gone home for the night already.

"But," Claire went on, drawing his attention back to her, "he finally admitted that he hadn't written a report because the meeting was only mentioned once, and to his knowledge, there are no known players named Ducos *or* Dubois. Since those names never came up again, he dismissed it."

"Hmm," Andrew said, setting his cup on the table and putting Finch out of his mind for the moment—though he'd certainly have a word or two with the man when he next saw him. "Why do *you* think it's important?"

Claire's eyes lit and he could almost imagine her rubbing her hands together in anticipation of unleashing her brilliance.

"Two reasons. First, *I* saw the name Ducos just recently. Not in any coded correspondence…" She shifted through a stack of notes on her table, plucking one from the pile. "Here. It's an invitation list to the Viscountess Balfour's annual masquerade, which is being held tomorrow night. The War Department is furnished with a list every year, as the Balfour ball is regularly attended not just by members of society, but by diplomats and expatriates from around the world," she continued. "Much political maneuvering is done there, I understand, particularly during times of war when official diplomats have been expelled from the country."

She smoothed the vellum out onto the tabletop and ran her finger down until, near the end of the list, it landed on *Miguel Ducos*.

"All right," he said, "but I'm not seeing how that leads us to San Carlos."

"It doesn't. Not by itself. But consider this," she said, going back to the original coded message that mentioned the meeting between Ducos and Dubois. "This is supposed to have happened only days after Rosalie's informant mentioned San Carlos being seen in Paris."

"Right."

"Oftentimes, messages are not the only things in code," she whispered. "Names are often disguised as well. It was only as I mulled the name aloud that something caught my attention. *Duke* de San *Carlos*." She emphasized the first and last syllables. "If you take into account the Spanish spelling of the title—"

Having learned Spanish at school, he knew *duke* was spelled *duc*, and thus Duc de San Carlos became…

"Ducos," he said.

Claire bobbed her head. "It very well could be. I did some digging, and discovered that San Carlos's full name is José *Miguel* de Carvajal-Vargas. *Miguel Ducos*."

The back of Andrew's neck tingled, as it did sometimes in battle. It was those times, he'd learned the hard way, that he should follow his gut. Perhaps this time it meant Claire's gut?

"Still," he said, "it's pretty thin."

Claire huffed a breath. "Let me thicken it up for you then. Let's say our theory is correct and Napoleon wanted to negotiate a secret treaty with Spain. Who would you think he would trust to represent him?"

Andrew thought for a moment, considering all he knew of the emperor and his tactics. "I would say only Talleyrand, Laforêt, or himself," he replied.

Claire was nodding, the light of triumph shining in her eyes. "My thoughts exactly. So I gave some thought to those names in relation to Dubois. And guess what I found?"

"I…" Andrew shook his head, coming up with nothing.

"Oh, come on. Guess."

Damn, she was alluring when she was smug. He cleared his throat, trying to rein in his thoughts before he embarrassed himself over another "man".

"I've no idea."

Claire sighed. "You're no fun."

Andrew just raised a brow.

"All right. Many times, the key to breaking a code is understanding the language and finding patterns within it," Claire said. "For example, the name Dubois means 'wood-cutter'."

"And?"

She smiled. "The name Laforêt means 'keeper of the royal forest'."

"I'll be damned," Andrew murmured. Ducos/Duc de San Carlos had held a secret meeting with Dubois/Laforêt... "When did you say the meeting took place?"

Claire looked back through her papers. "It was first mentioned a little over six weeks ago...just before Clarence was killed." She turned her eyes to him and he thought the blue seemed just a bit duller. "Do you think this is what Clarence and Uncle Jarvis were working on?"

"It could be." Andrew hated to see her self-satisfied smiles of moments ago give way to sadness. He wished they were somewhere private so he could take her in his arms. "But we'll have to prove it if we want to know for certain and catch whomever was responsible."

It seemed a monumental task, but that tingling in his gut told him he and Claire had the right of it.

"I imagine Napoleon would think it paramount to keep something like this absolutely secret until the treaty was signed, sealed, and delivered," Claire said, a thoughtful tone softening her voice. "I think that's why we've heard little to nothing about it, through your channels or Abchurch's. They are not going to commit any details to correspondence that could be compromised, not even in code."

"I agree."

She picked up the invitation list. "But a masquerade ball filled with diplomats and expatriates from all over the world..."

"...would be the perfect place to finalize details between the two countries and lay the groundwork to getting it ratified," Andrew finished for her.

THE VERY DEBONAIR LADY CLAIRE

"Exactly. You said yourself that your sources put San Carlos entering the country last week. I believe Miguel Ducos and San Carlos are one and the same, and Miguel Ducos is on this list," she said, tapping it with her finger.

"I've got to secure an invitation immediately," he said, thinking ahead to who he'd—

"*We've* got to, you mean?"

He looked over at Claire, whose lips had turned down into a frown that threatened belligerence.

Oh, no. There was no way in hell he was letting Claire anywhere near that ball, not with a dangerous plot of *this* magnitude afoot. A hard knot formed in his stomach at what might happen to her if San Carlos even suspected she knew anything that could scuttle the treaty that would secure his freedom and that of his king.

"Claire," he said, his head shaking his answer automatically.

"Don't you even think of forbidding me to go," she uttered, low. "I can see it written all over your face."

Andrew clenched his teeth. Of course she could. Because she'd be going over his dead body.

"Don't push me on this, Claire," he warned. "I'll have Wallace lock you in your room until the ball is over, I swear to God."

He wouldn't, of course, but damn it all! The idea of Claire putting herself at this kind of risk made him crazy.

"You wouldn't even know to go there yourself if it weren't for *me!*"

Andrew dropped his head, and his voice. He took a deep breath. "True. And it was brilliant of you. But you need to let me handle this now. I can't protect you and hunt for San Carlos at the same time."

"I don't *need* protection. I—"

"Yes, you do," he hissed. He'd die if something happened to Claire. Couldn't she understand that? "Even if it's from yourself."

Claire gasped. Not loudly, but enough to draw the eye of more than one of the code breakers, who glanced back at them curiously.

"This isn't the place," he said beneath his breath.

Her eyes flashed, but she firmed her lips and gave a short nod.

"Gather your things and go," he murmured. "I'll be there soon."

He strolled away, and was immediately caught by Greeves, who wished to discuss something one of their men had found in an Austrian diplomat's post.

From the corner of his eye, Andrew saw that Claire obeyed, though her movements were stiff and angry. Well, waiting for him in the carriage should give her time to calm down. That had been their custom of late, so they weren't seen leaving together. A driver would pick Claire up directly at the entrance to the building—so he knew she'd make it safely. Then they'd wait for him around the corner. He'd stay at Abchurch for an appropriate amount of time, and then follow.

As Andrew pushed out into the frigid night a quarter of an hour later and made his way to the next block over, he steeled himself. While he hoped Claire was ready to be reasonable, more than likely she would have worked herself into a dither by now, and he fully expected to be blasted with her arguments as to why he should take her to the ball the moment the carriage door opened.

But as he turned the corner, the ground seemed to fall out from beneath him and fear gripped him by the balls.

The carriage wasn't there.

And neither was Claire.

CHAPTER 13

Claire touched her fabric mask, ensuring it was firmly in place as she joined the crowds making their way into the Balfours' grand mansion on Berkley Square.

"I'll help you find your sheep, lass," rumbled a man's voice in a faux Scots accent.

She turned to a gentleman dressed as a highland laird—though she was pretty certain his plaid wasn't tied *at all* correctly—and smiled prettily at him. He, however, smiled directly at her bosom.

Claire tried not to roll her eyes.

The shepherdess costume she'd borrowed from Rosalie had been one of the least risqué the other woman had owned, but it still put rather a lot of Claire on display.

However, it was also the most practical for her needs. First, she had a wooden crook that she could use as a weapon if need be. Second, the large mobcap completely hid her shorn locks. And finally, it allowed for the most useful prop…

She held up the muff that she'd covered last night with white cotton wool and fashioned to look like a little lamb.

"I thank you, good sir," she said, waggling the tiny sheep, "but as you can see, I haven't yet lost it." She gave him a saucy wink and turned away.

As Claire pushed farther into the room, she clutched the little lamb to her, reassured by the weight of her muff pistol within.

Her smile didn't fade until she was out of the man's sight. Tonight, she intended to be seen as a frivolous peahen—and *not* as the kind of woman who might, say, speak several languages and be able to eavesdrop on a private conversation held in any number of them.

The anger that had been simmering since Andrew had forbidden her to attend the ball last night flared back to life. *She* was their best chance at overhearing proof of the Miguel Ducos/San Carlos plot. How dare he threaten to lock her away, even *to protect her from herself?*

Blast it all, her entire life had been ruined by a man who took it upon *himself* to decide her future without so much as consulting her. She'd be damned if she'd let Andrew replace Clarence as her self-appointed keeper.

As she circulated around the ballroom, Claire kept her eyes—but more important, her ears—open for anyone conversing in one of the languages spoken on the Iberian Peninsula.

She also kept a lookout for Andrew. Not that she had any inkling of what costume he might wear. She imagined he also watched for her. He wasn't a fool. He knew very well she'd be here tonight—the note she'd left him at the townhouse before she'd fled to Rosalie last night implied as much. Her best advantage to evade a scene was that he wouldn't know if she was here as Clarence, or as Claire.

A large male hand clasped her upper arm just above her elbow.

"A dance, Miss Peep?" a voice growled in her ear.

Andrew's voice.

Claire's stomach both flipped and melted, all at the same time.

"How did you know it was me?" she whispered as she turned to him. She pasted a smile on her face so that she appeared to flirt, if anyone was watching, but inside her heart hammered.

It picked up speed at the sight of him. Lord, he looked beautiful tonight, dressed in stark, close-fitted evening clothes of black.

He also looked furious. Anger simmered in his eyes, not the least bit hidden behind his simple domino.

"I'd recognize that décolletage anywhere," he said as his eyes dropped to her rather exposed chest.

Claire melted another degree. His voice had dipped low, and while he still sounded angry, passion colored his words. And for a moment, she was intensely glad she hadn't balked at wearing Rosalie's provocative shepherdess costume.

Not that she wasn't still irritated with him.

Andrew steered her toward the dance floor, where lines were forming. Despite the cold outside, the ballroom's multiple arched windows were open to combat the heat from the crush, and a gauzy red material—swagged with greenery in a nod to the Christmas season, no doubt—floated in the light breeze. Claire was grateful for the cool air, as she'd warmed significantly now that Andrew was near.

They joined the other dancers, pairing up across from one another, as the strains of violins signaled the beginning of an Allemande. Claire tucked the muff that concealed her pistol into her apron's pouch for the dance.

"How did you secure an invitation on such short notice?" Andrew murmured as he stepped toward her in the first move of the dance.

Claire met Andrew in the center of the aisle and touched her right hand to his as they bowed to one another. "Rosalie knows many people," she said archly. "And when I'd explained that I needed to be here to catch whoever had killed Clarence, she was only too happy to help."

Andrew huffed, as if he'd expected such an answer. His gaze held hers as they stood palm to palm, and Claire's breath snagged just from the intimate touch.

"Don't look now," he murmured, "but Ducos is three dancers up the line."

Claire started. That news certainly broke the sensual spell.

"You're certain?" she whispered as they circled one another in the dance's next step.

"Indeed," he said. "One of Balfour's men tipped me when Ducos presented his invitation, and I've been following him ever since."

The dance called for Claire and Andrew to turn away from each other at that moment, so she took advantage of the figure eight step that came next to cast a peep at Miguel Ducos.

The short, compact man executed his own steps just a few dancers away. As Claire skirted another figure eight around the woman next to her in the procession, she had to admire the duke's choice of costume.

He was cleverly disguised as…a Spanish duke in military court dress, with gold epaulettes, elaborate embroidery work along the cuffs, knee breeches, and lapels, and a bright red sash tied jauntily around his waist. The ensemble was finished off with Spanish crosses pinned to his jacket, a mask, and a bicorn hat with feathered flourishes.

Exaggerated military costume was popular masquerade fare, and everyone knew the *real* San Carlos was in prison in France, so…all in all, an inspired choice, really.

Andrew took her hand as they met once again in the middle, and pulled them into a twirl. The dance brought them closer, hands touching palm to palm and foreheads nearly grazing.

"Have you noticed him speaking overlong to any one person or group?" Claire murmured. She hoped she hadn't already missed her opportunity.

Another set of figure eights drew Andrew away from her and advanced them up the line. A bubble of anxiety floated into her throat. Was tonight's mission already for naught?

When a gliding step brought them face-to-face once more, he said, "No. He's mostly stayed to the edges of the room, taking it in." They touched hands, then Andrew's mouth turned down beneath his mask and his voice was harsh as he said, "You scared years off of my life last night, Claire. When I thought—"

The steps of the dance pulled them apart again. Claire joined arms with the woman next to her as a matter of course, but inside she fumed at the reminder of how he'd tried to keep her from coming tonight. Who cared what he thought when he found she'd left him in the cold? Served him right.

She'd almost *not* left him a note at the townhouse before she'd departed, either, but she hadn't wanted Andrew to worry…much.

She met him again in the center, and he took her hand for the twirl.

"You left me little choice," she hissed. "I will not be dictated to by you, or anyone. And at any rate," she continued as they touched hands in preparation to turn away from one another, "I'm here now, so let us drop the matter and do what we came here for."

Another loop with the neighboring woman, and they were once again together in the center for the twirl.

"Pax, Claire," he said, much as he had the first night when she'd insisted to remain as Clarence at Abchurch.

She relaxed as the ending strains of the violins echoed through the air and he turned her in the final twirl. He was coming around to accepting her part in this, which was good. But if they were going to have a chance at a future together, they would have to discuss his propensity to want to protect her at all costs.

If she could get over the fact that he'd been able to walk away from her in the first place.

After the applause for the orchestra, the line of dancers broke up. Andrew settled Claire's arm on his—rather possessively, she thought. She tried to tug away, wanting to follow San Carlos now that she knew what he looked like.

Andrew squeezed her hand. "No. We're just watching for now."

He must have sensed her frustration, because his mouth kicked up a half smile beneath his domino. "Don't worry," he said. "We're not likely to lose sight of him in that elaborate costume."

He had a point.

"Is it wise for us to be seen together?" she murmured as he pulled her into a stroll, loosely keeping pace with Ducos on the opposite side of the ballroom.

Andrew shrugged one shoulder. "If the killer suspects us, then he'd be looking for two men together. That makes your costume…"

His gaze dipped to her décolletage once more and his eyes flashed hot.

"...perfection."

The spark of heat that flew through her was so powerful, she half-expected her wooden crook to shoot lightning bolts.

"Isn't that why you came as Claire and not Clarence?" he inquired.

She swallowed, having to repeat his question in her carnally distracted mind. "Um, no, actually."

She told him her plan to get close enough to Ducos to be present to overhear any clandestine conversations.

Claire felt him go rigid, his muscles becoming taut where her hand rested on his arm.

"It's the only way," she said before he could mount the argument she saw brewing in his eyes. "Gentlemen are taught several languages as part of their education. Ducos will not speak freely to anyone if *you* or any other unknown man is hanging about."

She tightened her grip on his arm. "But me? No one expects a lady to know more than French. They're less likely to suspect me of being able to understand anything they say, so I have the best chance of learning what we need to know."

"Christ, Claire," he muttered, and she sensed him teetering on the edge of picking her up bodily and running for the exit, little lamb and all.

"You know I'm right," she said. "And I'm not giving you a choice." She knew it went against everything in him, but she was through being *protected*. She intended to do what she felt she must in her life. And if Andrew couldn't live with that... "I'm going after Ducos with or without you."

He shook his head. He took several deep breaths, no doubt grappling with his masculine instinct to shield her at all costs.

"All right," he said finally. "But I'll be close by. And if anything, *anything* at all makes you uncomfortable, just..." He looked her over. "Roll your shepherd's crook between your hands and I'll come to you."

She nodded.

"And if for some reason I don't, go immediately to one of the footmen."

That was an odd request. "Why a footman?"

"Because most of them here are actually Bow Street Runners," he said. "Apparently Miguel Ducos is not the only person of interest who is in attendance tonight. I've been told the authorities are also trying to trap an infamous jewel thief or two."

"Ah." Knowing that actually did make her feel better. She put on a brave front for Andrew, but her stomach churned at the idea of crossing men who had so much to lose. They wouldn't think twice about killing her if she were caught.

From the corner of her eye, Claire noticed Ducos change direction and head for the card room. Another man sidled up to him along the way. The hair stood up on the back of her neck. This was it. She knew it.

"He's moving," she said, as energy spiked through her. She let go of Andrew and quick-stepped her way through the milling crowd, making for the parlor that Ducos had just slipped into.

CHAPTER 14

Claire didn't look back to see if Andrew followed her. She knew he would, though likely some time behind so as not to alert anyone watching that they were about the same business. She only hoped her plan proved fruitful, as she doubted they would get another shot at uncovering this plot.

She slowed to a stroll as she reached the card room. Just before passing through the doors, she stopped to take a calming breath. She also plucked her little lamb muff from its pouch and cradled it beneath her arm like a silly prop for an even sillier costume. In truth, she just wanted easier access to her gun should she need it. Then she pinched her cheeks, pasted a smile on her face, and entered.

The Balfours' impromptu card room sparkled with light and hummed with conversation. Several tables were scattered throughout, filled with guests trying to best one another for a bit of coin. While more sedate than what she'd witnessed at the Devil's Den—and without games like hazard or roulette, which would be improper in a London ballroom—the room nonetheless reminded her of the gaming hell. Many women graced the tables, either encouraging the men or playing themselves.

Good. She should fit right in.

Her eyes sought out Miguel Ducos. He and another man had just joined a mixed group at a table in the far corner and were being dealt a hand.

It took everything in her not to cut a path directly there. But no. She needed to be circumspect in her approach, lest she draw suspicion.

She cut her eyes to the party at Ducos's table, who looked to be engaged in whatever game they played, himself and his companion included. She was going to have to take a gamble and work her way slowly around the room, hoping that no serious discussion took place between the two men until they'd settled in a while.

And so, against every natural instinct, Claire joined a table in the completely opposite direction.

Over the next quarter hour, she flitted from game to game, doing her best to make herself seem flighty and a tad ridiculous. She simpered, she cooed, she lost games on purpose and pouted mightily. And all the while, she made her way closer and closer to the table where Ducos still sat.

The Spaniard and his companion remained at their original table, but other people had come and gone from the seats near them—which was good for her. They should think nothing of it when she sat down.

She saw her chance when a silver-haired matron laid down her cards and gathered her reticule. Claire made her way over as the older woman departed the seat two down from Miguel Ducos. Her heart thumped like a jackrabbit, but she ignored it. It was now or never.

"Ooooh, what's this game?" she trilled as she lowered herself into the recently vacated chair, plopping her little lamb on the table in front of her.

"Faro, miss," said the liveried servant who must be acting as dealer and banker tonight.

Ducos flicked his gaze at her, but Claire dared not let herself look at him. Instead, she turned to the handsome gent on her opposite side. "Is it anything like loo?"

The man gave her a patient smile. "Not at all."

Claire twisted her lips. "How about piquet, then? Is it like piquet? I enjoy piquet."

She almost felt the man's eyes roll as he shook his head.

And her impression as a brainless flibbertigibbet was set.

Ducos looked away from her and returned to his hand of cards. Perfect.

"Ah, well," she said with an annoying giggle. "I'll give it a go anyway."

Play resumed, and Claire did her best to live up to that impression. She made silly mistakes and asked ridiculous questions, and all the while she kept an ear tuned towards Ducos. Problem was, he wasn't really speaking to anyone. He just played the game.

When the man sitting between her and Ducos decided to call it a night, Claire scooted over to his seat. "Perhaps this chair will be more lucky," she declared with a laugh.

Finally, she'd insinuated herself right next to the man she believed to be the Duc de San Carlos.

And still, nothing.

Had she missed whatever exchange might have happened by taking her time getting here? What if she'd been wrong about the man sitting next to her? What if he wasn't San Carlos after all? They'd have to start over again in their hunt for Clarence's and Uncle Jarvis's killer.

She fretted over all of that as she played her next cards, and as time passed without Ducos saying anything of interest, she began to wonder how long she should continue to sit here.

But then a tall gentleman, dressed in the colorful Andalusian costume of a matador, made his way to the table. He discretely tapped the man seated on the other side of Ducos on the shoulder. Without a word, that man stood and left the table, and the *torero* took his place.

"Ducos," the newcomer murmured.

Miguel Ducos leaned back in his chair, while keeping his cards fanned out before him like a shield. "*Señor Embaixador*," he replied softly.

Claire's breath stilled. The matador who'd joined the table was the current Spanish ambassador to London. Which meant she'd been right. Ducos *was* San Carlos. Her hand shook as she laid out her card, and she squeezed her fist to stop it. She had to stay calm. This was what she'd been waiting all night for, and she couldn't spoil it now.

She turned and laughed at something a woman on the other side of her said, angling her shoulder away from San Carlos to give him a greater sense of privacy in hopes he would be more free with his words. Then she settled in to listen.

With the noise of the room and the raucous game play around her, Claire struggled to follow the quietly spoken conversation, but she deduced right away that the men weren't speaking Spanish, but Galician—a sort of blend of Portuguese and Spanish that originated from Vulgar Latin in the Middle Ages and was still spoken in some parts of Spain. Luckily, she understood enough to get by.

"Recoméndolles que saca de Londres inmediatamente—" San Carlos was saying.

He was advising the ambassador to make preparations to leave London?

"Your play, miss," the dealer's voice pulled her out of the conversation.

"Of course," Claire replied, pretending to dither over what card to put down…and went back to listening.

"*Si, o tratado xa está en camiño, atravesando Catelonia coa axuda de Copons—*"

A burst of laughter from the table beside them drowned out the rest of whatever San Carlos was saying, and all of what the ambassador replied.

"*—segunda foi enviada con Palifax, no caso de que o primeiro sexa interceptado—*" she heard a bit later.

Claire could only catch snatches here and there of the whispered conference, but even so, she'd soon heard enough. Not only had hers and Andrew's theory been correct, it was worse than they'd thought.

She had to find him and tell him what she'd learned. Now.

When it came her turn to play, Claire pushed her cards into the center of the table.

"That will do it for me, I'm afraid," she said as she stood. She picked up her little lamb muff and waggled it. "I do believe I've been flee-ee-ee-eeced enough."

A few chuckles followed her as she left the table.

Claire discretely glanced around for Andrew, but didn't see him in the card room anywhere—which didn't surprise her overmuch. He'd likely concealed himself in case the killer was watching him, so as not to draw attention to what she was doing. So she made her way back to the ballroom, fully expecting him to rejoin her the moment she cleared the card room doors.

After a full turn about the place, she still hadn't found him. Unease snaked its way around her middle. It had cost Andrew to let her go after San Carlos on her own, to admit that he had to rely on her to protect herself as she carried out their mission. There was no way he wouldn't be by her side now that she was finished—not if he was able.

Still, she took her crook between her hand and rolled it between her palms in the signal they'd agreed to, hoping it called him to her side like the proverbial lost sheep.

But it didn't. Her unease flared into alarm. Where was he? And what was she supposed to do without him?

Go to one of the Bow Street Runners. That's what Andrew had told her to do.

And say what? Precious time would be wasted trying to get someone to believe her, she was certain. She had to get the information she'd gleaned to someone in the War Department right away.

But... Her stomach churned with fear for Andrew. She *needed* to find him, too.

In the end, the choice was made for her. As she turned to search out one of the runners-turned-footmen for help, her arm was caught in a punishing grip.

"If you want to see Sedgewick alive again," a familiar voice growled in her ear, "you'll walk out of here with me. *Without* making a scene."

CHAPTER 15

Andrew struggled against the ropes that bound him, twisting his wrists counter to one another in an effort to break free. The rough braiding bit into his skin, drawing blood. But the ligatures didn't loosen a bit.

Damn it all!

He hadn't been tied up or chained when he'd escaped his prison in Paris. When he'd been taken by French forces, Andrew had been treated as an officer and gentleman who might later be traded for one of Napoleon's own. He'd even been asked to dine with Marshal Marmont over several evenings—all in a failed effort to glean information from him about Wellington's plans, of course.

All very civilized, really, if one didn't count that the men who'd been captured with him had been shot dead on the spot—as *they* hadn't been officers—and that outside the locked doors that had held him were well-armed guards.

But that experience wasn't helping him to escape now.

He renewed his efforts, gritting his teeth against the pain.

Some minutes later, a cold sweat dripped down his forehead and stung his eyes, and his wrists were on fire. He needed a short break from the agony. Andrew let his body go limp against the hard wooden chair, and as he breathed in heavily of the foul-smelling air, he took in his surroundings.

He was in a small, bare room with dirty wooden floors, wooden walls, only one door, and a very small window set high above it. The awful stench—a sickening mixture of refuse and rotten fish—could only be the Thames, which meant they were very near the river. And given how long he'd been in the carriage before he'd been hauled unceremoniously into this place by two hulking men, he guessed they weren't far from Abchurch. Near London Bridge, perhaps.

He yanked against his bonds once more, but they were as tight as ever. After five years of war, was this tiny, stinking room where he was going to meet his end?

At least Claire was safe.

That was the only reason he'd gone quietly when he'd been ambushed in an alcove near the card room by two men dressed as footmen that he'd taken at first to be Bow Street Runners. Let the villains think they were safe by nabbing him. They couldn't know that *Claire* was his secret weapon. That by now, she may even have gotten the proof they'd been hoping for and be on her way to the War Department with it.

And all the while, by letting the blackguards take him far away from Claire without a fight, he was doing his very best to protect her.

He'd gladly die here if it meant keeping her out of danger.

The door handle lifted and the heavy wood pushed inward with a loud creak. A behemoth of a man appeared in the opening—the one who had tied these infernal knots once they'd gotten him into the carriage, as well as the ones that lashed him to the chair now.

Andrew straightened and braced his feet on the floor, preparing himself for whatever came next.

But what came next was a *shepherdess*, clutching a damned silly woolen lamb.

Claire.

Fear unlike any he'd ever known—even when facing certain death on a battlefield—racked him, and he had to swallow against the bile. *No!*

Another man followed Claire inside, one hand gripping her arm, the other holding a pistol to her side. He was dressed in costume as well, with a green mask that covered his face. He wore a suit of red, green, and gold triangles separated by gold piping, which marked him a harlequin—one of many Andrew had seen at the Balfour ball tonight.

Which meant the harlequin must have seen Andrew and Claire together, too, and somehow deduced that they were working together. Damn it all.

A third man, the other of the two that had brought Andrew here, stepped in last and closed the door behind him.

"Well," the harlequin said, "isn't this quite the little party? Not nearly as fashionable as the Balfours' ball, but much cozier, I should think."

Wait... He knew that voice.

"Pike?"

The harlequin laughed and used the hand holding the pistol to flip the mask up off of his face, revealing the code breaker who'd been working at the table next to Claire's all this time.

"You've got the right of it now, Sedgewick."

Pike? Andrew had suspected Greeves, Lord Marston's aide-de-camp and the man who knew most about Abchurch business aside from his late master, and who would have had the best access to the man. Or maybe even Finch, the code breaker who had resented Claire's abilities. But Pike?

"Now you know who I am, and I know who you are," Pike said, turning his gaze to Claire, "but what I've yet to discover is who this delectable creature is."

He pointed the pistol at her and Andrew nearly came out of his seat.

"I saw the two of you dancing, of course. I didn't think much of it until I noticed *you*—" Pike gestured at Claire with the gun. "—follow San Carlos into the card room. Now, remove your mask, dearie, and introduce yourself."

Claire clutched that damned lamb to her tightly with one hand like a frightened child and Andrew roared inwardly at his inability to help her. Her other hand trembled as she knocked the cap from her head before slowly pulling the mask down until it hung loosely around her neck.

Pike lost his grandiloquent smile as his face registered shock, confusion, and then...

"Barton? But how can that be?"

The man looked over at Andrew, then back at Claire. He raked her with his eyes, his gaze lingering on her décolletage. Then the hand that had been gripping her arm slid over and *plumped her breast.*

Claire gasped.

"But you're a *woman*," Pike said incredulously.

Andrew did roar then, shoving with his feet to try to rise out of his chair and get to Claire. He got about an inch off of the floor before the larger of Pike's henchmen strode over and punched him in the face so hard that the entire chair wobbled before he could right himself. Pain exploded in his cheekbone.

When the stars cleared from his vision, Andrew sought Claire out again. She no longer looked afraid. Her eyes spat blue fire as she glared down her nose at Pike. "Clarence was my brother. You'd thought you'd killed him weeks ago, didn't you? Before I took his place."

The man just stared at her for a long, dumbfounded moment.

Then the knot-tying behemoth said, "See, gov! I told you there weren't no way that cove survived a knifing by old Tom here."

Claire's chin dropped, but her eyes narrowed to slits. She turned her gaze to "old Tom" and Andrew thought the man would be wise to fear for his life.

Pike still had a bewildered twist to his lips as he stared at Claire. And then he started to laugh.

"You mean this whole time at Abchurch, it's been *you*?"

Claire nodded, once. Her jaw firmed, but he could see by the way her fists clenched that Pike's laughter shook and infuriated her.

"Oh, that's rich!" Pike chortled. "Here I'd thought you were the indestructible man. I mean, you'd survived being knifed. And then I poisoned your tea at least a half dozen times."

Andrew felt the blood drain from his face. If Claire hadn't detested tea...

"Why did you do it?" Claire cried. "What did my brother and Lord Marston know that made you feel they had to die?"

Pike stopped laughing then. He still had the gun pointed at Claire and he tilted his head to regard her.

"I'm not sure Barton knew anything, actually. I only knew that Napoleon was planning to treat with King Ferdinand, and that messages would necessarily travel back and forth between Paris and Madrid. I did my part to make certain that if those messages came to Abchurch that they got buried. But if one or two did make it through? Well, your brother, of all the code breakers in the War Department, had a reputation for breaking the unbreakable. He'd already spoiled things for the emperor at Vitoria—"

Andrew saw Claire's face go as white as her woolen lamb.

"—and I knew we couldn't take the chance that he'd be able to ruin this plot as well."

A horrid ache squeezed Andrew's chest as he realized the implications of Pike's words, and he saw from the way Claire's face crumpled that she understood them, too. Clarence had been killed because of the work *Claire* had done.

Her pallor went green, and she looked to be fighting off tears. His heart broke for her. Just as it boiled with anger. Pike looked ready to laugh again at her obvious suffering—even if the man didn't understand what upset Claire so.

"And Marston?" Andrew asked, trying to draw his focus away from Claire as well as draw out the conversation long enough that he could think of a way out of this damnable mess. But he couldn't see one, trussed up as he was like a damned Christmas goose.

Pike shrugged. "He caught me slipping poison into Barton's tea."

Claire once again squeezed her little lamb, probably imagining it was Pike's neck. Hell, *he'd* like to—

An explosion rent the air. Bits of wool flew in all directions as the acrid scent of saltpeter and sulfur burned his nose.

Before Andrew could even register what was happening, Pike fell to the ground with wide, sightless eyes—and Claire raised her—*lamb?*—and pointed it at the man who'd knifed her brother.

Another explosion rocked the room.

And suddenly, he understood. Claire's three-shot pistol must be concealed inside the damned sheep.

Old Tom dropped where he stood, which left one shot left for—

The largest of the three villains had roared and lunged toward Claire already. He was poised to knock the pistol from her hand before she could fire that third barrel.

"Claire! Get behind me!" Andrew shouted.

She spun, her skirts twirling around her in a move more graceful than any shepherdess he'd ever seen, and did as he said.

The henchman wheeled about more clumsily, but he corrected his course and went after Claire again. But this time, Andrew was between them.

The man lunged anyway, knowing Andrew could do nothing to stop him with his hands tied behind him and lashed to a chair.

Andrew shoved with all of his strength and threw his weight to the left. He couldn't get far off the floor, but it was just enough to overturn the chair and him in it, right into the path of the charging man.

The impact of the man's knee to Andrew's chest drove the breath from him. He squeezed his eyes shut and braced himself, pain jarring him as his left side hit the floor and the right absorbed the blows of the flailing man's feet.

Andrew felt a thud vibrate through the floor as the man came down hard behind him, which was followed quickly by the final, ringing shot.

Silence reigned in the small wooden room for a long, long moment.

And then Claire dropped to her knees beside him where he lay on his side, still tethered to the chair, his face now resting on the floor. Bollocks. He hurt everywhere. And he didn't know if his heart would ever beat normally again. When he'd seen that bastard rush at Claire—

"Are you all right?" she said, her voice shaking. Her hands flitted over his face, ran down his arms, and reached around him to tug at his bonds. "I'm going to have to find a knife to cut these ropes."

He groaned. "Inside my boot. I didn't have a chance to reach for it before I was trussed up."

Claire let out a breath, and wrinkled her nose. "Oh, good. I didn't relish having to search one of those bodies for a blade."

In short time, Claire tugged off his boot, retrieved his dagger, and sawed through his bindings. As she worked, Andrew noted that she kept her eyes fixed solely on her task, being careful not to let her gaze stray to the violent results of the past few minutes.

"There," she murmured as the last of the ropes gave way.

Andrew's muscles screamed with relief as he brought his aching arms back to their natural position. He gained his knees, and then pushed to his feet before turning to help Claire to hers.

But she'd already shot up. "We've got to hurry," she said, gathering her pistol from the remnants of wool scattered on the floor. "The treaty has already been negotiated *and* signed. Two copies are on their way to Madrid by differing routes in case one gets intercepted. We have to warn the War Depart—"

Andrew grasped Claire by the shoulders, gently but firmly turning her to face him. "Are *you* all right?"

She shook her head, even as her words said something different. "I'm fine, thank you."

Andrew cupped her face in his palms, still awestruck that they were both alive. He searched Claire's face. She wasn't fine, but he didn't think she understood that, yet. He'd have to let her be for now. "No, thank *you*, Claire. You saved us."

"*We* saved us," she insisted.

It would take days of discussion and dissection before they understood the whole of what had happened over the past few weeks, he knew. It would take him even longer before he got over the scare he'd had when he'd seen Claire pushed into the room at gunpoint.

But he didn't have time to dwell on his own feelings at the moment. They still needed to alert the War Department about the treaty.

Still…

"Pike deserved to die, no doubt. And I'm grateful that it was him and not us. But you shot the bastard before he told us what drove him to side with Napoleon. Don't you want to know what he stood to gain from it?"

Claire raised her eyes to his. They were so very blue, and as clear as a cloudless summer sky. He was reminded of afternoons spent wading in the stream near Barton Manor—he, Clarence, and Claire, when they were young and carefree. Before any ugliness came between the three of them. He wished they could go back there and start again. Do things differently than they had.

"I never cared about what he stood to gain from it," she said fiercely. "*I* only care that he'll never cause another person to *lose*."

CHAPTER 16

Claire nursed the brandy in her snifter, twirling the cut glass round and round in a slow, methodical motion as she sat curled on the settee in her library. It was nearing dawn, but the curtains had been pulled closed and the room was dark save for the fire burning in the hearth. Red and gold flames flickered distortedly through the lens of the crystal, enthralling and eerie all at once.

That's how she felt. Distorted, one step removed from reality, altered somehow...

Not even in the dark days following Clarence's death did Claire feel this awful sense of...nothingness. She supposed that by throwing herself into taking his place and solving his murder, she'd just distracted herself with a purpose.

But now...

Now there was no purpose. And nothing could distract her from the fact that her brother, her twin, a part of her very soul, had been murdered *because of her.*

If she'd not been so precocious, soaking up everything she could learn when she'd discovered her gift for languages. Or if she hadn't pushed her brother and uncle to let her translate and break codes for them, just because she wanted to feel useful. If she had only stayed in her place and left war things to the men, Clarence might still be alive.

Not to mention Uncle Jarvis.

And what of Andrew?

He'd almost been killed tonight, too.

Because. Of. Her.

A tear slipped down her cheek unbidden. She didn't even bother to swipe it away. The very thought of lifting her hand to her face exhausted her. If she could just lay her head down and sleep, would it be such a terrible thing if she never awoke?

The sound of the heavy oak entryway door closing in the foyer reached her, followed by the murmur of voices. Andrew must be back from the War Department, and be conversing with Wallace. Probably instructing the butler to pack his things so that he could be off to Wellington with what they'd discovered.

Back to duty. Back to war.

And she'd be left here alone.

No family. No lover. No purpose.

"May I have one of those?" Andrew said as he entered the library and saw her sitting there, still rolling the snifter absently between her palms.

"Of course," she said, and started to rise.

"No, no. I'll get it."

She watched him as he made his way to the sideboard. His strides had a hitch to them, where he now favored his right leg. His handsome face sported reddened cheeks from the chaffing wind outside, except for the ugly purpling bruise along his left cheekbone where one of those awful henchmen had planted him a facer. She was glad she'd shot the man. She only wished she'd had a four-shot barrel so she could have shot him again.

Still, the sight of Andrew's injuries pained her. They were her fault, too.

"I'm sorry," she croaked.

Andrew stopped, mid-pour, and turned back to her. His head

tilted, and his eyes turned down in the corners with concern as he heard the tenor of her voice. "Whatever for?"

All of the awful emotions she'd pushed down burst through the wall of numbness inside her. She couldn't stop her lip from quivering any more than she could stem the tide of sobs that crashed over her.

In the midst of that storm, she felt Andrew's arms close around her. He'd rushed to her side while her eyes were blurry with tears, and now pulled her to him. He held her close as she poured out her grief and her guilt about Clarence and Uncle Jarvis and almost getting him killed. He said nothing, only rocked her gently through it all.

At last, her tears dried up and her sobs were reduced to sporadic hitches. She rested her tired head against his strong, warm chest and closed her eyes. She breathed him in, filling her senses with him so she'd have a store to remember him by.

Andrew's voice rumbled in his chest, vibrating beneath her cheek. "Do you think Clarence would rather it have been you that was killed, instead of him?"

"What?" she said, lifting her head at his startling question to stare at him. "Of course not. Why would you say such a thing?"

"Why do you think Clarence went to work for the War Department?" he asked, rather than answer her. It was rather an annoying habit, answering a question with another question, she decided. Perhaps she should stop doing it.

"Because he wished to do his part to defeat Napoleon, I suppose."

"Indeed. And he did. He uncovered many a plot in his days working for Marston, things he likely never told you of," he said.

And then he proceeded to share stories of Clarence's successful missions that he'd learned when he'd briefed his superiors at the War Department. Claire's heart swelled with pride. She'd always thought Clarence was a hero, but it was nice to know others had, too.

"Do you think if Clarence had known about this treaty, that he wouldn't have given his life trying to stop it?" Andrew asked when he'd finished.

"But he *didn't* know. It was my—"

"*Or* that he wouldn't have died to save all those men at Vitoria?" Andrew interrupted.

Claire swallowed, understanding where he was headed with this. "He would have sacrificed in a heartbeat," she whispered.

"Without *your* involvement, thousands more would have been lost on the Peninsula, and we might very well still be mired in war there instead of having Napoleon on the run. It may be true that *because* of your involvement, Clarence lost his life—"

Andrew soothed his words with a touch, running his hand gently across her brow and into her hair.

"—but *because* of Clarence's death," he went on, softly, "we were able to uncover Napoleon's bid to turn the tide of this war back in his favor. You and I both know that Clarence would have given his life a hundred times over to prevent that. Or to protect *you* so that you could."

Claire heaved a breath. She understood what he was saying, but—

"I know of what I speak," Andrew said, tipping her chin so that she was looking up at him. "Tonight, when I let myself be taken to draw the villains away from you, I was glad to do it."

She gasped. "You went with those brutes without a fight? Why would you do that?" She already had to live with Clarence's death on her head. How would she have survived Andrew's, too?

"I was *glad* to die, just to keep you safe. So that you could continue doing what you do best, for the good of England. Clarence would have been, too. Because he loved his country. And he loved you."

Andrew framed her face with his hands, his eyes intense. "As I do."

Her heart tripped. Had Andrew just said—

"Well." His smile tipped in a half grin. "He loved you *differently* than I do, but that's not what matters. What matters is—" Andrew dipped his mouth to hers for a kiss that melted her toes. He waited until she'd opened her eyes again to finish his thought. "—I *love* you, Claire. And I want you to be my wife."

Tears sprang to her eyes once more. Goodness, when had she become such a watering pot?

Andrew was asking her to be his wife.

Did it matter anymore that his proposal was six years late? They'd been so young then. They both were and were not the same people anymore. Would the Andrew of today make the same choice?

As if he'd read her mind, he said, "If I could go back in time, I would never have walked away from you. I'm so sorry."

Claire touched his cheek. "I, too, wish that it were different, but I won't waste another minute of my life with regrets. I love you, too."

She turned her face to kiss his palm. Then she smiled against it. "As Clarence said, life is too precarious to live it without the one you love by your side."

As she spoke her brother's words aloud, any last vestiges of anger at him dissolved. Regardless of all that had happened in the past, she knew Clarence had loved her. That's what she would choose to remember.

And that's how she would move into the future.

"I would be honored to be your wife."

She lifted her lips for a kiss. *This* was how she would choose to remember Andrew on the long nights she was alone, waiting for him to return from war. This feeling of security wrapped in the strength of his arms, the sizzle of heat wherever their skin met. As they made love in the dawning hours of the morning, Claire did her best to savor every touch, every sigh, every moan of pleasure. And she tried *not* to think of the coming day, and how it would take him away from her for God knew how long.

But as they lay in one another's arms after, she couldn't put off the question any longer.

"When do you leave for France?"

Andrew opened his eyes, and she tried to memorize the sleepy, sated look in them and how the green softened when he was well satisfied, too. "I don't."

"What?" She scrambled to a seated position, uncaring of her state of dishabille. "But you said you were to rejoin Wellington as soon as Uncle Jarvis's murder was solved. Who will be taking word to him so that Napoleon's and San Carlos's couriers can be cut off?"

Andrew laughed, and rose up on one elbow. "Let's start with the easier question. Four teams were already dispatched in the night. One to Toulouse to meet Wellington with the news and set up a net to try to catch the couriers before they leave France. One to Catalonia to spy on General Copon, who you said is to aid one of the couriers through the Peninsula when he arrives. A third to track General Palifax, who we guess took a more northerly route with his copy of the treaty. And the fourth directly to Madrid to try to head the situation off diplomatically."

Claire blinked. "That was…quick. And thorough."

"The War Department is taking this bit of intelligence very seriously. Which leads me to your first question." Andrew pushed up into a seated position across from her, and she did her very best not to let her eyes drift down the expanse of his muscled chest.

"More than ever, the War Department is recognizing how valuable Abchurch, and the work the code breakers do there, is to the war effort. They've asked me to stay on and I've agreed. On one condition."

Relief bubbled up inside Claire. Andrew was staying in England. "What condition?"

He reached out and touched her face. "That when you're ready, you join me."

"Join you?" she asked. Damn it, she must stop doing that, she reminded herself. "I can't continue on as Clarence," she said. "I'll need to lay him to rest properly. It's only fair to him and to others who loved him to know that he is gone and to be able to say goodbye."

Andrew was shaking his head. "Not as Clarence, love. As yourself."

"Myself?" *Oops.* Well, it would help if Andrew started making proper sense instead of making such questionable statements. "A woman would never be allowed at Abchurch."

"*You* will be. You see, I told my superiors all about how invaluable your work was at Vitoria, and Greeves vouched for your skills in several other matters, as well. I insisted that if they wanted the best man for the job, they should have her."

Claire sat there, speechless in any language.

Then she said, "You're not going to hover over me all the time, are you, like some overprotective husband?"

He huffed. "I'll try my best not to. I confess, it will be incredibly hard for me. But you've proven to be quite adept at protecting yourself."

Happiness filled her. She wasn't going to be alone, after all. She *would* have family, love, *and* purpose.

And best of all?

"At least I'll never have to tie a cravat knot again."

A wicked grin flashed over Andrew's face and one eyebrow shot up. "Don't speak too soon, dearling," he said. "I have a few knots I'd like to show you…although they require a poster bed as well as a cravat or two."

A thrill shot through her as she tried to imagine what he meant.

A few hours later, she knew precisely.

And Claire decided cravats weren't so bad after all.

EPILOGUE

Claire and Andrew married by special license on the morning of Christmas Eve, and announced their surprise marriage at the Danburys' annual Christmas Eve ball. They thought it only fitting, given everything.

The only sadness to their day was when well-wishers asked after Clarence, having noticed he was not present to celebrate his sister's nuptials. Claire could not answer, but Andrew told people the story they'd agreed upon: that Clarence had fallen ill shortly after the ceremony, but hadn't wanted them to spend their wedding night fussing over him.

Shortly after the New Year, Lord and Lady Sedgewick regretfully announced the passing of her brother, Sir Clarence Barton, and entered a period of mourning.

The code breakers of Abchurch were shocked when they met Claire as herself, though Greeves insisted he'd always known something was fishy with the entire situation. Despite Claire's concerns, the men took to working with her rather well.

The Treaty of Valencay, as Napoleon's bid to usurp Spain's allegiance for himself came to be called, did reach Madrid. However, with the advance warning and the efforts of many, Spain refused to ratify it —after, of course, King Ferdinand was returned safely to them.

For her extraordinary service to the Crown, Claire was made an honorary Knight Companion in the Most Honourable Order of the Bath. While no one talked about precisely why she deserved such an honor, everyone agreed that she did. Even Finchy.

To celebrate, her husband had four new cravats made for her. She delighted in showing him her hard-earned knot-tying skills that very evening.

And he delighted in her, as well as the two sets of twins they later had, for the rest of his life.

The End

ABOUT HEATHER SNOW

Heather Snow is an award winning historical romance author with a degree in Chemistry who discovered she much preferred creating chemistry on the page, rather than in the lab. Her books have been published in six languages around the world, and have won numerous awards including: The Golden Quill, the National Excellence in Romance Fiction Award, The Write Touch Readers Award and the Book Buyers Best Top Pick. She lives in the Midwest with her husband, two rambunctious boys, three insanely huge dogs and one very put upon cat.

For more information about Heather's books, visit:
heathersnowbooks.com/veiled-seduction-series

A LIAR UNDER THE MISTLETOE

◈

CELESTE BRADLEY

Fearless Amie Jackham doesn't attend balls to dance, she's there for the thrill of robbing the lockboxes of the unscrupulous.

With the notorious Vixen still at large, Liar's Club spy Lord Elliot Hughes is taking the opportunity to clean out a few lockboxes for the good of Crown and Country—and leaving the Vixen's trademark lacy handkerchief behind.

Thief and spy were bound to meet eventually—and when they do, sparks fly in this sexy chase caper that runs through the snowy streets and glittering ballrooms of London's Christmas season!

PROLOGUE

"*Your Voice of Society declares that there is no need to clutch your reticules so tightly, my Lady Readers! The Vixen of Vauxhall strikes only at the strongboxes of the moneyed and miserly. Does Sir K— contribute to the orphanage not three blocks from his grand doorway? Does Lord P— pay his servants, or anyone else, in good time? Nay, your Voice of Society declares some fellows highly deserving of opening their treasure troves to find nothing but a lacy handkerchief left behind. Carry on, Dear Vixen, carry on!*"

CHAPTER 1

DECEMBER, 1814 — LONDON

*E*lliott dodged another drunken couple leaving the dance floor, and sent the apologetic gentleman on his way with a grin and a comradely slap on the back. Elliot didn't know him or the so-called lady with him, but he had long ago discovered that a tolerant geniality made him simultaneously well liked and forgettable.

He continued casually strolling the outskirts of the ballroom, a slightly inebriated fellow at loose ends. *It's only me wandering about, just another useless offshoot of a noble family, beneath any special notice.* He was as much background color as one of the potted palms.

Precisely the way he wanted it.

He had timed his arrival well, appearing somewhat late and well after the dreary receiving line where he would be forced to greet his host, yet early enough that the guests were still in and out quite actively and no one had actually asked for his invitation. Good thing, for he had no such thing on his person.

He doubted anyone at Lord Beardsley's bawdy event would stick so closely to the niceties anyway. What a strange way to celebrate Christmas! It was almost as though the very notion of a reverential holiday spurred certain members of Society to renewed debauchery.

Tonight, rum punch ran freely and Elliot was certain he caught the scent of opium smoke now and again. It was a decadent display, full of brightly colored ladybirds with high hems and low necklines who attended to the needs of their high-ranking protectors with bawdy energy. All gathering about a great, festooned evergreen tree that reached easily to the next story.

Just like my schoolboy Christmas holidays...except, of course, not at all.

Elliott prided himself that he fit right in, youngest son of the youngest son of the Earl of Breckenridge, with a mountain of lordly uncles and cousins, all quite healthy, mind you, between him and any sort of future. As Lord Elliott Hughes, too highborn for real work, too late-born for any chance at advancement, he disappeared into the crowd of young men with more rank than sense, more time than brains and nothing to do with themselves but to overindulge.

"Marry well," his father had advised before he passed away with as little fanfare as he'd lived. "Find an heiress who wants to be a lady."

Elliott's mother hadn't had anything useful to add, as she died when he was born.

It wasn't very good advice. He wasn't inclined to marry some status-hungry steel-monger's daughter. A feminine shriek of gleeful shock and horror rose up from behind a potted palm in Elliot's path. He veered well around it.

Certainly none of the women here this evening were bride material.

So he carried on. He was living the life everyone expected of him, drinking and dancing and spending the allowance doled out by his dutiful but indifferent uncle, the current earl. A ball here, a horse-race there, a card game or two in between.

It would be enough to drive an intelligent fellow mad with his own uselessness—if that fellow hadn't come up with much better way to pass the time.

As he strolled, he glanced into one of the side rooms set apart for gentlemanly cards.

"Oh, look!" he murmured to himself. "Lord Beardsley is at the gaming tables. What a lovely time to take in that gracious view from the upper floor." And find his lordship's study... and his lordship's strongbox!

Elliot slipped out of the ballroom as easily as he'd entered it.

No reason to remember him at all.

∼

Lord Beardsley likely believed that his eight-foot stone wall would keep the riffraff out of his garden. Miss Amie Jackham begged to differ.

From her small rucksack she removed a simple grappling hook with a lightweight line woven of leather strips. After a glance up and down the dark and icy cobbled alleyway, she easily tossed the hook up to catch on the top of the wall. Large cylindrical stone spikes marched across the top, surely intended to be intimidating, or perhaps hinting at Lord Beardsley's self-deluded personal endowment. The spikes only aided her attempt.

Taking the line in her black-gloved grip, she ran nimbly up the vertical, hand over hand on the rope. Once on top she kicked the covering snow away and poised lightly, gripping the squat pedestal of one of the spikes between her feet as she pulled her line up after her. She tossed the line down the other side, and quickly followed it to the ground below.

Around her, the artistically placed boxwoods slumbered peacefully beneath a blanket of snow. It was the coldest winter in decades, people said. Amie had to agree. The snow was lovely, but the chill crept into her home and her bed and her bones. Also, the snow made her leave footprints.

No matter. She knew this part of the garden was invisible to the house beyond because she'd been in that house just this morning, checking the view from every window.

She smiled slightly at the memory. No one ever looked at chambermaids, particularly in a house filling up with guests.

The other maids had given her a few curious glances, but there were so many new arrivals in the house already that they hesitated to question her for fear she served someone important.

Now, confident that no one could see this dark corner of the garden from any of the tall windows of the house, Amie didn't hesitate to strip off her clothing. Off came her trousers and boyish shirt and vest, along with her grubby cap. Clad in nothing but a short chemise that came halfway down her thighs, she shivered as she pulled the last item from her rucksack and shook it out. The pale green silk gown had been cleverly folded so as not to wrinkle but Amie had to take care not to allow the hem to drag in the snow as she dressed.

The precautions paid off. Moments later she looked entirely different. The neatly folded boy's garb, arranged in order for speedy dressing later, went back into the rucksack. She concealed the water-proofed leather bag behind a tree.

The line still dangled from the grappling hook but in the shadowed corner she doubted anyone would notice it. Best to leave it there. She might not be able to leave through the front door!

She had no mirror so she could only hope that the cap had protected her intricately braided hairstyle from her vertical gymnastics. It felt fine but she was perhaps not the best judge of fashionable hairstyles.

At any rate, this is not the sort of ball where a woman's hair stayed tightly up. She paused, wondering if she ought to be a little more mussed to fit in. *Never mind. Stop thinking,* she told herself.

Light on your feet, quick on the pull, nothing on your mind. Just as Papa had always told her.

She was a Jackham, born of a long line of night-burglars and jewel thieves. Nerves had no place in her life.

She stepped forward confidently, trotting toward the house with her skirts daintily lifted, nothing but a guest rushing back to the fun of the party.

Up the stone steps, across the terrace, through the glass doors, just stroll inside the house as if I belong.

There were already many guests visible through the ballroom terrace doors, so no one took notice of her. By the time she arrived inside she was slightly flushed and panting. Nothing odd there, just another woman fresh off the rowdy dance floor. She reached a drink off a servant's tray and stepped into the crowd.

Lord Beardsley's ballroom was very grand, and lavishly decorated for the event. Evergreen garlands and draperies of golden silk festooned every surface. More silk was hung to create little alcoves where one might find a fainting couch, a decanter of whiskey, or tiny cakes of opium on a hookah tray.

Amie saw that she timed her arrival well. Any earlier, the other guests might've been more observant, social hounds that they were. Any later, the party might be growing out of control. Already she spotted a few women wearing richly decadent gowns that seemed rather the worse for wear. One creature had her bodice ripped wide open at that moment. The woman only guffawed and tossed back her glass, breasts exposed.

Amie kept her revulsion to herself. Not her sort of party at all. She might be a thief, but she was still a lady!

She continued around the ballroom, slipping unnoticed through the press of guests who laughed a little too loudly, stood a little too close, or swayed a little too loosely in the dance.

She wasn't the prettiest woman in the room, nor the plainest, nor the best dressed, nor the worst. Utterly forgettable, precisely as planned.

On the other side of the great ballroom a staircase arched up to the doorways on the next floor. That was where she needed to be.

A tricky moment. That curving stair was intentionally in full view of the party, intended for grand entrances and exits.

Amie looked around her. She wondered if she could—

"Oh, there you are!" She widened her eyes fervently, gave a loopy grin, and clasped the muscled arm of an overdressed dandy staggering past. He was a pimply, sweaty-looking fellow, but he was good and drunk, which was all she required.

He stopped to look blankly at her, slowly focusing his gaze on her face. Then her breasts. But to his credit, his eyes did eventually return to her face. He smiled back, although he looked a bit confused. "Yes!" he said gamely. "Here I am!"

Amie leaned her bosom into his arm and squeezed his bicep. His jacket was padded. He likely had an arm like a chicken leg beneath his stuffed sleeve. That was all right with her. She didn't need a muscled oaf. She only needed someone who was still more or less upright.

"I thought you'd forgotten," she scolded playfully, giving him a little pout. "You promised you'd show me the conservatory." She batted her eyelashes.

He just stared at her. "But...it's winter."

Good heavens, what a clod.

She wasn't much of a performer, to be sure. She exaggerated her pout slightly, then more. Perhaps she wasn't convincing enough. She toyed with his cravat as she went on tiptoe, sliding her body up his side. "You told me that you would take me to the conservatory because you wanted to see me naked in the moonlight!" she shouted over the den.

The notion that he might actually have sexual satisfaction sometime in the near future seem to pierce the idiot's drunken fog. He began to nod emphatically. "Yes! Yes, I remember! I would never forget that! The conservatory, yes, let's go to the conservatory!"

Amie giggled sickeningly and then tugged his arm toward the arching stair. "It's this way, silly!"

"Ah, ah, yes! This way!" He stumbled along with her and even managed to pick up the pace on the steps.

At the top of the stairs, the hallway led off in two directions. One way would take them to the front stair and front door, where still more guests were arriving. The other led deeper into the house.

Amie gave a little yelp and pushed the dandy away, uttering the magic words. "There's my lover! I think he saw us!"

Wizardly words, indeed. In a flash, her companion had vanished, likely gone back down the stairs to lose himself in the crowd below. She ought to write a pamphlet—*How to Make a Man Disappear*.

She was well shut of him, for her only goal had been to appear as just another tipsy demi-rep looking for a dark corner.

No reason to remember at her all.

~

ELLIOT SILENTLY CLOSED the door behind him and lifted the candle-stub he'd lighted from a hallway wall sconce. The host's study was as ostentatious as his ballroom. Lord Beardsley was known as a libertine who denied himself nothing. Hence the plush carpet, the gleaming rosewood desk and the priceless art.

The house had thick walls. Elliot could barely detect the rousing country-dance tune now being played in the ballroom. He could likely fire a brace of pistols in here and no one in the house would know.

He went directly to the desk and sat in the chair. Then he reached beneath the inlaid lip of the desktop and slid his fingers to the right. There should be a—

His index finger touched a tiny brass button. A spring-loaded segment of the wooden trim popped into his hand. Within lay a heavy iron key.

Elliot hefted it in his hand and turned to a large box resting in a corner of the study. It had been brightly painted with pastoral scenes with some intention of making it look like a decorative piece, but when Elliot touched it, he could feel the cold iron beneath the thin skin of paint.

The strongbox was a good one. Solid iron, strapped with bands of more iron. Beardsley was so sure of its solidity that he'd not even bothered to carefully conceal it.

The lock was good as well. Elliot smiled. There was a large, obvious keyhole on the front. It was meaningless, a distraction. Elliot pulled a small lock-pick set from his cuff and turned his attention to a tiny hole concealed in the painted design of a wheel of a hay wagon. It required a tiny key that Elliot happened to know never left his lordship's watch fob.

Someone would have to know just where to look for that inconspicuous keyhole.

That someone would be Elliot.

He quickly sprang the miniature lock, which caused a two-inch square painted door to open. Behind that door was the large keyhole meant for the heavy key Elliot had found concealed in the desk. Elliot turned the key, listened to the thick bolts slide open and swung the weighty lid of the chest upward.

He grinned. "That will teach you to fire your faithful butler without reference because he skimmed a bit off the top of the household budget, you miserly wanker."

Not only had the furious butler spoken freely about the strongbox, he'd given Elliot some very interesting notions about might be found within.

The interior was filled almost entirely with stacked folios, each at least an inch thick with documents. Beneath those was a small wooden casket.

Elliot knelt on the floor, his candle planted in a dollop of wax on a small side table holding brandy and glasses. He gave a quick sort to the folios, making piles, scanning each page in the way he'd been taught—not so much reading as drifting his eyes over it for an instant, allowing a few key phrases to leap out.

Deeds and provenance for estate property and art treasures? Useless. A set of accounts, including income from Beardsley's estate...and then another, nearly identical set of accounts, that added up quite differently.

His lordship was keeping double books. Not of interest to Elliot, but he would be sure to alert the King's Remembrancer about Beardsley's rather monumental income tax evasion.

Finally, one slender folio revealed all that any Crown spy could wish. Several coded pages, which appeared to be two sides of a secret correspondence, presumably letters to his lordship and his lordship's own copies of his replies. The code was nonsense to Elliot's eyes, but no matter. He wasn't the one charged with finding the cipher. His job was to make a quick, neat copy and put the originals back where they belonged.

He used his lordship's own paper and ink. He was fast at his work, as were all the operatives of the Liar's Club. He was just one of a well-trained ring of thieves, infiltrators, code-breakers and yes, even the odd assassin or two.

A quarter of an hour later his careful copies were drying to one side while he bound up the folios, winding their cords precisely as he'd found them. Lord Beardsley wound clockwise, with a half-twist on the third round.

Elliot placed half the folios back in the iron box, the original left-hand stack in the very order in which he'd found them.

The wooden jewel casket he saved for last. Without really looking inside, he dumped the contents into his large, plain handkerchief.

Then he pulled a lacy lady's hanky from his pocket and laid it in the jewel casket.

The Liars were taking advantage of the fresh notoriety of the mysterious Vixen, concealing their activities in the wave of jewel thefts. Besides, as James, Elliot's immediate superior, said, "The coffers can always use a bit extra—all in the cause of national defense and whatnot."

There had been some recent activity in a once-defunct ring of highborn traitors. Every Liar who with a hand at lock-picking was being stuffed into a flash coat and weskit and sent out to infiltrate Society's ballrooms—and a few other rooms as well.

The timing was excellent.

Too excellent?

Elliot paused in his rifling to look down at the stones twinkling in the pile. A glamorous, mysterious thief hits grand house after grand house. A spy ring, led by some incredibly powerful people, needs to peruse a few secret files in a few grand houses. No one had ever seen the Vixen. Other than the trademark handkerchief, Elliot wasn't even sure how Society could be so sure the thief was female...

Unless someone with a stable of primarily male spies had needed the distraction of a female suspect?

"Knots within knots," Elliot muttered. He was a loyal sort and a patriot, but even he could only trust the brilliant, devious minds of his superiors so far! He could only hope that all his assignments worked in aid of the Crown and leave the deep thinking to others.

He replaced the jewel casket beneath the right-hand stack of folios, folded the bauble-stuffed handkerchief tightly and tucked the flattened parcel into the right breast pocket of his coat.

His copies, he folded down to half page and was preparing to fold them down to a size he could conceal in his cravat. No guard ever thought to search a man's cravat.

A floorboard creaked beyond the door of the study. Elliot didn't bother to turn or even hesitate. With a few swift motions, he had the strongbox shut tight again and the key back in the hidden slot of the desk.

With his copies stuffed roughly into his coat, he turned to the door with a loose drunken grin and bit of a stagger.

CHAPTER 2

"God, I've been found at last! I thought I'd die here, lost in the bowels of this bloody majestic house!" It never hurt to compliment a man's wealth, especially when displayed with such vulgar abandon.

It was not his host who stood in the doorway of the study. It was a girl—a woman, actually, but a young one. Lord Beardsley had no wife or daughter. The woman wore an evening gown, so she wasn't a maid.

Elliot casually lifted his candle-stub and lighted a branch of candles on Beardsley's desk. He needed to properly assess his new acquaintance.

The gown wasn't terribly fine but it was tight in the bosom and worn without petticoats. He could see the faint outline of her limbs backlighted by the sconces in the hall beyond. Not a timid Society miss, that was certain.

A prostitute? He secretly hoped not. She looked...nice, at least, not like a jade.

An amateur prostitute? A young woman attending a vile soiree like the one downstairs wasn't looking for a husband—she was looking for a protector. If she already had one, she'd be dressed more expensively.

If she'd had any idea what she was about, she would be dressed more temptingly.

Not that it wasn't a fine view, what with the revealing lighting behind her. She was pretty, with a fresh complexion and large green eyes, but then he'd always been partial to red-haired ladies with freckles that showed even through her powder. Really, very pretty.

It was too bad she was a whore.

All of that assessment flowed through his mind before the girl could do more than blink at him in surprise.

"Is this your house?" she asked. "I mean to say...are you Lord Beardsley himself?"

Elliot let out a breath. A girl on the hunt sneaking in to introduce herself. Pretty but possibly not too bright. Excellent.

"Not a bit like it, I'm afraid." He bowed. "Just any old bloke. Ordinary as mud."

She tried to hide her disappointment, but she didn't do a very good job of it. "I saw you come in here, so naturally I thought…"

You thought you'd put yourself in the great man's gun sights. Silly twit.

Beardsley was a first-class bounder, cruel and prone to violence, according to the intelligence Elliot had been given. The last place a young lady should want to be was in that man's bed.

Not his worry. After all, he was just an over-indulgent wastrel, soaking up another man's brandy. He slid a charming, slightly drunken smile onto his face. "I hoped Himself kept the good stuff in his study. Would you like a glass?"

She shot a look at the decanter on the side table next to the strongbox. "I dare not," she said, swaying slightly. "I'll be too much in my cups and then I might do something untoward!"

She was adorable. Alas, it was time to get out of this room.

"Shall we rejoin the dance?" Elliot offered his arm, bowing far enough to fake a stumble upon rising.

She batted her lashes at him and bit her lower lip. "Well… I was looking for his lordship.…"

For quite possibly the first time in his life, Elliott wished he were the sort of fellow he portrayed. The shining red hair and emerald eyes and charming freckles—not to mention the way she filled out her enchanting little dress—added up to quite an intriguing package. Elliot the wastrel would be just the sort to secure a mistress...

"...but I do dearly love to dance." She smiled invitingly.

Elliott didn't waste any time getting her out of the study and back to the ballroom. She snuggled into his arm as they walked down the hall, and when she squeezed his bicep and cooed over the bulk of his arm beneath his sleeve, he liked it. Dangerous master of intrigue or not, he was still a young man and young men liked it when pretty girls complimented their muscles.

∼

For all the balls Amie had attended uninvited, she had never yet taken the time to dance.

Speed was essential. Get in, get the brass, get gone.

This time, someone had beaten her to the strongbox.

It had been the dim line of light beneath the study door that had warned her. His lordship would have had a brace of candles blazing. Even a housemaid would have good light to assure a careful cleaning, not that any staff could be spared from such a well-attended ball.

The study door was unlocked, of course. She turned the latch slowly and soundlessly. No need to worry about creaky hinges in such a fine house.

She only opened it a few inches, but she gained a very excellent view of a figure in a formal coat kneeling before the open strongbox, sorting through the contents.

Blast.

What to do, what to do...

It could actually go in her favor. The competition had already cracked the lock. All she needed to do was to deliver him of his ill-gotten gains before he left the ball.

Silently, she stepped back and closed the door, thinking quickly. He'd looked youngish from behind. Fit as well—that had been an exceptionally well-muscled bum!

She had so little experience with distracting men. If this fellow was intelligent enough to crack that strongbox, then he would be far too clever to fall for her earlier gambit.

What would Ruby do?

When Amie heard the faint sound of the strongbox's spring-loaded locks clunking back into place, she bent over and shook her bosom a bit higher into her bodice, then straightened, pinched her cheeks, bit her lips and warmed up her eyelashes with a few practice flutters.

A creak and a rattle of the latch later, she opened the door onto the fairly believable scenario of a spoiled young gentleman sneaking a bit of his lordship's best brandy.

When he'd asked her to dance, she'd realized a waltz would be an excellent moment to try his pockets.

Then he'd taken her into his arms and every larcenous thought had drained from her mind. His hand on her waist was so warm...and the way his other hand held hers so gently, yet with total assurance. He took the lead and she had no impulse to do anything but follow him.

I'm dancing...

She gazed up at her partner in wonder. He was handsome. She'd been so busy thinking, always thinking, that she'd scarcely taken in his appearance. Now, so close, she could see the light from the chandeliers gleaming off his fair hair. Something about the way his cheekbones angled into his square jaw made her insides feel a bit unsteady.

He smiled down at her as if she pleased him as well, his gray-green eyes twinkling. Her blood began to heat in her veins. She took a deep breath to steady herself, but his clean, spicy, manly scent struck like a lightning bolt to parts better left unmentioned.

The music swelled. He swung her easily around the floor. The colors of the many brilliant gowns around her blurred in her vision, like a blooming garden seen through tears.

His hand slipped farther around, until it rested in the center of her back and then he was close—so close—

Mind your task, Amethyst.

Mama's voice, time-faded but true, snapped Amie back to herself.

Now, she wasn't dreamily chopping carrots in the kitchen, but risking everything she had for everyone she loved.

Right. On with the job.

∼

ELLIOT'S pretty partner was still a bit tipsy, for she suddenly stumbled and giggled, and turned left when she should've turned right. Elliot didn't mind one bit. It was a very pleasant collision. All sorts of soft places pressed against his body.

He was beginning to feel little inebriated himself. She smelled like apple blossoms and vanilla, like summer in the country. Outside it was the dark of winter. Inside, the candles were bright above them and she was a warm, soft armful. Once she'd landed against him, she didn't move away again. Their turn about the floor became less a waltz and more of a cuddle. Right in front of all concerned, not that anyone would care at this sort of party.

Being a spy for the Crown didn't leave much time for young ladies, especially not for dancing too close, or losing oneself in the scent of feminine warmth, or—

The music ended. Prompted by habit and the conditioning of his governess's oft-applied cane, Elliot stepped back, snapped his heels together and bowed, as one did to a lady after a dance. "Might I beg your name, miss?"

When he straightened, his warm, bright companion was gone. Though he looked sharply all around the ballroom, she was nowhere to be found.

A sudden thought chilled him. He clapped his hand over his secret left inner breast pocket. The thick packet of folded copies was a reassuring bulk beneath the silk of his evening coat.

Then he checked for the jewels in his right inner pocket.

At the complete and total lack of anything resembling pearls and emeralds held within the lining of his specially constructed coat, he gave a bitter laugh and shook his head.

Bloody hell. He'd been quite deliciously taken by a most delectable thief.

As he turned to leave the ball, weaving just enough to be believable but not enough to call attention to his exit, he quite honestly thought the dance might just have been worth it.

∽

IN THE LAST hour before dawn, Amie finally arrived at her own back gate. She'd come home the long way, as she always did after a job. Her father had drilled into all three of them that they ought not to lead possible pursuers to their home base.

So, even tired as she was, she'd given her imaginary shadow a merry chase through the alleys and side streets of London. Passing as a boy made this bit easier but she was careful never to pause, nor to rush in a suspicious manner or to remain exposed in the light from a window or lantern for too long.

Move from shadow to shadow, so that even if someone sees you, by the time they look back there will be nothing to see.

The months had not dimmed Papa's gravely voice in Amie's memory, nor his face, lined with pain and years and loss, or his eyes, filled with affection.

Papa had been known for three things in his life. Firstly, for being the finest rooftop man in London until a terrible fall broke both his legs. Secondly, for wearing the gaudiest, most dreadful weskits to ever see needle and thread.

And thirdly, for betraying a certain group of Crown spies to a French infiltrator, bringing about multiple murders with that treachery.

The other thing, of which the world had no notion, was that he'd been a loving and protective papa to three devoted daughters.

No matter what the world had thought of him, thief or failure or even traitor, to Amie he would always be the man who cared enough to teach her the true way of the world, to teach them all to survive.

When she finally let herself through her own back gate and

crossed the utilitarian garden toward the kitchen of the house she shared with her two sisters, she was exhausted and somewhat saddened. The ordinary house appeared sad and rundown in comparison to the glittering mansion she'd danced in only a few hours before.

It wasn't really that she wanted to attend that sort of ball, where people did questionable things for questionable reasons. It was only that it was a kind of life she would never live.

Her father had been as common as gutter mud but her mother had not. Lady Dorothea Montgomery had run away with a man she'd caught rifling through her grandmother's jewels and never looked back. She'd been happy with her little house, her rakish but devoted husband and her three little daughters.

Mama could never have known what she did to Amie with her stories of her sparkling life and her grand debut. They were simply her memories, told without regret or melancholy.

But for Amie, those stories caused a rift in her world. Although they were the grand-daughters of a duke, she and her sisters would never be presented to the Prince Regent at Court.

Amie would never waltz with a handsome young man—or tell him her real name. She would never spend giddy hours choosing gowns and bonnets and gloves.

Most of the time those activities seemed silly and wasteful to her. Yet once in a while, the glimpses she had of that other life while she worked a mark made her feel like a hungry child staring in a window at a grand feast, shivering unnoticed in the cold while others sated themselves in warmth and laughter and plenty.

Then as she came close to the house she could see into the window of her own kitchen. The room glowed even though candles were spare and the fire was as much for cooking as it was for comfort. Her two sisters, Emma and Ruby, bustled around the kitchen although it was still dark outside. And she didn't have to linger outside this warmth. It was rightfully hers.

Amie opened the back door and stood in the narrow entrance hall shaking out her boy's coat. Before the gathered mist could even drip to the floor her sisters were there for her.

"I'll take that," Emma said as she reached for Amie's rucksack.

"You look so cold." Ruby took off her own shawl and draped it over Amie's shoulders. "Come and sit down. Emma has just finished the baking."

Within moments, Amie sipped weak tea and munched on one of Emma's special biscuits—the ones she managed to concoct with almost no butter and only one egg.

Emma unpacked the rucksack with her usual efficiency. She shook out the green gown and examined it for rips or stains. "Oh, excellent. I wasn't sure those beads would stay on. I've re-trimmed this thing so many times it's a wonder the fabric has any integrity whatsoever."

Ruby, who was only eighteen after all, jiggled impatiently, almost dancing from one foot to the other. "Did you get anything?"

Amie tried to hide it, because Ruby was very easy to tease. But she couldn't keep the smile from growing slowly on her face as she bent over her tea.

Ruby spotted it once and clapped her hands in excitement. "I knew it. I just knew it!"

At that moment, Emma pulled the handkerchief-wrapped packet from the bottom of the rucksack, underneath the secret flap that would've withstood the searching hands of anyone who didn't know where to look. Emma laid it on the table and they all gazed at it reverently for a moment.

Why not take a moment to relish something so important? This was a new day. No more slipping into one house at a time, slipping out with a single silver candlestick or a porcelain dog from the mantel of a little used room. Goodness, last winter she'd been too terrified to steal anything but food from a few larders!

Then, patience spent, Ruby was on it with a leap, as Ruby was on everything. Amie and Emma sat back and watched their youngest sibling unfold the handkerchief and roll out a pile of gleaming jewels and shimmering pearls.

The loot gleamed in the dimness of the kitchen and the light of the two candle stumps that still burned.

Amie sat up and raised a brow. "Not bad."

Emma slid her a glance. "Didn't you know?"

Amie carefully didn't look at her sister. "It was dark and—" *I stole it from the man who stole it.* "And I needed to be quick."

She could have told them about the handsome thief in the study, but then she would have had to tell them about the dance. She'd been so intrigued by the combination of his flirtatious grin beneath his serious eyes. Heavens, he had smelled so good when she'd pressed close enough to pull the jewels from his pocket. The scent of him, that spicy mix of man and clean, light cologne, had made her thighs tighten beneath her gown.

Was it so wrong to want to keep the experience to herself a little longer? The interference hadn't mattered in the end, after all. She still ended up with the goods.

Meanwhile, Ruby parted the tangled strands of pearls with deft fingers and laid them out to one side. Emma bent to peer at them. "Matched. Excellent. The pink pearls will bring a good price, but we'll have to be careful. They're very easy to remember."

Then from the jumble on the table Ruby lifted a chain from which dangled an astonishing emerald in a square of rose-cut diamonds. It was the size of a horse's eye and glowed in the candlelight with a perfect green light. They all regarded it in appalled silence.

"Oh no." Ruby's eyes were enormous. "That must be at least twelve carats. Do we even know *how* to sell it?"

Amie made a slight face. It was a blow, to be sure. Important jewels, jewels that made a statement and were memorable, had led to many a thief's capture in the past. "Papa wouldn't touch that."

Emma tapped a single finger to her lips in thought. "If we knew a cutter..." She held out her hand and Ruby dropped the stone into it. Emma held it to the candle turning left and right. "The diamonds are easy."

She pulled a jeweler's loupe from her apron pocket and swiveled the lens free. She held the small magnifier to her eye. "They're not terribly remarkable, although good enough to bring a bit of coin." She turned the pendant over to look at the setting more closely. "It's beautifully made. A lovely design. Perhaps we should hold it for the future."

Amie nodded. Papa had always kept a stash of easily identifiable jewels. He called it his bribery box. A pretty something came in useful, to wave before a greedy magistrate's eyes, to dazzle and sway someone in authority just long enough to beat a retreat and disappear. That left the difficulty of disposal in the hands of some unsuspecting grafter.

"I'll put it in Papa's box." Amie reached for the gem.

"I'll do it!" Ruby took the necklace and bustled from the kitchen.

Emma watched her go with reluctance in her gaze. "I could learn to cut."

"Emeralds are too brittle. The job requires a master." Amie smiled wearily at her. "And we don't have time."

"No." Ruby reentered the kitchen and plunked down in her chair. "We can't go to a cutter. Even if we found one, we don't know if we could trust them. Papa claims cutters are more interested in the gems than in profit. If they saw something like *that*"—she indicated the emerald—"they'd never desecrate it."

Amie gazed at her sisters, looking from one to the other. She knew better than to let her concern show, but she knew them better than anyone in the world. *Papa claims...*

Ruby was the youngest, and although she had known Papa for the fewest years, she was the only one who still spoke of him in the present tense.

As if he were still alive. Concerning as that was, the more immediate issue was...

"Is it enough?"

Both Amie and Ruby gazed at Emma and waited. Emma sorted through the jewels touching each one, her lips moving slightly as she calculated the probable sale price. When she was done she sat back and let out a small sigh.

"We'll be able to keep the house. It will be enough to calm our debtors for a time...but only just." She brightened slightly. "Still, we should have enough left to buy a bit of food."

"Ham!" Ruby sang out. "Oranges!" She beamed at Amie with pride. "See, it is Christmas, after all!"

Amie found herself, as she sometimes did, riveted by her little sister's uncommon beauty. Ruby was all flashing dark eyes and shining black curls, vivid and lively. Her figure already stopped men in their tracks, whether they be dukes or dockworkers.

Emma had a quieter loveliness, like Mama's. The cool, restrained perfection of a marble goddess. *Those quiet ones are the ones you have to watch out for,* Papa used to tease Mama. *Or they'll run off with the first charming thief who comes along!*

Emma's hair was almost more blond than red and her figure elegantly slim. If Ruby bounced when she moved, then Emma danced. Both were extraordinarily beautiful, in their individual ways.

Amie tried not to compare herself, for she didn't believe sisters should compete. She herself was tall and freckled and blotched most dreadfully when she blushed. Emma claimed she looked like Mama, too, but all Amie could see in the mirror was Papa's ginger hair, his height and his early ability to climb anything.

You are not an extraordinary creature. You are not a goddess. You are only a rather good thief.

For the first time, the dismaying thought occurred to Amie that, had she not caught her handsome counterpart in the act, he might never have noticed her at all.

CHAPTER 3

*E*lliott could've been more discreet as he reentered his favorite establishment by using the front door. Then again, what was the problem? He was a young man dressed in evening clothes, wandering the streets of London a few hours after sunup, clearly a fellow who did not wish to go home. Where else would such a bloke go but to a gentlemen's club? Especially to an expensive but slightly disreputable gaming hell like the Liar's Club.

There was a short young man standing before the club door dressed in green and black livery.

"Isn't this a bit early for a formal doorman, Stubbs?" Elliott looked askance at the bright morning. "The other gambling hells won't open for hours."

The young man opened the door and waved Elliott inside. "It's good to see you again, my lord."

Elliott clapped Stubbs on the shoulder with a laugh. "You're the very picture of proper English staff, Stubbs!" He sauntered through the open door. "Job well done."

Perhaps it was Elliott's imagination, but he could swear that just before the door closed behind them he heard Stubbs mutter, "Been here twice as long as you, you silly toff."

Elliott didn't correct him. He wasn't a toff, at least not in any substantial way. He was more toff-esque, or toff-like, or possibly toff-adjacent. He himself wasn't someone, but he did know people who were.

This didn't usually bother Elliott, and it didn't bother him now. His natural ability to blend into Society was too useful a tool for his superiors to do without.

It was dead quiet inside the club and there was no one in the card room, and no one tending the bar. He could smell something cooking though, which meant Kurt was at work as always.

As Elliott passed through several layers of obvious and not-so-obvious doorways that led to the interior of the true club, the club with the real Liars, he could tell that not only was Kurt baking bread but quite possibly...almond biscuits?

Elliott was no slave to his stomach, but he'd danced and flirted and robbed and been robbed without ever making it to the actual dinner or any of the tidbits set out for the guests at last night's ball. His stomach growled a rather loud complaint about the drastic lack of almond biscuits inside it.

Instead of taking a left, as he properly should in order to promptly report to Sir James Cunnington, his immediate superior, Elliott took a detour to his right and dashed toward the kitchen.

He heard light, piping voices answered by a brief low rumble as he near the kitchen door. Once there, he entered the warm, fragrant glow of baking and bubbling cook-pots and giggling children. The ladies and gents of the Liar's Club had decided to celebrate Christmas at the club, for were the Liars not their family?

Now normally, one would not imagine small children enjoying the company of a large, scarred, hairy, monosyllabic giant wielding an enormous knife, but this was the Liar's Club. It probably seemed perfectly normal to the offspring of spies to coax sweets from Kurt the Cook, one of the deadliest men in England, the foremost assassin-in-residence.

Elliott, on the other hand, could be a very polite fellow when he wanted to be. Kurt glared at him from under bushy brows in inquiry as to his business there.

"Uncle Elliot!" One of the persons of negligible height impacted his leg and twined little arms around his knee.

Elliott picked her up, flipped her over his shoulder, then wiggled his fingers at the rest while she giggled into his back. "Good morning all. I have had a long night, working for the good of Crown and Country. Perhaps a tiny reward?"

Kurt uttered a short grunt that expressed his opinion of people who believed they deserved reward for simply doing their job, but he also ran a spatula under three biscuits on a tray fresh from the oven. He tossed them into a cloth, which he folded rapidly and threw in Elliott's direction in a single motion. Elliott snagged his reward out of the air and turned the motion into a flourishing bow, taking advantage of his proximity to the floor to deposit his flaxen-haired admirer on her own little feet.

"A thousand thanks, dear Sir."

Kurt didn't even bother to grunt this time but only sent Elliott an acid glare that made him laugh even as he scuttled to safety through the kitchen door. Kurt would never do anything to frighten the children, but these were Liar children and not easily frightened. And Kurt was incredibly accurate with a throwing knife.

Elliott burned his mouth on the first heavenly biscuit before he managed to slow down enough to blow his treat cool before biting in.

James Cunnington was Elliott's immediate superior and second-in-command in the Liar's Club. He stood over the desk where a lovely russet-haired woman bent over a pile of papers scribbling furiously. He looked up when Elliot sauntered in.

"You're late. Even for you."

Elliot lifted a shoulder. "Fell asleep after Beardsley's." Actually, he'd run himself ragged chasing after every carriage leaving the ball, trying to get a glimpse of his adorably light-fingered dance partner. Now he had no choice but to face the music. He handed off his coded copies to his superior. "Sorry."

James took them and flipped through the pages. "Neatly done. I'll get these to Fisher." Then he gave Elliot a stern glare. "But remember, Elliot, every moment counts." James turned back to the lady in the chair.

She, in turn, looked up at Elliott with a glint of amusement at her eyes. "He's grumpy. Something about the Vixen is bothering him."

Elliott raised brow. "So the Vixen is real?"

"More or less." James folded his arms and glared down at the gossip-sheets spread across the desk. "If you can believe *that* claptrap."

Phillipa rolled her eyes at Elliott. She might be James's beloved wife but she was also no stranger to the world of spies. Her father had been one of the lead cryptologists for the Liars at one time. "Gossip is a very reliable source. A gossip doesn't take sides. These tattletales don't care for anything but exposing secrets." She began to read aloud.

"What a fuss and flutter, Dear Readers, what a bang and bother! That wicked wisp of fog and fancy, London's very own Vixen, has struck again!

Poor Lord B—, if one may pity such an unpleasant fellow. He is wealthy still, although your Voice of Society happens to know he is poorer by a certain priceless emerald, among other trinkets.

Look no further than the Mistress of Mystery, Lord B—, for the source of your vexation! She holds your treasure as closely as she holds the hearts and imaginations of London herself!"

Phillipa set the newssheet down with a grimace. "Good secrets, ugly secrets or traitorous secrets. They simply don't have any other agenda than to expose them."

Elliott grinned at her. "And James still doesn't like it that they exposed the Griffin, does he?"

Perhaps he'd put a bit too much flirt into that grin, because James stepped between them, his large form entirely blocking Elliot's view of the delectably but entirely married Mrs. Dangerous Spy.

Men in love were so easy. Still, James had a fierce right hook and a murderous bent when it came to his darling Flip, so Elliot raised both hands and backed off a step. "And here I was going to give you one of my biscuits, hot from the oven."

Phillipa poked her head around her mountainous husband. "They're done baking? We can finish this later, darling." With a rustle of skirts and a patter of dainty feet, she was off to the kitchens to battle a passel of tots for a biscuit.

Which left Elliot alone with a jealous husband. This did tend to happen to him now and again.

Elliot thought it was about time he distracted his commander. "You know, I had begun to suspect that we created the Vixen as a cover for our own activities."

It worked. James snorted and dropped his bristling pose. "How brilliant of us. I'll keep that in mind for the future. But actually no, we are merely taking advantage of an existing situation. There is a real Vixen and she is becoming quite a problem."

Elliott rubbed the back of his neck. He knew he should report the events of last night. And he was going to. He didn't understand his own reluctance. So a pretty woman had flirted with him and lifted some jewels from his pocket. Only the jewels, not the evidence. He'd never broken character, and she likely thought him a burglar just like her. He'd done nothing wrong, except for those few moments when she'd been in his arms and he forgotten that he was a Liar and she was just a pretty demi-rep.

"So...last night—"

James interrupted him. "The bloody hell of it is," James burst out, "that every person that claims to been robbed by the Vixen is on our operations list."

Elliott's gut went cold. "Wait— *The* ops list?"

"The list where we keep the names of all suspected traitors." James was pacing now.

Elliott shook his head in disbelief. "How could that be? How could some night-thief have the same incredibly secret list that we have? *I* don't even know who is on that list, unless you tell me!" A sudden thought made him pause. "Are there Liars we don't know about?"

"I don't know." A deep voice came from the doorway. "Are there?"

James and Elliott turned to see their spymaster, the Gentleman, former right hand of the Crown, Dalton Montmorency, Duke of Etheridge. He glared at them both with his eerie silvery eyes.

Dalton didn't actually loom over Elliott, although sometimes Elliot felt as though he did. The Gentleman was an intense individual with a long strange history of his own. Not to mention being very wealthy, very titled, and according to all the ladies associated with the club, *very* handsome.

Personally, Elliott didn't see it. To him, the club's superior commander was simply scary as hell. He resisted the impulse to take a step behind James. After all, James was the sturdy next link in the chain of command, and therefore really ought to be first in the line of fire.

Too bad there wasn't a window Elliot could duck out of.

Dalton pinned James with his unnerving gaze. "We need to know who she is."

Well, damn. There it was. With a secret sigh, Elliott raised a hand like a schoolboy and wiggled his fingertips. "I think I know who she is." He took a step back when both men whirled on him. "At least, I think I met her last night. Which is why I came home with nothing but the documents—"

The gazes turned into glares. Elliot gave a cavalier grin and a shrug in return because, national security or not, he still thought fondly of that dance. "*She* robbed *me*."

∼

AMIE GLARED at the stout man facing her across the counter. "These pearls are very fine."

The pawnbroker, Connors, a part-time book-maker and full-time receiver of stolen goods, opened both hands in an eloquent shrug. "That as may be, Miss Amie. Only everybody knows there's some girl out robbin' places. Now, what harm do you think would come to me if I was caught tradin' in the Vixen's goods?"

Amie reached for patience and dripped a bit of honey into her voice. "Connors, you know me. You were one of Papa's dearest friends. If I tell you that I am not the Vixen, you can believe me. If you've seen the gossip sheets today, you know perfectly well that the house that was hit last night by the Vixen was in Grosvenor Square.

These pearls are not from Grosvenor Square. I will swear to you on my father's life—I mean, my father's grave." Papa would be the first to approve of the lie.

Connors smiled kindly at her, his amused paternal gaze making Amie's teeth grind. "Ain't been no report on what else was took from Grosvenor Square, other than that emerald. Could be pearls, could be not. What I know is, we got hired agents watching all our shops, though we be honest and righteous merchants. Them toffs want their jewels back and they want 'em now."

Amie tried to recall how her father had negotiated with this man. She fixed him with a confident gaze and kept her voice even. "You're going to buy these pearls. Let's be very clear about that. You know you are going to buy them and I know you're going to buy them. So the only question is, how much will you pay for them?"

Connors shook a finger at her teasingly. "None o' yer sass, Miss Amie," he said with a grin. "Maybe I'll buy 'em and maybe I won't. If I did, I'd have to figure in the risk. Vixen jewels are chancy. I'd have to hold onto 'em for a long time afore I dare sell them on. So I'm thinkin' I should only be givin' you a quarter o' what you're askin'."

Since she had asked for twice what she thought she could get, this meant that she was going to get half of what she really wanted for the jewels. Her heart sank. He was starting too low. If he'd meant to haggle her for a fair price, he'd have opened closer to the real value. She looked past his disarming, snaggletooth grin and his grandfatherly gray hair to the sharp glint in his eyes and the resolute set of his chin.

Blast it. He wasn't going to go any higher.

"You must understand how important this is to us!" She wished she had Ruby's theatrical talent. She would give anything to drum up some tears at this moment. "Without Papa—" Her throat tightened. "There's nothing left, nothing but the house itself. If I don't get a good price for these pearls, we could lose it entirely." Her voice actually broke slightly on the last word. Her eyes began to burn.

The tears were coming after all. She ought to have milked the moment for all the sympathy the man was capable of. She couldn't do it. Even though she knew it might help if she cried, she gritted her teeth and lifted her chin. She wouldn't weep before this man, who had once been so close to her father that she had called him uncle.

Blast Papa's felonious underworld friends! Not a single one of them had even offered her the piddling price Connors had offered her, and now she had no choice but to take it.

What a crew of thieves!

A few moments later she walked out of Connors's establishment with her reticule lightened by several strands of pearls, and unfortunately not made much heavier by the guineas within. She'd had no choice. She and her sisters could not survive much longer on frugality and the resilience of youth.

Papa's words rang in her mind. *They'll never forgive me, but you're safe. They don't even know you exist. But if they ever find you—especially if they realize how much you know about them...*

Amie believed him. That's why she hadn't allowed Ruby to come, even though her pretty sister would have charmed a bit more coin out of Connors. The less Emma and Ruby were openly involved, the less likely they would be to go down with Amie.

She'd been lucky so far. Furthermore, she would take happily take her chances in the magistrate's court. It was the Liar's Club she truly feared. If she were to be discovered by the Liars she was entirely confident she would end up floating in the Thames just like Papa. So bloated and blackened with drowning that he could only be identified by his ugly patterned waistcoat.

Poverty worried her. Prosecution frightened her. The Liars, on the other hand, that vindictive band of merciless assassins, filled her with black and breathless panic!

CHAPTER 4

*E*lliott couldn't believe it. He'd been loitering outside this pawnbroker's storefront for several hours, which wasn't easy to do without raising suspicion. He'd pretended at different times to shop for cigars across the street, or to wait upon a companion, impatiently checking his watch. He'd worn out shoe leather strolling nonchalantly on his way somewhere but in no great hurry. But there were a limited number of times one could casually stroll past the same shops in a day. Soon he would have to switch streets with one of his fellow Liars, Feebles or Rigg, who were staked out in front of other pawnbrokers.

It didn't always follow that a thief who targeted the highest in Society would try to sell their loot to a pawnbroker. A truly accomplished rooftop man—er, woman—would surely have a regular receiver. Furthermore, a practitioner of that caliber would have dressed to fit in better with last night's decadent but undeniably elegant crowd.

However, Elliot had recalled that his dance partner's gown had been a little tight in the bosom and, while it looked very nice on her shapely figure, was made of less than the finest stuff. Her jewelry had been simple, just a pretty amethyst pendant on a chain and demure diamond earbobs that upon recollection he realized were probably paste.

So, clearly not a rank beginner, but not an seasoned professional either—and therefore likely to take her ill-gotten gains to someone like old Connors, who had helped the Liars dispose of some of their own shady acquisitions in years gone by.

The boredom was getting to him. He was hungry and he needed to—

Suddenly, there she was, stepping out of the doorway marked with the sign of the three gold balls of a pawnbroker.

Elliot hadn't noticed her go in, but now he understood why. She was dressed as primly and sensibly as a governess in a gray walking dress covered by an unadorned brown coat. Drab, almost invisible, as common as a sparrow in a field. If it were not for the wisp of red hair that had come loose at her brow and now drifted across her cheek beneath her bonnet, he still might not have recognized her as his vibrant dance partner. This woman seemed pale, drained and weary.

Not that Elliot cared, of course. Her emotional state was of no concern to him at all. She paused outside the pawnbroker's shop, gave a tug to the wrists of her gloves, and lifted her chin.

He was too far away to know for sure, but he imagined a spark of grim defiance in her eyes. She was still pretty, even disguised as a bland upper-class retainer. In fact, he liked the way she looked at this moment. A woman like her didn't require feathers and paint to be attractive. She was rather splendid, even in her disguise.

As she marched away at what she probably imagined was a perfect pace of a servant on an errand, there was a lithe grace to her stride. That confident way of movement reminded him of the way she had danced last night, with her eyes closed and her body swaying to the music.

It wasn't that she was bold, or cheeky in any way. It was more that she could not quite hide her independent spirit.

He followed her, musing on how her grave carriage seemed as strict as a nun but somehow as direct as warrior. Furthermore, he didn't mind watching her walk away, not one little bit. The skirts of her gown swished very distractingly over her bottom with every step of her determined pace.

He already knew she had an agreeable figure. Lean and athletic, but for that tempting bodice. His arm had fit so nicely around her waist last night...

She turned the corner in front of him and disappeared from his sight. It was sheer habit that had him hurrying to catch up, and a good thing it was. He was so distracted by thoughts of the night before and of the drifting scent of apples and vanilla that he turned the corner too abruptly for proper stealth.

It didn't matter. She wasn't there.

Well now. Maybe she was a seasoned professional, after all. Elliott tugged down on his hat brim as if girding his loins for battle. With a small smile, he set out at speed. She can't have gone far. He could find her.

She might be an expert, but then again, so was he.

∾

AFTER AMIE LEFT Connors and his grasping betrayal behind her, she walked from the less respectable High Street to the Oxford Street shopping district. The shops became nicer, and she passed a confectionery and a purveyor of fine leather goods. In her upper class servitor guise, she looked entirely appropriate on this street, so there was no reason in the world for her to feel conspicuous.

Then why was it the hairs on the back of her neck were once again standing at attention? She felt exposed. *Watched.*

Some people might talk themselves out of that sensation. They might think to themselves, "Don't be silly. It's only your imagination. There's no one after you."

Amie knew better than that.

Better to look a fool than be a fool, Papa's gravelly voice whispered in the back of her mind.

So Amie turned the next corner a bit sharply, and then ran very quickly for a few feet. Then she ducked into a doorway. In the shadow of it, she hesitated for a long moment, looking down, pawing aimlessly in her reticule for nothing at all, while a few strangers passed and didn't give her a second glance. No one slowed. No one even looked her way.

She stepped out of the doorway to cross the street quickly just ahead of a wood wagon and then had to rush out of the path of a carriage. The horses startled a bit and the driver gave her a scornful glare, but because of her respectable clothing refrained from muttering curses in her direction. She walked quickly, moving alongside the carriage for the length of six storefronts, allowing it to block her completely from the opposite side of the street.

Then she entered one of shops randomly, pushing her way into the store as if the devil himself were after her.

Sundries. All the useful little things that everyone needs but no one ever thinks about buying until they run out. Shoelaces, corset strings, buttonhooks. Low investment, high profit margin.

Amie hurried to the counter, allowing herself to look flustered and a little bit worried. She leaned close to the woman who stood there, dressed in a respectable matrons gown with her hair tightly curled. The woman regarded her suspiciously, although she'd not yet spoken a word.

Old-fashioned, strict, precise with that little gold watch pinned just so to her bosom. A woman of stature in her own community. Judgmental. Of an envious nature.

That assessment no longer than a split second. Amie changed her story in that instant and leaned close to speak in hushed and tense voice.

"I need to speak to your husband."

The woman drew back. Her lips pressed together and her eyes narrowed. "Not another one. Get out of my shop."

"I have to speak to him! He has to know..." Amie placed a hand protectively over her navel. "He has to take responsibility—"

Before she could utter another word, the woman had bustled around the counter and taken a painful grip on Amie's upper arm.

"You hussy. I'll teach you to tell lies. My husband can't father children, you ignorant little tramp."

She was dragging Amie toward the door. Amie tried to jerk her arm free but the woman truly had a deadly grip. It must have been from stocking all those button-hooks. "So you'll throw me out in the street? Right in front of your own shop? What will the public think?"

The woman changed her tactics mid-yank. In no time at all, Amie found herself dragged to the back of the store and thrown forcefully into the alley behind.

The woman spat in her general direction, and slammed the heavy rear door on her. Amie took a moment to straighten her sleeve and push back a strand of hair that come free of her bonnet. Well, that had been considerably faster than trying to charm her way to the back exit.

She had probably lost her shadow, but still, it wouldn't do to go straight home. She might as well take a stroll through one of her favorite neighborhoods, which wasn't far from here at all. The houses were so pretty, and she loved the way the trees branched nearly over the street making it almost like a country lane. Even in winter, a charming sight.

She was strolling beneath the barren trees when the back of her neck prickled once more. *My goodness, I am having a day.*

So she hurried her steps a bit, turned the corner, turned another corner, ducked down the alley backing another more affluent street and ended up at the gate of a large mews behind a very fine house.

Oh yes, this would do nicely.

Although Amie appreciated the respite standing still in the shadows of the gate next to some skeletal rosebushes, she had been poised there long enough that she was beginning to doubt her own instincts.

She had taken position near the hinges of the gate where it would conceal her when it opened, and was considering the wisdom of moving along, when the latch rattled and the gate slowly opened.

Well then. Perhaps she was not so foolish after all. Papa would be proud.

She wished she wore her boy's trousers instead of her confining gown, but there were a few ways to get around that. Even as the gate continued to open she bent down and grabbed two fistfuls of hem and hiked them up. She tucked the wads quickly into the drawstring waist of her drawers.

I'm sure I look ridiculous, like a muslin mushroom. However, now she had all four limbs available for fighting. Best to get this over with quickly, before the chill turned her limbs entirely blue.

It occurred to her a bit too late that she ought to have concealed a stone in her reticule. Her belly rumbled. She was not thinking clearly from hunger.

A figure stepped through the gate. For the first time she actually saw her pursuer.

It was the thief from last night's ball.

∾

ELLIOT TOOK the first blow on hard on one shoulder. He'd blocked the strike almost by accident, turning when he heard a slight noise behind him.

The kick knocked him off balance. Before his opponent could close in, he threw himself forward and rolled away. His hat spun off into the snow. In a second, he was back on his feet inside the yard and backing away from his attacker who had emerged from behind the gate.

Limbs. Calves and knees and slender ankles outlined in dark winter stocking—and an exhilarating glimpse of bare thighs above the garters. Her white skin glowed against the black stocking-knit.

Oh, glimpses were good. He liked glimpses...

He was so distracted that he almost didn't block the next kick. Almost.

Instead he caught a dainty ankle in one hand just in time and pushed back, hard.

The lady thief fell back, for it was indeed the pretty redhead who had consumed most of his thoughts over the last two days.

She completed a very nice role backward roll herself, and provided him with tremendously pleasing view. Oh, those glimpses...

He realized that there was rather stupid grin spread across his face, but he just couldn't help it. Then she came at him. A whirl of blurred kicks and punches and—damn it, he had underestimated her!

He took a ferocious blow to the solar plexus and a knock to his skull before he pulled his wandering thoughts in order and began to take his opponent a bit more seriously.

She was good. Almost as good as he was. To be honest, if he didn't train every day, she might have had the better of him. It was almost as if she had learned her skills at the Liar's Club. There was a certain trick Kurt taught of keeping the knees spread and the hips tilted forward. She did it just like Kurt.

Minus the generally homicidal intent. And the knives, of course.

God, he really hoped she didn't have a knife. He was having such a good time.

She bit her lip and narrowed her eyes at him, but he didn't think he was mistaken about the curl of her lips at the corners. She was enjoying their tussle just as much as he was.

Knowing her moves, he stepped backward and then pretended to slip on the icy walk. She almost didn't take the bait, but he saw the shift in her shoulders when she decided to move in. He was ready for her strike and ducked. She over-extended. He rushed in close to grapple. If he hadn't had the advantage of height and size, he might not have gained the advantage. She was fast, but ended up wrapped in his arms all the same.

He grinned into her hair as she struggled. "I can't tell you how much I've enjoyed our dance." She twisted in his grasp, causing him to change his grip. Yielding flesh filled his hands. His gentlemanly reflexes shouted at him to release her with profound apology. His spy training wouldn't allow it. His animal instincts settled the vote in favor of holding on, so he held her all the tighter. "Alas, I fear it is time for the music to end."

His intention was to trap her arms behind her back and frogmarch her luscious criminal arse straight to the club. Instead, she kicked his feet out from under him.

Ow. He landed on his back on the hard snow-packed path. Because he knew better than to let go of an armful of furious woman with fighting skills, she came down with him. There followed a fascinating struggle, full of punches and squirming, where he wasn't sure if she was trying to kill him or make him fall in love forever.

Damn, he was smiling again.

He almost took a knee to the groin but managed to shift his weight and took it to the inner thigh instead.

Her low laugh gusted in his ear.

"Manners, miss!" It still hurt like blazes, so in order to protect his reason to go on living, he was forced to flip her beneath him. Not very chivalrous of him, but he persisted in subduing her struggles until he pressed her to the snow, straddling her with his hands pinning her upper arms down.

For the first time since he'd stepped through the gate, he had a moment to breathe. Beneath him, her chest heaved as well. For a long moment, there was no movement but the clouds of vapor they puffed into the icy air.

Her bonnet had come completely askew and dangled from the strings. It was now a crushed ruin behind her shoulder. Her brilliant hair streamed across the white ground, like sunset on snow. Her cheeks were pink and her vivid green eyes glared at him, snapping with emerald vexation. Damn, what a picture. The image was so arresting that when she squeezed her eyes shut and opened her mouth he hesitated a second too long.

She let out a piercing feminine scream of terror. It was a chilling sound, to be sure. He stared down at her in shock. She laughed up at him, a husky chuckle that rippled through his entire body.

She had a healthy set of lungs, and the house was not that far away. No more than a split second past before three burly footmen erupted from the back door of the structure. With the garden stripped of foliage by winter's chill, there was nothing to keep Elliot and his quarry hidden from three shocked gazes.

He gazed down at his delicious opponent in disappointment. "Now you've done it."

She didn't scream again but only batted her eyelashes at him with a wide innocent gaze. "You have it coming," she said calmly.

Then the husky footmen were upon them. They pulled him off with rough hands. Elliot didn't fight them, for the fellows were only doing as they should, defending a poor young lady being assaulted on the house grounds. He suffered their blows without resistance. Even when his face was buried in the snow and his hands were confined behind his back, he could hear the diabolical minx continue to work.

"I'm dreadfully sorry that I trespassed." She certainly sounded breathless, but the battle had been fierce. The tremble in her voice wasn't terribly convincing to Elliot, but the footmen seemed entirely hoodwinked. "I was only trying to hide from him. He's been following me all the way from Oxford Street and I simply couldn't run anymore."

Damn. Every word of it rang of truth because it *was* truth. She was brilliant. That was why she was hustled into the safety of the house while he, defender of the Crown, was the one frog-marched into the mews and tied to the door of a stall. The gleaming carriage horse inside the stall looked gently amazed and then nibbled on Elliot's hair.

"Do me a favor," he told one of his guards. "That lovely redhead. Get her name for me?"

The request earned him a cuff on the ear and a growl. Elliot let out a resigned sigh. He had the feeling he would be having a long night.

∼

AMIE SPENT no more than a few moments in the house all in all. One of the housemaids helped her inside, then called for the housekeeper. The briskly compassionate housekeeper took her to the lady of the house, who was a young woman not much older than herself.

The bell was rung for tea, but there was no need to wait on the sympathy. They were lovely, both of them. Amie felt rather ashamed of herself as she begged for a moment alone then, when they left her, ducked out of the nearest window. She sidled along the side of the house, and ran down the street in front into the blue-gray of gathering dusk.

It was a very nice house, she thought as she ran. Full of little treasures and keepsakes. Silver this and porcelain that. A part of her had not been able to keep from assessing the potential, but she knew she would never be tricking her way into that particular establishment. The Jackhams only robbed those who deserved it.

She threw away her bonnet as a lost cause and simply avoided people whenever possible until she was a mile gone. She slowed and pressed a hand to her aching side.

This time, she was certain no one followed her. Her gentlemen thief had been quite thoroughly detained. She almost felt sorry for him. Almost.

Her heart slowed to a more normal rhythm as she walked. She found herself with a silly smile on her face as she thought about their stimulating match in the snow. The blows had been serious and she knew they would both carry a few bruises, but she'd felt no actual fear of her life. She must be mad. He'd stalked her like a professional, had found her out when no one else ever had and had taken her down despite her skills.

It had been altogether the most stimulating adventure of her life.

And he still smelled astonishingly good. She smiled even as she reached a hand to massage her stiffening shoulder.

He'd fought well, and had bested her fairly. It was strange how easily she could predict his moves and evidently he had done the same. It was almost as if they had been trained by the same—

Liar.

Amie had to stop and lean against an iron fence as her heart rose in her throat and the breath left her lungs entirely. Oh, heavens. Oh, *no*.

He was a Liar. Trained by Liars, just like her father had trained her and her sisters. The same moves—dear God, the same *list*, the same *target*!

She swallowed hard, remembering the folded papers in his pocket last night, the ones she'd not bothered to pull. She'd stolen from a spy.

What had she done? She'd ruined everything! She and her sisters had managed to live their entire lives out of sight of the Liar's Club!

And now she had placed herself firmly in their view.

Did they know who she was? They must know something, for he'd been waiting for her outside the pawnbroker shop. He had clearly known where she was going to be, or close to it.

Connors's words rang in her memory, though she'd not listened well at the time. "We got hired agents watching all our shops."

They'd known to look for a thief on the trade, but not who she was, no, not her identity. If they'd known her name or address, they would've come to her there and taken them all.

This meant that it was quite possible they didn't know about her sisters. There was still time. Time to run. She pushed herself upright once more and picking up her skirts, ran for her life and the lives of her sisters.

CHAPTER 5

Fortunately for Elliott, trapped in the horse stall, it was not a long wait at all. The footmen who had tied him so securely to the stable post had scarcely left through the front door before a small shadowy figure slipped into the mews.

Feebles looked like a bundle of rags washed up in a sewer drain, but he was actually the greatest pickpocket the Liar's Club had. His weathered face grinned briefly at Elliott before he ducked his head and tugged at his cap with his usual unassuming air. "Will y'be wantin' that little rope problem taken care of now?"

Elliott sighed. Relief warred with chagrin. He really didn't want to stay here all night, nor did he wish to go through a great rigmarole with the magistrate. Still, he could not help but flinch at the hell he would catch back the club for not only being soundly defeated by a mere slip of a girl, but in ending up tied like livestock between a gelding and a nanny-goat.

"If you would, please." Might as well strive for a bit of levity.

Feebles, being Feebles, made no more remark as he whipped a small blade from a worn boot and sliced through the heavy rope as if it were string.

Elliott rubbed his wrists as the two of them slipped out of the mews into the dusk. There was no guard. Well, it was just a house, albeit a very fine one, not a military post. They took the wall rather than chance the gate again. The bracing run through the back alleys of London did much to cool the heat of Elliott's mortification.

They picked up Rigg on the way, the other Liar who'd been posted at a pawnbroker's to watch for the red-haired thief.

It was only then that Elliot thought to ask Feebles how the diminutive pickpocket had known where to find him.

"Oy, ye went right past me. I seen you following the lady and then I seen her give you what-for."

Elliott was sorry he asked.

Entering the club was synonymous with coming home. After the chill day, a fight in the snow, and a long dash back with frost crunching beneath their boots, it was almost miraculous to step into the light and warmth and delicious scents of Christmas baking.

Elliott's spirits lifted instantly. He was going to get his share of ribbing over today's loss, and he didn't look forward to making his report to the spymaster, but in the end this was his family. This was his home. Eventually, he would be forgiven. That was the Liar way.

On his way to face the music, Elliott sauntered past the room with the best fireplace, the one that had been taken over by the children as well as the evergreen tree. He poked his nose and grinned as the tiny flaxen-haired girl of no more than four slipped a hand into a jacket pocket draped over aspiring dummy and pulled out a handkerchief without setting off a single jingle-bell warning.

Elliott clapped and entered. The band of wee monsters gathered around him and he picked up the curly-haired tot to allow her to wave her hard-won handkerchief in high triumph.

"I did it, Uncle Elliott!"

"That you did, my candy-apple queen!" He swung her around until she shrieked and giggled, then he set her neatly back on her small booted feet. "I see your Jack has a jingle-bell on every pocket."

The oldest boy, Robbie, string-bean fellow of the great age of twelve-ish, folded his arms with a smirk. "There's eight pockets, including the weskit. I've got six down."

"Well done!" Elliott strolled around the dummy who wore an odd fashion of purple silk weskit, formal black dinner jacket only a bit ripped at the seams, and a lady's bonnet festooned cheerfully with holly and pinecones. He stretched his arms forward and cracked his knuckles with a show of warming up. "Shall I have a go?"

Robbie's eyes lit up. "I wish you would. Mother won't show me anything, for fear of encouraging me. And Father is afraid of Mother."

Robbie had been adopted a few years ago by James and Phillipa. He'd changed a great deal from the stunted chimneysweep child who had saved Simon Raines's lady wife in a moment of great peril.

Still, although Elliott understood the parental urge to preserve Robbie's childhood, the boy had never really had one, had he? Picking pockets was a damned useful skill for a Liar, and best learned young.

Elliott turned his back, made a grand gesture of crooking one arm over his eyes and started counting slowly backward from ten. There was a great rustle, pierced by shrieks and giggles and thudding little feet, as the assembled offspring filled the sparring dummy's pockets once more.

"—three, two, one!" Elliott whirled and took two steps to the dummy. In eight quick motions, his hands moving the same time, he emptied eight pockets in half as many seconds. Not a single bell sang out.

The assembled circle of children made appreciative noises. Elliott flourished a deep theatrical bow. "Thank you, thank you."

Robbie was gazing at him narrowly. "I saw what you did. I can do seven now, I think." He stepped forward.

"Only for Crown and Country, eh, old man?"

Robbie nodded seriously. Elliott made way for the master-to-be, and left the room with a cheerful wave. "Carry on, ye sticky beasties!"

It was silly and perhaps a bit pathetic, but his success with the jingle-bell dummy had put the jaunty back in Elliott's step that had been stolen by his grand, and now probably very notorious, defeat.

He wasn't angry with his opponent. If he was to be truly honest with himself, he'd enjoyed nearly every moment of their contest.

She really was quite astonishing...

Despite the fact that he truly had nothing to be ashamed of, Elliott felt like a naughty schoolboy called on the carpet in front of the spymaster. Dalton stood there by the small fireplace in his office with both hands braced on the mantle. His head dropped to gaze at the glow of the coals.

Elliot wasn't one to look too deeply into his loyalties. When he encountered someone new he rather quickly sorted that acquaintance into one of two categories: those he believed in and those he didn't. His masters at the spy academy had tried to drill logic and analysis into his head, but when in the thick and the dark, Elliot always fell back to on instinct. As yet, he had never been proven wrong.

"So what did your precious gut tell you about your lady thief?" Dalton remained where he was, his attention apparently absorbed by the glow.

Elliot let out a great long breath. "She is..." *Beautiful. Exciting. Tempting.* And if he was not much mistaken, she was also quite sad.

He had no inkling of why she should be so bereft, so he said nothing. His shrug did not seem to satisfy Dalton.

"Hmm." The man sent him a sour glance. "She bested you." It wasn't a question.

Elliott lifted his chin. "She's a good fighter. But no, she didn't beat me. I won the day. Until she outsmarted me."

Dalton shook his head, as if shaking off some inner memory. He sighed. "It happens to the best of us."

Elliott wasn't sure if the spymaster was referring to being beaten, being outsmarted, or being beaten and outsmarted by a woman. Considering Dalton's own clever and talented wife, Lady Clara, Elliott had the notion that his superior was speaking of the latter.

"You got lucky with the pawnbroker, but she's onto you now." Dalton straightened and turned to Elliott. "You need to widen the net."

"Agreed." Elliott nodded crisply. "If I may request more copies of the drawing of our target to pass around the club, we can ensure she sees no familiar faces. And I've had a better look at her now, so I believe I can give Lady Clara a few more details."

Dalton nodded and glanced over his shoulder at the petite brunette sitting at the large desk that dominated the office. "More copies, Clara?"

Clara looked up from the political cartoon she was working on and brushed back a lock of dark hair that had fallen over her brow. "Certainly. Lord Elliott, pull up a cushion. Dalton, darling, would you mind sending one of the children down to the kitchen? The scent of Kurt's baking has been wafting the halls for hours. I'm absolutely perishing for a biscuit."

Dalton frowned. "He's being very territorial about his kitchen at the moment. I'd better do it myself."

Elliott gazed ferociously at the carpet between his boot tips and struggled not to chuckle. One of the most dangerous men in the world nodded to his pretty little wife and scuttled off to fetch her a treat.

When he was gone, Clara gave Elliott a fond glare. "There is no need to laugh. You just wait, Lord Elliott. There will come a day when a woman will flutter her lashes and you will find yourself fetching her pretty floral pincushion from across the house."

Elliott bowed with an old-fashioned flourish. "That day is now, my Lady Clara. What may I fetch you? A cup of tea? A stool for your feet? Shall I mop your brow as you labor so hard?"

"Idiot." Clara rolled her eyes. "He could be standing right outside the door, you know."

Elliott smiled, but he did stop his carrying on. Flirting with the ladies of the club was a dangerous hobby of his. He certainly meant no harm by it. Rather, it was a means of staying in character. Most of his assignments were undercover in the ballrooms and gaming tables of the rich and bored. He fit very well into foppish and useless society. After all, it was from whence he came.

He pulled up a chair and settled next to Clara, who opened a drawer and pulled out her original sketch of the red-haired thief.

Seeing it again, Elliott realized he'd done little justice to the lady's snapping eyes and determined chin.

He continued to describe her from his new perspective of wrestling her down into the snow, a story which Clara enjoyed very much. However, she tweaked him ferociously when he began to wax eloquent about emerald eyes and fiery hair streaming across white snow.

"You're allowed to respect her fighting ability, Lord Elliott. But I don't think Dalton would enjoy knowing that you are, well, a bit smitten."

Elliott made a gentle scoffing noise. "Nonsense. Not possible. Absolute rubbish."

Damn. He couldn't even convince himself. *Smitten.*

At best she was a clever criminal. At worst, a dangerous enemy. Now he truly had to find her. It was time to figure her out, for good and all.

∽

AMIE SHOULD HAVE FELT safe when she at last entered the Jackham house. After all, she'd gone to enormous lengths to lose any possible tail. She'd walked for hours, running from doorway to doorway, dashing through shops. She'd even traded her warm brown coat for a thin blue one from a woman who seemed surprised but willing.

It was her last good coat, blast it. Ruby had her old one, for her sister had outgrown everything in the last year. Now Amie ached with cold and terror. With only part of her attention she caught the sweet smell of Christmas cooking and...what was that? Pine?

"Evergreen," Emma said as she looked up from the bowl she was whisking. "Apparently it's all the rage in fashionable circles to cut down a tree and bring it into the house to shed needles everywhere and then to drape bits and bobs all over it."

"According to whom?" Her voice sounded faint even to her own ears.

It was enough to make Emma look at her more closely. "Where did you get that coat? You didn't go out like that." She hustled forward. "Why it's naught but thin canvas! Oh, you must be freezing!"

"Who's freezing?" Ruby bounced into the room. There were pine needles in her hair. "Amie! You're white as a sheet!"

Amie let them coddle her. The fire and the hot tea helped enough that her hands stopped shaking and she could feel her aching feet again. However, it did nothing for the knot of fear that sank like cold lead deep in her belly. She took another sip of tea, hoping to melt that worrisome lump.

Her eyebrows lifted in surprise. "This is actual tea." She looked up, glancing around the kitchen. Belatedly, she noticed a ham on the table and a bowl piled high with potatoes and leeks. There were sacks by the stove that looked to be flour and even sugar. Oh, no. "You bought food."

Emma looked at her a bit sideways. "We thought we might as well. After all you were selling the jewelry today and...well, it's Christmas. I just thought we could have a few things the way we used to, like a ham and mince pie." She lifted her chin. "I should probably tell you now that there's a goose hanging in the larder. And I purchased a crock of redcurrant jelly. A small one. Well, fairly small."

Jelly. In winter. It was a mad splurge, to be sure. Amie blinked and her gaze slid to her youngest sister. "And we have a tree in the house?"

Ruby squirmed a little in her chair, her clasped fingers rubbing together in her lap. They looked to be sticky with pitch and bits of colored paper. She had several lengths of faded old hair ribbon draped over her wrist.

"I've seen— I've heard that other people have them in their houses. I remember hearing about it when I was little. Papa told me he saw one in a duke's house. It's ever so pretty, and it smells so nice. And I just thought— No, I should've gotten a simple garland." Ruby's face, usually so cheerful, took on a crestfallen frown. "I should have asked first."

"Ruby got it on credit. With a discount. I think she could talk a cat into swimming the channel!" Emma stood up briskly. "Yes, we went a bit round the bend. There's nothing to be done for it now. And what's the harm? You sold the jewelry, didn't you?"

Amie reached into her reticule and pulled out a handkerchief-wrapped bundle. It was all too small and far too light. Pinching a corner of it, she let the contents roll out onto the table. Her sisters leaned forward. There were a few guineas, a bit of silver, but mostly coppers gleamed in the candlelight.

"Oh." Ruby's voice was very small.

"Did you try Connors? And Becket?" Emma shook her head quickly. "No, of course you did. Those blasted old thieves!"

She'd failed so miserably. Amie's breath caught in her throat. "I'm sorry. I'm so sorry."

At her broken tone, her sisters swept her into their arms and held her close, petting her hair and murmuring denials. It felt good to be surrounded with reassurance, very good to be forgiven. It would likely feel even better if she could forgive herself.

There was still more. She hesitated. There was nothing they could do about it tonight. She could keep the real problem under cover just a little longer, and let her sisters enjoy the feast and the silly tree.

But the burden was too much to bear alone. And they should know. They should be prepared. They would be frightened, but they would be together and they would figure something out. Together.

She lifted her head. "It gets worse." Her voice was flat. "I was shadowed...by a Liar."

The fire still crackled. The oven still baked. The chill that swept the room had nothing to do with temperature and everything to do with dread.

CHAPTER 6

"We cannot leave." Ruby's tone was adamant. And since Ruby did not wax adamant very often, Amie and Emma were forced to take her quite seriously, despite her mere eighteen years.

Emma, as always, took the rational approach. "Ruby, there are many places we could live. We could move to the country and survive quite nicely, far from any possibility of being found by the Liar's Club."

Ruby looked at Emma with cool disdain. "We would be no safer in Staffordshire than we are in London. Papa always says it is easier to hide in a crowded city that in some village where everyone knows your business."

Amie and Emma shared a glance. Best to stay away from the sensitive topic of Papa. Amie added, "There are other cities. We could move to Edinburgh. Or Brighton. Or Leeds."

Both her sisters looked at her in horror. "Leeds?"

Amie backed down slightly. "Or...somewhere not Leeds. The point is that it might be best to relocate. I, for one, would rather like to live a long and happy life with my sisters."

Emma snorted. "Long and happy, yes. I rather hope we might have different futures then spending our spinster years together, but for the time being we must stick together."

Now Ruby and Amie stared at Emma.

"Different futures?" Ruby looked horrified.

Emma squirmed slightly. "I simply mean that perhaps some day we may do something else with our lives than to carry on the family business, so to speak."

Amie had never heard the like from Emma before. Emma was the criminal mastermind of the three. It was Emma who selected the targets, researched the events, decided on the costume, with a little help from Ruby, and generally carried the authority of being an excellent planner.

Something else? Something else…like dancing at a ball with a young man who knew her real name? Like a life not overshadowed by the constant threat of discovery? A life where the choices were more than steal or starve?

A life where she was not a thief?

Amie knew she had a rather highly developed sense of right and wrong, especially for the daughter of jewel thief. But she hated stealing even though she was rather good at it. That was why she was the one who insisted that their targets be entirely terrible people, who had probably come by their wealth by means of plunder rather than honest labor. It was a small lie to herself that it was somehow morally superior than being a cut-purse that targeted poor flower sellers in Covent Garden.

It must be better. She had to believe that. Except deep down, she rather didn't.

Ruby, who could be quite stubborn in those rare moments, folded her arms and sat back in her chair. "I won't leave. I don't want a different future. When Papa comes back, what will he think if he finds strangers in this house and the three of us blown to the four winds?"

"Well, three winds, anyway." Emma murmured.

Amie shot Emma a reproving glance. This was no time for sarcasm. Ruby's devotion to the dream of Papa's return was a fantasy that they could no longer afford to allow. *When Papa comes back.*

Not *if*. *When*. Poor Ruby.

She leaned forward. "Ruby, you know that Papa is gone."

Ruby lifted her chin and regarded her with scorn. "Say what you mean. You mean 'dead', don't you?"

"Don't be cruel, Ruby." Emma's tone was tart yet kind. "We all loved Papa. We all feel pain and abandonment and grief. Do not think for one moment that your loss is any greater than mine or Amie's."

Emma's cool but gentle reproof reminded Amie so much of Mama that her chest ached just that much more. Mama had died when Ruby was but seven years of age. Her youngest sister scarcely remembered anything of that time but that she'd been very much loved.

Emma, three years older than Ruby, remembered Mama a bit better. She even looked most like her. But Amie had had fourteen wonderful years with her mother. Those years left her richer than her sisters, surely, yet sometimes it seemed she missed Mama the most.

Mama had been practical and calm and yes, occasionally a bit tart. Papa had been a creature of recklessness and laughter and clever blarney. It had been Mama who had kept his feet on the ground.

Both her parents were gone. She was, in effect, the parent now. "Ruby, I know you want him to come back. I know that we were not allowed to say goodbye, or attend a funeral, or mark a grave for him. We feel unfinished by that. Our grief seems without end because we will never fully understand what happened to him."

Except that she did know. She knew more than the other two, at least. She'd saved them from that knowledge for nearly two years, but perhaps now was the time to tell the truth.

She looked down at her hands, clasping them tightly together on the table. "They did find him," she told them in a low voice. "A few days after he went missing there was a...a body pulled from the Thames. His body."

Both her sisters regarded her with widened eyes. Emma's indrawn gasp of shock rasped against the silence of the room like gravel.

"A body? I don't believe it! It could be anyone!" Ruby shoved her chair back with a scrape and with a defiant toss of her head, stalked from the room.

Amie started to rise to follow her, but Emma put a hand on her arm.

"Let her be. I'm not sure anything could actually convince her. I wish you had told *me* a long time ago, but I think I understand why you didn't."

Amie sank back into her chair and dropped her head into her hands. "I don't know what to do. I never know what I'm doing. If I thought that someone had ever written down the recipe for a life such as ours, I would follow it to the letter. Unfortunately, I believe we may be the first."

Emma scoffed gently. "Things are not so bad as that. So far we have made do quite nicely. Well enough, at any rate. And eventually you are going to tell me everything you know about Papa's death. But at the moment, we have a much larger problem."

Amie looked up. "Larger than Ruby never speaking to me again?"

Emma poked a finger into the pile of coins that still lay upon the table. "This isn't enough. We can pay the creditors a bit to aid their patience and we can lay in some food to last a few more months, but then what?"

Then what? It was always thus, with stealing and then inevitably spending. There always seemed to be a bit more stealing at her future.

"I have to go out again."

"Yes." Emma's voice was soft. "You'll have to go out again, even while the Liars search for us."

Amie shook her head vehemently. "No, not us. Only me."

Emma regarded her somberly. "If you should be recognized, it would be dire. I could go in your stead."

"Leave it, Em. You know it must be me. We could both be caught and convicted. What would happen to Ruby then?"

"All right." Emma sighed and relented in the face of Amie's ferocity.

Amie was prepared to pay the price should she ever be apprehended. But she would never give her sisters up. Never.

Shortly thereafter, in Papa's study, Amie carefully unfolded The List. She smoothed the creased sheet flat on the desk. Ruby's investigative notes were written in her tiny neat hand carefully between each name. Their youngest sister had even gone so far as to draw a decorative border on the paper, turning a list of scrawled names into something very nearly reverential.

"She's been at it again." Emma reached a finger to trace a line of tiny cats that ran down one side of the page. "These weren't here the last time I looked at it."

Amie shook her head. "Let her do what she likes. She's still just a girl."

Emma raised a brow. "I'm just a girl, for that matter."

Amie couldn't say the same. She felt as old as time, weighed down with responsibility and incessant dread. Papa had burdened her with a bit too much knowledge, and had assigned her with protecting her sisters from that same information. But how long could she continue to do so? When would they be old enough to share her worry and what would be the good of it if they did? Would they be in any less danger? Would their circumstances be any less real? Wouldn't she simply be parceling out her fears in order to have company in her misery?

She didn't always feel this way. While she felt enormous guilt about stealing, she had to admit to herself that there were moments...

She loved the balls. Oh, to stroll through those glittering rooms, to dance to beautiful music, to smile and laugh as if she were another person—a person without a worry in the world.

And then there was The Moment. The thrill of that moment! Her blood rushing through her veins, the heightened senses, the giddy reckless freeing excitement that came with getting away with it. No matter the crush of guilt after. No matter her fear of consequences. In that moment, she was brilliant and powerful and unfettered.

If she never went a-thieving again for the rest of her days, as she surely wished, it would be that moment she missed the most.

Emma didn't want to play the part of thief. She liked the triumph of a well-laid plan. She liked the organization, the plotting, the thinking of things through. She also liked the jewels. The beauty and the artistry of the jeweler and the stone-cutter appealed to her sister.

As for Ruby, Amie believed that the escapades served to keep Papa alive for their youngest sister. After all, what could be more affirming of his presence than to carry on his teachings?

Poor Ruby. Amie understood the lure of that fantasy. If Papa would return, they would be a family again. If Papa came home, they would no longer be alone in the world.

"The body in the Thames—" she blurted suddenly to her sister. "It *was* him."

Emma did not look up from the list, but her hands went still. "How can you be sure? You didn't see...did you?"

Amie shook her head violently. "No! Heaven's no, I could not have borne it! But I spoke to the woman who—" She swallowed hard. "The woman who prepares the bodies for a pauper's burial."

The pauper's burial was the resting place of the anonymous and unclaimed. It consisted of a churchyard burial with no witnesses, with only the most meager of a junior cleric's rote blessing, and bodies layered like logs filling in a single hole.

"What did you learn from this woman?"

Amie pulled her thoughts from the dark earth. "She told me of a man, a victim of unknown demise, pulled unrecognizable from the water. She told me that the only thing memorable about the—the person—was a particularly ugly and vivid weskit, patterned in violet and yellow."

"His favorite." Emma's breath caught slightly. Papa had been so fond of his ugly waistcoats, each louder and more vile than the last. Amie reached for her sister's hand, closing it gently into her own.

Emma took a deep breath. "So."

Amie exhaled in time with her sister. "So."

Emma pulled her hand away and quickly dashed away a tear or two. Then with quick, precise movements, she laid the list to one side and opened two of the most recent tattle sheets.

Amie gave a sigh. "I'd meant to pick and choose, to go slow." She looked at Emma. "I don't want any excess attention. As long as everyone stays focused on the Vixen we can shield ourselves under that umbrella. If we're careful."

Emma nodded. "Bless the Vixen. She's a clever one, choosing such wicked targets. It's easy to laugh at the rich losing baubles."

Amie knew what she meant. Regular folk enjoyed the tales of the Vixen. She was almost a folk hero to some, making her jabs at the wealthy and objectionable.

But they could no longer afford to ride the mysterious thief's coattails. Now they needed a big take, the prize of a lifetime. Gold, jewels, banknotes—anything of worth that could be carried out of London by three young women.

There would be no time to sell their plunder in the city, and no inside introductions to the buyers in a new place. They would need liquid assets, not simply jewels, to live on until they made the proper connections. Secretly, Amie rather hoped that they would not be required to connect themselves to thieves and pawnbrokers ever again.

Emma was humming a holiday tune to herself, as she scanned the tattle sheets and the list at the same time. Her left finger ran down the list even as her right finger ran down the page of the newssheet. Her fingers stopped moving. "Aha."

Amie leaned forward. There was only one name on the list with the required wealth that would be hosting an event this week. Amie felt her eyebrows rise. "Oh my, we are hunting big game."

"You're going to have to come up with a costume."

Amie regarded her sister dryly. "The frocks are always costumes." Giddy debutante or drunken demi-rep. Inwardly, she wondered what if she would ever be allowed to be herself outside these walls.

"A real costume. See?" Emma swiveled the newssheet for Amie's view. "A Grand Masquerade."

"Oh, for pity's sake!" Amie felt weary down to her bones. Blast it. Could it never be easy? "And where can I possibly find a wretched costume with naught but a week's notice?"

CHAPTER 7

The secret rear portion of the Liar's Club had gone dark, even as the false front business began to heat up.

It must be quite late. Clara looked tired, and Elliot's rear was getting rather weary of his chair. Or vice versa.

The first drawing was now changed and updated. Elliott held it by two corners and tilted his head, gazing at it critically. Not critical of Clara's talent, for that could not be denied. Her alter ego, Mr. Underkind, was not a famous political cartoonist for nothing.

Elliott just didn't feel as though he'd managed to convey his target's delicate features. "Her face is perhaps a bit thinner."

Clara raised a brow. "If her face is any thinner than this, then I fear for her health. She already looks as though she would arm-wrestle Kurt for a biscuit."

Elliott turned to her in alarm. "She's ill, do you think? Did I chase her through the cold when she is ailing? Did I lay out a sick woman in the snow?"

Clara drew back from his forcefulness. "I don't know, did you?"

Elliott looked at the drawing again, worry creasing his brow. "She certainly fought well. If she was ill, I should hate to face her when she's feeling better."

He tore his gaze from those haunting eyes and examined the rest of the drawing. "Yes, that's the necklace exactly. I saw it very clearly when I had her pinned."

"And what necklace is that?"

Elliott and Clara looked up to see Sir Simon Raines leaning in the doorway.

He grinned at them, a flash of white in a somewhat somber face. "What have you been up to Elliott? Did you steal something new?" He dropped his pose and strolled into the room, seeming like a man at loose ends.

Clara smiled at Simon. "If you're looking for Agatha, I believe she's in the kitchens, testing out Kurt's recipes for Christmas dinner."

Simon's face lit up as it always did in anticipation of seeing his darling Agatha. Elliott shook his head. The man was besotted.

Simon was just turning to go when his gaze fell upon the drawing and he halted. He frowned slightly and tilted his head sideways to see the portrait straight on. "That's odd..."

Elliott and Clara looked at each other. "Do you know her?" Elliott asked.

Simon shook his head slowly, still gazing at the drawing. "No. Not the girl, not really, although there is something familiar about her. But that necklace..."

Simon and his wife, Agatha, ran the neighboring spy academy. He'd once been the spymaster himself, so Elliot had no qualms about filling him in.

Clara stood and handed the drawing to Simon. Simon held it closer to the light and looked at it for a long moment. Then his blue gaze shot to meet Elliott's curious one. "You saw this very pendant, correct? And Clara drew it?"

"I did my best," Clara said.

Elliott nodded. "It's the very one, I'm sure of it. Of gold and amethyst. Why?"

Simon had the strangest look on his face. "If this is correct, if this is an accurate representation... I do believe this is the first thing I ever stole on a mission for the Liars. I never knew what became of it. I assumed it was sold on to fund the club."

He looked up with a bemused expression on his lean features. "I couldn't have been more then nineteen. In fact, it was the job where I met Jackham. We ran into each other in the dark, coming at the strongbox on the same night."

He looked back at the drawing, his expression gone sad. "He was my friend, you know. Before. We started the gaming hell together, as a cover for the Club. I...owed him."

Clary peered down at the drawing. "What could this girl have to do with Jackham?"

Elliott looked back and forth at the two of them. He knew who Jackham was, of course. Every Liar did. Jackham the Jackal, Jackham the Traitor, Jackham the man who had sold the secrets, identities and very lives of the Liars to the highest bidder. Good men had died. "He wasn't...trained, by any chance, was he?"

Simon looked up vaguely. He was clearly still lost in the past. "What? Trained? No, not in the way that a Liar would be trained. He might have picked up the odd trick, I suppose. He taught a few fellows in the club, the finer points of the Nuremberg strongbox, that sort of thing. In his day, he was a better thief than I ever was but it was his job to run the house in front. He knew it was a gaming hell and cover, but he thought it was a ring of criminals, not Crown spies. We kept him out of Liar business. I suppose I never really trusted him, not entirely. He was a secretive fellow. If I had listened to my instincts, I could have saved many lives."

Clara bristled. "Your instincts were correct. You did your best to keep him from Liar operations. What Jackham did, he did on his own. No one held a gun to his head and made him sell your lives to the Chimera. You have nothing to feel guilty about!"

Simon's lips twisted in a half smile. "Yes, milady. Very well, milady. Absolutely, milady."

Elliott smiled along with them at Simon's half-hearted joke, but the thick gravity that had fallen upon the room remained. He didn't want it to be true. He didn't want his lovely red-haired thief to have anything to do with the Jackal. But he had to ask.

"You said there was something familiar about the young lady?"

Simon looked up and nodded. "Yes, she looks a little bit like Dorothea...I don't recall her last name. Perhaps I never knew it. She was a woman Jackham was mad for when I first knew him. I never met her but he carried her miniature everywhere. 'My Dottie,' he called her."

Simon looked back down the drawing in his hands. "As I recall she looked a bit like this, but not as thin. And of course, she would be much older now."

"I saw this woman today." Elliott felt sick. "This is the thief that I believe is the Vixen."

Shock washed over Simon's features. "Oh hell. That bastard. So many damn secrets. He had a daughter all along!"

"Oh no." Clara's soft voice reflected the horror that Elliott felt. A traitor's daughter, rifling through the strongboxes of London. Her training had come from her father no doubt, a man who'd known so much more than anyone had imagined. A young woman in possession of information that could only have come from the Liar's Club, on the loose.

Dalton, when they reported to him, lined up before his desk like mortified schoolchildren, said nothing for a very long moment. Then he pushed back his chair and stood. "It makes sense. Too much bloody sense. And we let her get away." He looked narrowly at Elliot. "Twice. She knows you are onto her. She could be long gone. You said she was selling the jewelry."

Elliott writhed a bit inside but fought not to show it. "I saw her come out of the pawnshop and she didn't look pleased. If she did sell it, I don't think she got what she wanted."

"We have no other way of finding her." Dalton looked them all. "We cannot allow her to remain at large while in possession of such sensitive information. We could lose years of work should the contents of that list make it to the remaining offenders. They could pack up their operations, clean house, and hide the evidence! We'll never catch them if they have warning of our intentions!"

"I think she needs money." Elliott felt like a traitor for speaking, though not speaking would make him even more of a traitor, wouldn't it? "She's thin and threadbare. She tries hard to hide it, but I think she's on the edge. If she is about to run because of me, I don't think she'll get far on what she has."

Dalton nodded shortly. "Then it's possible she'll go out one more time. One last haul from the list, and she'll be looking for a big one."

Clara cleared her throat and raised her hand. "I know where I'd strike."

CHAPTER 8

"I'd really like to look now." Amie twitched beneath her sisters' attentions.

"Oh, no you don't!" Ruby gripped her shoulders and pushed her back down onto her stool. "Emma has to practice if she's going to be able to do this to you in a broom closet."

They would both be slipping into the house as maids early in the day tomorrow. The plan was to carry in a few dress and hat boxes, all containing Amie's costume, and then disappear into some little used room to wait for evening. Emma would help Amie dress in the elaborate guise, then slip out once more as a lowly maid.

Amie hated sitting still, possibly even more than Ruby herself did. She also wasn't fond of others making decisions for her, not even her dearest sisters. But a few more tugs and pins made Emma step back with a sigh of satisfaction.

"The hair is definitely the hardest part. I think that's it. What do you think, Ruby?"

Ruby came to stand in front of Amie and gazed at her critically. Amie crossed her eyes and stuck out her tongue, but Ruby ignored her. "It's good. It actually looks like a costume."

"They are always costumes," Amie muttered. She was tired and cranky from sitting on a stool—in whalebone stays! And bustles!—whilst Emma and Ruby did maddening things to her hair. And she was hungry again. Now that they had plenty of food, it seemed she couldn't get enough of it. "Is it teatime yet?"

Ruby looked at her with an understanding smirk. "Yes, pet. And for being such a good doll and letting us dress you up, I'm going to give you one of my lemon seed cakes."

It was childish to be so pleased with such a silly reward. Infantile, really. Amie slid a hopeful gaze toward Emma.

Emma shook her head. "Not a possibility, my dear. I baked them. I'm eating every crumb of my share."

Resigned, Amie wriggled on her stool. Her bum was numb. "Can I look now?"

They nodded, and Amie stood, wobbling slightly on the old-fashioned high-heeled shoes. Fortunately, she had small feet for her height. Otherwise Mama's old shoes would never fit.

She turned toward the tall looking glass with only mild anticipation. Usually, no matter what she did, she still looked like herself. Good or bad, the original Amie always seemed to shine through.

Not this time. Another woman gazed back from the glass. Another woman from another time. The rich sapphire silk gown was nearly thirty years out of date, which Ruby declared just old enough to make it a costume rather than simply out-of-date. It was an open robe style, clasped at the waist over a disturbingly low-cut lace petticoat which was meant to be seen.

The hidden stays made Amie's waist drop low and small until it reached her hips, which then bounded out, supported by the false-rump padding that tied beneath the gown. Her hair was piled high and luxuriously curled and pinned within an inch of its life. Her eyes seemed dark and enigmatic behind her mask.

She looked exotic, nostalgic, and rich. All with nothing but Mama's ball gown, Mama's shoes, and a mask that Emma had concocted from glove leather and feather trim, sacrificing a few stolen pearls as well.

"You look like her," Emma said quietly.

Amie lifted her chin. "Mama was beautiful. I am merely sufficient to escape notice."

Ruby clicked her tongue. "Not in that gown, you're not. Your bosom looks like a dessert tray."

Amie spared a glance at her bodice in the mirror, then looked away. "If I think about that too long I won't be able to go out in public like this."

Emma smiled at her in the mirror, her eyes full of understanding. "If it helps, your arse looks like a hippopotamus."

"I shall take that comment in the spirit in which it was intended," Amie said darkly. "Will my hair do?"

"Well, we didn't want to waste money on a wig. I think if I powder that, it will look quite passable."

"Because no one will be gazing at your hair when they can look at that bosom," Ruby said helpfully. Then she yipped and clutched her side, even as Emma's elbow returned to its former position.

Amie took a long breath, feeling the tightness of the stays that reached from her armpits to her hipbones. She looked nothing like herself. He would never recognize her.

"So we are entirely prepared."

Ruby bounced on her toes, her eyes alight. Emma nodded with calm assurance. "We are entirely prepared, Amie. Nothing can possibly go wrong."

∽

ELLIOTT ENTERED his rooms at the Liar's Club and shut the door behind him. It was time for him to prepare for tonight. Capturing the Vixen would be his redemption. He tried to remind himself that was a good thing. She was playing a dangerous game with dangerous men, and compromising the Liars' efforts at the same time.

She was very good. Likely she was on her way to a very successful career. Yet, it was a chancy business, thieving. One moment of inattention, one guard or footman breaking routine, one slip, one fall would bring a tragic end. Prison...or worse.

It would be a grand idea to redirect all that talent and skill into something more productive than simple thieving. She would, in short, make a magnificent Liar.

His preoccupation with his lovely red-haired target consumed his mind, so he didn't see the fellow in a chair by the fire in his sitting area.

"You need a haircut. Which works out nicely, actually."

Elliott turned at the teasing comment. "Good afternoon, Button. Are you here to trick me out in grand peacock style?"

Button rose and sauntered forward with his hands shoved deep in his pockets. He was a small fellow, with thinning gray hair and a pair of mischievous blue eyes in his puckish face.

"I'll admit that you make up a rather marvelous package of raw materials, and you have such a lordly way of walking." He shook his head. "But I didn't think I should dress you as a peacock. All those feathers can make for a rather awkward costume."

Elliott looked at him in confusion. "I need a costume? I thought I'd simply dress well and wear a mask."

"To a Grand Masquerade?" Button looked horrified. "Not on my watch!" He held out a large pasteboard box, presenting it in both hands with a little bow.

Elliot grinned at his theatrics. "The Golden Fleece? A new suit of armor? No, I've got it—the Emperor's New Clothes!"

Button pursed his lips but his eyes twinkled. "Wouldn't that be fun? But no."

So it was that Elliott found himself dressing in a blousy embroidered shirt, pointy hat, and full medieval hosiery.

"I look like a Prussian court jester."

Button stood back and tapped a finger on his chin. "Nonsense. You look like a huntsman. You have excellent legs, due to riding often. So many of the upper classes look like spiders in knitted hose."

Elliott had to admit that he did have very fit thighs. And the mask would surely hide his face. "Well, if this is my assignment…"

At which point Button flopped back down in the chair and laughed until he had to press his hands to his sides. "Oh, what a good little Liar you are! I cannot wait to tell my lady Agatha that she called this one entirely!" He looked fondly at Elliot. "I may be out one beribboned bonnet, but it was worth losing the bet to see your face just now."

Elliott sighed. "This is not really my costume, is it?"

Still chortling, Button pulled another box out from under the bed. "You are still a huntsman, but a rather more manly and intimidating version, I hope."

As Button handed him the new clothing, which Elliott much preferred, the little costumer managed to worm a few more details about his target from him. Elliot tried hard not to sound, well, *smitten*.

"I knew Jackham quite well." Button told him. "I found him gruff, but he always treated me fairly. Not everyone does, when one is different as I am. I sought out his opinion when I designed those secret pockets you all use."

Elliot paused in dressing. *So that's how she knew about my secret pockets!*

Button went on. "I liked him, and although he came to a truly unfortunate end, I can only judge the man that I knew. Until I was informed otherwise, I thought he was quite a good fellow."

Elliott frowned. "Yet we cannot excuse his betrayal, can we? To sell men's lives for no reason other than greed? I do not think that describes a good man!"

Button gave a sad smile. "I suppose it does not. However, I can attest that one's parentage does not always determine oneself. This lady thief of yours may be another sort of person entirely."

Elliott buckled the wide belt around his thankfully much more formfitting leather jerkin. "I liked her," he said quietly. "She fought me fairly and didn't cheat until she had no choice. She was smart and skilled and…"

"And pretty."

Elliott shot Button a glare. "So much more than pretty."

Button narrowed his eyes. "Hmm. Alright, let's take a look at you." He moved Elliott to stand before the mirror. "Oh yes, that will do nicely."

Elliott liked this costume much better. The dark green jerkin fit close to his body and the leather trousers with the laces down the sides, along with the high-top boots, made him look rather untamed. A man from another time.

Button handed him the mask and Elliott tied it on behind his head. It was a molded close-fitting half mask that covered from the tip of his nose on up. It was unadorned leather was stained to such a dark green it was almost black.

"You look a proper predator now." Button stepped back. "I almost feel sorry for your Vixen."

Elliott turned to regard Button as the man gathered up his boxes and wrapping in preparation to leaving. "It's for her own good," Elliot told him. "She's only going to get deeper and deeper in trouble on her own."

Button straightened and considered Elliott for a long moment over the top of his burden. "That may be. But let me leave you with one piece of romantic advice that I know is true. You will always regret the one you allowed to get away."

CHAPTER 9

Surprisingly, everything did go perfectly to plan. Emma and Amie had slipped unnoticed into the Earl of Chadwick's house early in the afternoon. They'd realized that the best place to prepare in the home of the childless earl was in the nursery.

The room hadn't taken long to find. The two of them spent their time carefully pinning and powdering Amie's hair until it was as white as Marie Antoinette's wig, with not a betraying red strand to be seen. Emma even powdered Amie's eyebrows using a bit of sugar water to make it stick.

Once they'd dressed Amie completely, her stays tied, her shoes buckled and her thievery tools cleverly concealed, Amie sent Emma on her way. Well before the party began, her sister blew her a kiss before she strode purposely out the door carrying an empty dress box as if she had every right in the world to be where she was.

Now, hours later, Amie stepped into the ballroom. The earl's house was much grander than Lord Beardsley's. The ballroom truly glittered and instead of just a few musicians, there was a full orchestra playing in the mezzanine. Truly, she could have fit the Jackham house and entire garden into the room!

The ball itself was far more elaborate and respectable than the one where she'd first seen the Liar. The dance floor was quite full already and there were quite a few women in bustled gowns and powdered hair, so Amie's costume wasn't even unusual.

She had to wonder if they'd gotten theirs out of the attic, too. Somehow she doubted it.

Steady on. Through the ballroom, up the opposing stairs and into the house. She decided she must be looking for a particular lady. She plucked a name from a conversation as she moved past. Lady Mantleworth. Should she be stopped, she would lower her intelligence, flutter inconsequentially, and claim she had become lost looking for Lady M.

On her way, she saw quite a few gentlemen give her a glance, and then another, without ever managing to raise their gaze to take an actual look at her face. Perhaps the bosom would come in handy after all.

She had marked the location of the study earlier in the day, as they looked for the nursery. She strode confidently toward it—no, wait. She was supposed to be quite silly, wasn't she? So she drifted toward it, moving vaguely as if she'd already begun celebrating her Christmas Eve.

The study door was locked. She leaned against it, fanning herself, as another couple walked down the hall from the guest wing toward the ballroom. When they had passed, she pulled two pearl-tipped lock picks from her piled and stiffened hair, careful not to dislodge any of the actual pins, and had the study door open in the blink of an eye.

Once inside the study, the strong box was not immediately obvious. Then she saw a large cabinet the size of a wardrobe between two bookshelves. Could it be inside there? It would have to be a sturdy piece of furniture to hold an iron strong box, but surely the earl could afford any sort of furniture he liked.

The cabinet also had a small lock which gave her picks no trouble whatsoever. Amie's swung the doors open wide and blinked.

This was no common strongbox. The grand Armada chest before her was as tall as she and thrice as wide. Clearly the earl intended to intimidate any would-be thieves.

There was just one thing. The large iron case, strapped with more iron, covered in iron-upon-iron ornamentation, was just like a sketch in one of Papa's journals.

The standard style iron Armada chest is a three-lock combination to be done in a specific order. The first lock exposes the second and the second lock exposes the third. Each lock operates its own set of tumblers. A three lock system will in fact operate six iron bolts that hold the door closed.

To Amie and her sisters, that paragraph was like a nursery rhyme they had learned before they were out of braids. She almost felt a fondness for the great monstrous chest, as if it were an old friend she had not expected to see again.

Three key holes. The first one would be small and hidden. From a wide leather garter strapped around her thigh, Amie took out Papa's ring of keys.

The ring itself was as large as an orange and held eighteen keys. It weighed a great deal. Ruby had wrapped it round many times with ribbon to spare Amie's soft skin from the teeth of the keys and to keep them from jingling as she moved. Amie unwrapped the festive red ribbon and tucked it into her bodice to use again when she was done.

The first of the delicate keys, of which there were six, did not work. Amie took a breath, calmed her nerves, and reminded herself to breathe.

"Light on your feet, quick on the pull, nothing on your mind."

Finally, the first lock slid to the turn of her wrist. Even as the bolt drew back, another small decoration flipped aside and revealed the second keyhole. Amie selected another size of key. Breathe.

At the turn of the key, several inches to the right another bit of decoration drew back and exposed the largest keyhole yet.

She took another breath and began to try the largest keys. On the ninth and last key, she was yet unsuccessful. Her hand began to tremble. It wasn't going to work. It was all for nothing. She was risking her life for a final score to save her family and she was going to fail. Again.

The key would not move. She dropped her forehead to the cold iron of the door and squeezed her eyes shut tight. Try again.

She started at the beginning with the large keys, this time moving each one in and out slightly hoping something would catch. Nothing happened. She tried the ninth key again. It had to be this one. But nothing moved.

Locks are very simple mechanisms, pet. There simply aren't that many arrangements for the teeth to take. I could make a million pounds tomorrow if I could invent a lock that fit only one key in the entire world.

Amie quelled her rising panic and stepped back to eye the door with a narrowed gaze.

And then she remembered. *A lock in the center of the door most likely manages vertical locks into the top and bottom of the strongbox.*

Of course! The vertical bolts were heavy and turning the lock would require lifting a shaft of iron by at least three inches. Amie took the key in both hands and turned hard. The iron bruised her fingers but the key began to move. Encouraged, she went up on tiptoe and put all her weight into the twist of the key.

She felt the bolts slide on their tracks and then, at last, clunk into place.

She'd done it. She reached out a hand to the heavy handle and hauled the great iron door open.

Surprisingly, the strong box looked nearly empty. There was a large jewel casket on a shelf above a tooled leather sack nearly the size of her fist on the floor.

She untied the top of the sack to peer inside and caught her breath at the sheen of the gold guineas that filled it near to bursting. Liquid assets!

A shiver went through her, a thrill of relief. Gold spent everywhere. No need to negotiate with pawnbrokers. In a few hours their bags could be packed and the ladies Jackham would never more be hiding in the London shadows, in constant fear of discovery.

Quickly, she rifled through the jewels, choosing diamonds and pearls. No significant emeralds, thank you very much!

She hiked up her gown and tugged her padded bustle sideways in order to reach into it. Ruby had sewn a clever purse into the padding. The leather bag and the jewels went inside. Amie dropped her skirts with a nod of fierce satisfaction. No one would find it there.

Before she closed the strongbox, she spotted something on a high shelf. Reaching it down, she found a single leather-bound folio. She opened it to glance through the pages. It was nonsense, gibberish.

It was code.

Furthermore, she found tucked into the back of the folio a stack of French land grants. She had enough French language to make her widen her eyes at the amounts. The paper franc had devalued in recent years, but land grants were forever.

The Earl of Chadwick was taking bribes from the French? Such a collection could be innocent, but then why hide it? And code? Code was always suspicious.

She gazed at the small stack of paper, perhaps twenty sheets of it, covered front and back with nonsense and then locked away in what was probably the most secure strongbox in London belonging to a very important earl.

Highly suspicious indeed, my lord.

Clearly, the earl was a very mistrustful person—and now that he'd been robbed, he would only increase his already formidable security. No one would ever lay eyes on these particular documents again, she would wager.

She bit her lip. She might hate the Liars for what they had done to Papa, but she knew they served a purpose. That was one of the things that made them so frightening—their indelible loyalty to the good of the Crown, no matter the cost.

If she managed to get her sisters safely out of the city tonight, might she be able to see this information then fell into the right hands? Not that she would ever lift a finger to help those animals, but she was an Englishwoman and a patriot even so. She would be helping her country, not the Liars.

On impulse, she rolled the documents tightly enough to fit into the compartment in her bustle. That left little room for anything else.

She picked up the small leather bag and pushed it into her bodice under one breast. She took up the jewels. These she stuffed beneath the other breast to rest cold and lumpy beneath it. Her bosom then levitated higher than ever. Blast it.

Within moments the study was just as she had found it. She patted a strand of hair into place, smoothed the silk of her gown, adjusted her bodice as well as possible, lifted her chin, and stepped out of study into the hallway beyond.

First she would save her family, then she would worry about the Crown.

"Good evening, Miss Jackham."

CHAPTER 10

His quarry looked astonishing and wicked, mysterious and alluring. She was a powdered and painted beauty from another time.

Oddly, Elliott found that he rather missed her freckles. Still, there was that expanse of creamy bosom to console him in his loss.

He spread his hands, indicating her costume. "My heavens, Miss Jackham. Is this all for me?"

She sidestepped and tried to evade him, but he knew perfectly well that other than instigating a full-on row in the hallway, she had no alternative but to play along for the moment.

Elliott bowed, then straightened and extended his arm. "A dance, Miss Jackham?"

"Oh. No, thank you."

Elliott smiled but allowed a little steel to enter his gaze. "Oh. Yes, thank you."

She looked at him warily, her green eyes dark as a forest behind her mask. Elliott merely waited, his arm proffered. After a long moment, she slid her hand to rest upon it. He could feel her fingers trembling.

They began to walk down the hall toward the ballroom. Elliott could hear her breathing and could nearly feel her pulse pounding. She no longer seemed like a cool and detached professional. She seemed like a terrified woman trying not to flee him.

He didn't want her frightened. He wanted her apprehended and properly trained, to protect herself and to be an asset to the Crown! He had not confessed this secret desire to James or Dalton. He imagined that they themselves had something similar in mind. She was too good to leave loose, too dangerous by half—yet Elliott believed that she could be reached. Some few thieves were spurred on by greed alone, but somehow he didn't think that that was her sole ambition. He hoped not.

Damn, that was an exceedingly enjoyable bodice. He thought the current style of gowns quite pretty. They looked comfortable and they did nice things for a lady's figure. But he had to admit that a few decades ago, they'd really known how to tempt a fellow.

The Liar and the Thief entered the ballroom just as the musicians struck up a new waltz tune. The orchestra was excellent and the music came falling clearly down upon them uninterrupted by the usual ballroom chatter and racket.

Elliott could not resist sweeping her into his embrace and melting into the crowd of other dancers on the floor. She stiffened in his arms, clearly still alarmed.

Alarmed by him? It must be his costume. He was a good fighter, but he knew that his foppish good looks and easy smile led most people to underestimate him. She seemed to see directly past his facade.

Perhaps it was his dark mask or his leather trousers but he felt dangerous tonight. When more dancers joined the floor, he pulled her close and then closer still.

~

AMIE SET ASIDE the largest portion of her mind to dance with him and to follow the music. Another small secret room she kept closed off. There was a panicked creature running in circles in that little room—

clawing at the walls, shivering and shaking and crying to be set free. She locked that fearful bit of her away.

Simply dance. That's all you are required to do at this moment. Dance... And think. Think fast. Think for your life.

Her captor did not seem inclined to cart her off to prison or to dump her in the Thames. His sole interest in her seemed to be this moment, this waltz, this dance of enemies in a glittering ballroom.

She risked gazing up into his face. The dark hunter's mask seemed to be setting a new sort of man loose in those gray-green eyes. Or perhaps it simply revealed him. She felt something inside her quivering in response, like a plucked string ringing in harmony with his.

She desired him. She savored this moment. As dire and fearful as it was, she knew that deep down she enjoyed the danger. Heat coiled and simmered deep in her belly. She breathed in his marvelous scent and closed her eyes, all the better to enjoy it.

I am in a great deal of trouble, yet I care not. She tried to think what Papa would tell her, what Mama would say. For once, there was no one speaking in her mind except herself—she was beginning to fear that herself was the last person she should trust.

Her feet stumbled in the unaccustomed heels. It was only a slight misstep but another guest trampled on her hem and she was pulled off balance. In another gown, she could've twisted and saved herself from a fall, but the uncompromising whalebone stays that did such unnatural things to her figure now prevented her from easy movement. She staggered, her arms flailing. She felt a strange disconnection from herself. She never fell. Where was her grace? Where was her catlike ability to squirm out of any situation? Who was she in this moment, fearless thief or damsel in distress?

Strong arms swept about her waist and caught her up. He set her on her feet to one side of the crush, her fearless Huntsman come to her rescue. No wait, it was her capture.

She was so confused. How could she love the feeling of his strength and his hands upon her? He was the enemy. He threatened everything she knew and loved. He threatened her very life and the lives of her sisters.

"Are you all right? Are you ill?" The concern is his masked gaze seemed strangely real.

She shook her head and pressed her hands against his chest trying to ease herself away from him. "I—I simply need a bit of air."

He lifted his head and shot his gaze around the ballroom. Was he looking for something? He pressed his lips together and seemed to come to a decision. "The terrace is just this way. Let us get you out of this throng."

He took her hand and guided her through the crowd to the doors at the end of the ballroom. The mullioned glass was lined in frost, but she could see that it looked out onto the terrace and the snowy grounds beyond. "Do you need a wrapper? Do you need your cloak?"

It was an excellent notion. Unfortunately, she hadn't thought to bring one. Or to own one, for that matter. *I gave away my good coat to escape you.* Then she thought about the grounds and somehow possibly reaching the wall past them.

She shook her head. "I'll be fine." He pushed open the terrace doors and led her outside. The terrace had been swept clean of snow and small decorative lanterns placed here and there, leaving enticing shadows. He led her into one.

She went directly to the stone balustrade and leaned her back against it, facing him, unwilling to turn her back on him.

The air was crisp and icy but there was no wind. After the heat caused by the crowd and her own physical confusion, it felt wonderful. This was exactly what she needed. A bit of quiet. A moment to think, to clear her head, to fix upon a plan.

Then he kissed her.

∼

HIS MOUTH WAS hot and hard. The large hand that he slipped around the back of her neck was warm and supportive. It was fair to say that he did not steal the kiss so much as begin it...

Wherein she decided to finish it. All by themselves, her arms flew up and her hands clasped behind his neck. She pulled him down to her even as she stood upon her tiptoes. The touch of his lips had opened a floodgate to a reservoir of something she had not even known she contained.

Something wild and fierce and heated erupted from her, obliterating her conscious thoughts before it. She could hear the small sounds she made in her throat as he deepened the kiss. His hard hands slipped fully around her and he pulled her tightly against him.

When he growled a deep and needful sound, it vibrated through her to resonate urgently in a place she'd ignored for most of her life.

Oh yes. Oh please. More...

His huntsman's cap fell off his head and onto the stones as she ran her fingers up into his hair. She tightened her fists to drag herself closer. But there was no closer. She could not... It wasn't...

Then his hot hand released one of her breasts from her low bodice. The icy air tightened her nipple but only for a moment before his heated palm covered it. He hefted her breast, lifting it.

His mouth left hers and he took her rigid nipple into his mouth.

Oh...

The throbbing between her thighs grew to almost pain, such a terrible, empty ache! He pressed her body back against the balustrade with his hips. She braced herself with her hands as he leaned her over his arm and devoured her nipples, one turn on another. She could feel the rigid thickness in his trousers press against her.

She had an idea what that was. She'd seen some of paintings Papa had brought home at the height of his career, before he had later sold them. She knew what men kept there, and she knew that women were made to receive it.

But no one had ever told her about the searing, blazing heat she experienced at the very thought of taking him inside her.

Then she felt him lift him up her skirt with one hand. For a moment she nearly panicked but he was on the wrong side of the garter with the keys.

Then again, what did it matter? He knew she was a thief. In that moment, she realized for the first time why he was able to reach her this way. He was her enemy, but he was also her equal.

There were no lies between them. He knew she was a thief. She knew he was a spy. They may be costumed and masked, yet she had never been more revealed to a man than she was at that moment.

Then his hand found her and his cool fingers slipped within her and slid in her dampness to find the center of her pleasure.

Yes. Yes I want that. I want him. I want his hand right there, right now.

There was no voice of logic. There was no canny plan. If she was captured, then her life as she'd known it was over. If she did manage to escape, she would never see him again.

Either way, this was her last chance to know him, to feel him, to slide her hands over his wide shoulders, to dig her fingers into his thick hair, to feel his mouth on her nipples and his hand bringing her pleasure beneath her skirts. It might be all she ever had to keep her warm through her future lonely Christmases.

I'm stealing this moment. That is, after all, what I do.

Then all thought was burnt away like paper before the flames he stoked within her. He made her writhe and tremble and cry out and then the starry sky above her disappeared behind the brilliant lightning of her shuddering pleasure.

CHAPTER 11

*E*lliott held her as she came quivering down from the peak of ecstasy. She panted and moaned. He kissed her brow and smoothed her hair. Gently he returned her bodice to its proper place and smoothed her skirt down.

The look of wonder in her eyes when she opened them surprised him deeply. She hadn't known of such pleasure. Virgin? Oh hell. And yet, he was glad as well. He wanted to be her first lover.

You want a great deal more than that, you nutter.

It was true. However, he could be patient. He could wait until she was through her training. Surely there would be occasion to meet. He could offer to be her sparring partner.

He held her in his arms and murmuring reassurances as she clung to him and blinked the surprise away.

Oh, he liked this girl. Admired her, desired her, found her endlessly fascinating. He wanted to know everything there was to know about her. He wanted to laugh at her jokes and learn how she took her tea and dance with her at their wedding.

Something cold stroked his cheek and he looked up, blinking. "It's snowing."

She looked around them and gave a soft, wondering laugh. "It's been snowing. Your hair is nearly as white as mine."

She smiled up at him then. The open, sweet smile took his breath away. Mask or no mask, she was the most astonishing creature he'd ever known.

"I should take you back inside. You'll surely be feeling the cold in a moment."

She cast a glance out over the grounds. He tipped up her chin with one finger and grinned down into her eyes. "You'll not be hopping the wall in that gown. Come on, dance with me again."

She bit her lip and then she tugged ruefully at her bustle. "I truly did underestimate this costume. I fear it is winning the battle."

He gazed at her in admiration. Snowflakes glittered on her cheekbones and across that tempting bosom. "It's a dreadfully clumsy gown, but you look very nice indeed."

She sniffed at his gallantry but the corners of her mouth quirked. *Oh, this woman...*

~

AMIE WASN'T AFRAID ANYMORE. She felt too powerful. That mad rush of pleasure to new and wondrous heights had left her with a dizzy feeling of invincibility.

She accompanied him back to the ballroom. She would allow herself to be foolish and silly for one moment more. One last, splendid moment. She had escaped him before. She could do it again.

The crowd had thinned slightly. Everyone had wanted to join the first waltz but now many had bowed out of the sprightly country dance currently being performed.

Surprisingly, he didn't pull her into it. Instead he pulled her close in a fast and dizzying waltz, increasing the speed of the steps to keep up with the new music. She laughed aloud. It was a mad, outrageous. She felt everyone staring at them. And she didn't care one little bit to be at being the center of attention.

More dancers joined them in their waltzing rebellion. They all moved in a circle together, orbiting around the central country forms, faster and faster. More and more people decided to defy convention. The entire floor began the same hectic waltz.

Amie's glee subsided somewhat as more dancers pressed close. She realized she and her Liar were walled in by the other dancers.

Something rang her inner alarms. The gentlemen were so tall, their partners so shimmering and grand. All the masks worn by the men seemed to have teeth. A lion, a bear, a wolf—all dancing and turning and seeming to snarl down at her.

Predators. Fear sparked through her. She flinched and tried to pull away but it was too late. She was hemmed in, surrounded, like prey by a pack, like a fox run to ground.

She was hidden behind them as she was danced off the floor and into a dark antechamber beyond.

~

SOMEONE LIGHTED the sconces on the walls. The room brightened and Elliot released his waltz partner and backed away, leaving her enclosed in the circle. Miss Jackham looked terrified once more, but more than that, she looked furious.

She stood in the middle of her masked captors and gazed from one to the next. Then she fixed on Simon, who wore a bear mask that revealed only his jaw and his vivid blue eyes. "I know you," she said with a small snarl. "I've seen you before."

Simon, who had stayed back a step from the others, moved forward. Agatha, gowned in russet silk and wearing an owl mask, refused to release his hand and moved forward with him.

"I am sure I don't know you," Simon told her. "I would certainly remember meeting the Jackal's daughter."

Elliott saw her stiffen at the epithet. "That name doesn't mean anything to me," she stated flatly. "And Lady Etheridge is not the only one who can draw. My father was almost as skilled as Mr. Underkind."

Dalton growled at the realization that Miss Jackham was aware of

Clara's political cartoonist identity—a fact that should not be known outside the Liar's Club.

Elliott cleared his throat and stepped forward. He spoke to Dalton, for he wasn't sure he was supposed to acknowledge or recognize the others in the room. "Did you find anything in the safe?"

Dalton, his hunting gaze fixed on Miss Jackham, now turned it on Elliott. "As empty as a cold heart," he informed him.

Elliott reached into two of his pockets simultaneously and withdrew an overflowing handful of jewels and a small leather sack that weighed heavily of coins. "Here is everything she had on her."

He heard Miss Jackham—*I wonder what her name is?*—gasp behind him and turned in time to see her hands flutter to her bodice before she jerked them down again to fist at her sides.

He carefully stepped out of range of those fists. The snapping rage and betrayal in her gaze would make any man wary. He felt sick to his stomach, but he was sure she would understand in the end. *I am not evil*, he wanted to tell her. *I am not cruel. I am merely very good at what I do.*

One of the ladies stepped forward, Lady Julia Ramsay, or to those in the know, the Fox. She was tall and elegant with her gleaming blonde hair pulled up high behind her mask of hammered gold. She was gowned in a Roman toga manner, one perfect shoulder revealed. The man next to her, Marcus—whom Elliott knew quite well, though one could hardly call them friends—leaned toward his lady. "The documents must be somewhere else."

The lady fixed Miss Jackham with a cold gaze. The Fox versus the Vixen. "Now does not seem like a good time to be uncooperative." Her tone was pleasant yet somehow also uncompromising.

Miss Jackham visibly fumed, then lifted her chin. "Turn your backs."

Julia tilted her head. "I shan't, if you don't mind." Her tone was distant and unconcerned.

When the gentlemen turned back around they saw Miss Jackham's hands held a slim folio of documents. Where ever had she kept them?

Elliott thought he saw an expression of growing respect on Julia's face.

Dalton thrust the considerable fortune of jewels and gold back into Elliott's hands as if disposing of a couple of used wineglasses. Elliot returned them to his pockets. He felt a strange need to keep his hands free—almost like a fight reflex.

Dalton stepped closer to Miss Jackham and reached for the documents. Miss Jackham made a small noise as Dalton loomed over her.

Elliott frowned. He didn't understand her terror. "No harm will come to you, Miss Jackham." He turned to his superiors. "Isn't that right?"

Dalton glanced at him briefly, his chilling silver gaze a dismissive flicker before he turned his full attention to the papers in his hands. Elliot looked at Simon, who gazed back at him without expression. Lady Julia, even though Elliott had been her first friend in the Liar's Club, gave him only a grave look.

Elliott's conviction of a positive outcome began to falter in the face of the thick, grim silence that was the only answer to his question.

Oh, bloody hell.

~

AMIE HELD VERY STILL, a deer in the circle of deadly hunters. Her worst nightmare had come to life—except for one thing. No one had yet asked her about her sisters.

"What's my name?" She looked at him, the one they'd called Elliot, trying not to flinch from him, from the knowledge he now had of her. Oh, how she wanted to cringe at the sight of her jewels and gold in his hands and the way he'd gotten them.

"I— I don't know." Elliot stared at her. "We know that you are Jackham's daughter."

"Is that it? I'm Jackham's daughter, so you see fit to kidnap me?"

The Duke of Etheridge, for yes, she knew him as well, gazed at her narrowly. His silver gaze gleamed behind the mask of a snow-white hawk. "We know you are a thief."

She laughed in his face. "And do you roll out the Royal Four for every thief in London?"

She saw Elliott twitch from the corner of her vision, but she did not remove her gaze from that of the duke. Etheridge was the spymaster. The others were there out of support for him, or perhaps due to curiosity about her. She knew how it worked. Jackham had been the responsibility of the Liar's Club. They had taken his betrayal personally and it would be they who meted out their twisted form of justice upon his offspring.

Etheridge stepped closer to her. "Your father should've protected you from such knowledge. He should've realized—"

"What he realized was that anyone connected to him would be tried, convicted, and sentenced without ever seeing a magistrate. What he realized was that the only way to protect me was to tell me everything so that even if he could not save himself, he could save me."

Dalton slid a glance sideways to meet the gazes of his companions. "I think you can see why we must seal the breach any cost."

"Cost?" She scoffed. "My father already paid the highest cost! How much more blood can he possibly spill for you?"

"Jackham should've thought of that before he took their gold." It was Simon Raines who step forward then. "I have sympathy for you, I do. I knew your father well—"

"You know nothing. He was the very best at what he did. You took away his profession and then you gave him what? Service work?"

Simon flinched from her. She saw it, and so did everyone in the dining room. "What's wrong, Sir Simon? Did I remind you of something unpleasant? Did I remind you that my father fell three stories because *you* made a mistake?"

"He forgave me for that." Simon said quietly.

"Yes," she spat out sarcastically. "Because there's so much forgiveness flowing at the Liar's Club!"

She turned back to Etheridge. Seal the breach, he'd said. Good. They would dispose of her and never, ever learn about Emma and

Ruby. In fact, the more furious she made them, the sooner they would go about it. All the better.

It was not an act, she realized. The rage boiled up in her like hot lava welling in a dormant volcano. It had been there for so long that she'd almost forgotten it was there.

"You don't know what he did—" Dalton began.

Amie was shaking with her rising fury. "On the contrary, I know precisely what he did. He gave me a full accounting after he was found out. It was the last time I ever saw my father before—"

"Before his body was found, you mean." That was Simon.

She shook her head quickly, shaking away the jolt of loss that always came when she thought of that night. "He didn't want anyone to get hurt. He only did it—"

"For his daughter." It was the woman in the golden mask.

"His secret family," Simon said sadly.

Amie lifted her chin. "His only family. You lot were just his employers, not his brothers. You never let him in, not really. Good enough to train you, but not good enough to be one of you."

"We cared about Jackham," the curvaceous brunette with Simon protested. "He was my friend."

Amie nodded miserably. "Yes, Lady Raines, he told me that, too. And that he'd been wrong to do what he did, that he'd take it back if he could, but by then he was in so deep—" She looked down. "Because of…because of me."

The golden lady tilted her head. "The Chimera found out about you, didn't he? Held your safety over your father's head?"

Amie gazed back at the woman in astonishment. "How did you know?" She had not even told her sisters that secret.

This time the woman almost smiled, although it was a grim sort of expression. "I am most familiar with the Chimera's methods."

"They didn't give him money," Amie insisted. "They weren't the giving sort. They were blackmailers, not benefactors."

Another man stepped forward. He wore a tiger mask, as did his red-haired lady. James Cunnington and his wife, Phillipa.

"He told me they gave him gold," James said. "He confessed it to the both of us when we were kept at gunpoint on a rooftop by Lady Lavinia Winchell. That was just before Jackham tossed her off four stories like a bag of sand."

Amie nodded. "I know that. He told me all about it. That was so you would look no further for his true motives. He also told me that he saved you both. He was ordered to kill your wife but he didn't. Instead, he killed off the alleged source of his supposed pile of gold. Does that sound like someone was in it for the payment?"

Phillipa spoke up. "No, it sounds like a man who would do anything to save his child."

Poor Papa. Amie straightened with pride. "There was no gold. He would never have sold you for so little. 'Honor among thieves,' he said. You might be criminals but you were *his* criminals. Somehow they learned about—" *Be careful here.* "About me. With that, they had all the leverage they would ever need, for my papa loved me."

She glared at them all, turning slowly in place, her chin lifted and her gaze defiant. "Do you all understand? My father loved me, and you murdered him for it!"

Her voice cracked and a hopeless shiver went through her. "Just as you are about to murder me."

CHAPTER 12

*E*lliot felt an icy flood of fear for her. Then Dalton shifted his weight, as if to move forward, as if to reach for her. It was more than Elliot could bear.

No.

Somehow he found himself in front of her, staring down his spymaster, the Royal Four and all their company. God, how intimidating. How had she stood there so defiantly against all those accusing eyes and toothy masks?

Because she is the bravest woman you have ever met. Button was right. Elliot would never forgive himself if he let her get away—unless it would save her life.

"Stand down, Elliot." Dalton's voice was a rasp.

"No, I don't think I will." An eerie calm seeped into Elliot, a warmth like sitting by a fire on a cold day, like facing the future with the woman he loved pressed to his back. He wasn't intimidated by Dalton, or Julia, or anyone else.

Elliot no longer needed another's moral compass to lead the way. He knew what he was doing was right. "You won't touch her, Dalton. None of you will. Because what you do to her now will set the precedent for the treatment of all the children of all the Liars forevermore."

"Jackham wasn't a Liar." That was Simon. "We never trusted him enough."

"Clearly the feeling was mutual, or he would have come to you and asked you for protection for his daughter." Elliot watched as Simon looked away and the understanding made him ache. "You made a bad call, Simon. Jackham did as well. I've been told that you left your post as spymaster because it was the only way you could keep your lady safe. You of all people must understand why he did what he did."

He spread his hands, reaching out to them all. "I'm telling you, this cannot be who we are. This is not how we should treat her." Elliot looked around at them all, Liars and the Four together. "It's a dangerous life. We all know that. The thing that makes it all right, the thing that keeps us living the life and running the risks is the very thing that makes us a family. My family."

He reached his hand behind him and felt her smaller one grip his. So cold and stiff, as if she believed herself already lifeless. "If there is one thing that I believe about this family, it is that we take care of each other's children. *We* keep them safe, together."

Dalton, who was father to one of the unruly creatures currently mobbing the halls of the club, looked taken aback. James, clearly thinking of his son, Robbie, nodded thoughtfully.

"It *is* Christmas," Phillipa said quietly.

Julia nodded crisply. "A good time to let go of the past, I should think." She stepped forward to stand before Elliot. "If you please?"

Elliot stepped back. He didn't leave Miss Jackham, or release her hand, but only moved to her side, to stand with her.

～

AMIE GAZED at the woman in the golden mask. She wasn't sure who she was.

"I also had to live down a notorious father," the woman told her. "A terrible man. Far worse crimes than selling secrets, I assure you."

Amie had no notion of what the woman spoke of. She'd thought the Royal Four were all men, but the other three—Wyndham,

Reardon and Greenleigh were present. By process of elimination then. "The Fox, I presume?"

The golden woman tilted her head. "You are very free with your knowledge, Miss Jackham. I wonder, have you told anyone else of the Royal Four?"

Amie inhaled slowly. She must lie, and she was a terrible liar. Think. "The things I learned from my father's journals never left his study, until this moment." True enough.

"And the Vixen's targets? Did they come from your father's journal?"

Amie blinked. "How should I know? I'm not the Vixen."

Beyond the Fox, the others stirred in surprise. The Fox narrowed her gaze. "Not? But the robberies this winter—all the victims were Liar targets. The information must have come from Jackham."

Stay calm. They're fishing. "I don't know who the Vixen is, I promise you. I only took advantage of the uproar to try to steal what I needed!"

James grunted. "That sounds familiar."

The Fox folded her arms and chewed on her bottom lip. She even looked beautiful doing that, when Amie knew perfectly well that she herself would look rather awkward.

The Fox went on. "The Vixen has robbed a royal fortune in jewels from five different houses. Jewels just like the ones Elliot took from you."

Amie drew back. "Heavens, no! Goodness, if I'd taken all those jewels, do you think I would be wearing my mother's old dress instead of a real costume?"

The Fox, clearly curious, took a good look at her gown, perhaps for the first time. "Yes, it is old. Even your shoes are old."

Elliot turned to look at her in surprise. "But you're so skilled!"

Amie looked around at them all. "Is that what this is about?" She shook her head. "I'm good at climbing walls and sneaking into houses! Until Lord Beardsley's ball, all I'd ever taken were silver candlesticks and curios and food from the larders! It was only for survival—but Papa's debts came due and…"

"Tonight, you cracked an Armada chest the size of a cart-horse,"

Dalton's tone was flatly disbelieving. "Are you saying that was the first time?"

Amie nodded. "Papa's notes..." Her voice trailed off. "Well, they're very thorough," she said quietly. "With sketches...and things."

Simon snorted. "Jackham was an excellent teacher, Dalton. Those are his lessons which I pass on to all the trainees."

"I don't believe a word of it." Dalton glared at Amie. She tried very hard not to quail from his eerie gaze. "She is the Vixen."

At that moment, the music from the ballroom ceased and the chatter grew to a fever pitch. Something was happening outside. Dalton looked Clara. "Will you please look into that?"

She was gone in a rustle of silk, her elegant parrot mask a flash of colored feathers as she glanced back over her shoulder at her husband. "Don't do anything until I get back."

Amie blinked at the serene tone of command in the lady's voice. *I don't know how to do that.* Emma probably did.

At the thought of her sisters, safe and sound and concealed, free to run and leave London far behind them, a peace came over her. It was all worth it.

She looked down at the hand that Elliot still clasped. What an unusual fellow, her Liar. He'd confronted his own superiors for her, had stood by her and fought for her—and he still didn't even know her name.

Leaning close, she went up on tiptoe to whisper into his ear. "Amethyst."

He turned to her in surprise, a smile lighting up his handsome face. *"How lovely to make your acquaintance, Amethyst."* His answering whisper was nearly soundless. No one else in the room could have heard them over the growing cacophony in the ballroom.

Amie took that little grace, that willingness of his to keep her name to himself for a little longer, and wrapped it up warm to keep near her heart. A gift to take out again some cold winter night, perhaps.

Clara slipped back into the room and went to her husband. She murmured something in his ear when he bent down to her. He straightened in surprise. Then he turned to them all.

"I believe I owe Miss Jackham an apology. It seems that in the past hour, the Vixen has struck a house a half-mile from here."

Amie heard Elliot let out a slow breath of air. He'd clearly believed her to be the Vixen as well.

The Fox put an elegant hand on Amie's arm. "Miss Jackham, although it is clear that you are not the Vixen, there is still the matter of the information your father has made you privy to."

Amie went very still inside. "I won't tell anyone what I know."

Phillipa Cunnington came to stand beside the Fox. "Oh, Julia, put the poor girl out of her misery and recruit her for the Liars. James is panting to see if she has any aptitude for code-breaking as well."

Amie blinked. "Me? A Liar?"

Elliot grinned widely. "I think it's a capital idea!"

Amie gazed closely at Lady Julia. "What if I don't wish to? What if I want to walk out of here right this moment?"

Dalton rumbled, but Julia held up a commanding hand without taking her gaze from Amie's. "Miss Jackham, you have done nothing that we plan to punish you for. Knowing all you know, clearly we would prefer to have you with us than against us."

Elliot began to speak but subsided at Julia's cool glance. "The decision is not yours to make, Elliot. It is Miss Jackham's. However, I cannot permit you to ponder it for long. We have much work to do and we would appreciate your assistance."

"Or she must leave London," Dalton interjected. "If she will not join us, she must be kept far from our base of operations. And under surveillance, of course."

Surveillance. That would surely lead the Liars to Emma and Ruby. Amie wasn't about to trust them quite that far. Join them and keep her sisters a secret? There would be time to understand the Liars, to truly determine if they could be trusted. If not, she would certainly be in a position to know if they ever learned of her sisters.

And...Elliot would be there. And more. There was the enticement of the hunt, the chance to use her skills, the taste of danger—yet for a good cause, without the bitterness of guilt.

She gave Lady Julia a serene nod. "I will join the Liars."

AFTER THE COMBINED power of the secret leaders of the British Empire left the antechamber, the air felt a bit thin. Elliot felt dizzy with relief and something else.

Elation. His own lady Liar! What a gift!

He picked her up in a great, laughing bear hug and twirled her twice around. "You were remarkable! Dazzling! I can't believe you held your ground in the face of them all!"

She gasped and pushed at him. "Put me down, you great oaf!" Nevertheless, she was laughing and blushing when he set her back on her feet. With one hand pressed to her heart, she gazed at him with shining eyes. "You saved me."

For the first time in his life, despite all the successful missions he'd run, Elliot understood what it meant to feel like a hero. "I did, didn't I? Damn, I'm good!"

She stepped closer and ran her palms up his chest and around his neck. "You are, Elliot." She tilted her head. "Elliot what?"

Oh, damn. She didn't even know. He stepped back and swept her his best courtly bow. "Lord Elliot Hughes, at your service." He straightened with a grin, but he remained wary of her reaction. It could come between them...if she wanted it to.

Her eyebrows were quite high. "*Lord* Elliot?"

He grimaced sheepishly. "My grandfather's an earl."

"Oh." Dismay filled her expression. "That's a dreadful difference in social rank."

His heart sank. "It isn't—I won't ever inherit or anything. It isn't real." She looked so serious. *Oh, God.* "Is that a problem, Miss Jackham?"

"I should say it's a problem!" She smiled then, an impish grin he'd not yet seen on her pretty face. "After all, *my* grandfather's a duke."

Oh, this woman! Elliot's smile grew until he felt his face would remain that way forever.

"You'll see," Elliot told her as they headed out into the earl's ballroom. "It will be wonderful for you to have a family. You won't be alone anymore. It will be just like having siblings."

Amie halted him in the moment of parting the curtains. "Elliot, I never actually said I didn't have siblings, you know." Then she held her breath. Perhaps it was an unfair test. She believed she could trust him, but there was so much at stake.

He froze and stared at her. Then he swallowed. "Well."

Amie waited, imagining the spinning clockworks in his mind.

Then he smiled. "Oh, let's not complicate matters. Shall we waltz once more before the earl is arrested? T'would be a disgrace to squander such a superb orchestra."

Amie smiled tenderly at him. What a good sport he was! She hoped he wouldn't realize that, whilst he'd spun her, she'd stolen this evening's loot back out of his pockets.

At least, not until after their dance.

EPILOGUE

"Your Voice of Society wishes you all a Happy Christmas, especially our dear Vixen! Lady Justice, pray you tend your scales and recognize that a certain someone is working for your benefit! And for those who believe that the innocent should be protected and that evil should not prosper, your Voice bids compliments and Christmas reveries come true to you all!"

The End

ABOUT CELESTE BRADLEY

Celeste Bradley is the *New York Times* bestselling author of more than 24 Regency historical romances, including the extremely popular Liar's Club spy series and the Wicked Worthingtons.

For more information about Celeste's books, visit:
celestebradley.com/books/

Made in the USA
Columbia, SC
17 November 2017